By Robin Saxon

Novels
The Royal Road
By Virtue, Falling

with Alex Kidwell
Sanguis Noctis Series
Blood Howl
Blood in the Sand
Bloodlines

Published by Dreamspinner Press
http://www.dreamspinnerpress.com

BY *Virtue,*
Falling

ROBIN SAXON

Dreamspinner Press

Published by
Dreamspinner Press
5032 Capital Circle SW
Suite 2, PMB# 279
Tallahassee, FL 32305-7886
USA
http://www.dreamspinnerpress.com/

This is a work of fiction. Names, characters, places, and incidents either are the product of author imagination or are used fictitiously, and any resemblance to actual persons, living or dead, business establishments, events, or locales is entirely coincidental.

ISBN: 978-1-62798-436-2
Digital ISBN: 978-1-62798-435-5

Printed in the United States of America
First Edition
December 2013

NEW ZEALAND

Rawene
Opononi

Auckland

NORTH ISLAND

Rotorua

Rangipo

Mt. Taranaki

Waiouru

Picton

Wellington

Arthur's Pass
National Park

SOUTH ISLAND

Fox Glacier

Queenstown

STEWART ISLAND

Chapter 1

Here I was.

My life had come to this.

Staring fifty meters above me to the top of the tallest tree in the forest.

It probably sounded like a metaphor for something—looking critically at the most important event of my life, perhaps, or thinking nostalgically of the good times amongst the bad. But I really was doing nothing but craning my neck, staring upward to look at the top of the kauri tree. Its trunk was a pale brown, smooth and ancient, and the top of it wasn't as leafy as I'd expected. Instead, it was bare limbs, twisting and curving over each other, providing a home for other plants of the Waipoua Forest as they nestled in and grew there.

Tāne Mahuta. The Lord of the Forest. That was the tree's name. It needed to have a name because it was the tallest kauri tree in New Zealand, if not the oldest. At an estimated two thousand years old, it must have seen so much history, I thought; how much pain and laughter and war had those old branches witnessed?

It wasn't witnessing anything particularly interesting with me standing and gawping at it, though, so I brought out my camera and took a few shots, then prepared to leave. I shuffled backward a few steps on the damp wooden pathway, raising my arms to try to get the whole tree in my view. I hit the button, but as the photo flashed past on my screen, I saw a person had blocked my view of the tree.

"Sorry," the man said, and I lowered my camera. Typical of me to see an approaching person through a camera lens first.

"It's no problem," I replied, though my words seemed to fall on deaf ears. The man was approaching the tree, getting closer than I had dared—not that the tree was in danger of falling over, but I'd just felt bad getting that close to something so ancient, like I might trip and fall and wreck it somehow. This man had no fear of that, his steps confident, but I noticed they faltered as he walked closer.

We were absolute strangers; the only words we had exchanged were polite apologies and forgiveness. I knew I should be leaving. My car was parked outside the five-minute walk through the forest, and I'd accidentally left it unlocked. But something caught my eye.

The man drew a small box out of his backpack, and I noticed fine creases at the corners of his eyes contained emotion he was holding inside. The box itself was plain blue cardboard. On top was a broad silver plaque, which displayed the name "Te Aroha Kokiri." When the man opened it, I could see a plastic bag full of fine gray sand.

No, not sand. Ashes. Human ashes.

Suddenly I felt very awkward standing around and eyeballing this poor man in what was supposed to be a very private, emotional moment for him. No doubt he knew I was still there, as there had been no leaving footsteps from me. I wondered if I could make a sneaky getaway.

Too late. The stranger turned just enough to catch sight of me from the corner of his eye. He didn't frown, or laugh, at the embarrassed look on my face. He simply raised an eyebrow, as if to say, 'You're not as subtle as you think you are,' and then he turned back to his work. The man scattered a pinch of the ashes at the base of Tāne Mahuta, then closed the box back up.

"I'm sorry," I said, quite uselessly, as the man turned to put the box back in his backpack.

"Sorry for what?" I saw a hint of a smile curve at the corner of his lips.

"Well, firstly, for standing around like a creepy person while you did that." The smile grew into a full-fledged laugh, his grin bright against dusky skin and dark eyes. "And secondly, for your loss."

My addendum caused his expression to sober slightly, though I could see I hadn't offended him, thankfully.

"Thanks," he murmured, zipping his bag back up. He looked at me, indecision clear in his face while he searched my eyes, trying to figure out if he could trust me, if I was the sort of person he could have a decent conversation with.

I almost went to apologize, but I kept my mouth shut. I knew I probably wasn't a terribly pleasant sight to look upon right now—I felt like shit, still, and I thought I might have looked even worse. I hadn't brushed my hair since stepping off the plane, so it lay in messy blond waves made worse by my habit of raking my fingers through it when I was stressed. My eyes were shadowed by purple bruises of exhaustion, and I hadn't shaved for about two weeks.

Weariness clung to me like a visible aura, so strong I was fairly sure it might actually be cut with a knife, just like my old friend tension. But the stranger apparently found something in my face that didn't immediately put him off, wonder of wonders.

"That box is my mum," he said, tilting his head to the side to indicate his backpack. "I mean, the ashes inside are. She died of a heart attack two weeks ago."

"I'm sorry," I replied, more genuinely this time. "That must have been difficult for you."

The stranger shrugged, not in a truly careless way, instead trying to casually pass off the emotion. He didn't want to share it with me, who was just as much a stranger to him as he was to me. "I'm scattering the ashes around New Zealand. She loved her country, so I thought she'd like it."

"I'm sure she would," I said. "That's a really nice thing of you to do." After hesitating for a moment, I then said, "I know this is probably going to sound *really* ignorant, and I apologize in advance, but Te Aroha Kokiri is an unusual name. I like it! I've just never heard it before."

There was that laugh again, this time in definite amusement at me. "That's a little ignorant, yeah, but you're forgiven." The man chuckled, but there was no ire in his tone. "You're in New Zealand, didn't you notice? Us Maori don't have names like John or Bob. Some of us do, but lots of us prefer the traditional names." He stuck his hand out. "I'm

Tāne." He pronounced it like "Tah-nay" and I liked it already; I'd noticed that the Maori language—Te Reo, I thought it was called—had a nice sound to it, very earthy and solid.

"Like the tree?" I gave him an oh so innocent look.

"Yeah, like the goddamn tree," Tāne huffed.

I took his hand, and shook it. He had a good handshake; firm and confident. "James Mitchell," I said, introducing myself. "You probably already noticed from the accent, but I'm here visiting."

Tāne, indeed, looked like he had already guessed. "We might be so inundated with American media 'round these parts that we get used to it, but we can spot one when we hear them," he said. "Let me guess: Alabama?"

"Texas."

"Huh. Those southern states all sound the same to me." Tāne gave me a quick wink, and I couldn't help but smile. The man had just scattered part of his mother's ashes around Tāne Mahuta, but here he was, laughing and carrying on a conversation with someone who had the definite look of a person who should be ignored. "So you're here visiting friends?"

I shook my head. "No, I'm here because…."

Because I needed a break. Because I needed to get away from my job, my life, my associates. Because everything I'd been doing had started to feel like a noose slowly tightening around my neck, and I'd needed to find somewhere I could breathe.

"I needed a vacation," I finished, well aware the answer sounded as lame out loud as it did in my head. "I'm, um, a banker." And that had been even lamer.

Tāne seemed amused by my obvious lie. "That's an awfully strange collar for a banker to be wearing, Father." The last word was emphasized so deliberately, it took me a few seconds to understand what Tāne meant.

My priest collar. Of course.

With a fumbling hand, I reached up and yanked it out from beneath my shirt lapels, embarrassed at my slip. The stiff scrap of material was promptly hidden and folded in my pocket. "I'm sorry. I'm not really a priest," I bumbled, and a split second later, I was well aware I'd just made it even worse. I should have just smacked myself over the head, which would have been more dignified.

"And not really a banker, either." Tāne gave me a considering look, then just shook his head with a bemused smile, uncertainty slipping in at the edges of his expression. "Well, hate to say it, but I should probably be going."

I'd never heard a more obvious excuse for leaving. Oh, Tāne most likely *did* have other things to do, considering what he'd said about his current journey to spread his mother's ashes around New Zealand. But with no mention of that, it was clear he'd just decided I was a crazy man and he should vacate the premises. I didn't blame him, what with my clumsy lies.

"Sure." I gave him the friendliest smile I could muster, because I didn't want him thinking I was going to bring an ax out of my jacket and murder him. Then again, maybe ax murderers did just that before they killed. What did I know? "Good luck with your trip. I hope it goes well."

Tāne bobbed his head in a quick nod. Then he was gone, and I was, once again, left alone with Tāne Mahuta. If trees could stare, I had the feeling it was staring disapprovingly at me.

"Oh, shut up, what do you know," I muttered at it.

TEN MINUTES later, when I was back in my rental jeep, I pulled out my map. I wasn't too far from Opononi, at least; maybe twenty minutes more driving. The sun was beginning to set—I already hated driving, and I really didn't want to attempt driving on the opposite side of the road, at nighttime, on what looked to be a narrow, winding path.

Before I left, I took a few moments to myself. I sat half out of the car with the door open, turned toward the forest. Many years ago, I'd been the kind of guy who had done this—just sat and appreciated nature for what it was: ancient, powerful, beautiful, the force that simultaneously killed us and kept us alive. These days, I didn't do much of that, but I did so now. This was the point of my trip to New Zealand, after all.

The Waipoua Forest was gorgeous. I'd never seen a forest like this back in Texas. Lush green framed the narrow road, near-vertical walls made up of dozens of different kinds of plants. Kauri, silver fern, northern rata, kowhai, kohekohe, mairehau—I knew their names because I'd memorized a little booklet of New Zealand flora and fauna on the plane trip over here, but I still had some trouble identifying them on sight. There were trees that looked a little like palm trees to my untrained eye, some willowy, and one kind had long strips of dead bark hanging from the trunk like a fur coat.

From somewhere in the dense forest I could hear birdcalls, some musical and trilling, some harsh and rasping, but all of them beautiful. The air was damp and chilly, but crisp, like a much-needed slap in the face.

I took a deep breath of that air, holding it in my lungs like it could scorch out the impurities of pollution I'd lived so long with. I loved my home state, but coming to New Zealand was a little like coming to a newly discovered country, fresh in the books of history, untouched and untainted by mankind.

With a slow exhale, I turned to properly sit behind the wheel of my car and slammed the door shut behind me. Before I started the engine, I ran a hand over the back of my neck to unclasp my necklace, tugging the pendant out from under my shirt. The heavy silver pentagram gleamed where it sat on my palm. I tucked it away in the same pocket I'd stored my priest collar in. Next, I removed the ankh ring I wore on my right hand, and the bracelet of various charms—a Celtic cross, a Norse rune, and a Buddhist lotus—from my left wrist. Those, too, were dumped in my pocket.

I wasn't a priest. I wasn't a banker, either.

I was, as I reminded myself for the fifth time today, and for the hundredth time over the past year, a con man. I prayed and I exorcised, I made charms and potions, I comforted and I forgave. I preyed on faith. I capitalized on belief. I made money pretending to be something that I wasn't.

And I was drowning.

Shaking my head to rid myself of my thoughts, I looked back again to the little path that led to Tāne Mahuta. Te Matua Ngahere was also nearby—I'd been told it was the oldest tree in the forest, and some estimated it to be up to four thousand years old, the oldest tree in New Zealand, possibly even the oldest rainforest tree on earth. I'd wanted to go see that, too, but it was starting to get dark, and the check-in time for my hotel was fast approaching.

The road to Opononi was as winding and narrow as I'd feared, and I spent every second of it clutching my steering wheel for dear life. Every once in a while a car would come up behind me and the driver would lean on the horn before swerving around me and speeding off with the kind of confidence one only attained by driving on the side of the road one always had. I attempted to make myself appreciate the scenery, but I was never able to go for more than one second of looking before my gaze went anxiously back to the road.

The dense walls of the Waipoua Forest parted as the road led on to more open land. Despite my fear that I would crash—or instinctively drift onto the wrong side of the road—my breath was taken away by the view. Green hills gently sloped down to the harbor, and the dying sun splashed over the blue sea stretching for a short distance before meeting the other side of the land. A quick glance at my map told me I was looking at Rangi Point, where sand dunes and grass with sparsely dotted trees met in a delightfully confusing mix.

Opononi itself was settled right on the harbor line, a tiny town that couldn't have more than a population of a few hundred. The main street seemed to boast only a few hotels, a general store, and a small collection of stores, no more than five.

I didn't know why, but it made me breathe easier. Something to do with the ocean air, perhaps, or the small size of the town—either way, I was smiling as I located my hotel and pulled into the gravel driveway.

"Evening," the hotel clerk grunted at me as I walked into the reception. He didn't look up from his television.

"Hello," I greeted. "Booking for Mitchell."

The clerk seemed to perk up at the sound of my drawl. "American, huh? What are you doing around these parts?"

"I'm not a fan of big cities," I told him.

"Yeah, well, bloody good on you." The clerk beamed at me, as if I'd somehow praised Opononi by insulting the big cities. "Lot more to see and do 'round here. Here." He handed me my room key. "You're in number seven. Take a left 'round the blue building and you're right in the corner. Oh, and here, take this too."

He turned to reach into a fridge behind him and then gave me a tiny jar, no more than two inches high and about the same wide. "Milk for the morning," he said.

I blinked at the jar. Did New Zealanders keep their milk in small jars? "Thank you," I replied. "Much appreciated."

With my keys and my tiny jar of milk, I got back into my jeep and pulled around the corner to my room. The hotel was a series of smaller cabins instead of one building block, and mine sat in front of the sharp edge of a steep hill. It was painted white, plain on the outside, though the website had assured me they had recently been refurbished.

It was nearly completely dark—and growing chillier—by the time I had lugged my suitcase inside, and I was glad to be inside. It had indeed been refurbished; the furnishings were simple, quite plain, but comfortable-looking. I collapsed on the couch with a groan, still jet-lagged from the long flight and the following three-hour drive.

I was shortly up again, though, driven by the need to put the milk in the fridge. I gave an amused snort as I shut the door, and then I turned to see if there was any coffee. I opened the cupboard and stared into it.

The daddy longlegs spider stared balefully back at me.

I wasn't normally bothered by spiders, but I did cringe a bit. Gingerly, I reached underneath it to get a mug and the jar labeled "coffee," and shut the door on the spider. Hopefully that would at least keep it contained. It could stay in there all it liked, as long as it didn't venture into the bedroom.

The preground coffee had to be broken up with a teaspoon before I added hot water, and I tried not to think about how old it was as I settled myself in front of the television, hot coffee in hand. The New Zealand news was on. I didn't really watch it; I just let voices and images wash over me as I dwelled in my own thoughts.

I wasn't sure why, but my thoughts took me back to Tāne. Not the tree, the person. The man who had taken time after spreading his mother's ashes to talk and joke with a complete stranger.

I envied his receptivity. Were I in his position, I likely would have offered the staring stranger an unfriendly frown and continued on my way. Though I was highly skilled in playing the part of an honest, friendly ear, truthfully I had long ago lost most of my will to open up to strangers. Most of them just weren't worth it.

For a time I lost myself in my thoughts and the bright screen of the television, slowly sipping on my coffee. I couldn't relax. For ten years my life had been hectic, and now that I was away from it, I still couldn't break myself of that mind-set of constantly needing something to do. The idea of dinner was considered and dismissed; I had not brought any food with me, and I wasn't sure if the Opononi stores would still be open.

Instead, I eventually retreated to my bedroom. Though I was exhausted from jet lag, sleep didn't come easily.

Chapter 2

THE SOUND of a *baa* from directly outside my window woke me up.

"Christ," I moaned unhappily, pushing my head against the flat pillow. I felt like I hadn't slept at all, and my eyes felt gritty even though I hadn't opened them yet. And I was *starving*.

The *baa* sounded again, a little further away. If there was a sheep wandering around outside, at least it was leaving. When I had read about the country, I'd formed an idea of New Zealand being positively overrun with sheep. The sheep-to-person ratio of New Zealand was higher than most countries, with four million people and thirty-one million sheep. I doubted my imaginings were true—or I hoped, for New Zealand's sake, that their main cities weren't constantly held up by herds of sheep belligerently wandering across the city roads.

I had never been a morning person, so I stumbled my way through a shower, brushed my teeth, and got dressed. My eyes still weren't fully open by the time I was drinking my morning coffee, though I did spare a smirk for the tiny milk jar as I used it in my drink.

As I put the coffee jar back in the cupboard, I spotted the daddy longlegs again. "Oh, there you are. Good morning," I said to it. "I thought you'd gone missing. You must have moved in the night."

As all daddy longlegs were prone to do, it ignored me. I didn't blame it; my morning conversation was intolerable.

"You wouldn't happen to know where I can get some breakfast?" I absently asked the spider. It, of course, did not know. "Well, you're useless, aren't you?"

I shut the cupboard door on my unhelpful friend and set out.

The morning air of Opononi was fresher than anything I'd ever breathed in my lifetime. I'd spent most of my life in Dallas, and while I loved the place, my lungs had long since resigned themselves to a diet of car exhaust and factory smog.

Here, my lungs almost ached from the purity of the air. I stood next to my jeep and just breathed for a few moments, shaking my head in wonder. I couldn't smell pollution; instead, the only things I could smell were grass and the ocean.

A third *baa* drew my attention to the hill my hotel cabin was set in front of. On the ridge of the incline stood a sheep, placidly chewing on grass. It swung its head to look at me, dismissed me, and went back to the clearly far more interesting activity of eating.

Still half smiling to myself in amusement, I got in my jeep and drove down to the main road. Driving there, it turned out, was mostly a superfluous venture, as I only had my foot on the gas for thirty seconds before I'd arrived at the main street. My only options, it seemed, were two hotel restaurants, both of which belonged to decidedly nicer hotels than I was staying in.

I chose the one that looked a little less upscale. While the hotel that sat at the entrance of Opononi, closest to the forest, looked very nice, my tastes ran more toward places that wouldn't cost me an arm and a leg.

The Opo Pub was obviously a bar for most of the day, but in the morning it welcomed visitors inside with a cheery sign advertising its breakfast menu. The interior of the bar instantly cheered me up a bit from my morning fugue; it was made of and furnished with dark wood, with sturdy chairs and tables set around the edges. A television set on the wall on the far side of the room displayed a sports game I'd never seen before, and below it was a roaring fire.

"Good morning." A woman behind the counter—which looked like it had been cut from a single, massive tree—smiled at me. "Are you looking for breakfast?"

"That I am." I glanced around the bar; I would be the only customer. Perfect.

"Take a seat anywhere you like. I'll bring you the menu."

I chose the table closest to the fire, shivering once as the heat from it began to warm up my left side. The waitress was there in a second, handing me a menu. I offered her a perfunctory smile in return.

"You sound American," she pointed out, lingering near my table.

"That's because I am."

"Oh!" She gave a brilliant grin. Women weren't my preference when it came to relationships. But Kiri—as her nameplate stated—was gorgeous in the most simple of ways: no makeup on her face, her hair in a loose braid. "Wow, I don't think I've ever had an American in here. Where in America are you from?"

"Texas." I was beginning to suspect that New Zealanders were very curious about foreigners, possibly because they were such a long, arduous flight away from most of the world. I didn't mind their curiosity. Far from it; it was actually starting to endear me to them. They were so open in their fascination.

"I've always wanted to go to America," Kiri sighed. "Especially Los Angeles. So, why are you visiting Down Under?" Her gaze lingered on my collar. "Come to see our churches?"

Damn it. I'd put my priest collar on. I hadn't even thought about doing so; I'd just gotten dressed on pure autopilot. But I didn't want to rip it off and frighten another poor person off when it was revealed that I was only pretending, so this time I kept it on.

"I'm off the clock, actually." I rubbed my fingers across the collar and smiled at her, automatically slipping into my old work persona. "Even priests need to take holidays occasionally, and I thought the scenery of New Zealand would be good for the soul."

"You're not wrong there." Kiri grinned as she tugged a notepad out from where it had been tucked into a wide belt. "Can I get you anything to drink while you look at the menu?"

I only needed to take a quick glance at the menu to make up my mind. "I'll have the bacon and eggs, please, and tap water with it."

She looked confused at the request of tap water, but rather than question it, she chirped, "No problem!" And then she left, leaving me, well, confused about her confusion. Did they not call it tap water here?

There was a paper called the *New Zealand Herald* lying on the table, which I picked up to glance over. I was more interested in the décor of the bar, though; people and their surroundings had always been more fascinating to me than the news of the world. There was a mounted deer head on the far wall beside the bar, a poster for a beer called Tui above the beer taps. Behind the bar hung a large white board, covered with scrawled names for a local raffle competition.

My gaze went back to the television. There were men in T-shirts and shorts passing a ball around. It looked a little like American football, just without the padding and far more tackling one another.

I heard footsteps behind me. Kiri cheerfully greeted the newcomer, and I heard the footsteps falter as they passed by my table. Despite my vague irritation that my peacefully solitary breakfast would now not be so solitary, I turned to look.

"Tāne," I said, surprised.

"Hey," Tāne replied. I'd spent the past ten years of my life learning how to read people, so his attempt to hide any reaction to seeing me didn't work. "Didn't know you were staying here."

"Likewise. I'm not a creepy stalker, I promise, despite appearances."

Tāne's expression eased at my pitiful attempt at a joke, though I saw his eyes dip to my priest's collar. Unlike Kiri, I'd told Tāne I wasn't really a priest, and I found myself hoping he wouldn't judge me too harshly for it. Of course, nobody could possibly judge me as harshly as I judged myself.

"Want some company?"

I raised my eyebrows at the question, but I nodded. "That'd be nice."

Tāne might just have been the one person in New Zealand I actually wouldn't mind disrupting my solitude—though to be fair, I had only met roughly seven New Zealanders so far, and four of them had been working for the airport.

He sat, and I noticed he started scowling as he caught sight of the television. "Bloody Wallabies," he muttered to himself, looking over the menu that Kiri had left on the table.

I couldn't help but ask. "Wallabies?"

Tāne opened his mouth to reply, and then seemed to remember he was sitting with an American. He laughed briefly, shaking his head. "Rugby, bro. You don't have it in America, do you?"

"We have something a bit like it," I replied. "We call it football. Except in football they wear a *lot* more padding."

"Wusses." Tāne wore a broad grin. His suspicion of me had apparently faded as he warmed to a topic he enjoyed. "Rugby's a *real* man's game. I'd like to see one of those footballers get into a scrum."

"I have absolutely no idea what that is."

Tāne looked like he was torn between amusement and a deep pity for the American who had not been enlightened as to the existence of rugby. He nodded at the screen. "Here, this's a replay. Watch this."

I did as instructed. Several men from both teams—one team in black, one in gold and green—crouched down low in several ranks facing each other, and then violently butted their shoulders and heads against the opposing team. A scramble ensued for a ball that had been put in the whole mess. When one of them retrieved it, the ball was passed from player to player.

I saw one player in black run toward a player in gold and green. "Oh, God, he's not going to tackle him without padding, is he?" I asked, horrified at the thought.

Wham. That was definitely a tackle, one so hard it sent the player in gold and green slamming to the ground. I saw a flash of blood streaming from the player in black's nose—I expected him to immediately head for the sidelines. Instead, he simply swiped an arm over his face and kept playing.

Perhaps Tāne had a point.

Tāne was laughing quietly at my look of mute admiration. "Fellas in black are our team, the All Blacks. The gold and green are the Australian Wallabies." He said "Wallabies" with such hatred that I wondered what the story was there. I knew Australia was geographically close to New Zealand, just to the northwest. I'd had a layover in the Australian city of Sydney, and the flight to Auckland had only taken three hours. Perhaps they had something of a rivalry?

"Who usually wins?" I sincerely hoped I wasn't opening a can of worms with that question.

"We do," Tāne said proudly. His tone then soured. "But sometimes those fucking Wallabies manage to win. We were missing Trent Barker in the lineup last night; he's built like a brick shithouse. He would have wasted them."

He was interrupted from continuing further by Kiri's arrival. She took his order, and set my water down on the table. "Tap water for you," she said, wrinkling her nose in bemusement.

Tāne took on the same expression. "Specifically tap water?"

"You know, just plain water," I tried to explain.

"That's just water, mate," Tāne said. He seemed to take pity on me and my strange American ways. "If you want plain water here, just order 'water.'"

"Oh." I wondered what they did when they wanted sparkling water. Or maybe they didn't have that here? "Good to know."

With an amused little smile, Tāne went back to watching the television. We sat in companionable silence while we waited for our food to arrive, and I watched both the television and his ever-changing expressions in response to it. He must be into rugby; one second he'd look elated when his team scored, and the next he'd look utterly dejected when they lost the ball.

I eagerly dug into my bacon and eggs when our food arrived. For the moment, my constant need to have something to work on wasn't so bad; I had food, I had company, there was a rugby game to watch, and cool ocean air was wafting through the open double doors. I was beginning to understand why all the travel websites called New Zealand *idyllic*.

"So, you staying here a while?" Tāne broke the silence to ask.

It took me a moment to process the question; I'd started to get absorbed in watching rugby players viciously tackle each other. And I didn't even like sports all that much. "Oh, no, I'm only here for the day," I said. "I have a loose schedule; I'm going to be traveling all over."

"I could show you around Opononi, if you want," Tāne offered. Despite my earlier lies, I didn't detect a hint of hesitation in his generous offer. I was amazed. "I mean, there's not actually much to see in the way of tourist stops, but I can show you them."

What kind of person could meet someone who lied about being a priest, see them *continuing* to lie about it, then selflessly offer their time and company? Tāne was either very kind or very stupid, and I was leaning heavily toward the former.

"That would be great." My surprise must have shown in my voice, because he laughed quietly. "I don't really know anything about this place. It's so small it's not in any travel guides."

Tāne shrugged. "Wouldn't be much to write about, anyway."

"Are you sure? I don't want to seem ungrateful, but you said yesterday that you were spreading your mother's ashes. I wouldn't want to intrude."

"Already did that here this morning," he replied. "My schedule's pretty open too. I've got two weeks off work, so I can take my time."

He was still turned toward the television; I noticed that his gaze grew distant. He was presumably thinking about his mother, whom he'd obviously loved very much. I could sympathize; I'd lost my father a few years ago, and there was nothing quite like the pain of losing a parent.

"I could use a distraction too," Tāne continued.

Fair point. What was more distracting than a foreigner who lied about being a priest? I was likely worth all sorts of entertaining mental hurdles.

"In that case," I said, "I'd be quite happy to be as distracting as you like."

Chapter 3

THE TOWN of Opononi, I learned, was actually quite charming.

I was used to big-city life. I'd been born in Dallas, raised in Dallas, and had lived in Dallas for all my life. In the past ten years, it had suited my purposes well.

Opononi was the polar opposite of Dallas. Where one had millions of people, the other had a mere few hundred, if that, and most of those few hundred lived on surrounding farms. Where one had pollution, the other had clean sea air. Where one had a hurried, big-city tempo, the other had a pace slower than an arthritic snail.

Don't get me wrong—I loved Dallas. I loved the ease of access and the people; I loved the streets and the culture.

But Opononi was exactly what I needed right now.

"Opo the Dolphin," I read, leaning in closer to squint at the weathered plaque. "Who came in from the open sea and lived along this shore, becoming so tame that children could ride upon her back." I glanced at Tāne and raised my eyebrows. "Really?"

"Really," Tāne confirmed. He looked, as I did, at the off-white stone sculpture above the plaque; it depicted a dolphin cresting above the water, a young child clinging behind her fin.

"Huh." I peered at the plaque again. "It says 1955 to 1956. It didn't live very long."

"One day a local found her at Koutu Point, dead in a rock crevice. She's buried under the statue."

I had a sudden, strange image of a team of archaeologists finding this place in a thousand years, long after the town of Opononi had lived and died. I found myself wondering what they'd think of this strange grave. Perhaps they'd assume the people here worshiped Opo as a goddess.

I noticed that Tāne was standing an odd distance away from the statue, unlike myself, who was mere inches from it. I quirked a smile. "Scared she's going to leap from her grave?"

Tāne gave me a faintly sheepish expression. "Maori didn't play with her, when she was alive. Some said she was a messenger from Kupe."

I would admit to knowing nearly nothing of the Maori spirituality, other than the strange coincidence of both it and the ancient Egyptian's sun gods being named Ra. "Who is Kupe?"

"The stories differ." Tāne shrugged. "One says he was a chief of Hawaiki who came here in 925 AD. After some not so great shit he did to his cousin, he took his wife, Kuramarotini, and escaped with her in the canoe Matahourua, slaying monsters on his way. Some say he discovered this land. Others say he came to this land on the canoe Aotearoa, and he found this land full of goblins and strange creatures. And *more* others say he stranded his brother-in-law and stole away his wives, and made the western coast sea rough so that his brother-in-law could not follow." Tāne exhaled a near-soundless laugh, shaking his head. "There's heaps of stories. Don't know if I believe any of them, but I was raised with them, you know? They kind of sunk into my bones."

I knew the feeling. Religion was an insidious thing, behind every corner of culture. Even if one was an atheist, one still found oneself doing a great many religiously inspired traditions without realizing the origins: throwing salt; knocking on wood; refusing to walk under ladders.

"Anyway, that's about all there is to see in Opononi," Tāne said.

Though I knew it was a very small town, I couldn't help but be surprised. I thought of Dallas: the amusement parks, the museums, the historical sights. "A dolphin statue? That's it?"

"Unless you really feel like walking around the three shops again." Tāne sounded amused. "Or visiting the hotel."

"I like it," I declared. I turned to face the ocean, letting the cool sea breeze wash over my face. The beach consisted of sparse gray sand and rock worn smooth by constant tide. The Hokianga Harbor was warmly blue under the midmorning sun. I looked across to Rangi Point again, at the odd contrast between yellow sand and green trees.

Opononi was quiet. The colors of it all seemed to strike me the most. I had only traveled from Auckland to here, a mere distance of one hundred and sixty miles—I had traveled much further around Texas—and one thing I had noticed was that New Zealand was incredibly *green*. Even in Auckland, the largest city in the country, the highways had been surrounded by rolling hills of trees, bush, and brush. Opononi was no different.

"You could try surfing, if you want," Tāne continued. He seemed content to simply watch the waves, standing with his hands in the pockets of his scuffed jeans. He looked good there, under the sun and next to the water, his short dark hair ruffling slightly with the breeze. He had put sunglasses on, so it was not in his eyes that I witnessed his smile, but in the curve of his lips. "Or I think you can take a boat out to Rangi Point, surf the dunes on boogie boards."

"I'm thirty-five. I think I'm too old to go surfing, water *or* sand."

Tāne lifted an eyebrow like I'd just said something incredibly ridiculous, but he didn't press the point. "Where are you off to next, then?"

My schedule really was fairly loose; I hadn't planned anything more than stopping at major parts of New Zealand. I had decided I'd just stop where I liked between those points, and if where I stopped had no hotel vacancies, I'd sleep in my car. "Rawene, I think it's called?"

I almost took offense at Tāne's snorted laugh, but since he was grinning when he looked at me—and not in a disparaging way—I assumed he wasn't laughing *at* me. "Your pronunciation is *bad*," he said.

From anyone else, I would have taken that as insult. From Tāne, though, I chose to take it as friendly ribbing. He had such an easy way about him that it was impossible to get high-strung for too long around him. "Oh? How do I pronounce it?"

"Rah-wee-nee," he clarified for me.

"Okay, then I'm going to Rah-wee-nee," I replied, exaggeratedly overpronouncing the town name. Before, I had been saying it like Rah-ween. Many places in New Zealand had Maori names, and though some looked simple to pronounce, I obviously wasn't thinking about the vowel sounds in the right way. "Where are you going next?"

"I haven't decided," Tāne said. "Maybe back down to Auckland. I only came this high up for Opononi."

"Why Opononi, specifically?" I hadn't managed to stop myself from asking, and I winced as the words came out of my mouth. "I'm sorry. You don't have to answer that."

"My mum used to come here for holidays when she was little." Tāne stared out at the waves. "Her and her brother and sister, and my grandparents, lived in Auckland for a while. She used to tell me stories about their shitty car struggling to get round the bends of the Waipoua Forest road. Mum loved it here. She used to tell me, my sister, and my dad the story of them breaking down on the road every Christmas dinner."

The only things I could think of to say were useless platitudes, so I said nothing. I simply stood by Tāne and watched the waves with him.

Then I began to wonder why Tāne was the only one of his family spreading his mother's ashes. He'd mentioned grandparents, an uncle and aunt, a sister, and a father. Surely *all* of them weren't dead.

I didn't want to ask, though. There was absolutely no way I was even going to go near the possible awkwardness of asking about his family when he might tell me they *were* actually all dead. I was sure they weren't. But I was going to avoid the potential awkwardness all the same.

"Have you ever been to Rawene?" I asked. "I think it's just half an hour's drive up the road."

"Nah, never been. But I wouldn't want to ruin your holiday by tagging along."

"Hey, you let me tag along with you this morning," I said. "Besides, you couldn't possibly ruin my holiday."

Tāne gave me a smile I couldn't discern the meaning of. "Already shitty?"

I surprised myself by laughing quietly. "No. Already *good*, thanks to you."

He fell silent, and I felt a hint of the awkwardness I had been trying to avoid. I wasn't usually this bad at conversation—when in my guise of friendly spiritual guide, I effortlessly charmed and chattered. Take off my mask, though, and I was apparently as conversationally graceful as an elephant.

"Really?" Where I'd expected Tāne to sound creeped out by my words, he instead sounded tentatively pleased.

"What, you don't have hordes of people falling over themselves to travel with you?" I'd admit to being surprised by that. I had only known the man for less than a day, and already I wanted to keep in touch with him for the rest of my life.

He wore that odd smile again. "Not really."

I wanted to express my doubt at that, and ask him if he was secretly a serial killer or had done something equally terrible, something everybody but me knew about, because I couldn't imagine that Tāne didn't have as many friends as he wished to make. But given that I'd only known the man for a short time, I decided not to pry.

"Well, you are welcome to join me," I offered instead. "We could find our way around Rawene together."

Tāne looked like he was internally debating it, then said, "You know what? Fuck it. Let's go to Rawene. I don't have to be in Auckland until tomorrow, and I've got no nagging family to make me go anywhere."

"Rawene it is." I clapped him on the shoulder, pleased he would be joining me. I had no doubt we would split up after visiting the town—unlike me, he actually did have a schedule, and I was sure the places he was visiting would be different than mine. But I was glad to have his company for a little while longer.

We made our way off the beach and agreed to meet outside my hotel in two hours. The walk back to my hotel was so simple I could have done it in my sleep: back across the main road, maybe twenty feet to the right, and up the driveway to my cabin. The gravel drive crunched under my boots as I trekked my way up it, and I kept looking over my shoulder back at the Hokianga, wanting to absorb as much of the sight as I could.

I had little to do to pass the time for two hours, so I planted my ass on the couch in my cabin. I'd accidentally left the television on; it was now playing what looked like a soap opera with frankly horrendous acting. Then again, weren't *all* soaps plagued by that very thing?

The overexaggerated emotional dialogue tugged me into a pleasantly mindless state, where I did not think about how Tāne hadn't mentioned my priest's collar. Nor did I think about the questionable state of his family, or any more of my travel plans. No, I became a couch potato to rival the best of them.

Eventually I started to feel guilty about doing so when I had a whole new country to see, so I managed to get myself off the couch. I had barely unpacked the night before, which left me only a few clothes to stuff into my bags before I was ready to take them to my rental jeep. Once I'd tossed them in the back, I checked out of the hotel and parked in a little pull-in park next to the beach.

As I sat with the driver's door open, turned sideways in the seat to face the ocean, I decided I could live in a place like Opononi. The clean air, the sea, the friendly people. I had no clue what I'd do for a living— I didn't know the first thing about farming, and I doubted I could cook or wait tables.

Okay, perhaps I wouldn't be moving to Opononi anytime soon, not when my unique set of skills was barely applicable here.

I found myself reaching into the bag I'd stashed in the backseat, then drawing out a battered packet of cigarettes. It was months old, because I was hardly a regular smoker in any sense of the word, and even though it seemed a crime to introduce chemicals into my lungs once more when I had so much fresh air to breathe, I really felt like a good sit-down and a smoke.

The cigarette was stale and burned a little too quickly, but the nicotine continued to relax me long after I had put it out, and before I knew it, two hours had passed. Tāne was pulling his car up behind mine. There was no need for conversation; I met his eyes through the windshield, he nodded at the road and pulled out again. I followed in short order, once again returning to gripping my steering wheel tightly in despair at driving on the wrong side of the road.

The drive was pleasant, thankfully on a flat road with a decided lack of tight curves. The road pulled away from the shoreline to meander inland, and I didn't see many cars coming the other way. The only ones I did see were farmers' trucks and well-worn cars bearing trailers behind them, passing by only one car every few minutes.

It was mostly farmland on the road—State Highway 12, my map told me. As much as I could, I watched it pass by—seemingly endless stretches of green paddocks dotted with cows and sheep. Every once in a while I saw a farmhouse set back from the road, usually in shades of white, red, and brown, with tin roofs and shuttered windows. We crossed a bridge over a thick river about twenty minutes into the drive.

I could tell we were getting close to Rawene when the road curved near to the Hokianga again, and sure enough, within minutes I started seeing the first buildings of Rawene. It looked to be about the same size as Opononi, though there was even less on the main road. We pulled up to a small parking lot on the side of the road, where the land met the ocean in a sharp curve. Where Opononi had been on a relatively flat line of beach, Rawene sat on a corner.

Before I stepped out of my jeep, I hurriedly took my priest's collar off. I wondered if I should just stash it somewhere, like under the car seat, so that I forgot about it entirely, seeing as I seemed unable to break the habit of putting it on.

Tāne and I stepped out of our cars at the same time, and I wandered onto the small grassy area that accompanied the very peak of the land. If I were to stand at the tip, water would surround me on three sides, but I was more interested in looking at the old cannon that sat a little way back from the shoreline.

"A World War II cannon!" I exclaimed, leaning in to get a closer look. My interest in the world wars was not something I often admitted out loud; not with my former job. I was supposed to be a man of peace. My grandfather had served in World War II, and I was the sole owner of all the fascinating things he'd brought back from the war. Unfortunately, I had never had much of a chance to sit down and study the wars in detail.

What I was about to say would no doubt sound incredibly ignorant to Tāne. But I was interested.

"I didn't know New Zealand was involved in World War II," I ventured, cringing at my own lack of knowledge.

If I had expected Tāne to get irritated at my insular American ways, or on behalf of his country, I was thankfully spared that bad reaction. Instead, he shook his head, sounding halfway torn between exasperation and bemusement. "James. Man. What do they teach you in those American schools?"

I wondered if that was a trick question. "America's involvement in World War II? And how we won?"

Now Tāne *did* look a little irritated. I immediately felt guilty, and went to apologize, but he spoke first. "America thinks they won it. Britain thinks *they* won it. Both of them kinda forget it's called a *world* war." He stopped himself and took a breath. A sheepish expression crept onto his face. "Uh, sorry. Everybody seems to forget that we were involved and lost a bigger percentage of our population than any other country involved."

"Really?" My eyebrows had shot up. "Were you attacked?"

"Nah. Australia was, though, by Japan. New Zealand and Australia, we sent all our guys overseas. There's lots of tales of New Zealanders at the time hating the *shit* out of the American soldiers who came here on break, 'cause all the women would get charmed by the foreigners and leave." Tāne was smirking now, his earlier irritation seemingly eased.

I smiled at the tale too. "You sound like you know quite a bit about the war."

"My granddad was there."

I brightened. "Mine too. I have all of his old memorabilia."

"Yeah?" Tāne looked interested at that, peering at me through his sunglasses. "That's pretty sweet."

The words "I'd love to show you someday" were on the tip of my tongue, but I held them back. However much I would indeed love to do that very thing, well, who knew if I would ever see Tāne again once we both left Rawene?

I found I didn't like that idea; I instantly felt a heaviness at the thought of never seeing the man again. The feeling surprised me, as I was not the kind of man who got instantly attached. There was just something about Tāne…. He was so incredibly easy to be around, like a balm for my guilty soul.

Tāne kept me from wallowing for too long. "Want to wander around a bit?"

I did. Side by side, we stepped onto the main road of Rawene. To my right I could see a few businesses: a café, and a few others that looked like offices. We turned to the left, where we walked past a gas station that doubled as a real estate office. I had to stop and look at the properties offered, glancing over the paper posters stuck on the inside of the window. Most of the properties were on farmland, though a few were in the town of Rawene itself, at damn good prices. There was no superfluous decoration on them, nor did they look straight out of a catalogue; they were functional, solid, and charming in their own way. One was even painted five different colors, ranging from pink to green. It might have been an eyesore, but I liked it.

For a moment, I was almost tempted to throw fate to the wind and inquire about purchasing one of the properties. I was a frugal bastard, and I had overcharged for my fake services; I had a nice sum of cash sitting in my bank account.

Not Rawene, though. The town had character, but I was fairly sure I'd get bored stiff if I hung around for more than a few weeks, and even that was dependent on Internet access and how many books I had to read. I was a man of very few hobbies.

Neither of us had any urge to wander through the residential streets, so we didn't leave the main road. A bright sign outside the café must have caught Tāne's eye, because he suddenly chuckled, pointed at it, and said, "We *have* to grab a bite to eat in here."

Though I'd had a decent breakfast, it was a few hours past lunch now, so I followed Tāne inside the café. I glanced at the sign on the way in, wanting to see what had attracted his attention. Possibly unfortunately for me, all I saw was a brand name I didn't recognize, written in bold, curvy, red script.

The café was seated right on the shoreline. We took a table near the window closest to the water, though my attention was drawn to a huge board on the other wall, covered in scraps of paper bearing ads, for sale signs, two missing pet notices, and, placed randomly among it all, pictures of old sailing ships with paragraphs of text underneath that I couldn't read from the distance.

Tāne seemed positively gleeful as I ordered a pie, though I had no idea why. I'd seen it on the specials board—"Pie with a side of salad"—and even though I had absolutely no clue why pie would come with salad, I'd ordered it nonetheless.

"What kind of pie is it, do you know?" I asked Tāne. "Apple, peach, or something else?"

Tāne just grinned widely at me. "New Zealand pie, bro."

"That doesn't tell me anything," I pointed out. Tāne looked too busy restraining his laughter to answer me, so I very immaturely rolled my eyes at him and turned back to look at the Hokianga. The gap of water seemed slightly narrower here, the land on the other side populated by a thick cover of trees. I could see only a few signs of population on the other side, though a quick look at my map informed me that there was a town called Motukaraka there.

I then said, "Why do I get the feeling you're conspiring with the waiter to bring me something that isn't food at all? Like some sort of joke against foreigners?"

"I would never do that." Tāne clasped a hand over his heart, putting on a show of looking terribly offended. "Who do you think I am?" I exaggerated my suspicious scowl at him, and he grinned at me again, the very picture of innocence. "We love foreigners; they bring in practically all our economy."

"Ah, so you're just using me for my money," I sighed. I had to work to restrain my own smile. "Fair enough."

Our food had apparently only needed to be heated up, because it was quickly put on the table in front of us. Tāne had ordered a sandwich; my pie looked decidedly... unpielike.

Oh, it was round and it had flaky pastry, but where I was expecting a *slice*, this was an entire pie, perhaps three inches across. Maybe they had tiny pies in New Zealand, like their odd, tiny jars of milk?

Not to be deterred by anything unfamiliar, I grabbed my knife and fork. "Seriously, what kind of fruit is in here?" I asked him as I cut into the pie, slicing it in half. The scent of cooked meat hit my nose, and it was so unlike anything I had been expecting I leaned back slightly in surprise.

Tāne started roaring with laughter. "Your face!" He gasped around laughs, leaning forward to grab my arm in his amusement. "Holy shit, your *face*, James. You look like you just found a dead rat in there."

Right then I wasn't focusing on the strange pie; I was much more interested in Tāne's hand on my arm. He had a strong grip, the hands of a man who worked with them for a living, little scars on his knuckles and joints. A jolt of warmth hit my gut, and I was suddenly thankful I wasn't prone to flushing, despite my pale skin.

My lack of response must have clued him in to the fact that I was staring at his hand. I looked up, and our eyes met. I wondered what he saw when he looked at me. Some ragged-looking foreigner in a rumpled shirt, dark circles below brown eyes, stubble so blond it was nearly invisible.

I was a very perceptive man; I had to be, for my job. And whatever he saw? He looked like he liked it.

Normally at that moment of seeing reciprocated interest, I would have gotten awkward and closed off. But Tāne made doing that impossible. Though his wide grin had faded into a small, curious smile, he squeezed my arm and neatly continued on with the subject. "It's not a dead rat, just so you know."

Laughter was not something that came often for me these days, but right then, I laughed.

"Well, thank God for that," I said, my thoughts still spinning. "We've got chicken pot pie back home, but I hadn't expected—what is this, steak?"

"Steak and cheese," Tāne replied. He still hadn't moved his hand away from my arm. "New Zealand's primo fast food. Well, either that or fish and chips; you can try that later."

"That's *weird*," I told him solemnly. "New Zealanders are weird."

Tāne chuckled. "Wait until you try Marmite."

I decided I didn't want to know what Marmite was. Instead, I tentatively speared what looked like a chunk of steak in sauce on my fork, added a cut of the flaky crust from the side of the pie, and chewed on it. It was *good*. The tenderness of the steak contrasted with the slight crunchiness of the pastry, and both savory tastes mixed nicely together. There was a hint of cheese in there somewhere, and I was soon eagerly getting more on my fork.

"This is good," I declared, much to my own surprise.

"Told you." Tāne took his hand away from my arm—I missed the contact already—to hand me a bright red plastic bottle he'd picked up from the table. "Here, put this on it. Tomato sauce makes it even more awesome."

"Tomato sauce goes on pasta," I told him absently as I took the bottle. "Wait, this is ketchup."

"It's tomato sauce."

"No, it's *ketchup*."

"*Tomato sauce*."

Neither of us were able to hold our serious, stubborn expressions for long. I returned his grin, my mood feeling lighter than it had for quite some time. "Okay, fine," I said, relenting. "If I'm in New Zealand, I'll call it tomato sauce, even though that's wrong and weird."

I still wasn't completely sure about the pie, but I started to like it more and more as I ate. The salad was fresh and green, probably locally grown on the nearby farms, and the big sliding door that took up one wall of the café was open, bringing in the air from the Hokianga.

It occurred to me that after we left the café, there wasn't much more to do in Rawene. We would leave, and that would be the last I saw of Tāne. New Zealand was a small country, but not so small that bumping into one specific person while both of us were road-tripping was a likely happenstance.

Once again, we ate in comfortable silence. When we were done, I paid and had to consciously think about *not* tipping—it wasn't done here—then we wound up sitting at a picnic table next to the World War II cannon while we digested. Neither of us had verbally volunteered the idea, we'd just gravitated there; Tāne was apparently as reluctant to leave my company as I was his.

I was turned away from the table itself to face the ocean, Tāne was turned toward the road. Every once in a while, the wind would drift past, carrying snatches of sound from the television in the gas station-slash-real estate office.

"I really think I could live in New Zealand," I mused.

"Yeah? You wanna become a Kiwi?" Tāne seemed bemused by the idea.

Kiwi, as I recalled, was a nickname for New Zealanders. I had been told that the name came from New Zealand's native bird, the kiwi—a small, fat, round ball of a brown bird, ground dwelling and flightless, with a long beak on it.

"I think I'd make a good Kiwi." The urge to laugh was tickling at my throat; I settled for a small smirk. "Don't you?"

Whatever Tāne's answer was, I didn't catch it. Prompted by the sound of a familiar city name, I was suddenly too focused on the television noise that I could hear. It sounded like CNN.

"... *in Dallas, Texas, but his current whereabouts is unknown.*"

I wondered if there had been a mass murder in my home city. I hoped not. Tāne, upon seeing that I obviously hadn't listened to his reply, turned his head to hear the television better.

A different voice started speaking on the television. "*Nobody has pressed charges yet, but there have been dozens of witnesses all saying the same thing, that this man came to them as a faith healer, a rabbi, an exorcist, or a practitioner of magic, depending on which religion the witness believed in.*"

Fear clutched at my gut. I didn't want to listen any further, but I felt like I couldn't move.

"*This all started to come out,*" the reporter continued, "*when multiple people realized that they had dealt with the same man, James Mitchell, in a position of power or as a guide in different faiths.*"

Then I really couldn't listen because the rushing noise in my ears was too strong. Guilt started as a sour taste at the back of my throat. I didn't dare look at Tāne. Instead, I started plotting how to remove myself from his company, quickly and painlessly, without looking like an asshole.

"Huh," Tāne said slowly. He didn't sound shocked, or angry. I wasn't sure what emotion was in his words. Perhaps a mixture of too many. "I wondered about the whole…." He pointed at my shirt collar. I had taken the priest collar off, but we both knew he was referring to it.

"Yes." My own voice was strangled. "That'd be me."

He didn't reply. Though I wasn't sure of his reasons for not speaking right then, I suddenly felt a desperate need to explain, even though my explanation would hardly help matters.

"I'm a con man," I said. "I don't believe in any religion, but I know how to take advantage of those who do. So I did. Any major religion you can think of? I've posed as it."

Saying the words felt good. They were barbs against my already exhausted guilty conscience, and I *deserved* to feel like shit. For ten years I'd taken advantage of something that brought joy and meaning to many people's lives. If anything, I probably didn't feel as bad as I *should*.

"I wondered why you didn't ask," I continued, keeping my head down. Staring at the ground was easier than staring at a fellow human being.

"Wasn't really my business, was it?" Tāne seemed to sense I was dissatisfied with such a simple answer, so he kept talking. "I thought you were lapsed. You looked guilty when you took it off, and I thought the lie about being a banker was just because you felt embarrassed over your ex-job. Hell, I don't know. There were plenty of other explanations."

He sounded hurt, I thought. Despite my name and my sins being splashed all over CNN, Tāne's personal upset struck me deeper right then. Perhaps it was because I could see his face and the fine lines of betrayal.

"I'll go," I offered, rising. I was caught awkwardly in a half crouch when Tāne grasped my arm.

"Seeing as we'll probably never see each other again," he said, "I'm curious. Why?"

I didn't have to ask what he was referring to. The problem was, there were too many answers. Why did anybody do bad things? Why did anybody deceive or hurt other people?

"Because I felt justified," I said.

Tāne's confusion didn't clear up, but he did let go of my arm. I immediately wanted the contact back. I wanted to sit back down and tell him everything, but my pride, however many tatters it bore, wouldn't let me. My guilt played a pretty heavy part in that too.

"Thank you," I told Tāne. "For everything."

Walking away was hard, even if I did know it was for the best. Tāne was a good man, a good soul, and he didn't deserve to have someone like me hanging around him like an unwanted leech. Now that my story had hit the news, I might get recognized, and I didn't want anybody but me having to deal with that.

I got back into my rental jeep, and I didn't look back. I didn't catch a last glimpse of Tāne as I drove away. I didn't honk my horn in farewell.

I just left.

Chapter 4

THE FIRST thing that struck me upon driving into Auckland was the sight of the Sky Tower. A strangely shaped building with a long, thin tower and a series of bulging rings near the top end and a long needle above that, it was the tallest building in New Zealand, and the tallest freestanding structure in the Southern Hemisphere. It was brightly lit in the dying light of evening, emphasizing just how much higher it stood above the nearby skyscrapers.

Auckland had about the same population as Dallas, but only half the size. The city itself, which I could see as I drove ever closer, was smaller in scope. The skyscrapers weren't as tall, and as a whole it seemed built much more for function than decoration.

I'd seen it—and the Sky Tower—when I'd first arrived in the city off my flight, but it seemed so much more striking in the evening, when the city was beginning to light up. Cities at nighttime had always been my favorite sight.

The drive from the outer suburbs of Auckland to the inner city added another two hours to the three-hour trip from Rawene, and by the time I was navigating the central business district, I had started to get royally weary of driving. I had thought driving on the wrong side of the road on country roads was bad, but it was nothing compared to the roads of the city.

Auckland's inner city, I discovered, was strangely small. I had booked a hotel two streets away from Queen Street, which the pamphlet said was Auckland's main inner-city road, the Times Square of the city. There had certainly been quite a few people wandering the street, smartly dressed and with the typical hurry of a big city.

After Opononi and Rawene, it felt strangely stifling to have cars inches away from my jeep's front bumper and rear end. I found myself scowling at pedestrians and cyclists, and then breathed an audible sigh of relief when I saw the sign for my hotel.

I'd built up quite a bit of money over the past ten years; life as a scam artist actually paid very well if you were good and knew who to target. And I'd known I would be in Auckland tonight, so I had booked ahead as I'd planned my trip. I hadn't spared any expense.

The Cook Hotel was a five-star luxury joint; not the kind I'd stayed in often. I typically preferred places where I didn't have to be scared of putting scuff marks on the floor or leaving hairs in the basin. The hotel in Opononi had been much more to my preference, even with the daddy longlegs hanging out in the cupboard.

But why not spend a night in a five-star hotel? Maybe I could visit the spa, or lounge around the bar and pretend I was part of high society. That certainly would be a change, considering I felt like little more than gutter scum right now.

A valet took my rental jeep, which I internally smiled at before I walked in the lobby. There was green marble everywhere: on the floors and in the pillars; even the ceiling was made of it, a dusky color shot through with veins of black and brighter emerald. It was offset with rich white-and-gold furnishings, smooth lines, and plush pillows on the couches.

With my stubble, uncombed hair, and wrinkled jacket, I felt more than a little out of place. I obviously looked it, too, judging by the subtle frown on the receptionist's face.

I told her my name and hoped to hell she hadn't been watching the news earlier that day. I was lucky—she processed my card and my booking with nary a glance up at me, politely welcoming and perfectly perfunctory. A bellhop took my bags to my room, and I followed with a weary eye. This might be a five-star resort, but I still didn't trust people not to make off with my luggage.

The bellhop didn't hang around and stare at me expectantly like I was used to, which left me feeling a little silly as he walked off, as I had my wallet half out of my pocket. I was so used to tipping culture it was just automatic now. I found it strange that New Zealanders didn't tip; then again, they probably paid their waitresses and service people more than a few dollars an hour.

The room was just as opulent as the lobby. One entire wall was floor-to-ceiling glass, giving me a breathtaking view of the city. The white theme remained, though the green had been replaced in favor of light wood and chrome. It looked polished and scrubbed within an inch of its life.

So much for relaxing in here. How could I possibly relax when I'd be worried about dirtying the place up?

I wound up gingerly sitting on the couch, the television going in the background as I stared out at the city with a bottle of beer from the mini fridge in hand. It was damn good beer, though as usual with mini-fridge fare, I wasn't sure it was *ten dollars* good.

If Tāne could see me now, he'd probably mock me for being a recluse.

The thought made me grunt, irritated at myself. I missed him, but our sudden, uneasy parting had been my own fault. Besides, I'd hardly expected him to accompany me for my entire trip around the country. He surely would have gotten sick of me before long.

A traitorous part of my brain made me remember the reciprocated interest in his eyes at the café. But mere interest wasn't a sure start of anything, so it wasn't as if I knew for certain that I was missing out on anything special.

I shut the television off, drained the rest of my beer, and went to stand next to the window. If I pressed my nose right up against it, I could see down onto Queen Street, which was only getting busier as the sun sank lower. It was nearly completely dark, and the city had lit up, luring me down with the siren's song of alcohol and entertainment.

I weighed my need for wandering against the possibility that people would recognize me from the news. If I stayed out of bright lights….

A humorless laugh escaped me. Who was I, Elvis? I wasn't going to get screaming hordes of people following my every move. But my guilt led me down the twisting hallways of paranoia, envisioning cameras and screaming accusations, maybe even calls to the police. I hadn't committed a crime here, and the last I heard none of my victims were pressing charges, so the police couldn't arrest me.

That entirely logical thought didn't make a dent in my anxiety.

I turned away from the window, and instead of heading out, I wound up wasting time, picking through my bags and searching for anything that might distract me. I hadn't brought much, just clothes and toiletries, a few books. None of the books looked particularly appealing to me right now; reading wouldn't be a sufficient distraction. When I looked through a side pocket of the bag I'd taken as a carry-on, I felt my fingers bump against the familiar shape of my cellphone, which I had kept switched off ever since I'd boarded the plane.

Though switching it on didn't exactly sound very appealing—I didn't want to know how many missed calls I had—I did it anyway.

Forty-five missed calls.

Wincing, I scrolled through the list of names. Most of them were old clients, some I hadn't spoken to or seen in years. But one name appeared more frequently near the end of the list: Damien Rookwell. My lawyer.

"Shit," I mumbled, a sour twist forming in the pit of my stomach. Unthinking, I hit the Call Back button.

Even as I had felt justified in my con work, I'd known that I was doing something wrong—hell, that had been half the satisfaction of it. I had felt that I was morally right at the time, but I wasn't a stupid man. I had known that there might be legal ramifications should I ever be found to be a fraud. So I had gotten in contact with a lawyer a year after I had started my con work. Damien Rookwell was expensive, but he was worth every cent. During our first meeting, when I had told him exactly what I was doing, he had simply nodded and told me that he would agree to represent me should the need ever arise.

For all those years, he had been the only person who *really* knew what I did.

After precisely three rings, Damien picked up.

"James! Jesus fuck!" I cringed, holding the phone away from my ear to spare my eardrums. "Where the fuck have you been? Did you know that your phone's been off?"

"Wow, really?" I muttered sarcastically.

"Don't fucking play smart with me, Mitchell," Damien cautioned. "I tried going by your place a few hours ago, but you weren't there. Where are you?"

"New Zealand."

There was a short period of silence on the other end of the line. I heard a sigh, then the sound of Damien taking a drink—scotch, I presumed. That had always been his favorite. "New Zealand," he repeated. "Great."

"I needed a vacation."

"Tell me you've at least seen the news."

"Yeah." I tried to inject some vigor into my voice so that I didn't sound as sullen as I felt. "Hey, at least they're not pressing charges, right?"

"Criminal charges, no." Damien paused, and the dread in my stomach sharpened. "Some of them are pulling together a class-action lawsuit, though."

"*Fuck*." That, I felt, summed up everything. I had no other words to say.

"Yeah, fuck," Damien echoed. "They're going to file for general damages. In other words, emotional suffering. And if their anger is anything to go by, they're going to try to get you for every cent you own, Mitchell. So how about you get your ass back on a plane and we can sort this shit out before it gets too big?"

I stood, my gaze going back to the window and the sight of Auckland's lights. "My return flight is in four weeks."

I didn't want to leave before then. Christ, the entire reason I was here was to escape everything back home. Only when I'd left, I hadn't known that I'd be running away from a class action. I knew I should do the responsible thing and go back, but that sounded about as appealing as repeatedly punching myself in the face.

"Two weeks." Damien didn't sound happy. "Fine, you stay where you are for now. Class actions take a long time to pull together, and we can talk about the settlement after you get back, if they've even got it to present by then. Just don't do anything stupid, and don't try to stay there, all right? And for fuck's sake, keep your phone on. I can handle everything for now, but I'm going to need your input occasionally."

"Okay." I pressed my fingertips to my temple, digging in; a stress headache wasn't too far off if I kept thinking about this. And like a coward, all I wanted to do was turn my phone off, contemplate becoming an illegal immigrant, and get some plastic surgery so I wouldn't be recognized. "I'll keep in touch."

"And I'll keep you updated." Never one for good-byes, Damien hung up after that, leaving me to stare at my phone.

Now I *really* needed a drink.

I got myself out the door. However much I didn't feel like socializing, especially after that call, I was forced to acknowledge that I did occasionally need it. And right then, it could be exactly the kind of distraction I needed. I would just stick to bars and refrain from doing anything particularly stupid, so I wouldn't end up in the spotlight.

Queen Street had the same look of the city itself—not overly given to flash and unnecessary decoration, but functional and solid. If I were to walk northwest I would wind up at the docks in Freemans Bay, as most of Auckland was built alongside a harbor. Wellington, I recalled, was much the same. The North and South Islands were long and thin—driving horizontally across them would only take a few hours in some places, so main cities such as Auckland had been set by water.

I kept my head down and my hands in my pockets as I walked the street. It wasn't nearly as busy as I'd expected; Auckland was the biggest city in New Zealand, and even though I'd known New Zealand was significantly smaller than the United States, I'd still expected crowds like New York or Los Angeles. That wasn't the case at all.

Groups of people milled past me, lulled into slower walks by alcohol and a Friday night. I kept my eye on the shops and the bars as I walked past, looking for something to catch my attention.

The bar I went into was chosen only for the green flashing light of the establishment's name outside. I'd started to like the color after seeing it so often—green in the nature, green marble. Inside, the bar was pleasantly small and relatively uncrowded, low music muffling nearby conversation.

The bartender greeted me with a friendly, "What'll it be?" Quick and to the point. I liked him already.

"Whatever's on tap." As he turned to get a glass, I let my gaze wander over the interior of the bar. A large mirror behind the counter made the bar seem bigger than it actually was. Posters for music tours and festivals were slapped on every available inch of wall, and I didn't recognize the names of half of the bands.

When the bartender turned back, I faltered. "Do I tip you?"

His friendly face split into a grin. "Nah. Not unless you really like me."

"Keep serving me beer and you'll be my new best friend."

"I hate to think how shit your old best friend was, then."

I didn't really have one. That thought struck me as entirely pathetic, however true it was.

I gave the bartender a nod and went to sit at the far end of the bar. There were a few groups sitting at tables, but nobody loud enough to distract me from my thoughts, which was a pity. At least there wasn't a television; the last thing I wanted was to see my face plastered all over the news again.

As I sipped at the beer, I pulled my map out of my pocket. Tomorrow I would be driving to a place called Rotorua, a smaller city in the upper-middle of the North Island. I could take one of two routes: one was a scenic route that would take me mostly through unpopulated land; the other cut through the middle of a few towns, like Ngaruawahia, Hamilton, and Cambridge.

From Rotorua, it would be a short trip to the Bay of Plenty. I'd planned to stay a day or two in Rotorua, then head to a place called Rangipo, the start of the Desert Road. Mount Ruapehu, one of New Zealand's more famous mountains, was on that road, and after that, I would drive east to Mount Taranaki and get a hotel nearby.

That seemed a solid enough idea for the next few days. Plan made, I then more casually perused the map, silently trying to pronounce place names like Paraparaumu and Waikanae. I was fairly sure that my pronunciation was appalling.

As time dragged on and the bar started to fill up, I felt less and less comfortable sitting there. Maybe it was my paranoia, or perhaps my vague guilt that I was in a new city, a new country, and all I was doing was sitting in a bar. I had not flown fifteen hours to drink beer.

I paid the bartender and went on my way. It was fully night outside, though I couldn't see any stars due to the brightness of the city lights. People and cars alike made their trundling way down the street, and I walked with no particular destination in mind.

Fate mockingly ensured I wound up at the foot of the stairs of a church.

It was a beautiful church. Stone spires reached up into the sky, topping the weather-darkened stone of the solidly built building. There was a bell at the very top, and the stained-glass windows were lit only by a mere hint of candlelight inside, a mellow contrast to the glaring city lights all around. It was a peaceful structure in the middle of a busy business district, separate but part of it all the same.

I sat on the steps, pulled out my cigarette packet, and lit one.

I felt justified.

That was what I'd told Tāne. It was the truth, the purest essence of it, but it was a lie by omission too. It wasn't the whole story; it didn't capture every aspect of why I had done what I had. But as a necessarily short explanation, it worked well enough.

I didn't react when I heard the creaking of the double doors behind me, but I did cringe internally. Only one person would be at a church this late.

A bemused voice came from my left. "I would tell you to put that out, but my job is to save souls, not lungs."

I bit back any number of retorts I had to that. "Good evening, Father," I said genially instead.

"Good evening." I heard a shuffle, the muted grunt of an aged man bending joints in ways that didn't work so well anymore. The priest sat next to me. Out of the corner of my eye, I could see him looking up at the sky, a small smile on his weathered face.

I remembered feeling that at peace with the world. Perversely, I hated him for being able to feel it when I no longer could.

"I'd offer you a smoke," I said, "but I think I already know your answer."

He gave a soft chuckle. "I gave it up many years ago. Don't let the title fool you. I'm as subject to temptation and nicotine cravings as anyone."

I made a wordless sound of agreement. I knew very well, in fact, but having a conversation with a priest about my lapsed status didn't sound like something I'd particularly enjoy.

"American, hmm?" he continued. "We're so inundated with American media I admit I barely notice the accent anymore. I'm Paul."

"James," I responded. "I'm on vacation."

I was halfway through my cigarette. I could get up and leave if I really wanted to; my nerves were on edge being so close to Paul, my paranoid brain growing surer by the second that he'd be able to *smell* my past on me. But as much as I wanted to leave, I also wanted to stay and attempt to pick up on some of that inner peace, like I could absorb it through osmosis.

That same paranoid brain expected a lecture on my past sins, and I was relieved to not get one. Paul didn't seem to know who I was.

He was apparently quite content to sit next to me and watch the passing life of the city, and after a while I relaxed somewhat in his company. The religious circles I had affiliated myself with had gotten a bit hellfire and brimstone at times; that Paul wasn't already asking if I believed and damning on my answer to the negative was surprising to me.

"Well, I'm going to take a wild stab in the dark and say that you might be in New Zealand for religious reasons," Paul said.

Damn. Maybe I'd gotten relieved too soon.

"Yeah? What gave it away?"

"There are three park benches along the street, yet you chose to sit on the church steps." Paul sounded gently amused. "And you're scowling up a storm, but you're not moving."

I didn't really want to answer. Paul seemed like a good guy, and the last thing I wanted to do was get my resentment all over him. He'd probably had a long day at work and just wanted to go home and put his feet up.

I settled on saying, "It's a long story, Father. Long and boring."

A long story that led to a class action currently being put together against me.

Christ.

He didn't reply right away, and I noticed he'd tipped his head back to look at the sky again. "I've lived in New Zealand for thirty years. I came out here from Ireland when I was thirty-two, and do you know what strikes me most about this country, spiritually?"

I shook my head, motioning him to go on.

"The *cleanliness*. If countries and cities have a certain spiritual buzz in the air, so to speak, New Zealand has something of a purity to it. As if the air is extra fresh here, as if there's nothing but potential."

I realized that what Paul had said might sound like spiritual bullshit to some people, but his words had truth to them. Those of us with long-held faith, those of us who were used to looking beneath the surface or closing our eyes and reaching out for something intangible—sometimes we tuned in on things like that. Whether it was real or imagined, I had no proof either way.

"I visited London once," I said. "It felt... like a great beast was sleeping underneath it."

Yeah. We definitely sounded crazy to nonbelievers.

"I loved London, don't get me wrong," I hastened to clarify. "But all that history felt like it had become a living, breathing thing."

"Really?" Paul looked interested. "I'll have to visit London someday. Some of the best churches in the world, there."

I only noticed that my cigarette had nearly burnt out when I felt the heat against my fingertips. With a muttered curse I went to stub it out, then, remembering where I was, grimaced and stood to walk over to a nearby trash can.

"I know what you mean about New Zealand, though," I said as I came back and reclaimed my former spot. "It does feel green."

Paul smiled sadly at me. "When did you lose your faith?"

Initial surprise hit me, and I thought he'd seen the news, but a quick run-through of our conversation made me realize I'd been pretty obvious about it. I sighed, twisting my fingers together. "Ten years ago. Shortly after I became a priest."

"I'm sorry, James." I felt the light pressure of a pat to my shoulder. "I won't ask what happened in your life to make you lose your connection to God. In my experience, with the people I've known, it's never a sudden thing. It's almost always a slow burn with a very sad ending. I hope you'll be able to find some peace of mind here."

I sat waiting for the lecture about how I was going to go to hell, but it never came. Paul never insulted my experience, and he never damned me. Just that small action made me feel like a piece of my stress broke off and lifted away.

"I hope so too," I replied honestly. "I miss it. I just have some difficulties with it."

"All the best, then." Paul stood, and I shook his hand when he held his out for me. "If you ever need someone to talk to, you know where to find me."

I surprised myself by answering genuinely. "I'll remember that."

I watched him walk away, for the moment feeling a bit lighter than usual. His understanding didn't ease my guilt about what I'd done, but it did make me feel a bit better about my own faith.

My purpose in coming to New Zealand had been twofold: one, to get away from the city I'd lived in; and two, to maybe find a place where I could rediscover my faith. It had always been a very important thing in my life, and even though I had lapsed, even though part of me resented it and my family and my parish for the division it had caused in me mentally, I did miss it. I missed the steady belief and the faith that a higher power would catch me if I fell.

There was a hole deep in my chest where my faith had once lain, and I had never felt more empty.

I watched the traffic and the people pass for a few more minutes, but my ass was starting to get sore and cold from the stone steps, so I started walking back to my hotel. I wasn't really in the mood to discover Auckland's nightlife. It seemed that most of the people swarming the streets were young, beautiful men and women in their twenties, and compared to them I felt like a bitter old crab of a man.

The hotel greeted me with a blast of overly warm air as I stepped into the lobby. I watched the numbers on the elevator slowly tick downward until it came to ground level, then watched the numbers on the inside rise as it took me to my level. My room was a hollow comfort; gorgeous but shallow, unfamiliar.

I fell asleep watching the far-off twinkling lights of the suburbs beyond the city, letting them lull me into a dreamless rest.

Chapter 5

NINE IN the morning found me in a café called Greenstone, sipping at my morning coffee and blearily watching people pass by the window.

I'd had a decent rest, finally getting over my jet lag, but I'd never been good at mornings. I would never be able to understand the people who actually felt *refreshed* upon waking up; the concept was utterly foreign to me.

In my postsleep haze, I hadn't cared about being recognized and stumbled into the nearest place that would serve me coffee, ordering the largest size they had. The largest size was apparently a regular coffee mug—I, coming from Texas, found that a bit strange.

As I slowly woke up, I studied the various things on the table for the lack of anything better to look at. The coaster under my mug had some sort of quote in tiny text on it, filling the coaster completely, so I lifted my mug to look.

God is, or he is not. A game is being played... where heads or tails will turn up. According to reason, you can defend neither of the propositions. You must wager. (It's not optional.)

Let us weigh the gain and the loss in wagering that God is. Let us estimate these two chances. If you gain, you gain all; if you lose, you lose nothing.

Wager, then, without hesitation, that he is. There is here an infinity of an infinitely happy life to gain, a chance of gain against a finite number of chances of loss, and what you stake is finite. And so our proposition is of infinite force, when there is the finite to stake in

a game where there are equal risks of gain and of loss, and the
infinite to gain.

Pascal's Wager.

I nearly rolled my eyes from the irony.

Once, I had quite enjoyed the philosophical argument. It seemed utterly rational and obvious. If you did not believe there was an afterlife, and belief was necessary for reaching it, then you would not get there, so you might as well believe.

I'd realized it was horseshit a few years after I'd lost my faith. It was all well and good to put things so simply, but the truth was, nobody could *make* themselves believe in something for the sake of belief. Faith had to come naturally; it couldn't be forced. A nonbeliever couldn't suddenly decide to completely and wholly believe. They had to feel it.

I shook my head in bemusement and put my mug back down. An immature part of me was tempted to rattle my mug a little to make coffee slop over the sides and stain the coaster so the words could not be read.

While I was in the middle of contemplating if I would explore Auckland some or if I would start the drive to Rotorua, I heard the doorbell jingle, then footsteps over the floor. It felt like déjà vu; it was how I had run into Tāne the second time in that little café in Opononi.

I snorted quietly at the little spark of hope I felt and shoved it down. There were 1.3 million people in Auckland; there was no way I would run into him again. Whoever was walking into the café, it was just someone I didn't know.

But that stupid little spark made me turn my head. The Greenstone Café was shaped oddly, with little nooks and crannies in the wall—one of which I'd parked myself in for the privacy, so nobody walking in would see me unless they deliberately approached. On the other side of the room I could see a man with his back turned to me. He wore a blue-and-green flannel shirt with light jeans, his dark hair was cut short, and his broad shoulders hunched inward slightly. As I watched, he paid for his order and went to sit down at a table near to the front window, his back still to me.

I didn't need to see his face to know it was Tāne.

Indecision tore at me. Should I go talk to him? Should I finish my coffee and attempt to sneak out without him seeing me? Or should I hide until he left?

I'd gotten no indication that he ever wanted to talk to me again. Tāne was a good man, I had seen that much, but even good men had their limits. Nobody was friendly to absolutely everybody.

And people like me? I was friendly to very few.

Tāne, though... I thought he could be different. I thought he might understand, if I talked to him. Even though I might never see him again, I felt like I needed him to understand.

Then again, this was the third time our paths had crossed. I wasn't sure I believed in fate, but that was some serious coincidence.

I made up my mind. I stood, coffee in hand, and clamped down on my dread as I walked across the café. I came to a stop beside Tāne and cleared my throat. He glanced up, looking politely inquiring at first, then surprised as he recognized me.

He inclined his head, giving me permission to sit. I did so.

We said nothing. Tāne's gaze was piercing, soul-searching, as he studied me, and I didn't look away, however much I wanted to falter under the strength of his scrutiny.

Then he lifted his glass of water to tap it against my coffee mug, a silent sign of forgiveness.

All the tension in my chest left me in one great drop. I wasn't sure what to say, but the tiny smile at the edge of Tāne's lips said everything for me. It seemed neither of us particularly wanted me to go on at length about what had happened in Rawene, and I was grateful for that.

"Hello again," I said instead.

"Three times we've met now," Tāne replied. "Do you think fate's trying to tell us something?"

I exhaled out a little noise of shared amusement. "If it is, I've never seen it be so obvious."

"Maybe you're just dumb and it needed to hit you over the head to get its point across." The corners of Tāne's eyes crinkled.

I arched my eyebrows at him in mock insult. "Thanks. That's really nice of you."

He just smiled some more and let that do the talking for him; it spoke eloquently enough. I wanted, desperately, to explain to him why I had done the things I'd done, but first I'd need to tell him exactly what I had done wrong, and the prospect of listing my sins didn't sit too well with me.

I resolved that if he asked, or if we spent much more time together, then I would explain. For now, all I knew was that we might only have a few minutes more, and Tāne didn't need them to be full of an awkward asshole attempting to atone.

The waiter delivered a plate to Tāne, who thanked him politely and set about grabbing a knife and a fork to eat with.

"So where are you headed to next?" Tāne asked.

"I hope I say this right—Rotorua?"

"Right enough," he said, laughing. "That one's pretty easy to say." He looked at me with a speculative gleam in his eye. "Through Hamilton, or the country road?"

I shrugged. "I haven't decided yet. Do you have a suggestion?"

"You rented that piece-of-shit jeep in Auckland, right?"

"It is not—" All right, it wasn't an especially great jeep. "Yes."

Tāne nodded to himself, chewing on a mouthful of the food he'd ordered. It looked like a pig in a blanket to me—meat wrapped in pastry. "I've got my ute, and I bet you it gets more kilometers to the liter than that jeep gets."

The metric usage took me a few seconds to work out; that must be the metric way of saying "miles to the gallon."

"A ute?" I laughed. "God, it's like you're speaking an entirely different language. I barely understood anything you just said."

Tāne pointed out the window. "That thing."

I turned to look out the window and immediately said, "Oh, a pickup truck." I had a reasonably decent knowledge of vehicles, and the pickup truck parked outside the café looked like an Isuzu, though I'd never seen that specific model before. It was a nice vehicle, though.

Tāne had it in bright red, and it was obviously used for utility as well as pleasure.

"It's an Isuzu D-Max LX Single Cab," Tāne said proudly. "Just got it last year. Isn't she a beaut?"

"It is nice," I agreed, still studying it. "Why did you get a pickup truck?"

"I'm a woodworker." I liked the warm tone of quiet pride in Tāne's voice. "So I need to haul around a lot of wood."

My face was still turned away—just as well, because the little smirk I couldn't stop was completely immature. A beat later I heard him snicker, and we indulged ourselves for a few seconds, giggling like schoolboys over the innuendo.

I turned back in my seat to face him. "A woodworker? I wouldn't have guessed that." Now that I knew, it seemed so very right. Tāne was one of the most down-to-earth people I'd ever met; with his strong hands and broad shoulders, I could easily see him with the strength needed for heavy work, and the delicacy required for little details.

"*Anyway*." There was still mirth in Tāne's eyes. "What I was going to suggest was we could go to Rotorua together."

"Pardon?" Surprise warred with genuine pleasure at the offer.

"Well, if you're going to see the biggest sights of New Zealand, from the top of the North Island to the bottom of the South Island, there's really only one route you can take," Tāne continued. "I mean, there are choices like picking one of two highways to get to your next destination, but we're not a big country. I'm betting I'm going the same way you are."

As much as I wanted to say yes, I couldn't help but say, "You'd sit in a car with me after knowing what kind of person I am?"

Tāne grimaced. "Do we really need to have a heart-to-heart about this?"

I wanted to say *yes*. I didn't like opening up about my feelings as much as the next person, but I thought knowing where I stood with Tāne would be helpful.

"You're sitting there overthinking, aren't you?"

"Yeah," I admitted sheepishly.

Tāne heaved a sigh. As he spoke, he ticked off points on his fingers. "I'm not asking just to be polite. I think it's shit what you did, but we all have bad shit we've done in the past, and I'm not going to judge until I know everything. You're weird and American, but I really do want to road-trip with you, even though we don't really know each other." He peered at the three fingers he was holding up. "That enough for you?"

I didn't tell him about the class action.

Instead, I said gratefully, "That's enough."

"Good, because I'm not doing that again." Tāne looked like he wanted to roll his eyes at me. I wanted to roll my eyes at myself too. "Now how about we put on some Enya and order some green tea?"

The volume of my own laugh surprised me. "You're on."

NOBODY WOULD be surprised to learn that we did not, in fact, play some Enya and drink green tea—though I privately admitted liking the latter, and Tāne had shiftily agreed, looking from side to side like he hoped nobody was listening in.

I returned the jeep to the rental service just outside the airport and had to reassure the very dismayed young man at the counter when I'd cut my month-long booking short. He thought there was something wrong with the car; I then had to stand by and watch him worriedly crawl over the jeep with a fine-toothed comb while I attempted to convince him it was just that my plans had changed.

When he finally released me from my exasperated repetition, I met up with Tāne in the parking lot and chucked my luggage into the back of the pickup truck, which Tāne then covered with a tied-down tarp.

His pickup truck—ute, I supposed I should call it—was surprisingly roomy in the single cab, had leather seats that I sank into, and the heating warded away the chill of the oncoming autumn.

My parents had always told me to never get in cars with strange people, but Tāne didn't feel like a stranger. He already felt like a good friend, the kind I could sit in comfortable silence with without the need for entertainment. I hoped he felt the same way about me, and from the way he pulled out of the airport car park without immediately engaging me in conversation, it seemed like he did.

Though we'd only known each other for a few days, I felt like I could trust him, which was why I hadn't hesitated at all when I'd accepted his offer. I felt like we could be friends—and maybe even more, a hopeful part of me whispered. There had definitely been a reciprocated spark in the café in Rawene.

So here I was, throwing my lot in with a Maori woodworker who was spreading his mother's ashes around New Zealand. We weren't exactly the most likely pair.

"Are you listening to Lady Gaga?" I stared at the radio, then at him, as Tāne pulled the ute onto the highway. "Seriously?"

"Shut up," Tāne said defensively.

"That's not even on the radio. That's a *CD*," I continued in growing glee. "You have a Lady Gaga CD."

"Shut up!" Tāne was laughing now. "It's not all Neil Finn and Bic Runga here. Most of our music is bloody American or European." Embarrassingly, I only recognized one of those names.

"It's okay," I told him very somberly, patting him on the shoulder. "Your love of Lady Gaga will remain a secret."

"Thanks," he said dryly. Then he offered, "Change the music to whatever you want; I'm not fussed."

I flicked through radio stations, passing through classic rock, pop, talk shows, and top forties. I couldn't detect any real difference between the radio stations here and the ones in the US, so I settled on keeping the top forties at a low hum, quiet enough that it wasn't disruptive but still loud enough to hear.

The suburbs of Auckland passed us by. They were just as green as Opononi and Rawene, though more dense with houses. Every house seemed to have a backyard lined with trees and foliage. Every street had more trees beside the road, some small, some almost towering over the roads. The green was just barely starting to get spotted with faint yellows and deeper oranges.

"So, do we want to go through Hamilton or the scenic route? That second one's mostly farmland and a few mountains, but there's a few towns on the way to stop and get lunch at," Tāne said.

"If you don't have any preference, the scenic route sounds good," I replied. Farmland and mountains might sound boring to a lot of people, but as someone who had lived his life in the middle of a city, I was actually excited at the prospect of seeing endless cows, sheep, and grass.

"Scenic route it is."

I unfolded my map and followed our route, keeping an eye out for place names as Tāne drove. He told me little facts about various suburbs as we went through them—"Wiri. I had a friend who went there for school, said it was shit."—"Manurewa. Couple of parks around here somewhere, I think, and not much else."—"Pahurehure. Sweet, we're nearly out of Auckland. Thank fucking God."

His commentary was simple and blunt, praising where it deserved and being none too kind where he had no love of the place. It occurred to me that I didn't actually have a clue where he even lived in New Zealand; the fact struck me as a bit strange, considering I was traveling with him.

I decided to voice this thought.

"I don't even know where you live," I said, a self-deprecating laugh under my words. "I never even asked. I'm sorry."

Tāne gave a bemused smirk. "Wellington, bro. I was born in Oamaru, and then we moved around a bit, but Wellington's been my home for the last nine years."

"Is it nice?"

Tāne shrugged. "It's where I live."

I knew the feeling. Dallas was a great city, but I'd accepted all of its charms and unique features as merely being part of my home. Where tourists would walk down the street and marvel at the architecture, I'd be too busy staring at the sidewalk and trying to avoid mowing fellow pedestrians down.

"Then I'm sure you can show me all the best parts of it." I said. "I'm not a fan of the tourist track. I like the out of the way places."

"Probably why you went to Opononi," Tāne said dryly. "That is *well* out of the way."

A thought struck me. "Hey, Tāne? In my hotel, the receptionist gave me this... weird little jar of milk. Is that normal?"

He laughed incredulously. "He gave you what? Nah, bro, we don't have milk in jars here. Sometimes in the really little towns they might still have milk delivery in glass bottles, but not jars."

I held my hand up, my thumb and pointer finger a few inches apart. "It was about this big. It was really difficult to pour."

That set Tāne off into a fresh peal of laughter. "That's just fucking weird. Don't worry, we have milk in normal containers like everybody else."

"Canada has milk in bags," I replied contemplatively.

Tāne just stared at me. It was a good thing the road was straight and relatively empty. "That's even weirder."

"I know!"

Tāne had turned his eyes back to the road, but he was frowning, apparently having real difficulty imagining milk in bags. To be honest, I did too. "Foreigners, man."

I nodded in solemn solidarity. Foreigners, indeed.

The houses along the road had started to vanish from sight about five minutes ago, leaving us with the vision of open road and lush farmland all around. When I excitedly pointed out the window at the sight of a paddock spotted with sheep, Tāne dutifully looked but didn't seem as enthusiastic as I did. He was probably used to the sight of a lot of sheep.

The scenery was much the same as I'd seen on the stretch from Rawene to Auckland, somehow distinctively New Zealand in a way I couldn't put my finger on. After thirty minutes I noticed a sign on the side of the road that announced we would soon be driving through Pokeno.

It was a town even smaller than Rawene, it seemed, the total drive through lasting maybe two minutes. I eagerly looked out the window nonetheless, taking note of homemade signs advertising garage sales, babysitters, and fresh fruit markets. The highway had officially transitioned from the Southern Motorway to the Thermal Explorer Highway a way back, though when I questioned him, Tāne didn't know why it was named so, either.

A short way out of Pokeno, we pulled over onto the side of the road to look at one of the fresh fruit markets at my request. I had lived off inner city supermarket food all my life, and while some of it was fresh enough, it hadn't been picked off the tree that morning like it was here.

The market itself was little more than a collection of wooden crates in someone's fenced-off farmhouse yard, reachable only by driving a third of a mile off the main highway.

The apples actually smelled like apples, I joyously discovered, and suddenly it seemed like all the apples I'd ever eaten in the past were pale imitations. Thankfully the lone aged woman guarding her wares with eyes as distrustful as a magpie didn't seem bothered by me picking the fruit up to sniff it.

"Tāne," I enthused, holding out an orange at him. "This is amazing—smell this."

Bemused, Tāne stooped slightly to sniff the orange. "I hope you don't think all our fruit is like this."

I would admit to slight disappointment. "Really? But there are farms everywhere."

"Nah. We export most of our good stuff, and the main cities suffer from travel time as much as any other country." Tāne examined a bunch of bananas as we shuffled along the line of crates.

We decided to pick up some fruit for the trip, and it was ridiculously low-priced. I had to restrain myself from buying an entire crate of apples; no matter how good they smelled, I wouldn't be able to eat them all before they rotted, and I wouldn't have the facilities to bake pies.

In the middle of selecting some oranges to buy, we wound up reaching for the same one, and accidentally knocked our hands together. As stereotypical as it might sound, I still felt a pleased little spark; our eyes met, and I could see he was feeling it too.

I thought this might be the perfect time to announce that I was interested—verbally or physically, though the idea of just kissing him appealed to me more. Unfortunately, the sight of the magpie lady hovering nearby was a bit off-putting, much to my disappointment.

I bought the fruit with the cash I had in my wallet; New Zealand had odd, almost plastic-feeling money, each note a different bright color. It looked a bit like Monopoly money to me, especially the pink five-dollar note. They also used more coins than we did, with one- and two-dollar coins colored gold to differentiate them from the copper or silver smaller amounts.

The magpie lady peered at me as I counted out fifty-cent pieces. "Aren't you the man on the news?"

I froze, dropping three of my coins from my suddenly clumsy fingers. "No, ma'am," I denied politely, bending to pick up the fallen coins. "Just someone who looks a lot like him."

That didn't deter her. "You are, aren't you?" She clucked her tongue, disapproval creasing her face—she still took my money, though. "You lied to all those poor people for money. You're lucky none of them are pressing charges, young man. I would."

If this had been the deep South, I probably would have gotten a high-volume rant about how I was going to hell. This lovely old Kiwi woman, however, just looked at me with so much disappointment it made me feel even worse than a rant would have done.

I stood there, clutched my bags full of oranges and apples, and said, "I'm sorry." I didn't need her to forgive me. After today I would never see her again. "If it helps, I'm more angry at myself than you possibly could be."

I couldn't discern her expression. She just shook her head and handed me my change. "I hope you apologize to them, young man."

"I will," I promised in a whisper.

I would. One day.

Just not today.

I walked quickly back to the ute, gritting my teeth against the sour taste of guilt at the back of my throat. Tāne was already there; I realized he must have made a quick getaway to give me some privacy when the magpie lady had started asking me questions. I gave him a wan, apologetic smile as I got back in the ute.

"One day you're going to tell me just what the hell happened," Tāne said as he started the ute up.

I leaned my temple against the cool glass window. "You'd have to buy me a lot of alcohol first."

"Consider it scheduled." Tāne nodded.

After he got the ute out into open road, Tāne reached across and laid his hand on my forearm. Though I was surprised at the contact, I was also grateful for it.

"I know the general gist of what happened," Tāne said softly. "But I also know that you're tearing yourself apart with guilt over it. Whatever happened, I'm okay with it because you're not that guy anymore."

His trust, above all others, seemed to be worth so much more. If a man as good as Tāne could forgive me without even knowing the details of what I had spent the past ten years doing, then maybe there was hope for me yet. Perhaps I hadn't fully damned my soul to the hell I still believed in, despite my doubt of heaven.

"I thought about kissing you back there."

Good one, Mitchell. Hell of a way to change the subject.

"Why didn't you?" Tāne very gently squeezed my arm.

I blinked at him in surprise. "That's not what people normally say. Aren't you supposed to say 'why?' or 'please don't'?"

Tāne's gaze was still on the road, though I could see him smirk. "I think we're both old enough, ugly enough, and intelligent enough to know why I didn't say either of those."

I'd tease him for calling me ugly, but my heart jumped in my throat, anticipation and hope making me single-minded. "The moment was ruined by the fruit seller. So you wouldn't mind if I did?"

"I'll just wait for the next moment, then."

Tāne seemed incredibly calm. I was hardly freaking out or reacting like a teenage girl asking out the boy she liked, but my heart was going faster than usual, excitement flooding through my veins. I turned my forearm and slid it back under Tāne's hand, bringing my fingertips to his wrist. His pulse was a little fast too.

"You are not the cool and collected Mr. Smooth you pretend to be," I said teasingly.

"My cover is blown," Tāne lamented.

"Should I shriek and jump around a bit? Then you really would be smooth, compared to me."

Tāne chuckled. "As funny as that would be to see, I'm pretty sure it's not necessary."

We drove like that for some time; his pulse under my fingers, his hand on my knee. I had never been so immediately comfortable with another person.

I did wonder what the hell I was doing. I wasn't a casual relationship kind of guy, and I didn't go for short-term flings. I had a month until my return flight and then I would need to fly back to the US. What was I thinking, pursuing a relationship on that kind of timeline? What was Tāne thinking?

I didn't think about it for very long before deciding I didn't care. We were just barely beyond the starting line and it was already good. I'd be a fool to let it go now.

Chapter 6

ROTORUA WAS a further three-hour drive away. The sight of farmland persisted for most of the journey, only breaking for the sight of low-lying mountains on the west side of the road, and a short trip over a similar low mountain range before we saw Rotorua in the distance.

I saw the collection of buildings as white shapes and orange roofs, but my gaze was drawn to the great lakes beyond. What looked like the biggest was, according to my map, Lake Rotorua, which the town curved along the shore of. In the distance, separated by only a very thin strip of land, was Lake Rotoiti. Two more lay beyond that—Rotoehu and Rotoma—but I couldn't see those two very well.

We turned onto a road that ran parallel to the main lake, and I smiled to myself as I watched it; it was one of the cleanest-looking lakes I'd ever seen, brilliantly blue and vivid. I figured this would be a great place to come for a summer holiday. It was chilly out, the beginning of autumn, but even so I was still tempted to strip down and jump into the lake.

The first thing Tāne said was, "Wind down your window."

Thinking he thought it was too stuffy in the ute, I did so and then recoiled at the stench that attacked my nostrils. "Jesus," I exclaimed. "Is that—?"

"Good old Rotorua air." Tāne grinned widely. I was starting to think he just enjoyed seeing me startled. "There's a lot of thermal geysers and hot mud pools around here, lots of minerals and gasses in the water that get near-boiled all day. Lovely, isn't it?"

It smelled like a mixture of burned rotten eggs and old oil. "I'm not sure 'lovely' is the word for it. People *live* here?"

"You get used to it," Tāne laughed. "After a day or two, you stop smelling it."

Aside from the smell, Rotorua looked like a nice place. I wasn't sure whether to classify it as a city or a town; there certainly weren't any skyscrapers, or even many very tall buildings, but it did seem a decent size. I saw shops and hotels alike along the winding waterfront road—Tāne had already booked his hotel before coming on the trip, but from the look of the vacancy signs lit up, I wouldn't have any problems finding a room on short notice.

The first thing we did was check Tāne in while I secured a room in the same hotel, a tastefully decorated white block of buildings two streets away from the waterline. I didn't feel the need to book anything expensive or lavish; the little single room five doors down from Tāne's booked room more than suited me.

We met up again outside in the little concrete-and-grass courtyard halfway between our rooms.

"So, what are we doing?" I asked. "You've got much more important plans than I do." I wanted to ask if he wanted company to wherever he would be spreading his mother's ashes next, but there was a chance he didn't want me to come along, so I decided to spare him the awkwardness of saying no.

"I'm going to the Waimangu Volcanic Valley," Tāne replied. That caught my interest, but again I refrained from asking. Luckily for me, Tāne said, "Do you want to come?"

To say I was surprised was putting it mildly. I hadn't seriously expected that offer. "Yeah, that'd be great," I said, the warmth in my words echoing the one in my chest. "Are you sure? I can guess how important this is to you."

Tāne didn't reply right away. "I want you to come," he said eventually. "My mum, she loved New Zealand. She loved showing it to people, like it was... fuck, like it was her kid or something. And that valley was one of her favorite places."

Honored beyond words, I simply nodded. "I'd love to come."

From our hotel it was only a short drive to the Waimangu Volcanic Valley. Tāne kept the box on his lap the entire time, one hand lightly curled around one edge to prevent it from tipping over as he navigated tight corners. It seemed a lot more intimate to me than what I would do with someone's ashes; I wondered if there was a different culture around funerals over here, or if it was just a personal preference of Tāne's.

We left the ute in the parking lot outside the visitor center and bought our tickets. Tāne grimaced at the entry fee, but very politely he said nothing out loud. "It was cheaper when I was a kid," he said quietly to me as we walked away with our tickets. "That's a bloody rip-off."

I was in the mood for a smoke, but seeing as the ticket seller had told us to allow two hours for the walk we'd be taking, I figured having a cigarette beforehand might not be a good idea. *Two hours* for a walk; I didn't think I'd ever walked that long to get to a destination before, but Tāne didn't seem to think it was a big deal. Maybe New Zealanders walked more?

We'd decided on the self-guided highlights track. The map they'd provided us with made the walk seem longer than Frodo's must have been to get to Mount Doom; when I mentioned this to Tāne, he muttered something I didn't quite catch. Something about everybody focusing on that movie instead of the other famous New Zealand movies.

The walk started off as a simple dirt track surrounded by greenery. It reminded me of Waipoua Forest, lush and dense, every square inch of forest floor covered with ferns or undergrowth; even the bark of the trees had other flora growing on it, as if they were so stressed for space that the plants had simply started growing on top of one another. It made for a slightly dizzying view with so much detail to catch the eye. I could hear birdsong coming from both the tops of the trees and the ground, quick chirps and drawn-out calls mixing with the buzz of insects and the gentle rustle of leaves in wind.

Our first destination, the map showed me, was the Southern Crater. Text alongside the map filled me in on the history of the place. This valley was New Zealand's thermal center, created by the volcanic eruption of Mount Tarawera in 1886. It was now a protected wildlife refuge and scenic reserve, with rare plants, plentiful wildlife, and steaming volcanic crater lakes. Waimangu, I discovered, meant "black water" in Maori. It was also the world's youngest geothermal system.

We turned a corner, and the Southern Crater came into view. "It's pink," I exclaimed in shock. "A *pink* lake?"

"Red algae," Tāne replied with a smile. I shook my head in amazement, studying the sight. The Southern Crater was set in a cradle of rock and plant, and at one edge I could see the surface of darker water, untouched by the algae that spread like a thick film over the rest of the crater lake, an odd contrast to the green around it.

After we walked through more dense, almost humid forest, the next destination was Frying Pan Lake. The name, I discovered upon seeing it, seemed incredibly apt.

I stood shoulder to shoulder with Tāne as we marveled at one of the largest hot springs in the world. It was pristine blue, bluer than any body of water I'd ever seen, and steam was flowing across the surface, twisting up and floating into the sky, exactly like the surface of a frying pan boiling water. Like the Southern Crater, it was set low in the land, the green, blue, and white the purest forms of those colors I had ever seen. My map guide informed me that the temperature of the water would be 130 degrees Fahrenheit, and that thirty gallons of boiling water entered the lake every second.

I felt humbled by the beauty of it. It was an odd feeling to experience, but my long-discarded faith tugged at my heart, emotion swelling, too large to contain. I felt Tāne bump his hand against mine, and after a moment of hesitation, I—maybe him, or maybe both of us moved at the same time—took his hand.

"I can see why your mother loved it so much," I said. My voice was hushed in reverence for the sight in front of me. The wind pushed the steam at us, blasting us with a hit of hot air from the surface of the lake.

"You haven't seen the best yet," Tāne promised.

Neither of us made mention of the fact that we were holding hands. It felt so natural—why call attention to it?

By virtue of the track being a one-way walk, we barely ever saw other people, and Tāne took my mind off my nervousness of being seen.

When the track grew narrow, he walked in front of me but never let go of my hand, and we laughed as we navigated obstacles like low-lying tree branches while trying to remain connected.

I did my best to read more of the map as we walked. I discovered that from 1900 to 1904, a geyser kept erupting in the valley at the height of what they said was four hundred meters. Having been raised on the imperial system, I wasn't sure if that was impressive or not until I read that the geysers had reached the height of the Empire State Building.

The Inferno Crater and Lake was just as beautiful; like the previous lake, it also had steam rising from the surface of the water, though this one was a much brighter blue, possibly due to the acidic nature of the water. We watched as great gouts of steam rose up to drift through the flora at the edge of the crater. I marveled and Tāne smiled at the familiar sight from his childhood.

Further on, the walk path provided little wooden bridges for crossing the stream that connected the Southern Crater to Lake Rotomahana, which was at the very end of the walk. We saw the Black Crater and the Fairy Crater, the latter of which plunged down deep with lava rocks for walls.

The Marble Terrace was a completely different sight again; the small pool of bright-green water was surrounded by rock that looked as if it had been coated in caramel, light-brown sweeping over shallow terraces of stone that had formed over many years as a result of the volcanic explosions.

Half an hour later, we reached Lake Rotomahana. Tāne held the box of his mother's ashes under his other arm.

"There used to be something called the Pink and White Terraces here," Tāne murmured. "The white ones were over there"—he pointed to the north of the lake, then about two-thirds down—"and the pink were there. My mum never called them that, though. She called the white ones Te Tarata, the tattooed rock. And the pink were Otukapuarangi, fountain of the clouded sky."

"Those are beautiful names," I replied, my voice hushed to match his. "But all I see is a lake. What happened to the terraces?"

"They were destroyed by the eruption back in 1886 that formed everything else here." Tāne released my hand to take the map, and flipped it over to show me a photograph of what the terraces had once looked like. They were sometimes referred to as the "Eighth Wonder of the World," the caption informed me, and the title was deserved. The grainy photo showed huge terraces of pale rock formed like a slope of pancake stacks, walled in on both sides by trees, descending into the water.

"It's a pity they're gone," I said, frowning at the lake.

Tāne just smiled. "But that eruption formed all the other beauty here, right? It's not a tragedy, or destruction. It just changed."

The profound wisdom in his words took me off guard. I didn't have anything nearly as intelligent to say. Instead, I turned and kissed him.

Our lips met in a way that felt as natural as our joined hands had. There was no hesitation, no surprise leading to awkwardness; we just kissed as if that was the only thing we had been born to do. It was gentle, almost chaste, a first exploration of how the other felt.

When I drew back, I said, "Sorry. That was just the smartest thing I've ever heard anyone say."

Tāne was laughing as he leaned in for another kiss; this one was briefer, more affectionate, like we had already kissed a hundred times. "Believe me, I don't mind at all," he said. "Maybe I'll try to say more smart things."

"Please do. It was really attractive," I said. I took his hand once more, holding it tight. As one, we looked at the lake. I said, "Is this where you're going to spread some of your mother's ashes?"

He nodded and tugged me after him as he walked down to the shore of the lake. Though Lake Rotomahana wasn't quite as dramatic as some of the other craters we'd just seen, I could easily imagine families playing at the edge of the water, throwing bread to the black swans gliding by.

Tāne let go of my hand as he crouched at the waterline to open the box. After a few whispered words I didn't catch, he took a small handful of the ashes and let them drift into the water, submerging his hand afterward to clean it.

When he stood and turned to face me, he had tears in his eyes. I grabbed him in a hug and he held me tightly, his shoulders shaking as he tried not to let the full force of his emotion loose. I wouldn't have minded if he had.

"Sorry," he mumbled against my shoulder. "Fuck. Sorry."

I just held him tighter. I had counseled a lot of grieving people in my previous line of work, and they were always the one kind of client I'd taken seriously. People could debate back and forth about faith all they liked, but grief was absolutely real. So I knew how to navigate my way around situations like this.

Tāne seemed like the kind of man who didn't really buy into platitudes, so I didn't give him any. I just offered myself as something solid that he could rely on right then, because he seemed to be lacking for that.

"Okay." Tāne pulled back from me, his eyes still damp but his composure mostly regained. He wore a self-deprecating smile as he swiped at my shoulder, where his head had been. "I'm cutting that shit out."

Again, I got the feeling that attempting to console him would only drag his embarrassment out. So I offered him my arm. "Shall we head to the shuttle, then?"

Tāne snorted with soft laughter. "Gentleman James," he teased. We walked arm in arm to the shuttle located near the lake that would take us back to the visitor's area—I was relieved we didn't have to walk the whole way back. My legs had started to hurt.

The shuttle ride back to the parking lot was uneventful, and I watched out the window the entire time, sad to see scenery pass by, never to be seen by my eyes again. Tāne was quiet, and although I wanted to speak to him, I decided to leave him in peace as he grieved.

I did wonder if that had really been his first time even showing a fraction of emotion about his mother's death. There were clues about Tāne that I was beginning to add up—the fact that he was carrying the ashes alone, that he hadn't spoken about his family yet. Estranged, I was guessing, or just not much love lost between the remaining living members.

When we got back to the hotel, evening was beginning to set in. We got takeout—McDonald's was everywhere, even in New Zealand—and had a quiet dinner in Tāne's room, commenting on the news of the day as we watched television. It was much the same as anywhere else: crime, sports, politics, and weather. A few of the news commentators had such thick Kiwi accents that I struggled to understand them, which was apparently a great source of amusement for Tāne.

I thought an early night would be a good idea for both of us, so I bid him good night when the clock rolled around to eight o'clock, and Tāne insisted on walking me to my door.

"Walking you to your door is a lot easier when you're only five doors down," Tāne mused. "But I feel a bit like I'm in school again."

"I never dated in school," I volunteered. To his credit, Tāne didn't immediately look like he thought I was insane, as a lot of people would have. "My family was Catholic."

Tāne peered at me in the dying sunlight, the orange cast of dusk lighting his eyes into a rich mahogany. "You've never dated?"

"No, I have," I hastened to reassure him. "Not until I was twenty-five, though."

"What, is that like the magic age you can start dating if you're Catholic?"

I couldn't help but laugh; the topic was dreary to me, but Tāne's confusion was more endearing than anything else. "No, that was when I lapsed. I was officially a priest at that point, but I didn't believe anymore, so I didn't exactly keep up the celibacy."

To his credit, he didn't pry, though I could see the curiosity in his eyes. And in that moment, I *wanted* to tell him.

I remembered his offer to listen, earlier, and my reply that I'd need alcohol.

Before Tāne could speak, I said, "There's a mini fridge in my room, and I bet there's alcohol in it."

Only the briefest flash of confusion lit his expression before he nodded. "Any decent beer?"

"Let's find out."

The notion of an early night was discarded as we went into my room and made a beeline for the mini fridge. We peered into it with frowns on our faces as discerning as the classiest of alcohol connoisseurs. "There's vodka," I pointed out. "Oh, I see some whiskey too. Crap brand, but it'll do."

"Baileys?" Tāne wrinkled his nose, holding the tiny bottle up. "Who the fuck drinks Baileys?"

"I drink Baileys," I said defensively. Tāne laughed, and I raised my voice to be heard over it. "It's good!"

"Yeah, okay, cocktail drinker," Tāne teased. "Bro, you're gonna have to chug that vodka to reassert your manliness."

I let him know what I thought of that plan with a simple, "Ugh." I had never chugged alcohol in my life, and I didn't think I wanted to start now. We gathered all the little bottles and the cans of beer and spread them out over the coffee table, then sank onto the couch. I turned the television on for some background noise.

I waited until I'd gotten halfway through a bottle of cheap whiskey before I said, "So."

"So," Tāne echoed.

I took a deep breath, but none of my courage came to me. I hadn't spoken about this with anybody—not my family, not my closest friends. I had deceived them all into thinking I was still religious, and I had hidden my "dabbling" into other religions from them.

"I'm gay," I finally said.

Tāne chuckled. "Yeah, kinda figured that one out."

I gave him a wan smile. "So did my very Catholic family after I told them."

"Ah." Tāne looked like he didn't really know what to say, so I kept talking to spare him the indecision.

"My father would have made a great priest, and so would my mother, if the church allowed women to be priests. They were both very, very devout. Good people with the best of intentions." I stared down at my whiskey bottle. "My two younger siblings and I were raised in the faith. It was everything to us. It was happiness, a support structure, hope in hard times. Our local church was our extended family, and we all knew we could count on each other if we needed help."

I drained the rest of the whiskey and leaned forward to retrieve another bottle; I didn't care which, I just went with whatever my hand came into contact with first, which turned out to be more whiskey. Just as well, since I didn't much like vodka, and the idea of drinking coconut rum straight was appalling.

"When I was growing up," I continued, "all I wanted to do was be like my father and help people. But when I was eleven, I started to get the feeling something was... wrong. When all my friends at that age started looking at girls, I wasn't interested."

"James," Tāne broke in, his voice uncharacteristically hesitant. "You know that it's okay now, right?"

"I know." I flashed him a faint smile. "Back then was a different story. I didn't really think about it much since I was never all that interested in relationships or sex anyway. I was like every kid who thought they were the odd one out for not being obsessed with those things. So I didn't spend my teenage years tormented by it. Mostly I just did my best not to think about it when the topic came up."

One corner of the label on the whiskey bottle had a slightly loose edge, so I picked at it with my thumbnail just so that I had something to do with my hands. "I joined the seminary when I was eighteen, on my quest to become a priest. And for a while it was good. Until I met Ezekiel."

Ezekiel had come from a family perhaps even more devout than mine. A year younger than me, he had joined the seminary in my second year, and our first meeting had shaken my very foundations. I hadn't noticed his old-fashioned style of dress; my first thought hadn't been about his thick-lensed glasses.

My first thought had been: *he's hot as hell*.

"I thought he was hot, and that wasn't something I was used to thinking about men," I continued quietly. "I remember being so upset by the thought that I could barely talk to him, but somehow we eventually became fast friends. I managed to repress my attraction, but I shoved it so far down that it festered like a badly healed wound. I didn't deal with it, so it just got worse."

I didn't tell Tāne the specifics, because I wasn't sure they were particularly relevant to the story. So I didn't recall Ezekiel's crooked grin, the way he shoved his glasses further up his nose whenever he got really into whatever he was talking about, or the little dent he'd get between his eyebrows on those dusty sunlight filled afternoons we'd spend in the library studying scripture. I didn't tell Tāne how I'd had daydreams about kissing Ezekiel, wondering what it would be like.

"Anyway. Obviously, as Catholics, we're taught that homosexuality is wrong. That wasn't even a question in my mind because I'd never been told differently. I didn't know why I was having those thoughts, but I knew they were sinful. I thought… maybe God was testing me, or maybe I'd been corrupted by the media or someone close to me. I tried to pray, to ask God to forgive me and help me find the right path again, but the thoughts just got stronger. I could barely stand to be around Ezekiel because of how much I wanted him. I felt dirty. Even worse, I felt like I was making *him* dirty by being near him. Eventually I thought it was best that I break off our friendship; I just couldn't think of any other way to get better."

I still remembered how upset Ezekiel had been. He truly had been my best friend, and I had been his—but I hadn't been able to explain to him why I couldn't speak to him anymore.

Tāne was silent. There was no judgment on his face as he listened to me, which was a relief.

I kept talking. "I graduated when I was twenty-five and became a priest. And…."

Tāne put a hand on my forearm, his grip light but firm. "And?" he prompted gently.

"And I got word the next day that Ezekiel had hanged himself in his room."

"Jesus." Tāne's eyes went wide.

"Yeah." My laugh was rough, the sound of it choked. Ten years later, I still hadn't fully gotten over it. "He left a note. It wasn't made public, but one of our teachers took me aside at the funeral. He knew that we were close, and he'd wanted me to know Ezekiel's last thoughts. He'd written that he was 'experiencing overwhelming sinful homosexual urges,' and he couldn't deal with it. So he hanged himself."

Tāne just squeezed my arm, a silent support. So I continued. "That was when I admitted to myself that I was having the same urges.

But it had been two months since I'd become a priest, and I'd elected to first work at a church in the inner city. I saw a lot of media on my commutes, and a lot of people outside my community, and it had slowly started to occur to me that maybe the rest of the world didn't think being gay was unnatural and evil. Maybe because Ezekiel had been the best man I'd known, or maybe I was just desperate to believe that I wasn't a sinner. Either way, I accepted it faster than most people in my situation do."

As I looked at the wall behind the television, I suddenly noticed that the wallpaper was decorated with kiwis. It was so distracting I temporarily forgot my place in the story. "So I went back to my family church and told them that I was gay. I pleaded with them to understand that it was natural, that it didn't matter what gender we loved. They told me that next I would be saying that it was okay to be attracted to dogs; I tried to tell them there was a difference between that and loving an adult who was fully capable of giving consent. I tried to tell them that homosexuality occurred in nature, and if animals didn't have souls, then they couldn't have sin, either. Nobody listened."

It had been, as I recalled, one of the most frustrating times in my life.

"Did *anybody* accept it?" Tāne asked quietly.

I shook my head. "No. I was forbidden from attending that church again. My family told me they never wanted to see me again, and they haven't contacted me since."

"Fuck." Tāne's voice was heavy. "I'm sorry, James."

I blew out a long sigh. "I was angry. At my family, sure, but mostly at God. I couldn't find any reason that being gay was wrong, so I started to believe God was wrong. And once you start doubting one aspect of your faith, it kind of snowballs from there. I started hating religion for blinding people like that, for tearing my life away from me."

"And that's when you started fighting back," Tāne murmured.

I nodded, unable for the moment to answer verbally. "I felt justified. Religion had hurt me so deeply that I... I felt *good* turning clients into fools. All I did was laugh on the inside at how stupid they were for believing, or at how ridiculous it was that they gave me money for saying the right words and acting the right way."

It had felt like revenge in the most twisted, satisfying ways. I remembered I had daydreamed about my clients one day finding out it was all a con, that the blessing and healing I had given them was fake. I had gleefully imagined their shock and their disappointment, their realization that maybe God's miracles weren't as real as they'd thought.

More than that, I had wanted them to hurt like I had been hurt.

"My immediate anger faded after three, four years. But by that point it had become routine. I mostly did minor services for branches of the Christian faith: confessions, giving advice, marriage counseling, grief counseling, baptisms. Some of the more extreme groups hired me to do exorcisms, blessing rituals, that sort of thing. I branched off into other religions, although the satisfaction wasn't quite the same, so I didn't do jobs for them as much."

"So why did you stop?" Tāne asked. I noticed that Tāne had moved on to a can of beer now. One and a half little bottles of whiskey weren't enough to get me even mildly buzzed, or maybe my topic of conversation was just particularly sobering.

"About a year ago, it just stopped feeling good," I sighed. "I thought about stopping, but by that point I'd gotten a lot of regular clients. I'd think to myself 'I'll stop in a week,' and then lovely old Mrs. Fieldman would want a blessing, so I'd move my quitting to the week after. Eventually I'd just had enough, and two weeks before I came here, I canceled all of my appointments and just left."

I imagined that had been the tipping point for the communities finding out I was a fraud. For ten years I had survived on community segregation—the Catholics didn't talk to the Buddhists about their religious guides, the Wiccans didn't talk to the Jews, and the Muslims didn't talk to the Southern Baptists. Those who believed so strongly in their religion that they hired people like me didn't tend to get on well with other religious groups. Tolerance was preached, but usually never followed in the hard-core crowd.

That was how I had been able to get away with it for so long: I had known lovely old Mrs. Fieldman and her very Lutheran family wouldn't speak about religious matters with non-Lutherans.

Apparently my sudden departure had caused enough of a ruckus in those communities that they'd all started talking to one another.

James Mitchell: uniter of the organized religions.

I made a noise that failed miserably at being a laugh. Tāne was silent, and I didn't blame him. If the situations were reversed, I probably would have gotten the hell out of here.

"What you did sucks," Tāne said frankly.

I winced, though I only showed it in the tiny frown at the corners of my lips. It hurt to hear, but it was fair too.

"I won't even try to sugarcoat it, because I know you'd see right through that bullshit," Tāne continued. "So, yeah, it sucks. It was wrong, and you know that now."

I just nodded dumbly. What could I even begin to say to Tāne? Fuck, he'd probably never even lied to anybody in his whole life; he just seemed that decent of a person.

"But I kind of get it." At Tāne's words, I finally looked over at him in surprise. "What your church did to you sucks too. It doesn't mean what you did is *okay*, but, shit, if that had happened to me, I'd be fucking angry too. I'd want to hit back too. Anybody would."

I could see a touch of anger in his eyes right then—not at me, but *for* me.

Tāne shook his head, and then he frowned down at his can of beer, presumably for a lack of anything better to scowl at. "I mean, I wasn't raised religious," Tāne said. "Well, I was a little. My mum's Rātana, it's a… what do you call it, a bastardized combination."

"A syncretic religion," I filled in.

"Yeah, that." Tāne waved a hand at me in thanks.

"A combination of what?" Even though we were only thirty seconds out of a rather harrowing conversation for me, my interest was piqued. I might have gone through a period of hating religious people, but my fascination with religion itself had never faltered, and it would serve as a nice distraction from my heavier thoughts.

"Old-school Maori beliefs and modern Christian," Tāne answered. "When all the European settlers came over here, they mostly converted everyone. There's not many left who still keep up the real traditional beliefs."

That struck me as very sad. From what I had seen of New Zealand so far, they seemed to do really well on preserving the Maori culture; better than other countries I could name that had had native peoples around long before settlers came in. The countries' anthem was always sung in Maori too, and all of the government and public buildings I had seen had their signs in both English and Maori. I had seen mentions of the language taught in schools, artwork of the mythology, Maori voices represented everywhere very strongly.

It seemed to me that, even growing up non-Maori in this country, one might have one foot in the culture, just because the country embraced its Maori heritage so strongly. But I also knew there would be some who disagreed with how well it was embraced, and in the end, I had no right—both as a foreigner and not a Maori—to say whether the situation was definitely one way or the other.

"So, your mother is Rātana," I prompted, interested to hear more.

"Yeah. But she always told me all the old stories when we were growing up, you know? Rangi and Papa, Māui snaring the sun, the Taniwha. Even if she's Rātana, those stories are still our culture. But if she'd turned her back on me because of something her religion dictated...." Tāne fell silent for a moment. "I'd be angry too."

His understanding was like a balm for my guilty soul. A tension in my shoulders I hadn't even been aware was there bled away from me.

"Thank you," I said softly.

I knew it didn't erase what I had done. It didn't make it any better. All those people I'd lied to and hurt were still feeling every bit as bad as they had five minutes ago. But the man who had somehow become the most important person in my life right now understood why I had done what I did.

I still hadn't told him about the class action, though. And I didn't want to, not right then.

I felt Tāne settle his hand on my knee, then grip tight. "What I do know is that beating yourself up over it won't help," Tāne murmured. "Yeah, there's amends and apologies to be made. But you gotta find a way to be cool with yourself."

I nearly laughed; it came out as a near-silent snort. "I wish it were that easy."

Tāne put his hand on my jaw, and before I could figure out what was happening, we were kissing. His lips against mine were warm and soft, a little chapped, reassuring and comforting. There was real strength behind his kiss, conviction, as if he was trying to prove something through it.

If he was, I wasn't sure I was getting the message. I was much more interested in deepening the kiss and finding his tongue with mine. I could feel him grin, which for a few seconds made kissing quite difficult—when I brought my hand up to the back of his neck and squeezed lightly, Tāne refocused, kissing me hard enough to push my head back.

It was a really fucking good kiss.

When we broke away, I wasn't thinking of much more than the possibility of another kiss like that. But even as my lizard brain chanted *kiss him, kiss him, kiss him*, the part of my brain that wasn't firmly entrenched in my own sex drive had some reservations.

Not every man thought with their dick first. I wished I could, because if I did, Tāne and I would probably be well on our way to having what would no doubt be fantastic sex, if the reciprocated interest in his eyes was anything to go by. But I had grown up with *no sex before marriage* beaten into me, which put emotional attachment well before physical attachment. I didn't do one-night stands. And since I was only here on a very short visa, I couldn't do a relationship, either.

I hated my rational brain sometimes.

With great reluctance, I drew away. "Tāne, I shouldn't," I apologized. "It's not fair to either of us, and—"

Tāne just tugged me back and pulled me to sit properly against him, our sides and hips aligned, his arm around my waist. "Shut up and watch some TV with me," he said cheerfully, effectively stopping any awkwardness before it could crop up.

I shuffled around to get comfortable, putting my arm behind his back to loosely grasp his hip. Tāne got the remote and switched the television on to the news, and together we watched the presenter interview the owner of a kiwi breeding program. We fit together so well that I found my eyelids drooping, pulled into lazy contentment by Tāne's warmth against my side and his understanding.

Chapter 7

I WOKE up with a numb arm and one hell of a crick in my neck.

I groaned before I even opened my eyes, and it took me a second to figure out where the fuck I even was. My head had fallen against Tāne's shoulder, his cheek was resting against my hair, and the television was playing some god-awful children's show. What had been a very comfortable position to fall asleep in was a horrible position to wake up in.

Gingerly, I opened my eyes a fraction. The sun was just starting to come in through the window, a tepid light that cast everything in shades of gray. It made me feel groggy and like I was still half in the dreams I'd been having, like it wasn't quite real. I blinked hard a few times, attempting to wake myself up, then started trying to pull away from Tāne as unobtrusively as I could.

"James?" My efforts were in vain, it seemed.

"Sorry," I said reflexively. "Just need to move my arm."

Tāne grunted and pulled away to flop over on his side, his legs hanging awkwardly off the couch. "Fuck, what time is it?" he rasped.

"Fuck if I know." I wasn't wearing my watch, and the clock on the wall was just a little too far away for me. "Morning sometime."

Tāne's next grunt was one of amusement. My arm started to tingle with oncoming pins and needles. Right then I couldn't be bothered moving anywhere, so I just sagged against the back of the couch and rolled my neck to try to ease the ache.

"So." Tāne's words were muffled against the couch cushion. "What's the plan today?"

I shrugged. "Up to you. I don't have anything booked."

"Right. I've got two stops we can do in a day."

"Yeah?" I rolled my neck to look at him.

"Desert Road and Mount Taranaki." Tāne finally opened his eyes with a frown, though it faded slightly when he caught sight of me. I hadn't realized it until right then, but I was smiling.

Looking at him, it was difficult not to. Tāne's hair was a mess, flat at the back of his head and sticking up too far at the front. He had this pinched expression on his face, like waking up was the worst thing he could imagine, and the sun was personally insulting him by daring to shine its light through the windows. His flannel shirt was rumpled, and he was twisted up on the couch with a boneless quality that normally only a cat could achieve—lying on his side with his legs at a right angle and hanging off the couch.

In short, he looked like someone I could very easily fall in love with.

The thought frightened and excited me at the same time. But instead of saying it, I just toppled myself over to lie on my front on top of him. I was met with a whoosh of air and a winded, muffled laugh. "Christ, your hip is bony," I muttered.

"Fuck you, then stop laying on it," Tāne retorted.

I grunted and dug my chin into his shoulder. "So what's at the Desert Road?"

"Nothing." I could hear the smile in Tāne's voice. "That's why it's called the Desert Road."

My own laughter was silent, but I knew Tāne could probably feel it. "Wow, that sounds really exciting. I can't wait to see nothing."

"Mostly nothing," Tāne amended. "For us it's really boring to drive down, but you do see Mount Ruapehu on the way. It's New Zealand's biggest active volcano."

"Wait. How active?" I asked suspiciously. "Don't tell me we're going to be dodging lava while we drive past."

Tāne gave another breath of a laugh. "It shoots out smoke every once in a while. Now, are you going to get off me so we can go get ready?"

"Nah," I said. "I was thinking of staying here all day. I've gotten used to the bony hip."

I was none too gently rolled off Tāne, but I just grinned at him from the floor. This was the best mood I'd been in after waking up in a long time, despite the crick in my neck. I was hardly going to complain about getting shoved to the floor.

Tāne shuffled back to his own room to shower and shave, while I did the same in my own shower. The bathroom was tiny but clean, and I felt almost human when I staggered out to start making coffee. The television was still on, though thankfully the children's program was finished and now a morning news show had started.

I studied my map as I drank my coffee and waited for Tāne. Seeing as I hadn't unpacked last night, all I would need to do to get going was put my bags back in Tāne's ute, so I spent the time looking at the roads we would be driving down. From Rotorua to Rangipo it looked like it would take about two hours to drive, and the Desert Road started from Rangipo. It wasn't all that long—fifty-two kilometers, my map said, which I figured was about thirty-two miles. It ended at Waiouru, and from there we would be heading toward Mount Taranaki, which was marked on the map as Mount Egmont too.

All in all, without stops, it would take about six hours. I thought I'd want to stop off at Lake Taupo on the way to Rangipo, as well as Mount Ruapehu. Of course, we'd also need food at some point, so this journey was definitely going to take all day.

Luckily for me, the idea of spending all day in a car with Tāne sounded quite relaxing. I just hoped he felt the same way.

What wasn't relaxing was the sound of my phone ringing.

I scowled as I snatched it out of my jacket pocket. The display read Damien Rookwell, which was at least better than the disgruntled former client I'd been expecting. I could deal with my lawyer, not with angry former clients.

"Morning," I grouched as I answered.

"You sound like you need some coffee," Damien remarked, a thread of bemusement in his voice.

"I'm working on it." I took another sip of the coffee I'd made— not the best I'd ever tasted, but when was preground hotel coffee ever good? "So what's up?"

"I have in front of me a list of names that are collaborating on the class action." I heard Damien shuffling papers. "You want to hear them?"

I really didn't. "Hit me."

As Damien read out the names, eleven in all, I recognized all of them. Miss Essex, the young woman who I had briefly given grief counseling to when her mother had died. Mr. Vaughn, the elderly man who had sought me out for on advice on whether or not his daughter was possessed. Mrs. Lane, who had paid me a princely sum for the baptism of her new son. Four on the list I had given marriage counseling to, two had been exorcisms, and two others had been prayer sessions. Not all of them had paid me a great deal of money, but it obviously wasn't only the money they were angry about.

"Okay," I said uselessly. "That's, uh…."

"That's not as many as I thought would try something," Damien said cheerfully. "This morning I was worrying about dozens or even hundreds of people getting together on this thing. Eleven's easier to handle."

"Well, as long as it's *easy*," I said dryly.

"'Easy' might have been overdoing it." Damien's tone dipped into seriousness. "Look, Mitchell, this is still serious. They're still deciding on what they want out of you, but my guess is? It'll be money and emotional satisfaction, a public apology or something. Probably a promise that you'll stay out of religious affairs for the rest of your life."

The latter stipulation wouldn't exactly be difficult. At that moment, I wanted nothing more to do with religion. Money and a public apology would be a lot more difficult.

"Let me know when they decide?"

"It'll be a while yet," Damien replied. "But I'm guessing they're not going to ask for just a few thousand bucks."

I grunted, finding a morbid amusement in that. "I doubt it." When my victims stated their wishes, I wouldn't be shocked to see a figure upward of a million. I didn't exactly have that much in my bank account.

"Just be glad nobody's trying to press criminal charges, Mitchell."

"I bet you'd be happier, though." Despite myself, I grinned faintly. "You'd be getting a lot more money out of me."

"True that," Damien said, laughing. "Look, I gotta go. Don't lose your phone."

We hung up, and I put my phone back in my jacket pocket. My coffee had gone lukewarm over the course of the conversation, and the thought of reheating it in the microwave didn't sound appealing, so I dumped it in the sink.

Tāne returned, and we loaded our bags up into the cargo tray at the back, which Tāne secured with rope and a tarp. Rotorua's traffic was just beginning to pick up as we drove out.

The sights outside were more green farmland; as a Texan I was used to farmland, but New Zealand's looked different. How, I couldn't say. I was starting to become familiar with New Zealand's version, and where I suppose a lot of people would have been bored by seeing nothing but farms and grass paddocks, I still enjoyed the sight. Especially when I got to tease Tāne about how many sheep there were.

It was a welcome distraction, taking my mind off my conversation with my lawyer. As soon as thoughts of trials and sums of money and public apologies entered my mind, I simply turned my head to focus on the scenery, staring at it hard, willing the unwelcome thoughts to go away.

We stopped off briefly on the shore of Lake Taupo. It had turned out to be a beautiful day, the sun warm but the wind crisp. We had a quick breakfast in Taupo, the town itself, which reminded me of Rotorua with its lake's edge community. The lake, I was informed, was the largest by surface water in New Zealand. I wasn't sure where it ranked in biggest lakes of the world, but it certainly looked big enough when we stood at the edge.

We reached Rangipo and drove straight through. The start of the Desert Road was a simple road lined on either side with tough-looking green-and-brown brush, high enough that it blocked our sight of anything else, and for a little while, it was the only thing to see. Even I got bored, then, so I dug a book out of the smaller bag I had placed next to my feet.

Ten minutes into the Desert Road, Tāne said, "James, look out the window."

I looked. So far, everything I had seen of New Zealand was green and lush, brimming with life and energy. But when I looked out the window, the scenery had transformed into something much different.

The grass was yellow, red, and brown, the flat expanse of it stretching as far as the eye could see. In the distance, I could see Mount Ruapehu, a craggy protrusion on the horizon. The top of it was covered with snow, the white at odds with the stark land all around. There were no trees, no vibrant green in sight, just hardy grasses in a surrounding I would have expected in Mongolia, not what I'd seen of New Zealand so far.

"Wow," I said to myself. It was just as beautiful as the forests, I thought, but its beauty was held more in its rough sparseness.

"Keep a look out in the distance; there's wild horses that live around here," Tāne mentioned.

"Really?" I was a grown man; I shouldn't have been so excited at the prospect of seeing wild horses. But I still sat up straighter in my eagerness, avidly searching every speck and rock for a hint of movement.

Tāne snorted a laugh. "Don't get too excited. I must have driven this road a few dozen times and I've never seen them."

That didn't dampen my excitement. If anything, it made me more determined to catch sight of the horses. "I'll find them, I swear to God."

Once we were opposite Mount Ruapehu, Tāne pulled the ute over to the side of the road. He retrieved the box of his mother's ashes from the back, and we stood at the edge of the grass, looking out over it toward the mountain.

I didn't pry into Tāne's thoughts; he seemed to be lost in his own mind, his head bowed, so I gave him the time he needed. While he thought, I wandered a short way across the rock and grass. When I looked up toward the horizon, I caught sight of something moving.

"Tāne!" I shouted, grinning widely as I pointed. "Look!"

Nine distant figures emerged from behind an outcrop of rock, moving swiftly away from us. But if I squinted, I could make them out—powerful-looking horses in shades of brown and gray, muscles rippling under their coats as they ran.

"Fuck me," Tāne said in wonderment. "They *do* exist. I'd started to wonder if everybody was just having me on."

Soon, the horses ran too far away for us to keep track of, but I still kept watching where I'd last seen them. Eventually I had to give up, and I made my way back to Tāne, shaking my head in pleased disbelief.

I stood by him as he shook a portion of the ashes on the ground, and together we walked back to the ute, shoulder to shoulder.

"Why here, if you don't mind me asking?" I said as I buckled my seat belt.

Tāne smiled a little. "Most of my family lives in Wellington, but I've got an aunt and uncle that live in Auckland. It's about eight hours' drive, and Mum always used to make Dad stop driving so we could get out and look at Ruapehu. She liked it best when it was winter; everything gets covered in snow here."

"And you never saw any horses?"

"Not until today." Tāne laughed, but he quickly sobered. "I wish she'd been around to see them."

I spoke without thinking. "Maybe that's why you saw them today. Maybe it's a sign." As soon as the words were out of my mouth, I cringed. It sounded exactly like something I would have said to a client, but despite that, I genuinely meant it. It seemed some small part of my faith was stubbornly holding on.

"A sign of what?"

"Whatever you want it to be." I tried to sound supportive yet casual, but I wasn't sure I managed it. I had done so just fine back when I had conned people out of money, but doing it genuinely was much harder.

Tāne glanced at me, only taking his eyes off the road for a second. There was a bemused arch to his eyebrow. "Is that Father Mitchell making a comeback?"

"God, no." I chuckled. "Just a man with a little faith remaining."

The realization was surprising, to say the least. I'd spent so long being angry at the followers of God that I hadn't really taken much time to think about God himself. I had assumed my faith was gone.

"Thanks, I guess. I'm gonna take it as a sign that we were just really lucky in our timing," Tāne replied. "But, really. Thanks." His smile was small but warm.

In all likelihood, yes, we'd just had fortunate timing. But a part of me wanted to believe we had seen those horses for a reason—that it had been a farewell of sorts, that there was a *meaning* behind the sighting. Perhaps that was just my human urge to read intelligent design behind pure coincidence.

We didn't see any more horses along the Desert Road, and twenty minutes later we were back to green farmland. From Waiouru we turned west, and while we drove around the bases of hills, Tāne periodically fiddled with the radio, trying to pick up stations. As the hours passed, I wound up dozing, my head lolling back against the seat and drooping to my chest in what was no doubt an incredibly embarrassing fashion.

An hour later, the road started winding near the edge of the coast—the South Taranaki Bight, my map informed me. The water was rough today, the waves topped with white crests. Specks of seagulls tumbled in the wind, and clouds gathered at the edge of the horizon. It looked like rain was on the way.

I could see Mount Taranaki in the very distance, but it took some time before it really came into view. It was snow-capped and dark underneath, surrounded by smaller green hills from which it rose like a pyramid. It wasn't the tallest mountain I'd ever seen, but it had to be one of the most beautiful.

We drove a short way up the side of it and then stopped off in what might have been a parking lot; it was little more than a big oval of gravel, with an even narrower road leading away from it to wind further up the mountain. Unfortunately, as we'd gotten further up the mountain, mist had closed in.

It left us barely able to see outside the gravel oval. Tāne stopped the ute at the edge of the trees, and we looked out the windows.

"Sure is a lot to see," Tāne said dryly. "Fuck. We'll get a hotel and come back tomorrow. We can't move on without you properly seeing Mount Taranaki."

So we drove back down the mountain to a town called Stratford, and went to the first hotel we could find. Since we hadn't booked in advance, we couldn't afford to be picky; we wound up in a place called Mountainside Hotel that at least looked clean and functional. I didn't require much from a hotel room—just a bed, a ceiling, and a working shower.

We wandered the town of Stratford until the evening, when we shared a dinner at a small restaurant. We both agreed to get an early night, so we retreated to our separate rooms for sleep.

In the morning, the mist had cleared off Mount Taranaki. We drove up as far as the winding road would allow, and I was glad Tāne was driving; the road was narrow and twisting, and not something I would have wanted to navigate while still unsure of what side I should be driving on.

Our next stop was Wellington. I noticed that Tāne seemed less and less talkative the closer we got to the city.

"You okay?" I asked as we passed a road sign that said "Bulls: 5km."

"Yeah, fine," Tāne muttered.

That was the most unconvincing answer I'd ever heard. "Really?" I prodded. "Are you sure?"

Tāne blew out a sigh. "I think we should split up while we're in Wellington."

I frowned at him, but didn't immediately voice the twinge of hurt I felt. I took a few seconds to think over everything we had done yesterday, searching for a reason I might have upset Tāne. I couldn't think of anything. "Okay," I said tentatively. Unfortunately I didn't do a great job at sounding agreeable.

"It's not like that," Tāne hastened to say. "Shit, James, it's not you. It's just… my family lives in Wellington, and I'm gonna have to go see them."

I desperately wanted to ask why Tāne was so reluctant to speak about his family, especially now that he didn't even want me to meet them. "Okay," I repeated. "But for the record, I'd like to meet your family."

Tāne's smile was rueful. "Yeah?"

"Yeah. They raised you, and you turned out great," I said. "Logic seems to follow that they'd be great too."

Tāne didn't answer immediately. He tapped his fingers on the steering wheel, seemingly thinking hard, so I left him to it. We arrived at the edge of Bulls and, hearing Tāne give a muted groan, I turned to look out the window.

Bank-a-bull. Market-a-bull. Unforget-a-bull. Lick-a-bull. It seemed like every second shop or service had the same kind of sign.

"That's... uh," I said uselessly.

"Yeah." There was a laugh under Tāne's word. "Not much to say about that, really."

Read-a-bull. Eat-a-bull. Live-a-bull. Bloom-a-bull.

It just kept going.

Treasure-a-bull. Afford-a-bull.

By the time we had left the town, I was chuckling quietly. I wasn't sure if the theme was tacky or cute, maybe a little bit of both, but it had definitely ensured that I wouldn't be forgetting the town anytime soon, even if I had never set foot in it.

"You can meet them if you want," Tāne finally answered. He sounded reluctant.

"Really?" I perked up at the idea. But I quickly started to feel guilty—his family was grieving his recently lost mother; they didn't need some ragged foreigner intruding on their home. "I don't have to. I know this must be a rough time for your family."

"Oh no, I've already decided." Tāne smiled a little. "If anything, you'll be an icebreaker."

"What, like, 'Hey, Dad, check out this weird American that started following me around'?"

That got Tāne to laugh. "Yeah, exactly. I'll just tell them you're my stalker."

"I'm sure that'll endear me to them." I poked his arm teasingly. "But thanks. I promise I won't be an annoying guest. I'll just book a hotel in the city and come when I'm called."

Tāne seemed relieved, and our conversation fell silent again. Not long after that, we reached the outskirts of Wellington.

Wellington wasn't as big as Auckland, but it was the capital city of New Zealand, hosting the political center. Part of the parliament buildings was a building called the Beehive, which I'd been told by Tāne was an extremely ugly eyesore. We didn't go into the main city; instead we headed for a suburb called Thorndon not far from the inner city. It was a hilly suburb, seemingly set on the side of a steep incline, with houses on one side of the road and trees on the other.

When Tāne pulled into the driveway of one of the homes, I started to get confused. "This isn't a hotel," I said dumbly.

"Nope. This is my house," Tāne replied as he stopped the ute. "I decided it'd be rude to make you pay for a hotel when I've got plenty of room in my place."

With Southern manners deep in my blood, I immediately started to protest. "No, Tāne, seriously, I can stay in a hotel—"

Tāne clapped a hand over my mouth. "You're staying," he said. "And that's that. Now get your shit and we'll put it inside."

I could hardly say no to that. Bemused and grateful, I got out of the ute to help Tāne untie the ropes and remove the tarp from the rear of the vehicle, and together we lugged our bags inside. The outside of Tāne's house wasn't really much to look at—it appeared on the smaller side, white-painted wood set under a dark roof, closed in on both sides by dense tree lines.

Inside was a completely different story.

I had never given a thought to what Tāne's house might look like, but as I saw it, everything made complete sense. It was Spartan but solid, dark wood floors with cream wallpaper. There were very few decorations: a few photos on the wall, and wood sculptures placed here and there. It was simple yet elegant, no space wasted.

Tāne must have caught me staring. "Sorry, it's a bit messy," he apologized.

I couldn't see anything that could qualify as a mess. Perhaps the few magazines scattered over a coffee table were what Tāne meant? "It's great," I said genuinely, and I made my way over to the kitchen, which faced away from the hill. It overlooked a portion of Wellington's harbor, and at the base of the hill, I could see numerous train tracks leading into a station. Beyond that, to the north, there were more green hills with houses dotted in among the trees.

"I did the floors myself," Tāne replied as he came to stand next to me. "I bought the place a few years back. It was a real fixer-upper, and there's still some rooms I'm working on between projects."

"There is nothing more attractive than a guy who works with his hands," I told him. "I'm just imagining you and a chainsaw out in the woods."

Tāne's grin was bright. "I hate to ruin your dream, but I buy my wood. I do use a chainsaw sometimes, though."

I snorted and bumped his shoulder with mine. "Leave me to my daydreams, man."

Tāne led me to a spare room that looked a little rough around the edges, and though he apologized profusely for the unfinished state of the room, I just waved him off. The bedcover was a shade of warm green that matched the trees outside the window, and even with patchy wallpaper and a chipped set of drawers, it looked warm and inviting.

The house was bigger than it looked; at the end of the hall there was a large workroom with sliding doors all along the harbor-side wall. The floor was concrete and the walls were plain, and there were all sorts of equipment and machinery lined up around the edges and in the very middle of the room.

"This is where I do my woodworking," Tāne commented. "It's not as big as I'd like, but it's enough for now."

I didn't reply; I was too entranced by a carving that sat half-finished in the clutches of several clamps on one of the long tables. It was a serpentine beast, fully two feet long, with a kind of head I'd never seen on any kind of lizard or snake before. The face was blunt, with two eyes set in flared eyebrow ridges. The mouth was a curious shape, like a flattened heart, and a long tongue protruded from it. All in all, it presented quite a frightening but fascinating visage.

"That's a Taniwha," Tāne explained. As he stood next to me, he absently brushed a few flecks of wood from the snakelike body. "They're an old story, one that changes depending on who you ask. Some people say they're kaitiaki, guardians that protect us, and others say they're monsters who kidnap people."

"It's beautiful," I murmured. The pattern had so far only been completed to just beyond the neck, and the legs looked a little rough, but it still looked perfect to me. "So you sculpt?"

"And I make furniture." Tāne waved his hand at a pair of chairs in the corner. "I work on commission basis."

The pay was apparently decent enough, if he could afford to buy a house and renovate it. Then again, I had no idea what New Zealand's housing market was like, or even its economy as a whole.

"You have a real talent," I said appreciatively. I had moved to look at a tiny sculpture at the end of the table. No more than two inches high and wide, its craftsmanship revealed a deft hand. "What's this?"

"It's a kea, a parrot native to New Zealand. They're pretty endangered, but they're cheeky little buggers."

"How so?" I bent down to get a better look. It was a fat-looking bird, more suited to the ground than long-distance flight, with a stubby beak.

"When we get to the South Island, I'll show you." Tāne sounded amused. But before he could say anything, his phone rang, and he looked none too happy when he looked at the caller ID. "Excuse me," he sighed before answering, and then he left the room.

I could dimly hear him greet the person on the other end of the line, but I tried not to listen in. Instead I wandered around the workshop to look at everything else; on a far table were little pendants for necklaces, dark wood inset with some kind of brilliantly colored shell that looked like abalone. A glance at a handwritten note underneath the pendants revealed that they were made of kauri and paua. Since I recognized kauri as a type of tree, the shell must be paua.

As he spoke to his family, I took the opportunity to pull out my phone and text my lawyer.

I sent: "How's everything coming along? –JM"

Not thirty seconds later, I received a reply. "Nothing new. Just a lot of paperwork."

I tried to take that as an encouragement. No news was good news, right? Did that saying even apply to the world of law, where everything took a very long time to happen? I replied with a simple "thanks" and put my phone away once more.

I knew I should tell Tāne. It wasn't fair to him, keeping him in the dark about this. He had said that he understood everything that I had done, and that it didn't color his perception of me—but could that change if he knew what was happening?

Tāne's voice rose, then fell into a tense-sounding murmur, then fell silent completely. When he came back into the workshop, his features were set more rigidly than I had ever seen on the normally mellow man.

"Everything okay?" I asked cautiously.

"I swear my dad has some fucking radar that dings when I'm in town," Tāne muttered. He pinched the bridge of his nose, and I frowned at how stressed he seemed.

"How bad is it?" I asked. "Your family, I mean?"

Tāne gave a faint laugh. "Probably not nearly as bad as you think. Shit, they didn't smack me around or anything; it wasn't like that. We just… most of us don't get on, and family get-togethers feel like pulling teeth. Dad's just gotten worse since Mum died, and I haven't heard two words from my sister."

I nodded. I didn't want to interrupt him in case he needed to let some steam off, and it saved me from blurting out everything about the class action.

"So, yeah, we barely talk to each other. They said they're too busy to come with me to spread Mum's ashes, which is a load of shit, since Dad doesn't do anything but sit on the fucking couch all day," Tāne continued. "And visiting them is the last fucking thing I want to do right now."

Chapter 8

OF COURSE, we ended up at Tāne's father's house two hours later. Except there was nobody home.

"Fuck's sake," Tāne muttered at the door, pressing the doorbell again. "I can't believe he's out. He *never* goes out."

I stood a few steps back from the door, feeling oddly guilty, like I expected Tāne's father to burst out from within and shout at me for starting to fall for his son. Tāne had never mentioned whether his family was okay with the fact that he liked men. For all I knew, they were even more homophobic than my own family.

"Where do you think he is?" I asked.

"Fuck if I know."

"You're saying 'fuck' a lot."

Tāne looked like he wanted to say it once more for the sake of it, but he wound up just sighing. "He's probably down at the marae."

And here was yet another moment where I looked like an idiot foreigner, but to preserve my dignity, I refrained from asking what a marae was. Since Tāne was heading back to the ute, it looked like I would find out soon enough.

We drove into the neighboring suburb and stopped outside a building on the outskirts of the shopping area. Behind it I could see a large area of cleared land, wooden posts driven into the ground to mark the fence line. Right in front, at the street, was a wooden building with a distinctive, fascinating design—it wasn't a square like most buildings, but instead a triangle, the two sides starting at a point for the roof and sloping shallowly to the ground. Two columns marked either side of the entrance, tall trunks with carvings similar to Tāne's Taniwha. To one side of the building was a more stereotypical rectangle building, surrounded by the grass of the open land.

I could see people moving between the two buildings, and a few more standing on the grass, chatting, socializing, and smiling. Though I still had no idea what a marae was, it looked inviting and comfortable, like it was used as a second home for many people.

As I closed the door of the ute, I noticed a woman standing next to one of the carved pillars. It was no exaggeration to say she was drop-dead gorgeous, and if I swung that way, I would have been thinking of ways to get her number. Instead, I was struck with the urge to become a photographer just to feature her in an artsy shoot. She was holding a cigarette as casually as any model and dressed in a professional-looking blazer and knee-length skirt, with her hair done up in a neat ponytail.

She watched Tāne as we approached, and just when I thought she was going to ask who he was, much to my surprise, they embraced. It was the stiffest hug I had ever seen.

"Sis," Tāne greeted her.

She flicked cigarette ash onto the ground, seeming more focused on doing that rather than paying attention to Tāne.

"Tāne." Her voice was throaty, much like Tāne's, and as I looked between the two I saw more similarities, especially around the eyes and the jawline. Tāne had mentioned he had a sister, but I'd never found out her name.

"James, this is my sister, Huia," Tāne introduced. "Huia, James Mitchell."

"And who the fuck are you?" Huia sounded bemused "Tāne didn't mention he was bringing someone."

"I'm a friend, ma'am," I answered, and I offered my hand to her. We shook; her grip was strong, which immediately endeared me to her a little despite the coldness between the siblings. "It's a long story. I'm on vacation, Tāne and I kept bumping into each other along the way, so we decided to travel together."

"And by *friend*," Huia said carefully, "you mean something else?"

Tāne and I shot each other a glance, and I could see his thoughts racing much like mine. We hadn't officially agreed we were dating so much as we had silently agreed to take it at our own pace. If there was a word for that, I wasn't aware of it.

Tāne grinned crookedly. "Sort of?"

She almost smiled back, and for a moment I could see something between them that wasn't stiff reserve. But then the door opened, and the moment was gone.

"Tāne!" A voice boomed; the man who had come from the door. He was taller than all three of us, with a solid weight to him but a hefty stomach that came from inactivity. He wore jeans and a T-shirt, the casual apparel contrasting sharply with his daughter's. "Shit, son, you didn't say you were coming this soon." He engulfed Tāne in a hug, and like the few seconds of familiarity I had seen between Tāne and Huia, I saw it in Tāne toward his father too. "And who's this pakeha?"

"Dad," Tāne protested.

Tāne's father was grinning as he said it, so I didn't take any insult. Though, honestly, I had no idea if I should or not. I introduced myself once more, shaking his hand. "James Mitchell."

"Hemi Kokiri," Tāne's father replied. He gave me a wink. "Nothing personal. It's just you pakeha all look the same to me."

"Americans?" I asked, still confused.

"White people," Tāne clarified in a mutter, rubbing his forehead. "Dad, enough with the racial slang, okay? James is a friend."

Even with the explanation, I still couldn't find it within myself to get offended. Back home, calling an African American by some of the nastier slang was incredibly insulting because of the history of the word, because of the continuing social oppression. Getting called a "cracker" didn't have nearly the same historical pain behind it.

"It's good to meet you, sir," I said nonetheless. Unfortunately, I couldn't follow it up with "I've heard a lot about you," since the only thing I knew about the man was that he was Tāne's father. I didn't even know what he did for a living. I didn't know what Huia did either.

"I'm going back inside," Huia said. She dropped her cigarette to the ground and stubbed it out with a precise stamp of her heel. She gave me a very polite, very distant, "It was nice to meet you, Mr. Mitchell," before leaving.

"Get me some lunch," Hemi called after her. She replied, but I didn't hear her exact words, only the exasperated lilt of her voice.

Tāne made a sound like a cut-off sigh and started toeing off his shoes. "Shoes off when we go in the marae," he told me.

I bent to follow suit, but Hemi's expression stopped me. The jovial smile had turned forced. "This marae is family and tribe only," Hemi said to me in a tone that tried to be polite but revealed its true insulted nature.

"Oh," I said, surprised and suddenly guilty. "I'm sorry, I didn't know."

"Dad, jeez, he can come inside," Tāne protested. "It's not an exclusive club. We can do the introduction."

"No." Hemi didn't say anything further, and he didn't need to. That single word spoke volumes.

"Dad—"

"It's fine," I hastened to say. "I understand completely." And I truly did—I wasn't sure if the marae was a religious building, but I had certainly been to enough churches and temples that weren't too keen on outsiders just traipsing in. "I can wait outside."

Tāne didn't look happy, but when he looked at his father, he also didn't look too keen on arguing further. "I'm so sorry, James," he said quietly to me.

Before I could answer, Hemi nodded at me, seemingly satisfied at my lack of insistence that I go inside. "See you around, James." He left to go back inside.

"Seriously, it's okay," I said to Tāne. "You go. I'll wander around the shops here."

Tāne still didn't seem too happy, but he gave a short nod. "All right. I won't be long. Meet me back here in an hour?"

"Sure thing." I smiled at him. Since I wasn't too sure about the attitude here regarding gay relationships, I carefully glanced around to make sure that nobody was looking before curling my fingers around the back of Tāne's neck. He relaxed a little at the contact, and I couldn't help but give him a quick kiss.

Unfortunately, just that one touch made me want to beg him to skip visiting the marae so we could go back to his house. Right then, all I wanted to do was spend time with him, the rest of New Zealand be damned.

But he kissed me back, we murmured a farewell before he went inside, and I was left on my own.

I started walking in the opposite direction, where I had seen a few streets of shops as we'd driven in. It was only a short walk, a few blocks away. I took the opportunity to study everything I went past—I hadn't noticed on the drive in, but we were in a suburb called Porirua. Without driving through it, I had no idea how big it was, but one thing I knew was that you could always make a reasonable estimate of the size of a suburb by its central shopping. Towns like Opononi and Rawene had maybe five to ten shops, including cafés. Porirua had a few streets' worth, and I could see what looked like a mall in the not too far distance.

Though the shops seemed nice enough, my attention was diverted by thinking about Tāne and his family, Huia and Hemi. They hadn't been what I had expected, though to be fair I wasn't sure what I had expected. Huia had been closed off, though I had seen that reserve crack a little. Hemi, on the other hand, seemed a jovial enough character, welcoming until it came to letting an outsider into the marae. I didn't know what to think about that—on the one hand, I wouldn't want to force myself into a cultural space where I wasn't welcome, but on the other hand, Tāne had acted like Hemi was just refusing me entry out of spite.

And then came the problem of why Tāne didn't like his family very much. I had seen that he obviously *wanted* to, but so far I couldn't see any one clear reason for his dislike. And Tāne didn't seem like the kind of man to give in to pettiness.

Before I knew it, the hour was up. I hurried my way back to the marae; I'd been absently poking through a bookstore on the far side of the collection of shops, and I'd definitely be late to the marae. I was, but thankfully Tāne was late in exiting too.

He came out five minutes later in a flurry of noise as the door opened, laughter and shouting, cheerful chaos sounding from behind him. I could hear a woman singing, and a man joining in. Tāne was grinning, his whole expression much lighter than it had been going in. Through the door I could see Hemi joining in the song, looking nothing like a man who had lost his wife very recently.

"You look like you had fun," I observed. I smiled a little, the atmosphere from inside infectious even though I wasn't participating.

Tāne laughed and shut the door behind him. "They're all mental," he said fondly.

"Who's 'they'?" I asked as we started walking to his ute. I couldn't imagine that everyone in there was related to Tāne, since I'd seen at least a few dozen people.

"Dad and Huia, obviously. Couple of cousins. But most of them are just locals." Tāne seemed to figure out that I had absolutely no clue what a marae was, so he explained, "It's a big melting pot of a few different things, but mostly they're cultural meeting spots for Maoris in the area. Not really like a church, more like a clubhouse, but even that's a bad explanation. I'll explain later, I'm *starving*. You hungry?"

I was. I didn't ask why I didn't get to say good-bye to Hemi and Huia, because I didn't want to come across as nagging. Once in the ute, Tāne drove us back toward the shops, and we stopped in at a little café, even though it was well after lunch and well before dinner.

As we ate, Tāne attempted to explain in more detail what a marae was. "It's not religious, but there's a bit of religion in it," he said. "As I said, it's not like church. We all follow different religions, or none at all in there. But we all share the same cultural traditions, you know? Like… I don't know, what's a cultural American tradition that dates back a long time?"

"Shoveling fast food in our mouths," I deadpanned.

Tāne grinned at me. "No, seriously."

I pretended to think. "Dumping tea in harbors." At his bemused look, I took pity on him and offered a serious answer. "Fourth of July. Families get together for a big meal with hamburgers and shitty salads."

"Okay, so, like that. We have a lot of traditions that go way back," Tāne said. "Like the hāngi. It's a big pit we dig in the ground to cook food in. There's others, but that's a good example. In the marae, we get together to celebrate our culture and our family."

"That sounds nice," I replied. From what I'd seen, they'd all seemed to really enjoy one another's company, like it was a second home. My old church, back when I'd really believed, had been like that—not just the services, but the gatherings we'd had outside of official church business. "How often do you go?"

"Used to be once a week, but I got swamped with work and couldn't go that much. And then Mum died, and...."

So it had been the first time he'd gone back to the marae since his mother's death, I presumed. But if he had come out grinning, he obviously hadn't been bombarded by shared grief and consoling. I knew Tāne was the kind of man to appreciate the lack of it, and they'd probably known that too.

"I'm sorry you didn't get to go in, James," Tāne continued.

"It's okay," I assured him. "Really. If it's a group formed around the Maori culture, I doubt they'd appreciate me wandering in."

"Nobody else would care," Tāne continued. "We love our culture and we love *sharing* it. But my dad, he's... he's not a racist, but he views the culture as insulated. He doesn't want anybody else coming in and ruining it."

In a way, I could understand. Maori were similar to Native American Indians, or the Australian Aborigines—they had once had land, and then settlers had arrived to take their land away from them. Their culture had been eroded, and their sense of identity had been muddled. Though it had been a very long time since it had happened, the long-term effects were still keenly felt.

"You don't have to apologize for him." I reached over the table to take his hand.

Tāne shook his head. "It just pisses me off," he sighed. "I'll talk to him, try to get him to change his mind. You can't come to New Zealand and not visit a marae; it's probably in all the tour guides."

"It is." I smiled, and he squeezed my hand. "Though the guidebook I have suggested that I visit the one in the museum here."

"Oh, man, Te Papa." Tāne brightened. "We should go. It's a great museum. It's probably not as big as the ones you fellas have in New York and Washington, but it's really great. We'll go tomorrow."

When the waitress came around, we ordered our food. While we waited, I released Tāne's hand, picked up a newspaper lying on the table nearest us, and idly flipped through it. New Zealand news seemed, for a lack of a better way to put it, a lot less dramatic than American news. Whenever I would look through an American paper, it was full of murders and mass shootings—though New Zealand obviously had crime, I certainly didn't see many headlines about it. Perhaps it was the smaller population, or maybe New Zealand just had a lower crime rate.

I turned to page six and was confronted with a tiny, grainy picture of myself.

"Fuck," I muttered and closed the newspaper. The sharp sense of panic wasn't quite as keen as it had been when I'd heard the news report in Rawene, but the shame was stronger. In Rawene, it had been on American media. Now I'd made my way into international newspapers. The article had been small, thankfully, only two paragraphs. It was a lot easier to stomach than a double-page spread.

"What?" Tāne asked, leaning in to peer at the newspaper.

"Nothing." I put the newspaper back on the opposite table.

"Seriously, what?" Before I could stop him, Tāne grabbed the newspaper and turned to the page I'd been reading. It took him a second, but when he saw it, he frowned. I couldn't interpret the emotions behind that frown, which made me nervous, even though he'd explained how he felt about it.

"They're still not pressing charges, right?" Tāne offered, like he was trying to make me feel better.

My laughter was an ugly noise. "Right."

"Look, maybe it's not as bad as you think," Tāne said, trying to reassure me. "If nobody's pressing criminal charges, that means that nobody thinks you really ruined their lives or did them serious wrong."

I glanced at the article. "Read a little further down."

I watched him do so, and I saw the way his eyes grew wide as he encountered the paragraph about the class action. I wasn't surprised that it had made it into the media this quickly—I especially wouldn't be surprised if one of the eleven behind the suit was drip-feeding information to the media. "Oh." He sounded *guilty*. Why did he sound guilty? "Shit. Sorry, I didn't see that."

"Don't apologize." I sighed, scrubbing a hand over my face. "I should be sorry. I should have told you."

"Look, it's not really any of my business—" Tāne started.

I cut him off. "There's no real details yet. All my lawyer has told me is there's eleven of my former clients putting it together."

"So, uh." Tāne looked hesitant. "Shouldn't you be flying back, then? Not that I want you to."

"This isn't going to criminal court, so it's fine that I'm here." I took a deep breath, trying to calm my nerves. "My lawyer said it was fine, at least. Honestly, I'm not all that familiar with how this kind of thing works. All I know is that I'm grateful they're *not* taking it to the criminal court."

"Me too," Tāne murmured. "I mean—shit, I have no fucking clue what to say."

I couldn't help but laugh a little. "It's okay."

"But you know, if I can help, I will, right?" Tāne looked so earnest, so *honest*, that I had to smile. "I don't know what the fuck I could do, but I'm here."

I reached across the table to grasp his hand, his palm warm and solid against mine. "Thank you." To the best of my knowledge, there was nothing that he could do. But the offer was appreciated.

But I was ruining a perfectly decently meal, so I tried to find another topic.

"Tell me about Te Papa?"

Tāne seemed to pick up on the fact that I didn't want to talk any further about it, so he started telling me about the museum. The chance to see and learn about New Zealand history sounded like something I definitely wanted to do, so we spent the meal talking about the Treaty of Waitangi and the Rainbow Warrior, historical New Zealand events that I had never heard of before. My bad mood easily slipped away in the face of Tāne's enthusiasm.

We made our way to his home just as the sun was beginning to set and the traffic on the roads was growing thick. Tāne switched the radio to a classic rock station, and we spent the drive debating the merits of Led Zeppelin versus The Beatles.

When I slept that night, in Tāne's spare room, it was blissfully without dreams.

Chapter 9

"DAD AND Huia invited us to lunch," Tāne told me in the morning.

I had barely shuffled out of bed, so I just stared at him and grunted in confusion. He replied with a chuckle, handing me a cup of coffee.

By the time I had finished half of it, I felt human enough to say, "Sorry, what?"

"Dad and Huia invited us for lunch," Tāne repeated patiently. "At Dad's place." From his tone, I couldn't tell if he was happy or wary about the invitation. Maybe a bit of both.

"Oh, yeah, that'd be great," I replied. I looked up at the clock on Tāne's wall to check the time. I'd somehow slept in till ten, which instantly made me feel guilty for wasting a few hours that otherwise could have been spent productively. "I'll go get ready."

Coffee cup in hand, I made my way back to the spare room. The bathroom was at the end of the hall, so I showered quickly, scraped off some of my stubble, and made sure my hair didn't look like a bird's nest. Once I'd done a passable job, I headed back into the kitchen, to be greeted with a kiss from Tāne.

I nearly spilled my coffee, I was so distracted.

He pulled back, wrinkling his nose. "Coffee and toothpaste do *not* go together," he teased, and I pulled him back in for another kiss. It was a much nicer alternative than talking.

"You sure it's okay that I come along?" I finally said. Our noses were still touching, since I was loath to distance myself too far from him. What we had was so casual, yet so domestic, that it was the most comfortable I had ever felt in a relationship. There were no expectations, and there was no hurry.

"Hey, *they* invited you," Tāne pointed out.

"I just know that you don't seem to have the best relationship with them."

Tāne smiled wryly. "It's a long story. And honestly, it's probably a bit stupid. Maybe you'll get it after lunch."

That sounded vaguely ominous, but I didn't question him again, though I still wasn't clear if he really wanted me to meet his family. Either way, he was right—they had indeed been the ones to invite me, and it would be rude to turn them down.

We drove back out to Porirua, heading toward the residential area this time. It was a nice suburb, as green as I'd come to expect in New Zealand. Tāne pulled the ute to a stop in the street outside a single-story white house. He let himself in, and I found it very strange that nobody immediately noticed the sound and came to greet us.

The hallway led to the kitchen first, where Huia was cooking. She was staring at a boiling pot with narrowed eyes, as if she expected it to strike at any moment. When we entered, she barely looked up. "Dad's in the living room," she said.

"Ma'am," I greeted. That made her look up at me.

"James," she replied, cut-off and formal. "Tāne, go say hi to Dad."

Tāne muttered something under his breath, but did as he was told. I followed, and we found Hemi seated on a couch in front of the television. From the looks of everything surrounding him—a nearly full ashtray, scattered food packets, the wear in the couch—he obviously spent most of his day there. The living room wallpaper, once originally off-white, had been stained yellow all up the wall and the ceiling closest to him.

It was dark in the living room, the curtains pulled, the only light coming from the television. Tāne immediately jerked the curtains open, only to be met with Hemi barking, "I don't want the light in here, Tāne, you know that shit hurts my eyes."

"It only hurts your eyes because you only *see* light once a week," Tāne snapped.

Hemi harrumphed. "I've got a condition."

"No, you don't!"

I wisely made the decision to go back to the kitchen, though it killed me a little inside that I hadn't been able to greet Hemi before they'd started arguing. I could still hear Hemi and Tāne as I left; they weren't shouting, but they were coming damn close.

Huia had a pinched look on her face when I came to stand in the kitchen. "Sorry," I said uselessly.

"What for?" she sighed. "It's not your fault."

"Are they always like this?" I shouldn't pry, but I was too curious. Besides, if Huia didn't want to answer, then she wouldn't.

"Dad is. When you saw him yesterday? He only gets like that when he goes to the marae. The rest of the time, he's like this," she said, nodding in the direction of the living room. "Tāne doesn't usually get going at him, though."

I wondered if Hemi spent all day on that couch. It looked like he did, but then how did he support himself?

Huia obviously picked up on the general direction my thoughts were going, because she said, "He lives on welfare."

"Oh." I immediately started to feel sympathetic. Though our own welfare system in the States could be terrible at times, I had known a few people who had needed it: those with disabilities, or out of work. It was a good system. "I'm sorry to hear that."

Huia gave a derisive snort. "Don't. He's not sick or disabled, and he could find a job if he wanted to. He just chooses to sit around on his fat ass, and has done so for the past decade." I was taken aback by the tone in her voice, and it must have shown on my face, because she softened slightly. "There's a nasty stereotype of Maori welfare squatters. It just pisses me off that my dad actually *is* one of the few people who do that."

For a lack of anything better to say, I said, "There's a stereotype like that in America too. It's just racists being assholes."

"Exactly," she murmured. She looked a little pleased that I agreed with her point of view, but her expression quickly turned to alarm as the pot started boiling over. "Shit!"

I got there before she did, switched the burner to a lower temperature, and swiftly took the lid off. Inside were what looked like potatoes, at a guess.

"Fuck," she groaned as she switched the burner off entirely.

"Not into cooking?" I asked, smiling.

"Not even remotely." She gave the pot a scowl and turned to put it on the sink and out of the way. "I'm a lawyer; I don't have time to cook."

Another lawyer in my life right now, then. At least this one didn't curse at me and give me bad news. Tāne had never mentioned she was a lawyer, but now that I knew, it made perfect sense. She looked like she'd just gotten in from the office—perfectly dressed and made up, and she hadn't bothered to get into more casual clothes to cook "Can I help? I'm not a *great* cook, but I manage."

Her carefully maintained distant expression eased enough to give me a smile. It was small, but genuine. If she had looked beautiful when I first met her, she looked infinitely more so with a smile. Just like Tāne. "I'd appreciate it."

Together we inspected the roast in the oven, checking that the carrots and pumpkin around it weren't going to get overdone before the meat was finished. Having pumpkin with a savory meal seemed strange to me, but I was assured that I'd like it. I mixed up a pesto sauce to go over the vegetables while she salvaged the potatoes, mashing them with butter. Tāne joined us while I was cutting some bread, and I realized I hadn't heard him and Hemi arguing for some time.

"James, you don't need to help, you're a guest," Tāne tried to protest.

I waved him off. "I volunteered."

"He's rescuing me," Huia said, and the siblings shared a quiet laugh.

"Yeah, who the fuck let you cook, Huia?" Tāne snorted. "You should have seen my face when you invited me to lunch. I was pretty sure it was gonna be takeaway."

"It almost was," Huia replied as she put some salt into the mashed potatoes. "Until Dad decided he wanted a home-cooked meal. I told him, 'What, you're going to ask Mrs. Ngapo next door?'."

"Shit, she can't cook either," Tāne said with a grin.

The sound of the television grew increasingly louder, until I could hear it loudly in the kitchen. Tāne and Huia fell silent, glancing at each other.

"The food's nearly done," I announced. They had been joking and easy with each other for a minute there, and I got the feeling that was rare for them. I didn't want it to end just because of Hemi's none too subtle way of saying *you're talking too loud*.

Huia nodded at me and started gathering the plates for lunch, while I was given the task of taking the roast pork out of the oven and cutting it. Tāne got the cutlery out, and after he went into the living room, I heard him ask Hemi, "Dad, do you want to sit at the table?"

I didn't hear Hemi's reply, but when Tāne came back, he didn't go to the dining table off to one side of the kitchen. Instead, he loaded one of the plates up with food and took it out to the living room.

It was wrong of me, but even I was starting to get frustrated with Hemi. I couldn't understand why he was like this with his children. My own parents had cut me off and had never spoken to me again after I had come out to them, but at least they'd had some kind of reason, as flawed as I might think that reason was. Hemi had two smart, beautiful kids, and he didn't seem to notice.

We all gathered in the living room with our plates on our knees. Lunch was a quiet, uncomfortable affair, and it was so dim in the room I could barely see what I was eating. I wasn't sure I liked the pumpkin, but I ate it anyway.

"So, Huia." I attempted some conversation. "You mentioned you were a lawyer? Where do you work?"

She brightened, seeming relieved for the break in the silence. "I work at—"

Hemi turned the television up even louder.

Only my manners kept me from snapping at him. As it was, I just gritted my teeth and shot Huia an apologetic look—but her gaze was already down once more, fixed on her food. She didn't look scared, but angry and resigned.

We finished our lunch to the uncomfortably loud sound of the television, though I barely listened to it. My thoughts were louder, swirling around the topic of Hemi as I internally ranted at him and wished I could do so externally. Tāne and I took everybody's plates after we all finished, and together we worked to rinse them, shoulder to shoulder by the sink.

He opened his mouth to say something, but I got there first. "It's okay," I said.

"No, it's really not," Tāne said quietly, barely audible above the television.

"It *is*," I insisted. "You know why?" He shook his head. "Because soon we can leave."

Tāne apparently hadn't been expecting that answer, because he burst into a laugh. "Yeah," he said, still laughing quietly. "That's pretty much the one good thing about this situation."

Huia joined us, and despite her perfectly manicured nails, she helped us with the dishes.

"Huia, would you like to have dinner with us tonight?" I asked on a whim.

She looked startled at the offer. "Sure. I can drive Dad to—"

"Not him," I corrected. "Just you."

The correction only made her look more surprised. "Just us three?"

I nodded. "Tāne offered to take me to Te Papa. I thought maybe we could meet you in the city afterward for dinner? My treat. If you're free, of course."

"I'm free," she confirmed. "Yeah, sure, that sounds like it'll be nice."

"Great." I smiled at her, trying to lift the mood somewhat. It was becoming rapidly obvious that her distance with other people might be something she learned from Hemi; if that was the case, I wanted to see if I could make her smile a little more. She and Tāne were so much alike, though Tāne was much more ready with a laugh.

We finished up the dishes, and Tāne and I said our good-byes to Hemi first. He managed to tear his eyes away from the television, but he didn't do much more than give us a vague wave farewell. We said good-bye to Huia between our parked cars, and she shook my hand as we parted.

"She's nice," I said on the drive home.

"She is," Tāne replied. "When she feels like she can be. I think she feels like she's learned from Dad that it's not usually worth the effort."

I could understand. With a father like that, I might have turned out the same way. Luckily for me, my father was an incredibly outgoing man, confident and energetic. I had learned all my people skills from him. Still, I wondered where their mother had been in this equation. Had she been like their father? I couldn't think so, not from the few stories Tāne had told me about her.

"Not you, though?" I asked.

"I'm a little closed off." He laughed quietly. "Mum was great, but you can never get fully well-adjusted if one half of your parents aren't."

I could see that. I had yet to hear Tāne speak of any friends, and usually people with close friends mentioned them fairly often. So I could safely assume he didn't have any. I remembered when he first told me he didn't have many friends; it had struck me as odd. Now I was beginning to see why.

"Well, I'll try to get Huia comfortable enough to loosen up around me," I said. "I promise."

WHEN IT came time to fulfill said promise, I wasn't sure how successful I would be.

Tāne and I had spent the rest of the day at the museum, Te Papa. He'd been right in saying it wasn't as big as the Smithsonian, for example, but it was still impressive. I had seen natural history displays before, so the section on New Zealand history was my favorite. There were a lot of Maori relics, old wakas—canoes—weapons, documents and records, little bits and pieces of the history of the culture. There was a model marae we were allowed to walk around in, though we still had to take our shoes off. On the inside, it was a low-lying wooden building, much smaller than the main building at the Porirua marae, but beautiful nonetheless.

We spent a few minutes in the "earthquake box," a small house— complete with interior furnishings—built on hydraulics to simulate the sensation of an earthquake, and all the while a television in the corner played footage of earthquakes. Wellington, I learned, was right on a major fault line, and as such experienced a lot of earthquakes. As the house shook, Tāne and I laughed and grabbed on to the walls in order to avoid falling over.

I saw an enlarged version of the Treaty of Waitangi—the document that had been signed by the native Maori and the settlers in order to come to a peace settlement over land disputes. Though I knew nothing about the treaty itself, I didn't have to know details to know it would be controversial. Such things always were.

Te Papa was set right on the harbor, so when Tāne and I emerged from the museum, we walked to the edge of the wooden wharf to admire the bay while we waited for Huia. There were restaurants set along the wharf, some industrial boats further along the way, and I saw groups of people here and there, walking and enjoying the evening.

"I could see myself living here," I said absently.

"Yeah?" Tāne looked interested. "Why Wellington?"

I gave him a bemused look. "You're one of the top reasons on the list."

He grinned back at me. "Of course. I'd be insulted otherwise. But why else?"

I hadn't seen much of the city yet, or indeed much of anything else. But the harbor alone was almost enough to make my mind up. I could see myself coming out here every day just to relax, maybe on lunch breaks if I worked in the area, or on evening walks if I lived nearby. The wharf was old but sturdy, and huge, extending for what looked like a few miles around the curve of the harbor. Old ship equipment was sporadically placed for flavor, and the whole atmosphere was just very *freeing*. I didn't know how else to describe it.

Unfortunately, the explanation I voiced wasn't nearly as explanatory as my thoughts. "I just really like this harbor."

Tāne snorted, bemused. "Then you'd better be rich, because living on the harbor costs a *mint*."

"Really?" I'd admit to some disappointment at that, but I should have anticipated it. Housing by water always cost a lot. "Then I'd just work near here."

"What would you do?"

It was an interesting question. Since the job I'd held for the past ten years wasn't exactly a business I planned to get back into, I would need to do something else. And I had no clue how I'd manage to get a visa with this scandal hanging over my head. Then again, if nobody was pressing criminal charges, nobody could *legally* refuse me entry into a country after I dealt with the class action.

Before I knew it, I was seriously contemplating the details of moving over here. It was perhaps a bit premature, but I'd already fallen in love with this country. That Tāne was here would also be a big bonus.

"While I was scamming people out of their money, I got a degree at college," I volunteered. "Religious history."

"Seriously?" Tāne laughed. "While you were angry as hell at religion?"

"I've never been angry at religions or mythology," I said softly. "Just its people."

"Maybe you could teach," Tāne mused. "Or work at a museum. I bet there are plenty of jobs you could get with a degree like that."

I didn't know how true that was, but the idea was quickly endearing itself to me. I felt like I couldn't go back to Dallas, even if it was the only home I'd known. What if I went down to the supermarket and saw Mr. Johnson, the Anglican man I had prayed with when his wife was in hospital? What if I went to the library and saw Miss Dhawan, the young Hindu woman whom I had helped find the materials for her Ishtalinga? I'd like to apologize to them all sooner rather than later, but continuing to see them afterward would just be awkward.

But thinking about it would have to wait, because Huia arrived then.

"Evening," she said.

She'd clearly come straight from work, her hair swept to the side in a neat ponytail, heels a mile long. Tāne and I had done our best to dress up, or at least upgrade from his usual flannel and my usual old jacket. Tāne, it turned out, looked *very* good in a casual suit jacket and slacks.

"Hey." Tāne smiled at her, and she actually smiled back. The lack of their father's presence was already doing wonders.

"Ma'am," I said. Huia rolled her eyes at me, but she didn't lose her smile.

"You can drop the Southern charm, James. Tāne might fall for it, but it's wasted on me."

"Oh, it's not an act," Tāne said dryly. "You should hear him talking to strangers. Ma'am this, sir that. He's so *polite*."

Huia studied me for a moment, approval in her eyes. "Where are we eating, then?"

Tāne and I had decided on a restaurant not far from where we were standing. The front of the restaurant looked out over the harbor, with outside seating spread across the wooden slats of the wharf. The outside lighting was just starting to come on with the setting sun, and it looked to be filling up fast.

We ate and had a few glasses of wine, and over the course of the dinner, I got to see Huia slowly relax into our company. If I had to hazard a guess, I'd say she and Tāne didn't spend much time with each other outside of their father's company, and their tense relationship with him had spilled over into their relationship as siblings. But a good dinner, good wine, and a third party to tell them funny stories about America helped break that tension.

At least for tonight. I was under no illusion that my taking them out for one dinner would permanently fix their relationship.

Still, our conversation remained light. Huia never asked what Tāne and I were to each other, and the topic of their mother never came up. That was just fine with me—I hardly expected Huia to trust me after a few hours. But she was Tāne's sister, and she seemed like a good person, so I automatically wanted to help however I could.

When we parted ways, Huia even gave me a careful hug. I could see Tāne over her shoulder, and he looked utterly astonished. "I think you should come back to the marae tomorrow, James," she said.

I was fairly sure that was the very opposite of a good idea, but I replied, "Yeah, sure, if you want. I don't have anything scheduled."

Tāne frowned. "What, so he can sit outside again?"

"I'm going to speak to Dad." Huia's features were settled into fierce determination; I could only imagine she faced down judges with the very same expression. "I'll make him let James in."

"Why?" I said before I could stop myself.

Her sudden insistence on this made no sense to me. I wasn't part of the family; I probably wasn't even in her list of friends yet. Huia had absolutely no reason to go out of her way for me.

She scrutinized me for a moment. "Because I saw you on the news before I met you. I didn't read much about what happened, I just know your face."

I didn't visibly cringe, though it was a close call. Instead, I looked away. We had been walking through the city as we spoke, and I just now noticed that we had come to a stop beside a metal sculpture with what looked like braille popping out of it. "I thought that would make you want to never see me again."

Huia twitched her lips into a smirk. "I'm an atheist, James, and I have no love of religion myself. I don't agree with what you did. But you technically did nothing illegal. The Church of Scientology charges its members; nobody thinks they're sane, but they're still allowed to do it. If you were a furniture dealer and had sold 'oak chairs' that were actually cardboard, yes, you would have provided a false service. No court could accurately judge whether your religious services were real or not."

"I know," I said awkwardly. "Nobody's pressing *criminal* charges."

"Ah," she said delicately. "Class action?"

"Yeah," I sighed. "I've got a lawyer back home working on it."

"Is he any good?"

"I guess I'll find out." I smiled wryly. "I hope so, for my sake."

"Look, I can tell you're struggling with it. Not just the case, but your emotions about everything you did," Huia said. "That's why I'm going to get you invited to our marae. It can really help take your mind off things."

Right then, it didn't matter *how* it helped. I was just pleased it was even an option. "Thank you."

She nodded at me, and we started walking again. I noticed Tāne shooting us baffled little looks, to which I just smiled. And when we finally saw her to her car and then stood watching her pull out of the car park, he said to me, "Okay, did you do some spell on her? I haven't seen her like that for years."

I told Tāne my theory about how their relationship with their father had spilled over into their sibling relationship, and how sometimes things like that just needed an icebreaker.

"Huh. Well, then, I guess we're going to the marae tomorrow." Tāne looked like he wasn't sure if he should be dubious or hopeful, but he still grinned at me. "I'm gonna need to teach you a few things before we go."

"Like what?"

"*Things*," he replied sagely.

THINGS TURNED out to be a list of Maori words, a rough outline about various ceremonies, and things I absolutely should not do while in the marae. I'd never been good at languages, so just memorizing a small handful of everyday words was hard enough, and incredibly specific words were even harder.

Hongi and hāngi, for example, were two different words, but as we drove up to the marae, I was having a hell of a time remembering which was which.

"Hongi's got one O in it, like nose," Tāne tried to coach me. A hongi was a nose kiss; Europeans kissed each other on the cheek in greeting, but the Maori lightly pressed the tip of their noses together. And a hāngi was a food pit, a traditional practice of cooking food underground.

"Okay. And what's kia ora again?"

"Hello." Tāne laughed quietly. "Don't stress about it too much. Nobody's expecting you to rock up and suddenly start speaking perfect Maori. But a few words here and there is gonna gain you a lot of friends."

It was about respect, I knew. If I went into the marae and showed that I respected their culture enough to learn about it and participate in it when I was invited, it would show my respect for it. More than anything, I wanted to avoid offending anybody.

"One last thing," Tāne said as he pulled the ute to a stop near the marae. "You'll be asked to introduce yourself. You'll give your name, where you're from, that kind of thing. But the important part is telling them a little bit about yourself." He turned to face me, clasping one hand to my shoulder. "Be honest, James."

"I'm not sure it's a good idea that I be honest," I admitted. "What would I say? 'Hello, my name is James Mitchell, and for the past ten years I've been taking advantage of religious belief to scam money out of people'?"

"If that's what you need to say, then yes." Tāne looked perfectly somber. "The introduction is so they can get to know who you are, yeah, to see if you're a good person. But more importantly, it's about being honest."

I hadn't been *honest* very much for the past ten years, not even to myself. Not until I'd gotten here and had actually started thinking about things. So the prospect of being honest to a group of strangers wasn't exactly something I was looking forward to.

"Hey." Tāne's murmur drew my attention back to him. He cupped a hand over my cheek and drew me in to touch the tips of our noses together. It was a lot more intimate than I had expected, and the unfamiliarity of it made me smile. "It's gonna be fine. You'll do great."

I doubted that. In fact, I wouldn't be surprised if I got kicked out of the marae as soon as I told them what I had done. It would be well within their rights. If *I* was judging who got to be let into the marae, I'd probably kick me out too.

"Come on." Tāne's voice was soft as he drew back. "I see Huia."

Dread began to settle in the pit of my stomach as we got out of the car and approached the marae. Huia was waiting outside, and as we got closer, she nodded at me. "I got Dad to agree," she said as she greeted us. "He's not somebody who makes decisions around here, but it's important that he doesn't strongly oppose you coming in."

"Thank you," I said genuinely. "That means a lot."

"Does it?" Over the rim of her sunglasses, she narrowed her eyes at me. "You look like you're going to throw up."

"He's just nervous," Tāne said cheerfully, slapping me on the back.

"The worst that can happen is that your introduction doesn't get accepted." Huia shrugged. "Of course, then everyone would be annoyed that they had to spend a few hours this morning getting ready for it."

I frowned at her. "Who spent a few hours? Why?"

"The kids who perform the haka got here early," Huia said. "And then there's the cooks. Oh, and a few people wanted to decorate the marae with some American stuff, because they think it's funny."

"I had no idea an introduction was such a big event," I said slowly. Now I felt even worse.

"It doesn't have to be." Huia rubbed her hand over her mouth, trying but failing to conceal a little amused smile. "But Dad saw you on the television, and he might have mentioned it to everyone."

"Oh, fuck," I groaned. I contemplated looking for the nearest hard surface to bang my head against, but that would be a bit too melodramatic. "So why are they even letting me in?"

"It's probably the scandal," Tāne said, laughing. "Everybody loves gossip. And they want to know why you ran away here, why you're coming into a marae. You're also a foreigner; foreigners are funny."

I *could* take offense to that, or resent it, but Tāne's genuine amusement lifted some of the darkness out of my mood. So I just scrubbed my hands through my hair absently, probably messing it up, and tried to prepare myself. "Okay. Do I just go in, or...?"

"Nah, give them a few minutes," Huia said. She withdrew a packet of cigarettes from her pocket, and I gladly bummed one off her, and together we stood and smoked while Tāne wrinkled his nose at us. The nicotine didn't ease my nerves completely, but it did help a little, and by the time I stubbed the cigarette out, I was feeling somewhat braver.

Though I still had absolutely no idea what I'd say.

The door to the marae opened, and a woman I didn't recognize stuck her head through it. She only looked at me for a moment, then clucked her tongue at Huia, motioning that they should go in.

I, however, was indicated to stay at the gate.

"What everybody's going to do is the more formal version of the ceremony," Huia said to me before she left. "Sometimes if you're on your own you'd just walk in and introduce yourself, but the ceremony is important. Just go with it, and you'll be fine."

Tāne touched my shoulder and smiled at me encouragingly, then they both left to go inside. A moment after they entered, a woman about Huia's age exited and came to stand near me.

"Ma'am," I greeted her, my nervousness somehow well hidden.

"Good morning. I'm Alice," she murmured to me. "Do you know what's about to happen? We've got a few minutes."

I answered in the negative—Tāne hadn't explained the formal ceremony to me, possibly because he hadn't been expecting it. So Alice explained everything to me, and I did my best to memorize everything.

The pōwhiri—the welcoming ceremony—was an old custom to extend the graces of hospitality, to join together the host and the visiting party. One important aspect of it was the removal of tapu from the visitor; a concept I got the feeling would take a very long time to properly describe, but Alice simply explained it as a kind of sacred energy that should not be touched or interfered with. First, I would be welcomed with the karanga, the call.

Another woman came to stand at the entrance of the marae. Everything was silent for a few seconds, and then the woman at the marae step suddenly called out, her voice clear and strident.

"Haere mai rā, te āhuatanga, i ō tātou mate tuatini, e haere mai!"

Just before, Alice had told me that it meant: *Welcome, to the representatives, of our many dead, welcome!*

We had started walking slowly toward the marae, and Alice responded to the call in kind, though her words were different. Traditionally this ceremony was for a meeting between two tribes, and normally the visitors would have a representative of their own doing the call, but Alice had told me she had volunteered for me.

As we grew closer, the women's words intertwined.

"Haere mai rā e kui mai, e horo mā i te pō."

Come old women, old men from the underworld.

"Karanga rā te tupuna whare hi te kāhui pani."

Call, ancestral house, to those who mourn.

"Huhuingia mai rā o tātou mate hia tangihia i te rā nei."

Gather our dead to be wept over today.

"Ki nga iwi e, karanga ā!"

Call to the tribes!

It sounded like a funeral to me, but Alice had explained that honoring the dead of both sides was an important part of the welcome ceremony, as it invoked the spirits of the dead and shared memories for both callers, then cleared a spiritual pathway between the visitors and the hosts. It was a dedication to the ancestors, and those that surrounded the marae. We reached the steps, and a different call was taken up, one to welcome us as guests.

Their voices were beautiful, strong and powerful. I actually felt myself start to get a little choked up with the sheer emotion and spirituality of it.

We stopped in front of the steps and remained in respectful silence for a short time. One more verse was sung by the woman greeting us, then a small group of kids, maybe nine or ten of them, came filing out. They were dressed in brown flax skirts, and the boys had their chests bare, while the girls had woven flax shirts painted in reds and whites. All of them had their lips painted black, as well as a symmetrical design that curved from the bottom of their lips down to their chins. I'd learned last night that the design was called a tā moko— on children they wouldn't be permanent, and few Maori got them tattooed today.

They looked *fierce*, even though none of them could be more than thirteen. It was a little startling, and even more so when some of them stared at me with wide eyes. It wasn't the wide-eyed stare of curiosity. No, it was a challenge.

I instinctively hunched my shoulders. Who gave children the right to be so scary?

One voice rose, then, calling out in a long, unwavering chant, the words elongated and flowing. The others started a different chant, and it seemed that the leader was acting as a caller of sorts, and the others were responding in kind. Their verse was strong and unflinching, their movements much the same, strong beats of their feet against the ground, slapping of hands against thighs. It was utterly enchanting to watch.

When they fell silent, I was left feeling a little dazed. And when they filed off, I heard some of them giggling to one another, no longer the oddly powerful little figures they'd presented before.

We were indicated inside. I made sure to take my shoes off first.

Inside, the marae's walls were uncovered, leaving them the same rich brown wood that made up the outside. Along the top of the walls there were distinctive red, black, and white patterns, and massive ceiling beams had the same patterning carved into them. The inside was relatively bare, save for a community noticeboard on one wall, and some kid's artwork next to it.

All along one wall were three rows of chairs, with two dozen people sitting in them, staring at me.

My anxiety level peaked sharply, but I forced it back.

Tāne had told me there was no such thing as a head of a marae; instead, they were run and cared for by a group of trustees. I assumed the man standing by the microphone was one of said trustees. I was ushered to take a seat beside Tāne.

The man spoke in Maori, so I was hopelessly lost as to what he was specifically saying, but Alice had given me the broad strokes earlier. He chanted for a minute first, a prayer to invoke the protection of the gods and to honor the visitors. He then spoke an acknowledgement to the ancestral house, and thanks to Mother Earth, to the dead, to the living. After that, he spoke about the purpose of the meeting.

I was entranced by the rhythm and flow of the language, and the ceremony itself, but when I took a quick glance to my left, I saw several people looking so bored they were almost asleep. I suppressed a smile. What was interesting for me was obviously common for them.

It was then that I noticed the American decorations Huia had mentioned. On the opposite wall was an American flag, a cut-out picture of the Statue of Liberty, and what looked like tiny pizza stickers scattered around a sign that read "Kia Ora!" I was torn between thinking it was cute, because it had obviously been done by kids, and having to suppress a groan.

Two other men spoke, though Alice hadn't told me what they would say, so I assumed their speeches were more informal. The third speaker then nodded to me.

It looked like it was my turn.

Time seemed to pass impossibly slowly as I stood and walked to the microphone. I could hear everything: someone in the back row clearing their throat; a little sigh; the cars outside; a bird in the tree next to the building. The microphone put off a burst of static as I adjusted it.

"Hello, everyone. My name is James Mitchell," I said. At least I managed to stop my voice from shaking.

They all stared back at me.

"I'm from Dallas, Texas. I was born there, and I've lived there my whole life."

For a moment, I wished someone would reply. They weren't supposed to, so I knew nobody would, but it would have done wonders to ease my tension.

"And I'm honored to be here. Tāne and Huia Kokiri suggested that I should come, so thank you for agreeing. New Zealand is a beautiful country, and I'm humbled to be invited to take part in your traditions."

This was it. I couldn't put it off any longer, not without starting to repeat myself.

"I'd tell you what I do for a living, but right now I don't do anything, because for the past ten years I've posed as guides and gurus for various religions to scam money off people."

I could have heard a pin drop.

"I used to be a devout believer, but my faith was shaken when I came out as gay to my family and church and they rejected me. I was angry for a very long time, and I believed that conning others was a just revenge. But I know better now. I now know what I did was wrong."

I drew in a deep breath, unable to look at any of the people staring back at me. I didn't want to see whatever expressions might be on their faces.

"So I stand before you now as a man who is searching for a way to right his wrongs. I'm not a very good man, but I'm trying my best to be."

My extended silence signaled to the elders of the marae that I was done speaking, and the first man who had spoken stood. Before we had come, Tāne had instructed me to put some money in an envelope as a gift, a small donation to the marae. I gave that envelope to the man before me, and he clasped my arm, then leaned in to press his nose against mine.

"You are welcome to our marae and our family, James Mitchell," he said. "Now let us eat."

Cheers and laughter arose from the congregation, and my breath left me in a shaky rush. I was grinning so hard it hurt, my eyes stung, and I felt like I might break down into weeping from happiness at any moment.

"Thank you," I whispered to him.

The man just winked at me. "Save your thanks. Now you have to greet everybody else."

Chapter 10

HE HADN'T been joking. I had to go around and nose-kiss each and every single person in the marae. There were a lot of hugs, a lot of names exchanged, a lot of older women pinching my cheeks and cackling to themselves for reasons that were lost on me.

It felt like a family reunion, like I had known everybody in this room for years. Even Hemi, who still looked dubious at my inclusion, hugged me like we were family who hadn't seen each other for an age.

I'd loved my parents, and I knew my parents had loved me. But I had never been welcomed like this.

It was enough to make me feel a bit overcome, so by the time the greetings were done, I had to excuse myself to go to the bathroom, which was in a different building. The warmth of the sun shook me back to steadiness a little, but once I reached the bathroom, I still had to take a length of toilet paper to dry my eyes. A quick look in the mirror confirmed that I looked like shit, but at least I looked like *happy* shit. That was something of an improvement.

"Hey. You okay?" Tāne came up behind me. He wrapped his arms around my waist, pressed his chest against my back, and settled his chin on my shoulder.

"Yeah." My laughter left me as a short, slightly hysterical burst. "Yeah. I'm okay. That was just... a lot more emotional than I expected."

"It can be that way for a lot of people, doesn't matter where they come from or what their lives are like," Tāne murmured. "It's just how the pōwhiri goes."

"It was beautiful." I met his gaze in the mirror and wrapped my arms around his. We looked good together, I noticed. "Everything about it."

He grinned crookedly. "Was that a double entendre I just heard?"

"Absolutely." I turned my head to kiss his cheek. "But I do mean it. Thank you. I need to thank Huia too."

"We'll find her," Tāne agreed. And then for a little while, we simply stood together while I calmed myself down. I felt the same way I used to feel after a particularly emotionally charged church service, like I was vibrating with spiritual energy and resolve, like right at that moment I could do anything, overcome anything.

Someone banged on the side of the wall, and both Tāne and I jumped.

"You better not be doing anything I wouldn't want to see in there!" a woman called, and I heard a group of other women burst into giggles as they passed by. They sounded so genuinely amused I couldn't even be embarrassed. Tāne and I exited the bathroom to the sound of more laughter, and though Tāne had turned red, I just grinned at everyone.

We were ushered to the space in the middle of the grass between the buildings, where several men were digging a pit. "It's for the hāngi," Tāne explained. "What they do is dig a hole, then heat up some rocks that they put at the bottom of the pit. The meat and vegetables go over the rocks in wire baskets. Then you put some heavy cloth over everything and then dump the soil back on top. The rocks cook the food over a few hours, and then the men dig it back up."

It sounded like a combination of baking and steaming. It also sounded delicious. We hung around and watched as the fire in the pit heated the stones, while women came and placed an enormous amount of food in wire baskets wrapped in wet white sheets down on the grass. It seemed like I could see a little bit of everything—potatoes, carrots, pumpkin—which I still found strange—onions, as well as pork, chicken, and lamb. The men laying down the hāngi doused the fire and swept away the ash with a hose, which made huge billows of steam bloom from the pit. They hurriedly put the food in it, covered it with blankets, and started shoveling the soil back on, presumably to trap the heat. Just the sight of it being prepared made me hungry, but now I had to wait hours for it to be done.

That task completed, we were whisked away to join the group of people sitting around tables under the shade of the dining hall roof. Tāne and I sat next to each other, and the next few hours passed in a blur of conversation and laughter.

There were all types at this marae, I learned, from retail workers to business owners, from young to old. People from all walks of life and from every background I could think of all united together in the marae. I was told stories from the cultural history, and coached in a few new Maori words, while they laughed gleefully over the way my accent mangled the words.

Finally, the food was ready, and this time I helped dig up the hāngi. When we lifted up the blankets, the rush of air that greeted us was still warm. We used the blankets to transport the hot wire baskets to the kitchen, where a group was waiting to take them off our hands.

Not five minutes later, the food was being served in the dining hall. Three long communal tables sat all of us, and I rubbed shoulders with Tāne and Huia as we sat down to eat. The food was served on massive wooden plates, sometimes artistically, sometimes just a pile of food. Either way, it all smelled *amazing*.

To the best of my knowledge, different foods took different times to cook. Yet somehow everything was perfectly done. What was more, it was excellent food.

The talking didn't slow down as everyone ate. If anything, it increased as everybody talked louder to hear one another in the enclosed space, making others speak even louder, and continuing the chain of effect. I ate so much I was sure I actually waddled my way out of the room.

It was a lot quieter outside, which was a relief—it was nice to be among such cheerful people, but even I needed a break. I sat at one of the tables outside and took some time to breathe. Though the marae wasn't part of what had once been my religion, everything had felt so incredibly spiritual. The karanga, especially.

I looked up at the sky, picking out the shapes of animals and landmarks in the clouds. It reminded me of one of the final straws that had broken the back of my belief. What had led me astray hadn't been solely what had happened with my parents and my church. It had also been skepticism.

I remembered a day like this, staring up at the clouds, and wondering *why* we saw faces in the clouds, in clouded marble and tree trunks. I'd asked my friend Beth, an atheist, and she had told me that our minds were wired to recognize faces, but sometimes our brain got tripped up and saw vague shapes as faces. That was why the simple smiley face was recognizable to us, even though it looked nothing like a human face.

Beth had laughed after she'd replied, and had told me about how, when she was a child, she'd believed that waterfalls were actually operated by extremely short men who resided inside the boulders and watched out an invisible window, manually pumping water. Her mind at that age had been unable to comprehend how waterfalls had really worked, so she'd assumed a person was right there, that an intelligent mind was the cause. That had gotten us talking about the tendency of children to draw faces on the sun in their drawings, or to believe that the house would get sad if they left for too long. Children were animists; they saw life in inanimate objects.

And that had gotten me thinking. What if we were all like my friend had been? Instead of a simple waterfall, which we would later grow up to understand, what if we looked at the bigger picture? What if we looked at the universe and couldn't understand it, so we saw an intelligent mind behind it, operating it? What if our brains, wired to recognize pattern, sometimes went overboard and saw miracles, luck, and a spiritual helping hand where there was none?

The thought had become so insidious that I'd started to think about it every time my thoughts had strayed to God. Eventually that, and my anger, had ensured I'd stopped being religious entirely.

But now, as I sat with the distant sound of laughter and family behind me, I wondered: What if I had been looking in the wrong places? What if I shouldn't look to the huge and the inexplicable, but the small and the familiar? What if religion and God were found in moments like these—acceptance, companionship, and the gift of love?

"Having a good time?" Hemi's voice broke me out of my thoughts. To my surprise, he sat down in a chair close to me and looked out across the grounds, as I was doing.

"Yeah," I replied. What else could I say? I wasn't going to dump all my emotions on him. He wouldn't want that, and he wasn't the kind of man I would want to share with, either. "Thank you for agreeing to let me come." I wanted to say more... much more. I wanted to demand to know why he treated his children like shit; I wanted to tell him to stop doing it. I wanted to know why Tāne was the only one spreading his mother's ashes. But it wasn't my place to come in and fix their family. That was up to them. To *him*.

Hemi only shrugged in response. I couldn't tell if he was truly unconcerned with my being there, or if he just didn't want to say anything more on the topic. "So how did you and Tāne end up traveling together?"

"We met in Waipoua Forest," I said. "We were both looking at Tāne Mahuta."

Hemi gave a grunt of a laugh. "His mother's favorite tree."

I hadn't known that, though I supposed it made sense, given what Tāne had been doing there. "And then we saw each other again in Opononi, and for the third time in Auckland. We both decided it would be easier to just travel together."

"Right." Hemi still didn't look at me. "So. You're queer."

The frankness of the statement, along with the terminology, caught me off guard. Some portions of the LGBT community might have been trying to reclaim the word, but I had never been *in* the community. Part of me still feared being so open. "Yes, sir."

"I still remember the day Tāne came out to me and Te Aroha." Hemi's voice held too many emotions in it, both negative and positive, for me to untangle. "He just came right out and said it. 'Mum, Dad, I'm gay.'"

I could assume, at least, that they hadn't kicked Tāne out or cut off contact with him. But Hemi didn't sound all that happy.

"And now I have to rely on Huia for grandkids," Hemi grumbled. "And you've seen her. More concerned with a career than family. Damn girl should just settle down and have some kids."

I opened my mouth to reply, but wound up closing it again. I *could* say that, if Tāne and I stayed together long-term, then we could adopt. I *could* say it was none of his business if Huia chose her career right now. I wasn't afraid of Hemi, but I really didn't want to antagonize him.

"What did your folks do when you came out?" Hemi asked.

"They kicked me out, didn't answer my calls, and never spoke to me again," I replied flatly.

That seemed to give him pause. But the only answer I got was a grunt, and I had no idea what that was supposed to mean. Disapproval? Understanding? Satisfaction? I didn't particularly care to find out.

"I'm going to go back inside," I said. "It was nice talking to you, sir."

All I got was another grunt.

TĀNE AND I spent another few hours at the marae before we went back to his place. We were just in time for dinner, but with the massive lunch I'd eaten, I still felt like I didn't have any room for more. But we put together a light dinner for the sake of it, crackers and cheese and a glass of wine, and spent the evening on the couch watching movies.

We decided we would head out to our next destination in the morning. Tāne wanted to keep going, and I didn't want to have to spend any more time with Hemi, so we agreed easily—though I did admit to him that I'd be sad not to see the marae again.

"We'll come back when we're done with the road trip," Tāne assured me. That made me smile.

The next morning, we were up excessively early, at 3:00 a.m. I groaned the whole time we got packed and ready, but Tāne was strangely cheerful. He drove us down to the ferry terminal at the harbor, just outside the city, and I tried to be a good road-trip partner and not fall asleep in the passenger seat.

"God, why are we up so early?" I moaned pitifully as Tāne turned the ute into what looked like a large parking lot.

"Because the ferry leaves at six, and you need to get your car into the queue an hour and a half before," Tāne replied. I looked at the clock; it read 4:00 a.m., so we were, for some reason, half an hour early. Tāne picked up on my frown. "It's good to get here early, so you're near the back of the parking in the ferry. That way you don't need to sprint to your car when the ferry stops on the other end, since you won't be first out."

I grunted. It was too early in the morning to actually understand what he was saying. Tāne just laughed at me, hitting me in the shoulder. "Come on, James, wake up! The ferry's sweet as, I used to love going on this thing as a kid."

"Sweet as what?" I asked groggily.

"What?" For a moment Tāne and I just stared at each other, both of us confused. It took him a second, but he broke into a grin. "Oh. It's a saying. It's just 'sweet as.' It's like 'awesome.'"

I snorted in laughter, accepting that explanation. And when I sat back in my seat, looking out the front window of the ute, the bright lights in the still-dark morning made me remember what I'd been dreaming about last night.

"I had weird dreams about faces in the clouds."

That made Tāne chuckle. "Whose faces?"

I hadn't remembered up until he asked me—the faces had been my parents. The memory of the dream came to me as clear as day then, and I sighed. "Family."

"Ah." Tāne's hand was still on my shoulder. "Want something to cheer you up?"

I wasn't actually in a bad mood, though the idea of getting in a *good* mood was something I welcomed. "What have you got in mind?"

We left the ute parked and walked a short distance to a store near the ferry terminal, open at this time of the morning. I got myself a green energy drink that promised to have more caffeine in it than coffee, and a donut. By the time we got back to the ute and I'd gotten halfway through the drink, my eyes were open wide.

The cars around us grew in number. Tāne and I passed the time by listening to the radio, and we were so into a David Bowie song that we nearly missed it when the cars around us started to move. Slowly, we moved up the line and drove into the back of the ferry.

The Interislander ferry—according to the tour guide I had—took three hours to get across the Cook Strait, the strip of ocean diving New Zealand's North and South Islands. The guide also boasted that it was one of the most beautiful ferry rides in the world. The boat we were on was called the Arahura, the Maori word meaning "pathway to dawn."

As we made our way to the passenger levels, I noted that the Arahura was in incredibly good condition. Everything was clean and nicely decorated, and there seemed to be a lot of on-board activities, from game rooms to cafeterias. Space was narrow, as all ships seemed to be, but the close quarters didn't bother me. Of course, the first thing Tāne and I did was head out onto the outside deck.

The ferry wasn't moving yet, but the sun was just beginning to come up, lighting the edges of the waves in the water, which were rocking the boat gently. I could see Wellington off to the side, the city curling around the harbor. The air was fresh and still chilled from the night, and if the energy drink hadn't woken me up, the air certainly would. I drew in a deep breath, absently smiling as Tāne and I moved to stand near the rails.

"I went on this a couple of times when I was a kid," Tāne said, nostalgia thick in his voice. "I always loved it. Dunno why. I'm not actually a huge fan of boats. I think I just liked the cafeteria."

I grinned at him. "In my books, that's a perfectly valid reason to like a boat. We should head over there."

Tāne nodded enthusiastically. "Absolutely. I wonder if the food is still the same."

The food, it turned out, was not exactly the same as Tāne remembered, but that just made him happier, since he had different things to pick from now. I wasn't sure why Tāne was so excited about the little packaged food items, but it did make me smile at him fondly when he spent ages deliberating over which meat pie to pick. I went with a sandwich myself, and a bottle of orange juice, and I teased Tāne about his love of meat pies as we found a booth with a table.

The ferry started moving not long after we sat down, and I was glad we had picked a window booth, since I was able to watch the scenery as the Arahura slowly moved past. Not long after we pulled away from the city, the ferry moved through a narrow gap of green hills dotted with white houses, and past a steep cliff with a lone lighthouse on it.

Then we were out into the open ocean. Tāne and I went onto the deck once more to watch Wellington vanish into the distance, seating ourselves on two of the outside chairs. I pulled out a book I had with me in my bag, and Tāne played games on his phone. The ocean air was obviously doing me good, because I felt so relaxed I thought I could drift off at any moment, warm in the sunlight and content with Tāne next to me. I leaned my shoulder against Tāne's, occasionally reading him a passage from the book, or looking at his phone to see a new high score he had just achieved.

We spent a couple of hours with nothing around us but ocean, but eventually Tāne nudged me, murmuring, "Here comes Picton."

Picton was the town that the ferry arrived in at the very top of the South Island. We stood once more and watched the South Island get closer; from a distance it just looked like a mound of green growing ever larger to our eyes.

To my surprise, we didn't just stop when we got close to land. Instead, the ferry turned into a narrow channel with sloping mountains on either side, light and dark green dotting the landscape. Tāne told me we were in the Marlborough Sounds, which led into the Tory Channel, and Queen Charlotte Channel after that. The Arahura slowly wound its course through all of them, sometimes leaving me astounded that a ferry of such decent size could navigate through such tiny pathways. It *was* beautiful, as promised, nothing but rolling hills and water.

I found myself smiling. Looking at the beauty of nature had always made me feel like my faith was close in those moments, and now was no different. I didn't think about the past. I didn't think about my skepticism, or organized religion, or what I had done. I just took in the incredible sight around me and marveled at the majesty, thanking a higher power that I was alive to see it.

The town of Picton eventually came into view, nestled between the same green mountains we had been traveling through. Tāne and I remained on the deck until the call to go to our cars came, after which we headed back downstairs to the lower deck. After waiting for the cars in front of us to leave, we eventually drove out and into Picton, where we pulled into a park on the side of the main street to look at our map.

We'd be driving to a tiny town named Arthur's Pass today, in the middle of the Arthur's Pass National Park, which was in Canterbury. It hadn't been on my list of things to do, but Tāne told me the scenery was spectacular. The drive would take five hours, which would put us into Arthur's Pass before dinnertime. The drive out of Picton took us past Mount Pleasant and a lot of green countryside that now felt as familiar to me as Dallas. We turned off the highway at Spring Creek and started to follow a winding river.

For much of the next few hours, there was absolutely nothing to see outside of a few lonely houses and farms. In the distance, huge mountain ranges framed the land either side of us. We drove along a road called Upper Buller Gorge Road, a narrow pathway with trees crowded in close to the road and the sharp slope of cliffs on one side. Here and there nature closed in around us, going from open farmland to winding trails between the mountains.

When we finally got into the Arthur's Pass National Park, the greenery on the mountains started giving way to the occasional patch of brown grass and stone. We looped around a rushing, rocky river and past gray cliff faces with purple lavender sprouting. If we hadn't been looking for it, we might have missed the turnoff for the town. Four streets seemed to make up the entire town, and the buildings were still distant from one another.

We were lucky enough to get a hotel room before it started getting dark, and I groaned as I got out of the car, my legs and back aching. I was getting too old to sit around in a car for half the day. We got a quick dinner from a nearby supermarket and hit our beds early.

I woke up at dawn, craving a cigarette. Though all I wanted to do was stay in my warm bed, the need for coffee drove me out of bed to clumsily pull on some clothes and my boots. I groggily stared at the little coffee machine as it gurgled, and my mind started wandering to other vices. Nicotine. I wasn't a regular smoker, but sometimes it just felt damn good to have a cigarette, and early morning cigarettes were some of the best ones. When my coffee was done, I gathered the mug close then headed outside, where I could see sunlight starting to streak across the ground as the sun rose on the other side of the building.

And then I rounded the corner of the cabin.

In front of me was a mountain, the top of it coated in snow-lit pink and orange in the dawn light. The trees and rock still looked dark, making the snow resemble a beacon in the dim early morning. Across the parking lot was a lake, the clear blue water reflecting the mountain, only disturbed by the lazy path of a few black swans. Around the lake were trees, a few of them starting to turn orange and red with autumn. To the side of the lake was a long wooden cabin, a chimney at the top piping smoke, and a fat orange cat seated on the deck railing.

"Holy shit," I heard Tāne murmur behind me. The crunch of his shoes on the gravel road came to a stop beside me. "Now *that's* a sight worth remembering."

I hummed in agreement, unable to think of anything to say that would properly sum up the sight. Instead, I struggled to light up a cigarette with one hand, and leaned against the side of the cabin, still staring at the mountain. It was freezing cold, and I couldn't tell apart my exhaled smoke and breath.

"Looks like they do breakfast there," I said, nodding toward the cabin. "Hungry?"

"Always." Tāne grinned at me. He waited until I finished my cigarette, and I had a temporary crisis as I debated where to stub it out. The thought of just leaving a cigarette butt there felt awful to me, like I'd destroy the beauty, so I shamefully kicked it under the gravel. I put my mug back in my room and joined Tāne outside once more.

The orange cat jumped down from the railing to curl around our feet as we approached the cabin, and then followed us inside, where it was warm and smelled amazing. The woman behind the counter was in her sixties; she had gray hair pulled into a loose bun, and a ready smile. "You boys looking for some breakfast?"

"Yes, ma'am," I said fervently. As soon as the smell of cooking food hit my nose, I realized that I was starving. The woman—Marlene, her nametag read—ushered us to a table outside on a wooden deck right next to the lake and promised to bring us coffee in a minute; even though I'd already had half a mug of coffee, the promise of decently brewed coffee was damn good. I laughed as the cat decided to make itself at home on my lap, vibrating with purrs as I stroked its back. "I've changed my mind," I said to Tāne. "I want to live *here*."

"I know, right?" Tāne smiled, turning in his seat to face the lake. "But I'd get bored in a week. I'm too used to city living."

"Me too," I sighed regretfully. "Are there any big cities near here? Maybe I could just drive out here on weekends."

"Christchurch is about two hours from here. But you wouldn't want to live there." Tāne grimaced.

"Why?"

"They've had two *huge* earthquakes lately." Tāne shook his head, looking sad. "A lot of people died in the last one, and thousands of homes were destroyed. They're still getting aftershocks."

"Jesus," I said sympathetically. Tāne had told me that Wellington experienced a lot of earthquakes, but it wasn't a New-Zealand-wide phenomenon, just in certain areas. "That's terrible."

"Yeah," Tāne sighed. "Everybody's just waiting for it to happen again. If I lived there, I would have moved out by now. But it's home for a lot of people, and lots of people don't want to leave."

Our coffee was brought out by Marlene then, who gave me an amused smile at the sight of the cat on my lap. "Don't feed him anything," she stage-whispered. "He's already fat enough as it is." She took our orders, and bustled away once more.

The peaceful atmosphere left me thinking about the marae, which in turn made me think about Huia and Hemi. I hadn't gotten a chance to say good-bye to them—I didn't mind not saying good-bye to Hemi, but I would have liked to speak with Huia again. Then again, Tāne had reassured me we would be going back to Wellington, so it wasn't the last time I'd see her.

As far as we had planned, we didn't have much to do today, only a bit of sightseeing, which would mostly be done on the road to our next location. Tāne hadn't told me where he was going to spread his mother's ashes in this section of New Zealand.

When our food came out, it smelled heavenly. I'd ordered bacon and eggs, and Marlene had also given me toast and a little bowl of tomato soup. I tucked in eagerly, then sipped on what was honestly the best coffee I'd tasted as I watched the black swans paddle in the lake. Every once in a while, the cat on my lap would sneak a paw up in search of my bacon, causing me to keep pushing my plate further away toward the middle of the table, out of reach of sneaky cat paws. By the time I finished, I was nearly groaning at how full I was. The sun had risen more, and the sunlight was warm, though the air was still cold and would likely stay that way.

"If I moved to Wellington," I mused, "do you think we could take vacations down here?"

It didn't even cross my mind to ask if we would take vacations together. I felt so comfortable with Tāne I didn't even question that we would remain together if I found a way to live in New Zealand.

Judging by the grin on his face, Tāne didn't question it either.

"Fuck, yeah," Tāne said emphatically. "On long weekends we could take the ferry over and drive down, spend a few days here. Talk about the perfect way to destress. And it looks like there's some great wood around here; I could even take some back for my job."

Without fully thinking about it, I reached across the table and took his hand. I should probably ask and make things clear. Just in case. "If I did move here," I said cautiously, even though Tāne, by all accounts, seemed to agree with me, "would you still want to be with me?"

Tāne gave me a look. "That's the stupidest question I've ever heard." For a brief second, I worried that he meant he wouldn't want to be with me. Tāne obviously saw that in my expression, because he rolled his eyes and turned his hand palm up to grasp mine. "I just started talking about our future vacations, didn't I?"

That he had. I smiled ruefully. Tāne wasn't in the business of saying things he didn't mean, so if he had talked about future vacations with the two of us, then he obviously wanted them.

"Sorry," I apologized. "Temporary lapse in brain function."

"I forgive you," Tāne said generously. "But if you need it spelled out, then, yes, if you moved here, I'd still want to be with you."

My logical brain had actually started working, so I hadn't needed it spelled out, but it was still nice to hear. "Good," I murmured. "Because I really am thinking about it. If I can't be charged over anything I did, then I'd have a good chance at getting a visa. I think. Fuck, I'm not really sure how class actions affect my long-term chances at doing anything." Not much, I didn't think. Though I didn't have any work experience in my degree—I was hardly going to use the experience I had on my resume.

"It'd kind of suck if you had to leave and I never saw you again," Tāne agreed. From his expression, "kind of suck" was an understatement.

That sealed the deal. "When I fly home, I'll start looking into visas," I said. It felt crazy—I hadn't known Tāne for that long, but here I was, thinking about a way to stay in this country permanently. I told myself if it didn't work long-term between Tāne and me, then I would still be living in a country I had fallen in love with. But half the reason I was thinking about this was Tāne.

Tāne smiled at me, a wealth of meaning behind the simple expression.

I didn't want to imagine a future without him.

Chapter 11

AFTER WE left the hotel, we resumed driving.

Until we started heading toward our next destination, it seemed that Tāne didn't have any one particular place in mind for his mother's ashes; we drove west for a while, curving around mountains and cliffs. Then a little south, past rivers and small lakes. When Tāne stopped the car, I saw nothing but trees around us.

We were halfway up the side of a mountain, stopped at a little gravel area for cars to park in, so we could appreciate the view. We stood for a while at the edge of the slope, looking down upon the patchwork of farmland and forest. Tāne knelt to scatter some of his mother's ashes, and when I asked why here in particular, he just shrugged and said she had liked the whole area.

After that, we started heading toward Fox Glacier. I was told it was one of the most accessible glaciers in the world, and also one of the very few to end in rainforest only 980 feet above sea level. It was a three-hour drive, and I spent most of it looking out the window and poking at the crossword in the newspaper I had bought on the ferry.

There was a small town near Fox Glacier, called by the same name, which seemed to have mostly been set up for tourism to the glacier. There was one hotel, which we checked into—and we were told we were very lucky to get a room, as Fox Glacier sometimes saw up to a thousand visitors a day during the busy tourist season.

We drove into a valley and left the ute in the parking lot to walk further into the valley. Like the sight that morning, it seemed that we turned a corner and were suddenly confronted with the incredible view of the glacier. Settled into a narrow valley of gray and green mountains, the glacier looked like a torrent of water had started streaming into the valley but had been suddenly frozen halfway down. It was white and gray with age near the bottom, and bright-white and blue where the newer ice had formed. It was also huge, more than eight miles long, though we could only see the very end of it.

We weren't the only people there. There was also a group of six, led by a man in ice-hiking gear. Before I had the chance to comment, Tāne hurried over and spoke to the man. He came back grinning.

"Come on, James," he said happily, "we're going with them."

"Going where?" I didn't get an answer; I was instead dragged over to the visitors' reception, where the man—the tour guide—handed us both a pile of equipment.

"Both of you are in good health, right?" the tour guide asked us.

I stared at him. "Wait, Tāne, are we going *climbing* on that glacier?"

"Hell, yes, we are, to both questions," Tāne enthused. "Get your gear on, James."

The tour guide snorted in soft laughter, offering his hand to me, which I took. "Brian Salter, but just call me Salter. I'm the glacier guide here. What we do is we go on a half-day trek across Fox Glacier. We walk alongside it for a bit, and then when we get to the newer ice, we take a path across."

"James," I said. No particular expression crossed his face, so I assumed he didn't recognize me. "And yeah, we're in good health."

"Good." Salter nodded at us. "Get the gear on. We're heading out in ten."

I blinked down at the pile of equipment we'd been given, and between us, Tāne and I managed to figure out what everything was for. We pulled on thick leather boots and knit caps for warmth, a fleece-lined jacket, and a belt from which hung some sort of strange device made of leather belts and sharp metal pieces. I was informed it was called an instep crampon, which would help us walk on the ice without slipping.

"Are we really going to go walk over a glacier?" I murmured to Tāne, surprised. "Isn't that dangerous?"

"Not with a guide." Tāne beamed at me. "Man, I've always wanted to do this, I just never got around to it."

Tāne looked so happy I decided to cut any hesitations or complaints right there. I didn't want to be the buzzkill of the party, so I just laughed quietly, shook my head, and said, "All right. But if I slip and die, it's your fault."

"Got any life insurance?" Tāne joked.

"Yes, actually, but right now it's not set up to go to you." I hit him in the shoulder. "So don't get greedy."

Tāne clasped a hand to his heart. "Me? Never. I'm only greedy about one thing." With that, he leaned in and kissed me quickly, then somehow managed to practically skip off despite the heavy gear he was wearing.

I followed at a slower pace, clomping over gravel to join up with the tour group. Two of them were speaking excitedly in Mandarin, and the other four in Spanish. And without preamble, we set off. Before we reached the glacier itself, we walked for a time over rocks and chunks of fallen ice as the glacier loomed ever larger in our vision. I was glad for the thick jacket as we neared the ice.

We stopped at the very edge of the glacier, in front of a well-worn path through it, as Salter told us to put our instep crampons on. Since none of us knew how to, he had to gather us close and show us—and even then, I still spent longer than I should have trying to buckle them on. Salter eventually rolled his eyes and helped me.

And then we set off onto the ice. I grimaced heavily at the first few steps, holding my arms out for balance as I tried to get used to the unfamiliar feeling of metal hooks on my boots digging into ice. Tāne was ahead of me, grinning madly, and the other tourists were behind me, some of them showing the same awkwardness I was. It didn't take long to get used to it, though, and before long we were all making a quick pace along the ice as Salter informed us about various landmarks.

When we paused, I took the opportunity to look around us. We had reached what looked like the narrowest gap in the valley, and all I could see was gray mountain and white ice stretching out up the gorge far into the distance. It looked so strange against the trees in the distance, two wildly different environments that had no business meshing. The group stopped for a time to catch our breath and rest our legs, while Salter told us that Fox Glacier, along with New Zealand's West Coast, was part of the South West New Zealand World Heritage Area.

We walked further among ice ridges and crevasses, sometimes jagged, where large chunks of ice had broken off, sometimes smooth and beautiful to behold. Soon we were led out into the middle of the glacier, where we could see what Salter called the icefall, which resembled a thick waterfall of ice.

"It's fucking freezing," Tāne grumbled next to me.

I snorted and bumped him with my shoulder. "Don't whine; this was your idea."

"Yeah, well." Tāne couldn't stay scowling for long; his expression lit up. "It's cool, though, isn't it?"

"Positively freezing," I deadpanned.

He laughed. "Now who's the whiner?"

"It's amazing," I said, smiling over at him. "Truly. I didn't even know something like this could exist. A whole bunch of ice right in the middle of the mountains? It's crazy."

"Who wants to go down an ice hole?" came Salter's booming, cheerful voice. Tāne and I looked askance at each other.

"Who wants to *what*?" one of the tourists asked, sounding just as dubious as I felt.

Salter clomped over a short distance to a feature I hadn't noticed before: a giant hole in the ice. I felt the bottom drop out of my stomach as I approached and leaned over to look down. I couldn't see a bottom to it, only what looked like an endless tunnel of blue glasslike ice, just wide enough for an average-sized man to fit into. "You really let people go down there?" I asked.

"On good, cold days like this, yeah," Salter replied. He knelt down to start pulling some things out of his backpack: rope; hooks; what looked like climbing equipment. "When it's warmer, the sides of the ice are slicker, which makes it dangerous. The ice around us all moves too, so you never know when the glacier could twist up and squish someone when they're in the hole."

Every single one of us paled.

"Fuck no," one of the Spanish men said emphatically. "Fuck that."

"What he said," agreed one of the Chinese women.

"I'll go!" Tāne volunteered.

"What?" I yelped. "You heard him—you could get turned into a pancake!"

But Tāne had apparently made his mind up, because he was already at Salter's side. "It's perfectly safe in cold weather like this," Salter assured us all. "The ice moves less. Even if it did decide to move in big chunks, it would be slow enough that we'd be able to pull anybody out long before anything bad happened."

That only reassured me slightly. But I supposed I had to trust that Salter knew what he was doing, so I didn't voice any further complaints as Salter got Tāne strapped into the ropes and coached him on how to walk down the wall of the hole. We all watched as Tāne walked backward over the edge of the hole—he got a little divot between his eyebrows when he was concentrating, and it made an appearance now, along with a frown at the corners of his lips. I moved as close as I dared, cringing as I watched him move down.

"This is awesome!" Tāne shouted up at us when he was halfway down. I suspiciously eyed the sides of the tunnel, listening for any creaking or groaning sounds that might signal the ice shifting. "I feel like I'm in some crazy sci-fi movie!"

That made me laugh; I saw my breath freeze into steam as I did. "What, on an ice planet?"

"Like that one we watched at my house, with the big bug tunnels!"

"Why would being in one of *those* be cool?" I shouted back. Tāne was getting increasingly further away.

"Because…." Tāne's voice got even quieter, and I couldn't make out the rest of his words. I sighed, but I didn't worry, because from the look of the rope he was nearly at the bottom.

Salter nodded at me. "Just a few more—"

A ripping noise caught my attention. I jerked my head up just in time to see the rope snap. It slithered toward the edge of the hole and fell into it.

"Tāne!" I cried, falling to my hands and knees at the lip of the tunnel. "Tāne?"

Behind me, the other tourists gasped and moved forward. Salter shouldered them out of the way.

I craned my neck, trying to spot Tāne, my heart slamming too hard inside my chest, my blood thundering in my veins. I called Tāne's name again but heard no answer.

I didn't know how far he'd been from the bottom when he'd fallen. What if it had been too far? What if he'd injured himself? What if he was *dead*?

Beside me, Salter worked quickly and efficiently to secure another rope to the outcropping of rock, and I tried very hard not to yell at him. He should have checked the rope; he should have made sure there was nothing to split it on the ground. But yelling wouldn't help right now.

For the first time in a very long time, I prayed.

I didn't bow my head or close my eyes—I wanted to keep an eye out for Tāne. But my lips moved as I silently recited a prayer, as I desperately pleaded with all my strength for Tāne to be okay. If God couldn't spare me from my family, if God couldn't save Ezekiel, then he could at least do this one thing for me.

Just this *one* thing.

Salter moved to crouch next to me, letting the new rope down the hole. "Tāne," he called, obviously careful about how he directed his voice. "If you can hear me, grab the rope and tug once."

A second ticked by. The rope jumped.

My breath felt like it had been punched out of me, but Tāne still wasn't in the clear yet. He could still be injured.

My mind went a little numb as Salter started calling down instructions for Tāne to secure the rope to his climbing gear. Salter stood back, and with the help of two of the others, started hauling the rope—and Tāne—up. I hurriedly moved back from the edge of the hole, not wanting to impede progress in any way.

Finally, I saw the top of Tāne's head, and then the rest of him as he climbed out. He looked shaken and pale, but he was standing easily. All I wanted to do was tackle him in relief, but I stayed cautious, just putting a hand on his arm in case he was hurt.

"I'm okay," he said hurriedly, his voice a bit breathless. "Just winded. I'm okay, honestly. I only fell a little way."

"You sure?" Salter said, squinting at him. "Helicopter's on its way anyway. Standard procedure."

I hadn't realized Salter had called for a helicopter, but I was grateful nonetheless.

"I'm sure," Tāne said, "Just—"

I grabbed him before he could say anything further. I didn't squeeze him as hard as I wanted to, just in case he was bruised, but I still gripped him tight in my relief.

"Jesus fucking Christ, never do that again," I hissed. "I nearly had a fucking heart attack. Fuck."

Tāne shook a little with laughter. "Me too," he mumbled, burying his face in my shoulder. "But I really am okay."

I could hear the buzz of helicopter blades in the distance.

"You two go," Salter announced. "We'll wait here until you get on the chopper safely, and I'll take the others on the walk back."

"That's really not necessary," Tāne protested, though I noticed he'd started to shiver a little. I wrapped him tighter in my arms, and then, after a thought, I shrugged off my jacket to wrap it around his shoulders. "James, come on, you need that. I don't need—"

"Let him coddle you," Salter said sternly. "And when you get back to base, you'll have two more people coddling you and feeding you hot chocolate. Get used to it. We've got to make sure people are safe."

Tāne grumbled under his breath, but didn't complain any further. Which was just as well, because if he'd kept going, I might have smacked him. Gently.

The helicopter landed on a flat patch of ice not too far away, and Salter helped us get across the ice. We squashed ourselves into the back two seats while the pilot watched, and then he gave us headphones once we were settled.

"Hey, check it out. This way you guys get a free air tour," the pilot joked.

I felt recovered enough to laugh somewhat. Tāne did too, though our laughter was a bit faint. The helicopter took off, and I held Tāne's hand the entire time.

But as we flew, the view *was* magnificent. As worried as I was about Tāne, he seemed more interested in leaning over me to look out the window to see Fox Glacier from the air, so I did too. It was even bigger than I had imagined now that I could see it from a proper distance, and despite what had happened, I still found it beautiful. It did take some time for the pounding of my heart to slow down, though.

When we landed, we were ushered inside the visitors' center, through to a back room where Tāne was wrapped in a blanket, given hot cocoa, and sternly told to sit down on the couch. I too was given a mug, and when I sniffed it, I was fairly sure I could get drunk off the fumes—that wasn't just hot cocoa. We were left alone after one of the employees double-checked that was okay.

"Well," Tāne said after a moment, "that was a bit overdramatic."

I nearly choked on my laughter, struggling to swallow the sip I'd just taken. "It wasn't *overdramatic*. You fell. It was an accident."

"Yeah, but the response was a bit over the top." Tāne looked bemused, clearly attempting to underplay what had just happened.

I just shook my head. "It scared the shit out of me," I confessed.

Tāne extended one hand from a lump of blankets and patted the couch next to him. When I sat, he wound his arm around my waist and pulled me close. "Sorry," Tāne murmured.

"It's not your fault," I protested. "I was just… yeah, scared." I smirked a little, rueful. "I even prayed." Wasn't sure if I credited God with the fact that Tāne was going to be okay, but the praying had certainly made me feel better.

Tāne chuckled, pulling me closer against him. "Yeah?"

"I'm pretty sure nothing miraculous actually happened." I shrugged. "But it made me feel better."

At the time, I hadn't had the brain power to think about anything more than the immediate. I'd only been able to contemplate the present, not the future. But now that I could think properly, other *what ifs* started popping up.

What if Tāne had died down there? What would I do with my future? Would I still have moved to New Zealand?

I didn't know how to answer any of those questions, because I didn't want to contemplate them. For now, I just wanted to focus on Tāne being alive and well.

"Shit. How much whiskey do you think they put in here?" Tāne muttered, staring down at his drink. "I'm gonna be wasted by the time I'm finished drinking it."

I couldn't help but laugh. "I'll be the designated driver, then. You keep drinking; it's good for you."

Tāne had stopped shivering, and his eyelids grew heavier the more he drank. As I sat next to him and sipped only very occasionally at my own drink, I watched him—probably more carefully than the accident warranted. I just didn't like being confronted with my own, or anybody else's, mortality.

As soon as Tāne was declared well enough to leave, we took off our gear and I got him into the car, where he proceeded to grin stupidly the whole drive back to the hotel. I just smiled fondly at him when I wasn't clutching the steering wheel and hoping I didn't run us both off the road. He was clearly under a mixture of fading adrenaline and alcohol, which meant he'd crash when we got back to the motel.

I didn't want to leave him alone, so I took us both to his room, where he proceeded to fall onto the bed. I did my best to be quiet and unobtrusive as I tugged his boots off. I thought he was asleep, but he murmured, "Get up here."

After getting rid of my own jacket and boots, I tentatively sat on the bed next to him. Tāne cracked open his eyes to roll them at me and tugged at me to lie down. I ended up on my side, facing him, both of us on top of the covers—which I quickly saw to, yanking them down so I could pull them over us. Tāne rolled over to put his back to me, and it was the most natural thing in the world for me to shift closer, draping an arm over his waist as I pressed in close behind him.

He was okay. I just had to keep reminding myself of that. He was right here and barely had a bruise on him. He was fine.

It was only just after lunchtime, but I let him sleep. And after a time, I drifted that way too, though I never fell fully asleep. I listened to the sound of the occasional car passing by on the road, the birds in the trees, and the rustle of leaves outside. It was quiet here, more quiet than I had ever experienced living in a big city.

I woke properly when I felt Tāne start to stir, though he didn't wake up, so I crept out of the hotel to go buy some food. I figured a quiet night in might be the best way to go, and since there weren't exactly many fast-food joints in Fox Glacier—I hadn't even seen a McDonald's—I went to the supermarket instead, and got a few things I could put together for a meal.

Tāne was on the couch in front of the TV when I got back. He looked groggy and still half-asleep, but fine nonetheless, though my paranoid gaze wouldn't stop looking for any sign of him not being okay. He fixed me with a *look*, and I shrugged, returning that look with one of my own that said *get used to it*. But I didn't fuss over him, because he obviously wasn't the kind of person who enjoyed that kind of thing.

"Just, one last time," I said as we ate, perched shoulder to shoulder on the couch. "You're okay, right?"

"I'm okay, James," Tāne replied. He briefly rested his head on my shoulder. "Promise."

Chapter 12

THE NEXT day, we were scheduled to head south through Milford Sound and into Queenstown. The first thing we did, though, was go to the local shops to buy some warmer clothes. I hadn't anticipated it being this cold, and apparently neither had Tāne, but the further south we drove, the colder it was getting.

I took over the driving responsibilities for the day—Tāne insisted he could drive just fine, and I was sure he could, but I still wanted him to take it easy. The drive itself was a lot less perilous than my first drive through Waipoua Forest had been; the roads were mostly gentle curves, though we did go through and over a lot of mountains. The West Coast of the South Island, I was told, was one big mountain range, stemming from a major fault line running the entire way down the west side of the island.

Most of the first half of the drive was through narrow mountain gaps. We stopped off at a small gravel area along the side of the road to stretch our legs.

I noticed Tāne was halfway between grinning and looking around him with trepidation. "What's up?" I asked.

"Just looking out for something. It's nothing to worry about," he said dismissively. We went over to a picnic bench at the tree line, and I had a cigarette while he relaxed. The air was cool but the sun was warm, and it was a damned nice day.

I heard a vague thump, but thought it was just some kind of wildlife, so I didn't pay much attention. Tāne, though, started laughing between curses, rising off the bench. Alarmed, I turned to look at what he saw and was greeted with the sight of a fat green bird perched on top of the ute, putting its best effort into removing the antenna.

"The hell?" I said, too surprised to react right away. Then I stood and moved toward the car. The bird fluttered back and landed on the ground, eyeing me up. It looked familiar, but I couldn't place it at first, then I realized I'd seen the shape of it carved into wood. Tāne had a figure of it in his workshop, and he'd explained to me that it was a kea.

He'd also called them cheeky little buggers. I could see why.

"This is why you don't leave your car unattended in this area," Tāne said, laughing. "Fucking keas."

As I watched, the kea boldly returned to the ute antenna, hooked its curved beak around the base of it, and tugged. Another kea came from the trees and set about apparently trying to remove the rubber lining from his windows. I was laughing as I chased them away again.

"They seriously have some kind of grudge against cars," Tāne explained as we stood near the ute, having a staring competition with the two birds. "Or anything humans leave out. They'll destroy your car if you give them the chance. I even heard a story about a kea making off with a tourist's passport."

They were beautiful birds, despite the bent for destruction. Probably about twenty inches long, they resembled a parrot but weren't nearly as brightly colored. They were a muted olive green, brighter on their wings, and as I saw one fly overhead, I could see a flash of brilliant orange underneath its wings. "They're kind of cute," I admitted reluctantly. "Even if there are now four of them looking like they want to rip the ute to shreds."

"We should probably head off." Tāne chuckled. As I got back into the ute, I kept my eyes on the keas, and I peeled out of the parking area before they got the idea to launch themselves back on the car.

It took us another couple of hours to reach Queenstown. I'd noticed Tāne texting back and forth with someone on the way; I didn't ask who, but from the mix of a smile and exasperation on his face, I would have guessed Huia. He also booked a motel along the way, though it took a few tries to find a place that wasn't booked out, and then he went right back to texting Huia.

Queenstown, like so many of the cities and towns we had visited, was built along water. Lake Wakatipu was an oddly shaped lake, long and narrow and shaped like an S, and Queenstown was built around the front of the lower curve. It was a beautiful sunny day, and the lake looked clear as we drove the road that wound next to it. Queenstown, Tāne informed me, was famous for its ski slopes. Neither of us had any intention of actually skiing—and nor would we get the chance, as it was only just into autumn—but I thought I'd like to see the mountain nonetheless.

We drove through one of the main roads in search of the motel Tāne had booked—most of the ones we passed were lit up with "no vacancy" signs. We had to pull in to a side road for our motel.

The desk clerk took one look at us and held up a key. "Booking for Kokiri," he said, clearly more interested in his book.

Tāne took the keys, and we walked down a cramped orange-wallpapered hallway to find room number twenty-one. It wasn't the nicest motel, I had to admit, but I had certainly stayed in worse over the years, so I was hardly about to complain. I opened up the door, and we went inside.

Only to find Huia sitting in our room.

"Jesus," Tāne yelped. "What are you, a fucking movie assassin?"

Her laugh was throaty. "I try my best." She was dressed more casually than I had seen her before, in jeans and a long sweater, her hair pulled back in a simple ponytail.

"No, seriously, what the fuck?" Tāne demanded. He dumped his bags on the floor near the bed—the *only* bed, I noticed. "Are you trying to give me a heart attack? How did you know where we were?"

Huia cast Tāne a bemused gaze. "You told me the name of the hotel when we were texting. And I was nearby for work that's just finished up."

I laughed at the look on Tāne's face. "Oh," he said. "Well, whatever, you're still a fucking movie assassin. Why are you here, though?"

Huia cast her gaze down to the floor. "I'm here to help spread Mum's ashes."

Tāne's defensive posture fell away. Hesitantly, he went to sit next to Huia. For a while, he looked like he had no clue what to say, and I busied myself with putting our bags away. Eventually, he said, "I'd really like that."

I wondered what had made her change her mind. More to the point, I wondered why she hadn't been doing this with Tāne to begin with. But asking would be incredibly rude of me—it wasn't really any of my business.

"Do you remember the last time we came down here with Mum and Dad?" Huia asked Tāne, a smile in her words if not on her expression.

"Yeah, on Mum's birthday." Tāne chuckled. "Damn, that was a while ago. What, like ten years?"

"Something like that." Huia did smile then. "We went skiing. She hated it, but we loved it, so she came along just for us."

At that point I decided I was intruding on a private conversation, so I went outside under the pretense of having a cigarette. There was a little secluded backyard area just out from the kitchen, so I took my book and my cigarettes and went to sit in the sun. I could hear the vague murmur of their voices inside; I was glad they were getting a chance to talk away from their father.

Half an hour later, they came outside and sat in the other chairs. Huia lit up a cigarette, and Tāne slouched back in his chair until he was nearly falling off it. Birdsong occasionally reached our ears, traffic humming on the road nearby. We sat in comfortable silence for a time before Tāne said, "James, me and Huia are gonna head out to go do the ashes, if that's okay?"

I got the meaning: he wanted it to just be them. "Yeah, of course," I said, surprised he'd even felt the need to ask. I wouldn't want to rob them of some private mourning time together, nor would I want to intrude. I was just honored that Tāne had so far let me in on so many of those moments. "You guys go ahead. I might wander around the streets."

Tāne stood and kissed my cheek. "Have fun," he murmured.

When he drew back, Huia was watching us both. She wasn't smiling, but there were distinct creases around the edges of her eyes. "We won't be long," she said, and she sounded *fond*.

It looked like she approved, then.

That was a damn sight better than Hemi's attitude.

They left, but I wound up staying in. Maybe I was just feeling lazy. I parked my ass on the couch and watched some television. The hotel didn't get many channels, but the news was enough for me. I dozed in the sunlight streaking across the room and lost track of time to the sound of news reporters talking about the weather, which was apparently unseasonably cold.

The noise of the door opening woke me from my half sleep, and I blinked groggily at Tāne and Huia as they came back in. The sun had shifted, and a glance at the television confirmed that they had been gone about an hour and a half. Huia's eye makeup was smudged, but I pretended not to notice. She muttered something about going to the bathroom to clean up, which left Tāne and me seated alone on the couch.

"How was it?" I asked.

Tāne, when I looked closer, looked like he'd been crying too. I reached across to put my hand on his knee, concerned, but he just smiled at me. "It was good," he said quietly. "It was really good."

I didn't press him for more than that. Huia came out of the bathroom with her makeup wiped off, and together we vegged in front of the television for a while. I had no real reason to be tired, but I certainly felt it. For the past week we had been traveling nonstop, and while sitting in a car was hardly physically taxing, it was still curiously tiring.

A few hours later, we went out to the nearest supermarket to get some food for dinner, just bits and pieces that didn't involve a whole lot of cooking. It turned out Tāne had indeed been texting Huia on the drive here, and he'd told her we were going to Queenstown; she had been in Wanaka, one of the next towns over, on a business trip to meet a client. But the client had canceled at the last second, after she'd already arrived, so she'd figured she might as well join us in Queenstown.

She confessed to me that she was glad she had; she'd felt horrible about not being able to go with Tāne to spread their mother's ashes. Huia didn't explain why she'd refused in the first place, but I got the feeling there were a number of reasons: work; time; family relations. In the end, it wasn't my business. I was just happy they were getting along.

When the hour grew late, Huia retreated to her own hotel room. Though Tāne and I had shared a bed for a nap after Fox Glacier, we hadn't truly *slept* in the same bed—and with only one bed due to Huia's meddling, it looked like we'd be doing that now. I could have offered to sleep on the couch, or Tāne could have, but when we looked at the one bed and grinned at each other, it was obvious we were all too happy to share.

With the television on—because Tāne said that he liked a bit of white noise in the background while he slept—we slipped under the covers after we'd gotten dressed for bed. I twisted and turned to get comfortable, and wound up on my side, facing Tāne, who was watching me with a bemused expression.

"You're not gonna be an annoying sleeper, are you?" he teased.

"I'm fine once I get settled," I insisted. I hit the pillow a few times, stretched my legs to the tune of Tāne's jokingly exasperated groan, and finally went still. "See?"

He laughed. "Yeah, and now I'm wide awake again, because you made such a racket."

"Oh, shut up." I grinned crookedly at him as I closed my eyes.

I felt him move, the slide of skin against sheet, then he closed his hand over the top of mine. I tangled my fingers with his and opened my eyes again to look at him. He looked content, his eyes closed, his posture relaxed.

And I was a man. No matter how much I wanted to wait until I knew for sure that we'd have something long-term, my lizard brain still perked up at the fact that we were in a bed together, especially at the sight of Tāne in his shirtless state. The light from the television was dim, but the blanket was only pulled halfway up his torso, which afforded me a nice view of faintly lit dusky skin, the electronic blue light clinging to the lines and angles of his muscles.

I wanted him. God, I wanted him. I wanted to roll him over, under me, to kiss him until he was breathless and so much more.

"Tāne?" I murmured.

"Mm?" He cracked open an eye to look at me.

"I want you." I couldn't be more eloquent or honest than that. "Not right now. Because there are things I want to wait for. I want to know we'll be together. I want to not be weighed down with a boatload of personal issues. But, fuck, I want you."

His eyes were darker than usual in the low light. He took my hand and raised it to his lips, then pressed a kiss to my knuckles. "I know."

I didn't actively think about moving closer, but I was there in a quick motion, pressing our legs together and my lips against his. Our kiss was gentle and lingering, aching with the restraint of it. "Seriously. I want you," I repeated.

He laughed softly. "I know. Me too." Tāne kissed me again, then tilted his head to kiss my jaw, sending a shiver over my skin. "But we can wait. I'm completely cool with waiting."

I didn't know many people who would say that and truly mean it. "And just for the record, I intend this to be long-term," I whispered.

Tāne smiled at me, the blue light revealing the curve of his lips. "Good."

"Good," I echoed, closing my eyes once more. "So you're stuck with me, you realize that?"

Tāne just hummed happily, sounding like he was starting to drift off into sleep. "Absolutely. Do you hear me complaining?"

I didn't. And I'd never felt happier.

Chapter 13

AFTER QUEENSTOWN, we did an about-face to the north again and headed up to Lake Tekapo, which would be our final stop.

We'd said good-bye to Huia with the promise that we would see her again in Wellington. She actually hugged both of us—and not a pathetic sort of hug, either; it had been a real, genuine hug with a strong grip and a complete lack of awkwardness.

I found myself reluctant even to drive to Lake Tekapo in the first place. It would mean I would be one step closer to the final leg of my journey. After Lake Tekapo, we would drive up to Picton to take the ferry back across, and in Wellington I would take a plane to Auckland, where I would depart the country.

Once we got to Lake Tekapo, I would only have two more days left in Tāne's company.

I was planning on coming back, of course. There was no other option, in my mind. But I didn't know how long it would take to get a visa. What if it took years? What if the class action made it impossible? What if the only way Tāne and I could be together was with a long-distance relationship with occasional holiday visits?

"Stop thinking, James."

I turned to look at Tāne. He was driving again today, looking as whole and healthy as he ever had. That morning, even I and my constant worrying had been forced to admit that the only injury Tāne had was a slight bruise to one knee where he'd come down on the bottom of the ice tunnel. So I had let him drive again, much to his bemusement.

"I can hear the gears turning," Tāne continued gently. "And I know. We've got half an hour till we get there. And then back to Wellington tomorrow."

"And then back to my home halfway across the world," I sighed.

"Yeah." Tāne's response was muted. He sounded like he was trying to be upbeat about it, but failing. "But you'll be back." That, at least, he sounded sure of.

"I wouldn't know what to do with myself if I couldn't come back," I admitted. The thought wasn't one I wanted to entertain. I loved Dallas, but now it felt like it held too many memories. Too many people to remind me of the terrible things I had done. Too many opportunities to be reminded of the past, my family, and my failures.

But I did need to go back. I had things to do.

"I have to deal with this class action. And then I'm going to find some of the people I lied to," I said, staring out the window. The scenery on the way to Lake Tekapo was flatter than it had been on the West Coast, fewer mountains and more farmland, which was even more abundant in the South Island than it was in the North. "And I'm going to apologize."

"Yeah?" I could see Tāne look at me. He frowned suddenly and looked back to the road. "I wish I could come with you."

"You don't need to," I reassured him. "It's probably something I should do by myself anyway. I got myself into this mess alone; I should solve it alone."

"You never *have* to be alone for anything," Tāne said softly.

I briefly settled my hand on his where it gripped the steering wheel. "I'll show you around Dallas someday," I promised. I smiled faintly. "Just not when there could be a spectacle following me around." My smile vanished quickly in favor of a grimace. I didn't think there'd be paparazzi following me around, but I also knew I wasn't going to be ignored. Religion was important in the Southern states, and I had flagrantly used it against people.

Honestly, I had no idea how big it would be. Just thinking about it was nerve-racking enough.

But I had to face the music sometime.

We drove through a town called Twizel, then briefly around the shore of Lake Pukaki, before arriving in the town of Lake Tekapo. The lake itself seemed to stretch out as far as the eye could see to the north, with only the dim gray of mountains in the background to mark its eventual end. We booked a hotel, then parked the ute near the lake's edge and sat on the grass, facing the water.

It felt wrong to spend my last visit to a new town feeling so melancholy. I wanted to enjoy it. I wanted to explore the town and its surroundings. I wanted to marvel at the clear blue of the water and the sky, to breathe in the clean air and find some more New Zealand food, so normal here but so foreign to me. But all I could do was stare at the lake and do my best not to let the dread in the pit of my stomach grow too chaotic.

I was sure I was being the worst kind of downer, but when I looked at Tāne, he seemed perfectly content to sit and have a quiet moment. His eyes were closed, dark lashes resting against his cheeks, and he'd tilted his head back to enjoy the sun. The wind was ruffling his short hair, and a hint of a smile was curving at the corners of his lips.

I'd known he was beautiful, but right then, it struck me all over again.

"I'm coming back," I said.

He opened his eyes and looked back at me. I saw the moment where he heard and processed my words, relief easing into his expression. And then I saw the little grin. "We are the most morose assholes right now," he teased.

Despite my mood, I chuckled. "God, we are," I agreed ruefully. "We should actually *do* something instead of just sitting here."

Tāne jumped up, and I took his offered hand to help me stand. "Any ideas?" he asked. "I'm open to suggestions."

I cast my gaze out across the lake. A bright sign caught my eye, and I started to smile. "How are you at rowing?"

BOTH OF us were *awful* at rowing, it turned out.

Getting the hang of synchronization was more difficult than it seemed. Tāne would put his oar into the water, and I would catch on a second too late, then my oar would send our rented canoe spinning in the opposite direction, and neither of us was managing to actually make it go forward.

I couldn't stop laughing. "Tāne, we *need* to work out a system," I announced.

He enthusiastically dug his oar into the water again, sending us rotating to the left. "Who needs a system?" he called back gleefully. "We're getting somewhere!"

Somewhere was about ten feet from the pier and still in relatively shallow water. The canoe we had rented from the lakeside store was bright yellow and red, the oars colored to match. Our life vests were the same lurid shade of yellow. The instructor who had given us the canoe had asked if either of us knew how to operate one. Tāne had answered yes.

"I'm beginning to think you've never been in a canoe in your life." I laughed, leaning forward so I could poke his back.

"I have!" he replied defensively, twisting to look at me over his shoulder. "When I was seven."

"Seven!" That just set me off into more laughter. "You probably weren't even allowed to have an oar!"

Tāne grinned widely at me. "The camp leader had both of them. Okay, we'll figure this shit out, bro. I'll count, and on every even number, we row, okay?"

That turned out to work decently well, after a few false starts and hiccups. We made our way out into the middle of the lake; there was barely any wind, so the water was calm, with only the smallest of ripples marring the surface. Lake Tekapo, at my best guess, was about two miles across at the widest point, and perhaps eight miles long, so when we let our canoe gently drift, I could see the land on either side of us, a mile away. To the east were mountains, as well as to the far northwest.

But I kept looking back at Tāne, who was more compelling than any of those sights.

His back was to me, so I could only see the back of his head and his short dark hair. I could see the broad line of his shoulders, clothed in his usual flannel and the life vest. His shirt was rolled up to his elbows, baring strong forearms and capable hands, muscles that bunched and released when he moved the oar.

"I can feel you staring at me," Tāne said, a smile in his voice.

"I can't help it." I leaned forward to tug at the back of his collar, straightening it. "Even when all I can see is your back. You're one of the most attractive people I've ever seen."

He sounded like he was muffling laughter. "My *back* is attractive?"

I snorted. "Shut up. You know what I mean."

"You give the weirdest compliments," he said fondly. "Man, we should have brought some food out here. I'm hungry."

Tāne, I had learned, was always hungry. I had no idea how he ate so much and managed to keep in shape. Last night in Queenstown, we had cooked up steak and vegetables; I had roasted some potatoes in the tiny tray and temperamental oven that the motel had offered in its little kitchen, but about half of the tray had been left over. After we'd all finished dinner, I'd witnessed him stealing the tray to keep eating off it. No man should be able to eat that many carbs and not gain any weight.

We spent a few more minutes relaxing and then headed back. The return trip was easier now that we had settled into a rhythm, and we made good time. The motion of rowing was oddly soothing, as was the quiet interrupted only by the sound of sloshing water.

After we reached the shore and had given the canoe and the vests back, we made a quick detour back to the hotel to pick up the box with Tāne's mother's ashes. Then we returned to Lake Tekapo and wandered around the edge of it for a while in silence.

Finally, Tāne stopped at an outcropping of rocks. "I guess this is it," he murmured. "This is the last of her ashes."

I stood next to him and put my arm around his waist. "Do you want me to go?"

"No." Tāne leaned against my side. "No, I want you here."

Resting my cheek against his shoulder, I nodded. Tāne opened the little blue box and bent to set it down at our feet after he'd taken out the bag inside. There was only a handful of ash left. Tāne just held on to the bag for some time as we stared out at the water.

"Mum," Tāne said, his voice wavering, "I love you. I know I screwed up sometimes, but you were always there for me, even when I did stupid shit like get into fights at school. You just put a Band-Aid on me and told me to kick their asses harder next time."

I smiled to myself—Te Aroha Kokiri sounded like a hell of a woman.

"And I know our family is a bit fucked up. I know Huia and Dad should be here with me right now. But Huia was here last time, so, um, I guess don't blame her too hard?" Tāne slowly undid the bag. "I love you. Again. And I really fucking miss you. I wish you were here to meet this guy I met." He glanced across at me, his smile wobbly. "I think you'd like him."

"I'm sure I would have loved her," I murmured.

That made him laugh a little, the sound more like a hitched sob. "See, Mum? He's a gentleman." He paused to rub a hand over his eyes. "Anyway. I guess this is good-bye."

Slowly, reluctantly, he tipped the bag upside down. The ashes filtered through the air into the water, dull gray swirling with blue until they were carried off by the current. I held him tighter, and we stood there for what felt like hours, until the air grew cold and the sun started to sink.

THAT NIGHT, after dinner, neither of us even attempted to go to the other room we had booked. Through silent agreement we wound up in the same bed again, in the same position that we had taken after Fox Glacier—me pressed close against Tāne's back, my arm resting over his waist. I kissed the back of his neck and we settled in.

I wanted to do more. I wanted to slide my hands up under the T-shirt he wore to bed, feel his skin under my fingers. I wanted to kiss him until we grew short of breath. I wanted to slowly strip him naked to see his skin against the dark sheets, and I wanted to touch him until he was lost to ecstasy. I wanted to do so much more than just lie here together—but I didn't want to do any of that until I knew for damn sure we'd have a future.

Instead, I just held my hand over his hip, idly rubbing at the jut of bone with my thumb. Tāne took my hand with his and pressed it lightly against his stomach.

Nothing in particular prompted my words. There was no special moment, no revelation. No one overwhelming thing that led to me saying it.

"I think I love you."

If I had ever said anything true in my life, those words were the truth. I felt it so keenly, lying here with Tāne warm and solid in my arms, that *not* saying those words would have felt wrong. Perhaps it wasn't the most romantic way to put it, but it was from the heart nonetheless.

Tāne didn't reply right away, but his hand remained clasped with mine. I let him have the time; words like that shouldn't be rushed, nor should those feelings. And though I was leaving the country late tomorrow, right then I felt like we had all the time in the world, like this hotel room was a suspended moment in history that would last exactly as long as we both needed it to.

Finally, he murmured, "Me too."

It would be more romantic if I left it at that. But I couldn't resist. "That's a little narcissistic of you."

He started shaking in laughter. "You know what I mean."

"I do." I kissed his shoulder blade, smiling.

The warm glow of contentment settled into me as I got comfortable. I closed my eyes and squeezed Tāne's hand, then let myself drift off into sleep, having never felt more peaceful than I did at that moment.

WHEN WE arrived at the airport the following night, I was already contemplating how difficult it would be to be an illegal immigrant.

We had traveled most of the day, starting early to drive to Picton, and taking the ferry back. All told, it had taken us about eleven hours, from six in the morning to five in the evening, and even though my flight was at eight, we decided to head straight to the airport.

I was sure I scowled the whole way there.

Huia had met up with us when we'd gotten off the ferry and followed us in her own car to the airport. So now we sat in the domestic terminal, at a café near the security gate, sipping on coffee and trying to think of anything to say.

I wasn't being very successful at coming up with conversation.

Then again, I didn't need to. As always, Huia was remarkably blunt and got straight to the point. "Are you coming back?"

"Huia," Tāne groaned.

"It's a valid question," she replied sternly. "I've seen you date a fair few men, and none of them have ever put that look on your face. You're happy. I want to know if James intends on *keeping* you happy."

"I want nothing more," I confirmed. "Honestly, right now, I have no idea where to start. There's things—important things—I need to do once I get back to the States. And I have no idea how long that will take, or what my visa options will be. But I want to live here. I know that."

Huia scrutinized me for a moment longer before nodding. "What do you have to do when you get back?"

I hesitated in replying. Talking about it so openly with anybody but Tāne still felt strange to me. But I'd need to speak to my own victims, and that would be a *lot* worse than talking to someone who I knew had forgiven me. So talking to Huia wasn't going to be nearly as hard as what I had coming.

"I have to see this class action through," I sighed. "My lawyer says I'll have to do a public apology. But I want to find some of the others that I wronged, the ones not pushing the class action, and apologize to them too. I don't know how much good it will do. I don't think most of them will forgive me. But I know I have to at least let them know that I'm sorry."

"If you need advice, just call me." Huia reached out to grasp my arm, squeezing once before letting her hand fall away. "I've handled class actions before. They're scary, but if you handle them right, both parties usually walk away happy."

"Shit. Glad it's not me doing that," Tāne murmured, shaking his head. "Call me before it happens, okay? I'll give you a pep talk. We both will."

I took a second to look at both of them. They really looked like siblings now, their body language a lot more at ease with each other. They probably still had a long way to go, but I was glad to see the start of it. "I will," I promised both of them. "We can have a conference call, and I'll weep in terror while you two tell me to stop being a baby."

That made Tāne grin. "We'll do that."

Seemingly sensing that I needed a distraction, Tāne and Huia offered to show me around the airport until my flight was called. So we wandered from shop to shop, and I took great amusement in looking through a tourist store. On display were New Zealand flags—both the official version with the Union Jack and the unofficial version with a simple black background and silver fern logo—stuffed sheep toys, little kiwi figurines, dish towels that bore the words "Kia Ora" or "Aotearoa."

I was in the middle of examining a set of coasters when I heard an announcement over the loudspeaker. I tensed, listening for the number of my flight—and when it was announced, I held back a miserable sigh.

It was time for me to go.

"That's me," I said ruefully, gathering my carry-on bag. Huia immediately pulled me into a hug.

"Good luck," she whispered to me.

"I'll need it." I laughed lowly, hugging her back. "Thank you."

She stepped back, and then I was engulfed by Tāne. I held him tightly, because I didn't want to think about letting go. "You'll be back," Tāne said, sounding like he was trying to convince the both of us.

"I'll be back," I promised. Despite the lead weight in my gut, I still only narrowly restrained myself from making a Terminator joke. Instead, I turned my head to kiss his cheek, but Tāne wasn't having any of that. He hauled me into a proper kiss instead, the kind that made my head spin and my blood pressure rise. It probably wasn't entirely appropriate to be having that kind of kiss in the middle of a crowded airport, but I didn't care.

Huia gave an exaggerated disgusted noise in the background, which made both Tāne and me grin, making it impossible to keep kissing. Instead, I leaned my forehead against his, wanting to keep close.

"I'll call," I said. "And e-mail. And text. You'll probably get really sick of me."

"Not a chance," Tāne said. "I'll reply to everything even if it's three in the morning."

Out of the corner of my eye, I could see a crowd gathering around the security gates. I had to check in half an hour before the flight was set to leave, which meant I had to go through right then. I still didn't want to, but the prospect that I'd be able to stay in touch with Tāne cheered me up a little bit.

"Okay," I sighed, reluctantly pulling back from Tāne. "I should head off."

"Have a safe flight." Tāne's voice was tight, and he was blinking a little too rapidly. The sight of him made my throat tighten up. If this went on much longer, I was absolutely going to cry in the middle of an airport.

Huia saved me; she gave me a light shove in the direction of the security gate. "Piss off, James," she said, laughing. "Go on, go get your flight. Call us when you land."

Though it was the last thing I wanted to do, I gave them both a final hug. "I will. Absolutely." And with that, I started walking toward the gate.

I turned back for one last look. Tāne was waving. Huia had put her arm around her brother's shoulders, and as she saw me looking, she lifted a hand in a wave too. Tāne's smile looked a little pained. Behind them was a view of Wellington through the window, bright and beautiful and clean, green trees and yellow sun.

I swallowed around the lump in my throat and left.

Chapter 14

MY HOME, I discovered, didn't feel like home anymore.

I had a nice apartment just outside the inner city of Dallas, on the eleventh floor of an apartment building. It had a great view, three bedrooms, two bathrooms, a fireplace, and a spa. It was minutes' walk away from any convenience I'd need, mere blocks away from numerous restaurants, with a theater right next door.

And now I would rather be staying in any of the tiny, cramped hotel rooms I'd had in New Zealand.

It was spring in the States, and the trees were beginning to blossom—a sharp contrast to the slowly reddening leaves I had seen in New Zealand. It was comfortably warm, not the chill I'd gotten used to. Dallas was packed and busy, traffic and people everywhere, loud voices and city pollution.

By the grace of God, luck, or simple coincidence, I hadn't been recognized at the airport or on the taxi ride home. I had managed to get to my apartment without a single comment or strange look, which made me wonder if the media was done with me in its fickle, quick-moving way. And now I sat alone in my expensive apartment, the American accents on my television sounding both familiar and strange all at once.

I had to call my lawyer. But that didn't sound like a particularly good idea to me at the moment. All I *really* wanted to do was go curl up under my blankets and hide.

I had texted Tāne as soon as I had gotten into the taxi outside the Dallas airport, though I hadn't gotten a reply yet. Given that it must be the middle of the night for him, that was to be expected.

I already missed him. Maybe that was ridiculous, given that only about a day had passed, but I did miss him. I just wanted to be back in New Zealand, I wanted to be back on our road trip. I was already thinking of just booking another ticket and getting a tourist visa for six months.

But eventually my money would run out. I couldn't keep going for six months at a time, no matter how enticing the idea of that was. I would have to settle somewhere, and I would have to find a job. I would have to actually work on a real visa to get me back into New Zealand, even though the thought of doing all that sounded exhausting and more than a little scary.

Eventually, I turned the television off and retreated to bed, where I spent the night tossing and turning, too jet-lagged and too awake to sleep.

THE NEXT morning, I finally called Damien. Or rather, he called me.

He wasted no time in getting straight to the point. "They've given a settlement offer."

"Christ," I mumbled. I had been in the middle of my usual morning coffee routine, but now I actually had to pay attention. I dragged a hand over my face, scratching at the stubble I'd been too lazy to shave, and blinked hard a few times, trying to get my eyes properly open. "What is it?"

"Mitchell, I'd strongly suggest that you try to get this dismissed."

"That bad, huh?" I said wryly.

"Trust me when I say that you don't have their asking price in your bank account." Damien didn't sound happy. Then again, when did he ever?

"Okay. Give me a second." I tucked my phone between my ear and my shoulder and took my empty coffee mug with me to the sink. I just needed a second to think. If I didn't get this case dismissed, then it would move to a deposition, and I'd have to sit and have my history rehashed by lawyers in endless questions that just asked the same thing in different ways. But if I didn't fight this, then my former clients would take me for everything I had.

I should fight. I knew I should.

But I was done trying to pretend that I'd had good reason to do what I had. I was done trying to defend myself. I was done *hiding*.

"I want to settle," I told Damien. "I don't want to drag this out and have it go to trial."

"No," he replied, sounding incredulous. "Trust me, James, you should move for a dismissal. It's almost always the smartest option. That shit takes time to go to trial, and in that time, memories fade and tempers cool down. The plaintiffs probably don't have a lot of money—*they're* the ones that can't afford to have this go on too long."

It was logical and smart; if I was a genuinely wronged party. But in my case, that just sounded like a cold move.

"I've taken enough of their money." I dumped the mug in the sink, and with my hands free, I took hold of my phone again, pacing back to the living room. "I've caused them enough grief."

"They want 1.2 million dollars," Damien said.

That gave me pause. That was more than I'd been expecting. And Damien was right, I didn't have that in my bank account. I wasn't poor, but I wasn't a millionaire either. The selfish miser in me wanted to say, "Fuck it, let's go to trial, then."

"They're not going to get that amount. Surely they know that." I grimaced.

"I don't know. But *we* know that, and *we* also know that instead of 1.2 million, they're just going to get every last cent you've got."

I'd be broke. I had no idea how I'd live or feed myself, pay rent, or buy gas. "Do you think I could convince them to leave me enough to get by on while I find a job?" I asked.

"Jesus, I don't know. I still say you should—"

I cut Damien off. "I want to settle," I repeated, more firmly this time. "So schedule a meeting or however this goes."

The silence on the other end of the line sounded grudgingly accepting. "Fine. I'll call a settlement conference. It'll just be you, me, the plaintiffs' lawyer, a judge to oversee, and maybe a few of the plaintiffs themselves."

Great. I'd have to look at them while accepting defeat. Apparently I still had some rebellious pride left somewhere, because the thought of that stung—even if I hated myself for feeling that way. But largely, I supposed it could be satisfying. I would finally be getting the chance to put everything behind me. That had to be worth it

OVER THE next week, I did very little. I attempted to look for a job, though very few employers even called me back, and those that did seemed to change their minds as soon as they got a look at me. I tried to spend as little money as I could, and mostly I only left my apartment for food.

I kept in touch with Tāne, though every time I contacted him just made me miss him worse. We spoke of irrelevant things: what the weather was like in Wellington, how Huia and Hemi were, the difference between American football and rugby. We never strayed onto the topic of the class action, and for that I was grateful. Our conversations were a point of joy in my day, and every time I hung up the phone, my day felt that much worse without his voice in my ear.

I missed him. His voice wasn't enough—his tinny laughter over the distance of the line wasn't enough. I wanted him beside me. I wanted to be back in New Zealand so badly that I dreamed about it every night.

But before I could go back, I had amends to make.

Two days before the settlement conference, I started making some calls.

"Mrs. Johnson, hello, it's James Mitchell. I—"

Click. Dial tone.

"Mr. Chandra? Good morning, it's James Mitchell. I'd like to speak with you about—"

Click. Dial tone.

"Miss Braithwaite, it's James Mitchell—"

"You'll roast in hell for what you did!"

Click. Dial tone.

An hour and twenty attempts later, I wanted to give up. Unfortunately for me, my contact list was a lot longer than just twenty numbers. I had barely gotten a sixth of the way into it, and the rest of the list had started to look like a mountain I just couldn't climb.

But I had to do this. So I didn't give up right then and there like I wanted to; I shrugged on my jacket, pulled a baseball cap low over my eyes, and headed out.

Though the streets were packed as usual, the baseball cap obviously did the trick, as I wasn't recognized. Once or twice I thought I saw somebody trying to look more closely at me, but whatever they saw or didn't see, they didn't stop in their paths. I still felt paranoid, though, and I kept my head bowed and my shoulders hunched as I walked.

My first visit would be to Mrs. Gallagher. She had been one of the first people I had ever ripped off, actually—I'd still been nervous back then about getting exposed as a fraud, but too angry to care about what happened. I had never identified myself as belonging to a specific church, and I had never taken advantage of any of the legal rights afforded to priests. I had relied solely on implication. Back then, I would have said that trusting me was her own fault. But with a class action looming over my head, something that could very easily go to trial if the plaintiffs weren't happy with what I could give them, I was nervous.

Mrs. Gallagher was a middle-aged single mother of three. When I had met her, ten years ago, her husband had recently divorced her, and she had wanted guidance from God about how to live her life. At the time, I had simply given her the advice of common sense—I had never willingly given my clients bad advice, and I had never deliberately told them things that would hurt them. My anger had been satisfied enough by the gleeful idea that I was tricking them. So I had told her to turn to her family for support, to look to her friends, and to take advantage of any help the government would give single mothers. I had done a bit of cold reading to tell her that God wanted her to make peace with the fact that her husband had cheated; I hadn't known beforehand that he had, but the signs had been obvious.

She had thanked me profusely and told me I must be gifted to receive such a clear line to God's love. Then I'd taken a few hundred dollars off her and had laughed all the way to the bank.

I wasn't in a laughing mood right now.

Mrs. Gallagher opened the door four seconds after I rang the doorbell, and the look on her face sent a lead weight dropping into the pit of my stomach. First polite inquiry, then recognition, then anger, and finally betrayal.

She wasn't one of the eleven people bringing the class action against me. I knew I would see them soon enough. No, I was seeking out the ones who weren't on that list—just because they didn't get in on the class action, it didn't mean that they didn't feel betrayed. And it didn't mean that I could just forget about them.

"Ma'am." I greeted her as politely as I could. I knew I didn't need to introduce myself.

"You've got some nerve, showing up here," she said coolly. "I should slam this door in your face and be done with you."

"You probably should," I agreed. Mrs. Gallagher clearly hadn't expected that; surprise mingled with betrayal in her expression. "But I just wanted to say that I'm sorry."

Her bark of laughter was a little too loud. "And you think I should forgive you?"

"I just—"

"Get out," Mrs. Gallagher snapped. "Get off my doorstep and don't contact me again."

And with that, she really did slam the door on me.

MY NEXT visit was to Mr. Parker—though I knew him better by his first name: Daniel. I had met him about five years into my con work; at the time he had been nineteen, a dedicated eclectic pagan. He had focused on a mixture of Greek and Norse deities, and I had helped him with a ritual to worship Zeus.

I knew a lot of people—especially in the Southern states—would disregard paganism as a lesser religion, or would laugh and call it silly.

I regarded it with the same weight I did any religion. Belief, after all, was just as powerful no matter what you directed it at.

Daniel looked decidedly different when he opened his door. Gone were the symbolic pendants, though the tattoo of Thor's hammer remained on his wrist. He looked more mature, like he had done some growing up. The T-shirts with band names were gone, replaced by an expensive-looking business shirt and tie.

"James Mitchell?" He blinked at me. "Holy shit."

"Mr. Parker," I said, schooling my voice to sound strong and confident even though I felt anything but. "I don't require much of your time. I assume you've seen the news."

Daniel laughed, a little disbelieving. "Yeah. Yeah, I did. It's been all over the place. I mean, don't get me wrong, it's pretty funny to see the Christians all riled up, but it's...."

It was then that I knew he still practiced, because his expression took on the same touch of betrayal that Mrs. Gallagher's had. I hadn't been sure before, but now I was. "I'm here to say I'm sorry," I said quietly. "What I did was unforgiveable."

"And yet you're here looking for forgiveness," Daniel pointed out.

I faltered. I wanted to protest that I wasn't, that I just wanted to let people know I was sorry and leave their forgiveness up to them. But that wouldn't be telling the truth. I *did* want people to forgive me, because only then would I feel like I could forgive myself and start to move on.

"I guess so," I admitted.

"I don't know if I can give it to you." Daniel was brutally honest. That didn't surprise me—he'd been blunt when I'd met him.

I nodded. "I understand." Part of me wanted to plead with him, but I knew no amount of begging would change anybody's mind, and nor should it. "I just wanted you to know that I realized what I did was wrong."

Daniel looked like he didn't know what to say, and the long pauses between our sentences were getting more awkward by the second. "You're going to go talk to everybody else you did work for?"

"I am," I replied.

He snorted quietly. "Good luck with that. And good luck with the lawsuit, I guess." He seemed briefly sympathetic. "Don't go to anybody who owns a gun."

As he shut the door, I cringed. That was actually some good advice.

PEOPLE ALWAYS say that the third time was the charm. I didn't know how true that was, but I hoped it was the case as I made my way to Mr. Guthrie's house. He was someone I also knew better by his first name, Josiah, though everybody called him Jack.

Jack had been a neo-Nazi in his youth. He still bore the tattoos and the scars of that life, though he'd gotten the majority of the tattoos covered up. On the backs of his hands were two tribal patterns that had once been swastikas, and around his neck was a band of black that had previously been barbed wire. He was a big man, tall and broad, and he looked intimidating until you got to know him. Seven years before I met him, he had fallen away from the neo-Nazis and had turned to Catholicism instead.

We had been friends, of a kind. I had never let anybody in too close after what my family and my church had done, but I had been a regular fixture in his life for about a year, around the sixth year of my scamming. He and his wife had lost a child, Evelyn; she had only been two at the time, killed by a deadly bout of pneumonia. Every month for a year, I had attended Evelyn's grave with them to pray for her and to console them.

He was one of the people I felt most guilty over, not only because my prayers for a dead child had been false, but because he and his wife had just been such good people. I didn't want to imagine what their reaction had been to the news. Just like I didn't want to actually knock on their door.

But I made myself raise my hand and knock, because I owed it to them.

Then again, for all I knew, they'd be better off never seeing my face again.

Linda, Jack's wife, opened the door. Her eyes grew wide, and before I could open my mouth to say anything, she darted away. Two seconds later, I heard a very distinctive click, and the shadowed shape of a double-barreled shotgun appeared at the end of the door.

"Jesus!" I yelped, throwing my hands up to show I wasn't armed.

"You *bastard*," Linda hissed. The rifle was shaking—I doubted she actually wanted to kill me, but that didn't ease my fear any. Triggers could still be pulled pretty easily. "I saw you on the news. Do you have any idea how I felt when I saw that? How Jack felt?"

"Ma'am," I said, placating, as calm as I could be with a gun pointed at me. I saw Linda's gaze dart around behind me, but they lived in a residential area, and the street was empty. There would be nobody to notice the man with his hands raised in front of their door, nobody to notice that something strange might be going on. "Please, I just want to talk."

"Linda?" Jack's voice came from the hallway. "Linda, who's—" His voice cut off as he obviously noticed the gun. He opened the door fully, rage in his eyes, fully prepared to beat off whoever was threatening his wife. But his anger changed when he saw me, no longer a protective anger, but a betrayed one. "Linda, put the gun down."

She seemed reluctant to do so, but she lowered the muzzle of the weapon. The safety was clicked back on, and I heard a thud, perhaps the sound of the gun being put back in its usual resting place. I relaxed only marginally.

"Mitchell." Jack didn't sound happy. "I suppose you should come in."

"I don't need—"

"Come in." Jack's tone brooked no argument. I meekly followed them inside. I was led to the living room, where Jack directed me to sit on one of the couches. Linda disappeared into another room, but Jack sat across from me. "What do you want?"

I didn't know where to start. I had too many things I needed to apologize for to him. "I wanted to say sorry," I said quietly. The only noise in the room was the muted ticking of a wall clock, which just added to my anxiety. "A little while before the news came out, I'd stopped what I was doing."

"And what *were* you doing?" Jack asked me, his voice hard. "I want to hear it from you, not the media."

I took a deep breath. "I tricked a lot of people into believing that I was a guide or an advisor in a lot of different religious groups. I was a con artist. I didn't believe any of what I was preaching."

Jack bowed his head. The top two buttons of his shirt were undone; I noticed a small tattoo on his right collarbone, an 88. I still remembered being confused by its meaning until he'd explained it to me—the eighth letter in the alphabet was H, and two of them stood for Heil Hitler. He had mentioned quite a few times that he was going to get it covered up with a tattoo of a cross, but it remained unchanged.

For a lack of anything better, I said, "You never got that covered up?"

Jack's broad shoulders jerked once in a sad kind of laugh. "I'm not Catholic anymore, Mitchell."

"Why?" I blurted out, surprise warring with concern and a deep dread tightening the back of my throat. "You were so devout. It made you so happy."

"That year?" Jack finally looked up at me, and I wished he hadn't. Jack looked like a bodyguard, the kind of man you wouldn't want to even look at the wrong way; seeing him with tears in his eyes was like a punch to the gut. "I appreciated what you did for us, Mitchell, I really did. But something felt... wrong. I couldn't explain it. Something just felt off every time you would come with us to her grave. I thought it was something wrong with my faith. I thought I was starting to doubt, and that wrong feeling was like a splinter. It contaminated everything else."

He didn't need to explain further. Somewhere in the back of his brain, he'd felt like there was something wrong, and it had been me, my fake prayers and my fake faith. But instead of figuring out that there was something wrong with *me*, he'd assumed that he had been at fault instead.

I had indirectly driven him away from his faith.

"From there it was just downhill." He shrugged. "I couldn't stop wondering why I felt so weird during those times. I started *actually* doubting. And then I couldn't bring myself to go to church, because I was sure everybody else would know my heart wasn't in it anymore."

"Fuck," I whispered. "Jack, I'm... I'm so sorry. I never intended that to happen."

"No. You *intended* to rob us of four thousand dollars over the course of that year for goddamn grief counseling." Jack's expression tightened, grief nearly hidden behind anger once more. "We nearly went broke."

I hadn't anticipated this. I had known people would be angry, but I hadn't thought I would actually destroy people's beliefs. I hadn't thought I would drive people to near bankruptcy.

All the guilt I'd been trying to ignore suddenly came crashing right back down on me. I had done an okay job of not constantly thinking about it in New Zealand, but I hadn't known the reality of it, the *depth* of what I had done. Now that I did, there would be no pushing this guilt to the back of my mind.

"I'm sorry." Saying it was useless, but what else could I say? "I'm so sorry, Jack."

He didn't say anything. After a few moments, Linda came into the room. She didn't sit, but she stood near Jack, her face like thunder. She hadn't been as devout as Jack but had always worn a little cross necklace given to her by her mother. She wasn't wearing it now. I didn't need to be told why.

"I think you should go." Her voice was gentle, at odds with her expression.

"Of course." I couldn't deny the relief I felt. I stood, rubbing the back of my neck as I tried to think of something, *anything*, to say.

Jack followed me to the door, but his hand on my shoulder stopped me before I could leave. "Mitchell?" He looked like he was working up the courage to say something; it was almost certainly something I didn't want to hear, so I braced myself. But he surprised me. "I forgive you."

"You what?" I said dumbly.

"I forgive you." He obviously had great difficulty saying it, but he forced the words out. "I don't know why you did it. I don't know how you justified it to yourself. But I forgive you."

I had to look away to hide the sudden burning in my eyes. How was it possible that he had fallen away from his faith but was still a better Christian than I had ever been?

"Thank you," I whispered. "You didn't have to say that."

"Yeah, I did." Jack pulled his hand away from my shoulder. He didn't look angry anymore, just deeply saddened. "I get the feeling we're both victims in this, Mitchell. I'm still not happy. I'd still beat the shit out of you if I thought I could get away with it. But you're not as good an actor as you used to be. I can see you're torn up about this."

The burning in my eyes turned into a tear tracking down my cheek, which I hastily scrubbed away. "Thank you," I said again.

"I'll see you around, Mitchell," Jack said. He took one last look at me and then closed the door behind me.

I could only hope everybody else would be as kind.

THE MORNING of the settlement conference, I didn't want to get out of bed. The sun was shining in through the windows, the birds nearby were singing—it looked like a beautiful day, the kind of day I'd normally enjoy.

Not today.

It took a lot of effort to force myself out of bed and to stumble toward the coffee machine, but I eventually managed. I tried not to think as I stared at the coffee machine, because if I let myself start thinking, I'd probably put myself into one hell of an anxiety spin. So I couldn't think about how I might be damn near broke by the end of the day, I didn't think about how the hell I'd survive after this, and I certainly didn't entertain any notion of the angry plaintiffs lynch mobbing me. I just made myself get dressed, shaved, and out the door.

The settlement conference was being held at my lawyer's firm, in a spare meeting room that was on the fifth floor and down the end of a hallway that seemed to go forever. Damien had advised me to arrive an hour early so that he could brief me on everything that was going to happen, so when I pushed the door open, only he was inside. That didn't calm my nerves any.

He was dressed to the nines, a light-blue tie complementing his gray pinstripe suit and white shirt. I'd gotten similarly well dressed, though perhaps not quite as well as him; my suit wasn't nearly as expensive, but it looked good enough. I'd even managed to brush my hair.

"James," Damien greeted me, waving me over to the chair next to him. The table in the middle of the room, a twenty-seater furnished with dark oak, looked positively forbidding. "Come on. We've got a lot to run through and probably not enough time to do it."

Gingerly, I sat, eyeing the stack of paperwork next to him. I had provided Damien with as much paperwork as he had asked for: proof of transactions, proof of service, even ID. Ten years of paperwork was on the table, and the thought of having to even look at any of it sent that nausea in my gut churning to life once more.

Damien eyed me warily. "You need a bucket or something?"

"No." I waved him off, nodding at the paperwork. I took a deep breath, trying to calm my nerves. "Let's just get started."

I didn't pretend to understand legal jargon. Honestly, before now, I'd never even paid attention to things like class actions, settlements, trials. They had just been things that happened on the news sometimes, things other people had to go through. But now I sat and I nodded my way through Damien's explanation of what was going to happen, doing my best to figure out exactly what the hell he was talking about.

He dumbed it down a bit for me. I'd have to buy him flowers after this for that one small token of kindness.

The hour passed by too quickly, and two minutes before everybody was due to arrive, I found myself glancing anxiously at the clock. I kept thinking surely five minutes had passed, but when I looked, only thirty seconds had dragged by.

I heard footsteps in the hallway. Damien hurried to tidy the scattered papers.

The door opened to a man that looked every inch the essence of *lawyer*, from his sharply cut suit to his slicked-back hair. I almost smiled at the picture he made—as if someone had taken the global stereotypical image of a lawyer and made it flesh. But as he walked in, I saw flaws in that perfect image: lines of stress on his forehead, a paler band of skin around his ring finger where he had once worn a wedding ring, a harried expression on his face.

"I'm Simon McCullen," he greeted, "the representative for the eleven plaintiffs. They'll be here in five minutes. They're waiting in the lobby."

I wanted to say they could stay there, if they wanted, while I sorted this out with McCullen. It would certainly be easier.

Instead, I forced a wan smile and held out my hand. He took it in a firm shake. "James Mitchell, but I suppose you know that already. This is Damien Rookwell, my lawyer."

"Yes, we've spoken," McCullen muttered distractedly. He sat across from us; his file of paperwork was much slimmer than mine. "Mr. Rookwell tells me that you want to settle."

"Here and now," I agreed. "I just want this over and done with."

McCullen seemed to smile, though it could have been a trick of the light. "I'm not sure my clients would appreciate that kind of attitude, Mr. Mitchell."

Damien shifted forward in his chair. "Oh come on, Simon, it doesn't fucking matter what his *attitude* is—"

I cut in. "It does. I'm sorry, Mr. McCullen, you're right." A little politeness went a long way. As did contrition, I assumed. McCullen *was* right; the eleven victims gathered today would want to see me apologetic, not weary and absolutely done with all of this. It wasn't them that I was sick of, it was *this*, it was *myself*.

McCullen made a little *hmm* noise and opened his file. We sat in awkward silence for a minute while I resumed my clock-watching duties, and when the big hand struck on the hour, McCullen stood with a polite "Excuse me."

He left, presumably to retrieve the plaintiffs.

"Oh my God," I groaned pitifully, leaning back in my chair, passing my hands over my face. "I'm going to puke."

"I thought you said you didn't need the bucket," Damien huffed.

"That was before. This is now. I'm going to have to look at their faces. I'm going to have to talk to them."

"I thought you said you'd been going around apologizing?"

I managed a vague shrug. "It's different. I didn't *know* they were angry at me. I know these people are."

I wanted to talk to Tāne. He had managed to calm me down and get me smiling whenever I started to think too hard about things. His mellow, even presence would have helped me a lot right then, and it also would have given me much nicer things to focus on. But Tāne wasn't there, and I didn't even have enough time to text him.

"Well, it's not gonna be a good look if you throw up all over the plaintiffs, so try to contain yourself," Damien sighed.

Maybe it was the tense mood or maybe it was the absurdity of the image, but I started laughing. No, that certainly wouldn't be a good thing to do, although it might get them out of the room quicker.

My laughter was cut short when I heard the sound of many footsteps approaching, and the nausea came right back. I stood, doing my best to not fold my arms defensively or hunch over. I wanted to at least present a polite image when they entered.

And then, there they were.

None of them looked like they were two seconds away from throttling me, which was a positive sign. I could see old anger in some of their faces, though, sadness in others. Determination in all of them. Mrs. Lane, whose son I had baptized, seemed to be leading the pack. She stood at the forefront of the group as they filed in, and she took the seat directly to the right of McCullen.

God. What did I say?

"Good afternoon."

It didn't seem like enough. It *wasn't* enough, but until the conversation got started, there wasn't much that I could say.

They all sat, so I sat too. Every second of silence seemed to stretch painfully long, but in reality, it didn't take Mrs. Lane any longer than two of those seconds to answer me.

"Mr. Mitchell." Her tone was cordial, polite, which I was grateful for. She had worked in banking, I recalled, so she was probably used to sounding polite when all she really wanted to do was yell at someone. "Shall we get right to business?"

Damien answered for me. "Absolutely."

For a moment all I could hear was shuffling papers. I was relieved that nobody seemed inclined to strike up any kind of small talk, which would have been rather painful.

"All right, I'll get started," McCullen said. "James Mitchell. You've been asked here because eleven plaintiffs have gathered a class action against you. The filed complaints are emotional distress and providing fake services for monetary gain. Nobody wants to take this to court, but we will if that becomes necessary."

"I don't want it to go to court, either," I said. My voice was even, at least. "Mr. Rookwell, my lawyer, indicated to you that I have said I'd like to settle, for whatever the asking price."

Some of the people around the table seemed surprised. Either McCullen hadn't told them or they hadn't believed him.

McCullen made that little *hmm* noise again, and I started to wonder what it meant. Was he just buying time while he thought, or was he trying to make a point with it? "The plaintiffs are asking for reparation of 1.2 million dollars and a public apology."

I'd heard the number before, but I still probably went a bit pale just from hearing it.

"From that look," McCullen said, "I'd hazard a guess that you do not have that amount ready to give."

"Uh." I cleared my throat. "No. Not exactly. But I do have savings. I'm willing to give whatever I can as long as there's just enough left over for me to live until I find a job."

"And how much can you pay?" McCullen asked.

Some of the plaintiffs seemed to perk up a little, clearly interested in my answer.

"Roughly six hundred thousand." I'd been saving up to buy a house. I supposed that was off the list now. "Six hundred and twenty-four thousand, to be exact. I'll pay six hundred and ten thousand."

"And are you willing to make a public apology?"

"Yes, in whatever way is asked of me."

"Then, gentlemen, I will need a moment with my clients." McCullen nodded at us and turned to speak to the eleven around the table. I wasn't sure why they bothered speaking in low tones—I wasn't more than three feet away from McCullen, and I could hear him clearly. But I did the polite thing and pretended not to listen.

They talked about whether my offer was enough. And I was surprised to hear that none of them really seemed to get angry about the fact that I couldn't pay what they were asking. I knew that I hadn't seriously ripped off any of them; the most I had taken was five thousand, from Miss Essex, whom I had given grief counseling to. Split eleven ways, my offer would give them each fifty-five thousand.

I supposed that monetary compensation for past bills wasn't the real issue here. Emotional damages, they'd said.

Money didn't buy happiness, but it certainly went a long toward it.

The murmuring between the plaintiffs continued on for a few minutes. Damien made himself look busy by shuffling his papers, and I was left staring out the opposite window. All I could see was the gray of a neighboring skyscraper.

"Mr. Mitchell?" McCullen's words drew me back from my thoughts. "The plaintiffs have agreed that that amount will be sufficient. In addition, they want the public apology to be made within the week."

I nodded. "Of course."

And that, it seemed, was that. McCullen pushed some papers at me to sign, and none of the plaintiffs spoke while I did so. Then, one by one, they filed out of the room without so much as a word to me.

It was… strangely disappointing.

"I'll be in touch." McCullen shook my hand and left in much the same manner, leaving Damien and I to pick ourselves up out of the chairs and make our way to the door. I deliberately stalled, not wanting to run into anybody as I left, and by the time we exited the building, everybody was gone.

"That was strangely underwhelming," I said, feeling a little dazed.

Damien's laugh was a quiet, brief sound. "It always is. It's not like the big dramatic scenes you see on the TV, man."

"I guess so." I shook my head, the urge for incredulous laughter bubbling up. "So, what now?"

"Now you look into doing that apology and wait for McCullen's call about the money."

Our walking had taken us to my car, which I had parked on the street. It was a beat-up old thing, but it served its purpose. "I'll call you tonight about the apology. I'm going to need some advice." All I wanted to do now was go home and sleep, possibly for a week.

"You do that." Damien clapped a hand to my shoulder. "Look, James, you did good in there, even if you did go against my advice. You can handle the apology. Whatever you need, you call me, okay?"

I managed to summon up a smile for him. "Okay."

TWENTY-FOUR HOURS later, I pulled my car into the parking lot of a local news station and saw a group of reporters already waiting at the door for me. They hadn't seen me arrive, so for now I was safe. But I had no idea how I was going to get into the building without being mobbed.

Yesterday, I had called several of the news stations in the area to let them know I wanted to set up an announcement. All of them had offered the use of a conference room in their buildings, and I had picked the smallest station, hoping to avoid some attention that way. Unfortunately, it looked like news had spread, because among that group of reporters I could see a few from stations I hadn't called, cameras and microphones both bearing the distinct lettering of at least three other stations.

A knock came at my window, making me jump. A young woman stood next to my car, motioning for me to roll the window down. When I did, she said, "Come with me. I'm here to escort you."

"Oh, thank God," I muttered as I stepped out of my car. When I had called the news station, they had been a lot more helpful than I had expected, possibly because they were eager for the spectacle I was going to give them. They had told me that they would assign someone to direct me, and they'd also told me to park at the back of the parking lot, closest to the back door, so that there wouldn't be a media frenzy as I tried to walk in. Without a further word, she led me to the door that looked seldom used. It took us into dim hallways that also looked like they were barely used. I was just grateful I'd gotten inside without any hassle. "Thank you, ma'am," I said to my savior.

She didn't give me more than a passing glance, entirely businesslike. "I'll take you to the conference room."

I did, however, get more than a few lingering glances as we started to walk through areas with cubicles and proper offices off to the side. Some people muttered as I passed, some outright glared. I was relieved none of them approached me to throw a punch. In this part of the country, people were very emotionally involved in their religion—which wasn't to say that people anywhere else weren't, we just took it to a whole new level in the Southern states.

The news station I'd picked, though, was left-leaning. I thought they might be kinder, not toward what I had done, but about the fact that I was gay. The last thing I wanted was to get slurs yelled at me while I was trying to explain myself.

My guide paused outside a door marked "Conference Room #1." "Mr. Mitchell?"

I broke myself out of my thoughts. "Yes?"

"We're here." She studied me for a second, a rueful smile touching her lips. "You might want to brace yourself."

I suddenly remembered that I had forgotten to text Tāne. I had done so last night, but my typing had apparently been somewhat incoherent in my exhaustion, as he had called me shortly after, sounding bemused. We'd talked briefly about the settlement, but he'd obviously picked up on the fact that I had just wanted to sleep. So we had traded good-byes, promising to talk the next night.

I gave my guide a nod. "I'm ready."

I wasn't. I wanted to run away, but it was now or never.

She opened the door and a roar of noise came from within. Cameras started flashing, bright white bursts that made me squint against the glare of them. My guide led me past the horde of reporters to a long table at the front of the room. "Mr. Mitchell!" the reporters were shouting. "Mr. Mitchell, over here!"

Another woman appeared at my side. "Helen, get him into place," she told my guide. "Mr. Mitchell? I'm Violet Bligh. I'll be sitting right next to you and directing the questions."

"Ma'am," I said, having to raise my voice to be heard. "Much appreciated."

I sat down, and Violet positioned herself at my left. The crowd noise began to die down, shouting replaced by the click of cameras, the tap of fingers against phone screens, and the scratch of pencil on paper. I looked at Violet, and she nodded.

"Mr. Mitchell would like to make a statement and a public apology, as per the agreement in his settlement," she announced.

I cleared my throat, nerves rising again. "Right. Yes," I said uselessly.

I hadn't prepared a speech. I hadn't prepared anything ahead of time. I'd thought that coming here and speaking from the heart would be the best idea, but now I wished I had a script to read.

"Well, you obviously already know who I am," I said to the crowd. "My name is James Mitchell. For the past ten years, I have been providing religious services to individuals within various religious groups, though I did not believe in any of those religions myself. I faked everything I did, and I charged good money for it. Three weeks ago, I stopped my practice entirely."

"Why did you do it?" one of the reporters called.

Another reporter called out. "And what do you have to say about the accusations leveled against you that claim you did this all because you're gay?"

I blinked in surprise. The room was hushed once more, some reporters on the edge of their seats to hear me answer. I hadn't realized that was part of the rumors. Butterflies were forming a tornado in my stomach, but I felt strangely Zen as I answered, "What I did wasn't solely because of my sexuality, but it is true that I am gay."

I wished I could have closed my ears to the noise that happened then. A good deal of it was indignant; some of it was even disgusted. Half of the room, however, was quiet, merely watching me with speculative looks.

"I realized it while I was a seminary student." Again, a few murmurs sounded. "And I hated myself for it. I had been raised to believe that being gay was a sin, that it was something dirty and shameful. I felt so guilty about it that I tried not to think about it. My best friend at the time, though I didn't know it then, was also gay. He hanged himself just after I graduated."

A ripple seemed to run through the reporters, but none of them spoke. "It was at that time that I moved into the inner city to work at a church here. And because I was exposed to a much wider range of opinion, I learned there was a sizeable population of people who believed being gay was natural and absolutely nothing to be ashamed of." I pretended not to hear the muttered response to that one. Getting angry would do no good.

"Shortly after I came to believe the same, I came out to my family and my church. They all rejected me. My parents have not contacted me since, and any attempt on my behalf to contact them has been met with refusals to acknowledge me."

There were other low words then, but they were from people shaking their heads in disbelief, looking sympathetic. A few even looked angry on my behalf. I smiled a little at them, grateful.

"I was angry," I admitted. "I had just lost all of my family and friends because of something that didn't even affect their lives. I was angry at them and at God—for making me gay, for making being gay a sin, for anything and everything. I wanted to hit back. I wanted to prove to myself that their religion wasn't real; I wanted them to look like fools. That was when I started my scam work. I believed I was entirely justified at the time. But in the past year or so, I started to doubt what I was doing, and I eventually stopped.

"By that time, I had started to feel incredibly guilty about what I had done. I realize now that everything I did was reprehensible. And that is why I am here. I want to apologize."

I looked at one of the film cameras pointed right at me. "If I have wronged you, I am truly sorry," I said, addressing the people I knew would be watching this, the people I had lied to and taken money from. The people who were waiting for this. "What I did was wrong. I had no right to lie, no matter what I had experienced. If there is any way I can make it up to you or if you'd just like to speak to me, please contact me. I do not intend to take part in any religious establishments anymore, as I feel doing so would be a mockery of their faith, something that I do not wish to partake in. I will spend the rest of my life feeling guilty over what I have done; I can only hope that by doing this, I will bring some closure to those I wronged. Thank you."

When it became apparent that I was done speaking, the roar of noise from the reporters threatened to deafen me. I couldn't help but still be surprised by the number of them there—my story wasn't that big. But it seemed that everybody loved a scandal. Either that or reporters were just a noisy bunch.

Questions were thrown at me, and Violet waited patiently until there was a break in the noise, long enough for her to say, "Now that Mr. Mitchell has finished his statement, we will take questions. First question," she called. "You, in the purple hat."

"Mr. Mitchell," the reporter said eagerly, "you have allegations from 127 witnesses that you scammed them, but some people are estimating that the real numbers are in the thousands. What do you say to that?"

I didn't mean to scoff a little. Unfortunately, I did. "I'm not sure that in the thousands is an accurate number. However, the number would be a little higher than 127."

Voices rose again and Violet picked another reporter. "Is it true it wasn't just Christian denominations that you dealt with?"

"Yes. I also dealt with Jewish, Hindu, and various fringe religions like paganism."

"What was the biggest fee you took from a client?"

"Is it true that you offered exorcisms?"

More questions were shouted, and I did my best to answer them politely and diplomatically. Yes, I had offered exorcisms—I had done them too. No, I had never deliberately injured a child; where on earth had *that* question come from? No, I did not have AIDS or HIV.

Just as I was beginning to get tongue-tied from the increasingly strange questions, Violet seemed to know that I'd had enough.

"That's all the time that Mr. Mitchell has for questions," she said, her voice hard. Violet stood and took me with her. The reporters started shouting again, hurling questions at me, but Violet motioned for me to stay silent. Some of the reporters tried to follow us down the hall, only to run into Helen blocking them off. The noise faded as we walked away, and by the time we turned a corner into the next hallway, the reporters were no more than a distant murmur of sound.

I let out a shuddered exhale, roughly scrubbing my hands across my face. "Christ," I muttered. I felt like I could jump out of my skin, adrenaline racing through my veins.

But it was done. It was over.

And now I could focus on moving on.

Epilogue

Six Months Later

I HAD been lying again—but this time it was for a good cause.

I hadn't told Tāne that I'd be arriving in Wellington today. We had spoken every single day of the past six months, either through e-mail, texts, or phone calls. Sometimes we'd had nothing to talk about, because neither of us had had anything particularly eventful happen that day, so we'd sat in silence and watched different channels of television together, commenting on what we were watching. Surprisingly, it had never gotten awkward, and he was probably the only reason I hadn't gone insane from trying to work through the visa process.

Living in Dallas for the past six months hadn't been easy. Many people still hated me. I had been refused service in stores, had gotten spat at on the street, had been called any number of slurs and insults by complete strangers. A number of times, a reporter or two had followed me around, trying to get additional comments. But the chaos was fading. Every day, fewer people felt the need to comment or glare at me.

The issue of gay rights had become a local hot topic. For every person on the news who insulted me, another would debate the harmful attitude toward homosexuals in religious communities. For every criticism, there was a protest against bigotry. It hadn't been my intention to raise that debate, but I was grateful for it. If even one family with a child in my old situation changed their hateful stance against homosexuality, I would be happy.

Still, I couldn't help but wonder. For every one person that was willing to change their beliefs, there were ten that just used bad press to reinforce their negativity. While it was a good thing that it was being discussed, I knew all too well that the homophobes really set in their ways would just be looking at the chaos and nodding to themselves: *See, gay people are bad. Look at what he did and look at what talk about him is still doing.*

The very nature of my mind—prone to overthinking and anxiety—led me to speculate on whether I had actually made situations *worse* for people. Maybe there were kids like I had been, kids with families who thought being gay was a sin, families who would only have their beliefs made even stronger and more vitriolic with the waves I had made in the local news. I would be held up as every example of why being gay was wrong, and with that, I could have caused kids who loved their own faith to doubt themselves or get into that same cycle of self-hatred that I had.

It wasn't a pleasant thought. And believe me, I hadn't wanted to think it.

But I was glad to get away from all of it. I had gotten some work experience in while I was in the process of getting my visa, though I hadn't actually told Tāne that I had managed to procure a work visa. I wanted to surprise him.

Now I was here, back in Wellington, smiling as I drove my rented car down to Porirua. I had a week before I started my job, and tomorrow I would be moving into the apartment I had leased. To be able to work in New Zealand, I'd needed to get myself a work visa, which meant that an employer had to sponsor me. Needless to say, I'd gone through a lot of job interviews on the phone, most employers winding up reluctant to hire me when they could just get someone who actually lived in the country.

Eventually, however, someone hired me. It wasn't the most glamorous job, nor did it pay the best. But it was something.

I was now a secretary for a car retailer. Seeing as I didn't know the first thing about cars, I had a lot to learn, and I got the feeling that the only reason I'd even been hired was because I'd gotten on really well with the boss I'd been interviewed by. Whatever the reason, I was happy to have it. The work visa would last me a year, and at that point I'd need to reapply for another one, and so on until I could get resident status.

I parked outside the marae, still smiling to myself. It was more of a grin, now, but either way my face was starting to hurt from the constant pull of muscles. I just couldn't stop. I had an apartment, a job, and in five minutes, I would have Tāne again.

Tāne had mentioned that he'd been going to the marae every Saturday, and I had carefully timed my flights so I would arrive in the early afternoon. As I entered, I could see there were a few people that I recognized. I hurriedly put my finger to my lips before they could say anything, and they grinned at me, clapping me on the back as I walked past. I exchanged a few silent hugs, which nearly made me tear up—the difference between how I was treated back in Dallas and here was remarkable. Granted, these people hadn't been personally victimized by me, but they had still accepted me wholly.

I was pointed in the direction of the grassy area between the marae and the dining hall, so I crept that way. When I got outside, I could see Tāne, Huia, and Hemi, all three with their backs to me, standing by the hāngi. I moved as silently as I could, and when I got close enough, I clapped my hands over Tāne's eyes. "Guess who?"

He obviously wasn't expecting me, because he didn't recognize my voice. He sounded exasperated when he said, "Fuck, Mike, get your hands off—" He was interrupted by Huia's laughter as she turned and saw me. "Wait. *James?*"

Tāne spun around, and I barely had time to see his face before I was nearly tackled in a hug. "Holy fuck!" Tāne laughed against my ear, squeezing me as hard as I was squeezing him. "Fucking hell, you bastard, why didn't you tell me you were coming?"

I didn't answer with words, but with a kiss. I grasped his face with both hands and tugged him in, then kissed him until we both ran out of breath. "I got a work visa," I said, grinning widely. "I got an apartment, and a job. I'm here. I'm here for good."

Out of the corner of my eye, I saw Hemi nodding approvingly, his hand falling to Tāne's shoulder briefly. Something had obviously changed there—a small change, but it was something. Huia leaned in to kiss me on the cheek and said, "I'm glad you're back, James."

"You're really gonna live here?" Tāne asked. His eyes were wide, hopeful.

"I'm really going to live here," I confirmed. I laughed again; I couldn't seem to stop. I was just so ridiculously *happy*. "I even got a place in Thorndon near you. It's a five-minute walk away."

Tāne kissed me again. His skin was sun-warmed, his clothes smelling faintly of the hāngi smoke blowing around us. I could hear a few people in the dining hall singing as they cooked, and still more crowded in around us, welcoming me back and asking me how long I was staying.

It was good to be home.

ROBIN SAXON, born and bred in New Zealand, lives in the Midwest with partner Alex Kidwell. When not writing or daydreaming about ideas for more stories, Robin is usually found playing MMOs like *World of Warcraft*, reading, drawing, and fussing over their cats, Starsky and Hutch.

In the rare times when they are not being pestered by their cats, Robin also listens to heavy metal music and enjoys everything from classics like Chaucer to urban fiction, as well as cooking vegetarian meals and inflicting them on Alex.

Visit Robin's website, http://www.saxonandkidwell.com, find Robin on Facebook, https://www.facebook.com/robin.saxon.77, or e-mail Robin at robin_saxon@yahoo.com.

Sanguis Noctis Series
by ROBIN SAXON and ALEX KIDWELL

http://www.dreamspinnerpress.com

Also from ROBIN SAXON

Robin Saxon
The Royal Road

http://www.dreamspinnerpress.com

Also from DREAMSPINNER PRESS

ANYTHING COULD HAPPEN

B.G. THOMAS

http://www.dreamspinnerpress.com

FILTH
M. KING

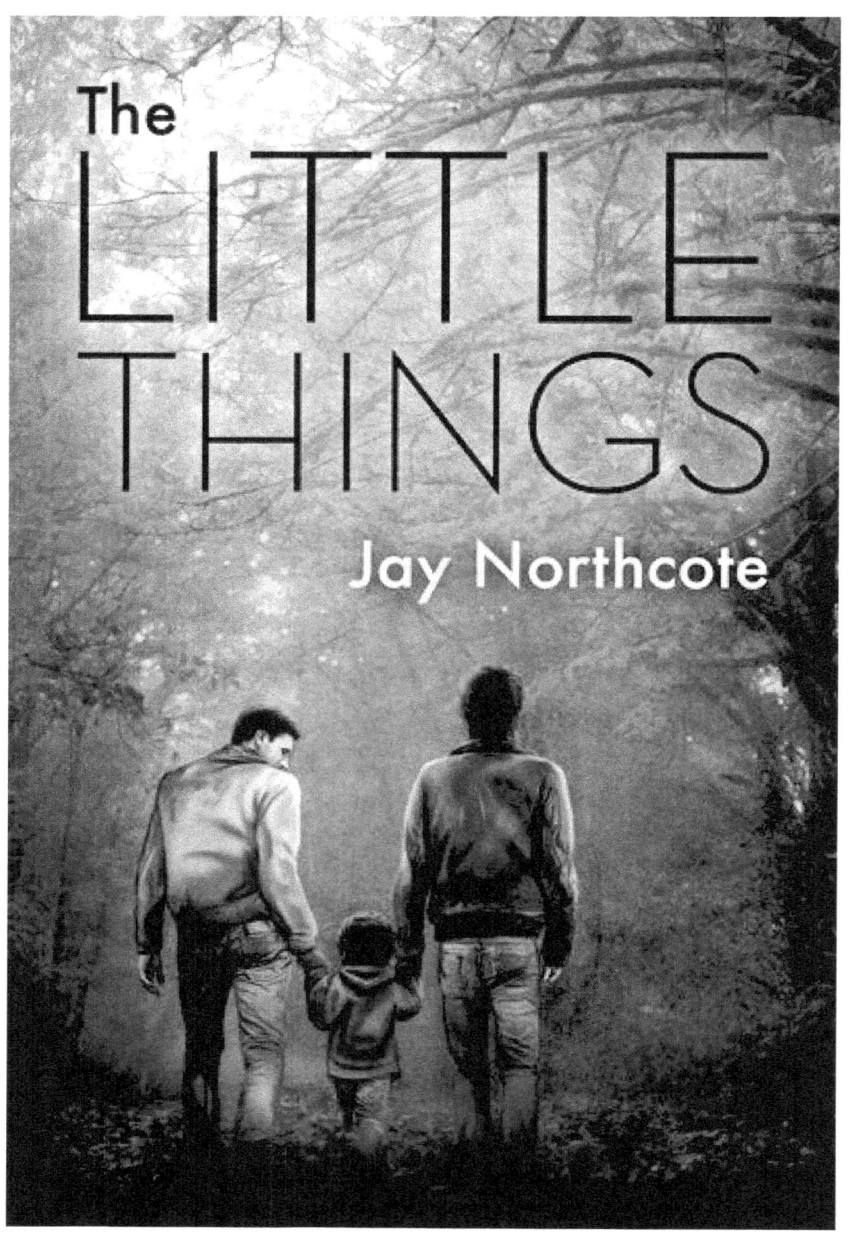

http://www.dreamspinnerpress.com

Also from DREAMSPINNER PRESS

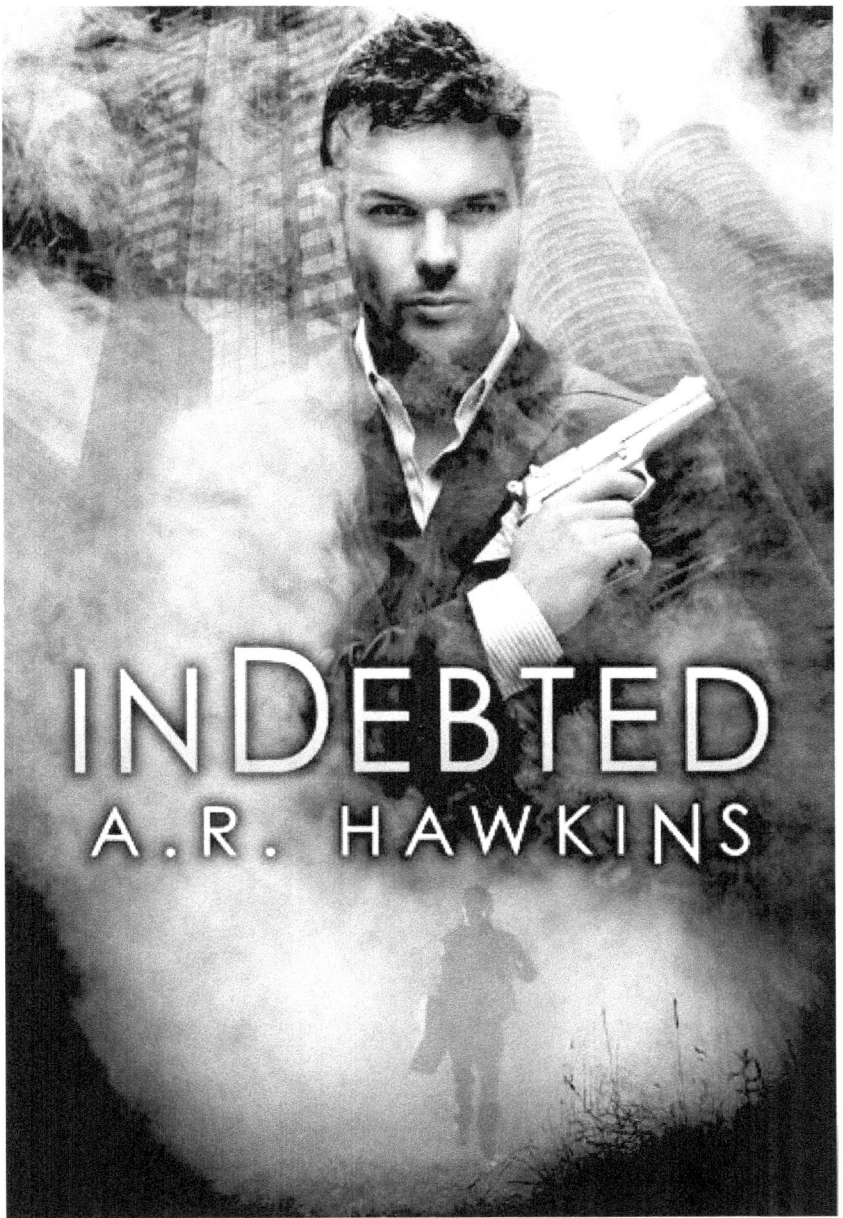

inDEBTED

A.R. HAWKINS

http://www.dreamspinnerpress.com

www.ingramcontent.com/pod-product-compliance
Lightning Source LLC
Chambersburg PA
CBHW060057260626
47160CB00005B/1700

ARIEL TACHNA
Contemporary M/M Romance at its Finest

Chase the Stars

"…Ms. Tachna has the talent to take everyday life and weave it into something special that leaves the reader sitting back just feeling good and wanting more." —Hearts on Fire Reviews

"Ms. Tachna remains one of my favorite authors. She allows her characters time to grow and develop and doesn't force strange circumstances to push or pull her characters in ways their behavior doesn't indicate is realistic for them." —Mrs. Condit

Inherit the Sky

"…a well-crafted, beautiful book that I would recommend to anyone looking for a love story that takes courage." —Guilty Indulgence

"I enjoyed this excellently researched and written book very much and hope there will be additional stories about all of the characters on and near the Lang Downs sheep station." —Mrs. Condit

"This story is beautifully, realistically handled." —Joyfully Jay

Overdrive

"After reading this story, I wonder when exactly Ariel last raced over the Sahara because all the details are there, making this story authentic from every angle." —Joyfully Jay

Seducing C.C.

"…a great comfort read." —Blackraven Reviews

"…a seductively sexy and romantic story." —Night Owl Reviews

Once in a Lifetime

"… a coming-of-age story that introduces heart-pounding firsts and nostalgic lasts." —¡Miraculous!

NOVELS BY ARIEL TACHNA

Château d'Eternité
Fallout
Her Two Dads
Inherit the Sky • Chase the Stars
The Inventor's Companion
The Matelot
Once in a Lifetime
Overdrive
Out of the Fire
Seducing C.C.
Stolen Moments
A Summer Place

THE PARTNERSHIP IN BLOOD NOVELS
Alliance in Blood • Covenant in Blood • Conflict in Blood • Reparation in Blood
Perilous Partnership
Reluctant Partnerships
Lycan Partnership

WITH NICKI BENNETT
Checkmate • All For One
Hot Cargo
Under the Skin

WITH MADELEINE URBAN
Sutcliffe Cove

NOVELLAS BY ARIEL TACHNA

Healing in His Wings
Rediscovery
Rose Among the Ruins
Why Nileas Loved the Sea

WITH NICKI BENNETT
Something About Harry
Tying the Knot
THE EXPLORING LIMITS SERIES

AVAILABLE AT DREAMSPINNER PRESS
http://www.dreamspinnerpress.com

CHÂTEAU
D'ETERNITÉ

ARIEL TACHNA

Dreamspinner Press

Published by
Dreamspinner Press
5032 Capital Circle SW
Ste 2, PMB# 279
Tallahassee, FL 32305-7886
USA
http://www.dreamspinnerpress.com/

Cover Art by Anne Cain
annecain.art@gmail.com

ISBN: 978-1-62380-606-4
Digital ISBN: 978-1-62380-607-1

Printed in the United States of America
First Edition
March 2013

Château d'Eternité previously available as a free short story, published by Dreamspinner Press, June 2012.

To Jaime, who helped me make Russ and Quentus believable.

CHAPTER ONE

RUSS PETERSON stared down at the invitation, bemusement and curiosity filling him.

You are cordially invited to

a two-week retreat at

château d'Eternité.

That was it. No explanation, no dates, no details. Just the embossed card in his hand.

Oh, and a round-trip plane ticket to France in his name, as well as a first-class ticket on the TGV from Paris to Marseille and the phone number of a car service in Marseille.

He was tempted to toss it all in the trash. He couldn't find a name anywhere on the envelope other than the one on the invitation: château d'Eternité.

There was a solution to that. He sat down at his computer and typed the name into the search window, waiting to see what came up. Images displayed first, pictures of a house that could have come out of his Renaissance history books, with fanciful turrets and spires gracing the towers and a beautiful mishmash of styles that suggested renovations over time. Architecture wasn't his forte, but he'd learned enough as a sidebar to history to place most European buildings in the correct century, anyway. He got lost once he crossed into Asia. Scrolling down a little more, he found a couple of travelogues from people talking about their amazing visit to château d'Eternité and how it had opened whole new worlds to them. He couldn't find an actual Web site for the organization or person who ran the retreats, which seemed odd, but the travelogues were on reputable sites, so he figured he could trust them; especially when while reading through them he found enough differences in description and detail to feel like they hadn't all been written by the same person.

The dates for the tickets corresponded rather freakily with the two weeks of vacation he had agreed to take because his boss had threatened to fire him if he didn't use some of his accrued days. Russ didn't think his boss could get away with that, legally, but he'd chosen two random weeks in March and then promptly forgotten about them.

It wouldn't be so bad, maybe, if he had someone to plan a vacation with, but he'd never met anyone, male or female—he didn't really care which—who would put up with him for more than a month or two.

Maybe going to France for two weeks wouldn't be such a bad idea. It would be a change of scenery, if nothing else. It wouldn't cost him anything, and it wasn't like he'd made other plans. He could take the books he'd planned to read on the development of guns and their impact on warfare in the late Middle Ages and the Renaissance to read there, if nothing else. Then when people asked what he did on his vacation, he'd have something impressive to tell them instead of saying he'd sat around his apartment and read for two weeks.

IT WAS a lot colder in France than in Arizona.

That was the first thought that crossed Russ's mind when the plane landed in Paris. Even with his warmest sweatshirt on under his jacket—more layers than he ever needed in Tucson—the wind bit through him, licking at his ankles, hands, and chin, swirling up his pants legs and down the back of his shirt and leaving him shivering. Fortunately the inside of the terminal was warm while he waited to get his bags, and the line for taxis was short. The driver spoke very little English, but Russ remembered enough of his high-school French to ask for the Gare de Lyon, *s'il vous plaît*. If the man rolled his eyes at Russ's butchering of the pronunciation, he still took Russ where he wanted to go, and that was the important thing.

Navigating the train station was another exercise in frustration and freezing. The platforms were covered, but while the vaulted roof would keep out the rain and the three walls blocked some of the breeze, the fourth open wall did nothing to hold in the heat. He found a café and ordered coffee to warm up while he waited for his train to arrive. The waiter spoke enough English to ask where he was going. He answered only "Marseille," figuring the waiter wouldn't have heard of the château d'Eternité.

"It's nice in Marseille this time of year," the waiter agreed. "Is too cold to swim still, but the beaches, they are beautiful, and the flowers have started to bloom."

Russ doubted they'd be blooming up in the mountains, but he settled for smiling and agreeing. "That will be pleasant, I'm sure. I can sit in a café near the beach and read."

"A very agreeable way to spend a vacation," the waiter replied, giving Russ his coffee and the check.

Deciding he might as well start, he dug his book out of his backpack.

"*Guns, Germs, and Steel*," the waiter read from the cover of the book when he came back to check on Russ a few minutes later. "That is not light vacation reading."

"It is for me," Russ said, feeling defensive. "No messy emotions to get in the way, just historical fact and interesting theories based on those facts. Of course, someone else could take those same facts and come up with completely different theories. That's where the joy comes from."

3

"And none of us will ever know the truth," the waiter replied.

Russ smiled ruefully. "Not until someone invents time travel."

THE TGV was every bit as nice as Russ had been led to expect, rolling quietly out of the station exactly on time and picking up speed as soon as they cleared the Paris city limits. He pulled his book back out of his backpack and settled in to pass the three and a half hours to Marseille in the best of all possible ways.

When they slowed down to pull into Marseille, he looked up, finding it hard to believe the time had passed already, but he dutifully put his book away and retrieved his suitcase from the luggage vestibule at the end of the car.

He'd made arrangements with the car company mentioned on the invitation to pick him up at the train station and drive him up to the château. They had assured him a driver would meet him.

Stepping out of the train, he took a moment to appreciate the sun on his face. It still wasn't as warm as Tucson, but it was definitely warmer than Paris had been, and he could smell the salt breeze off the ocean over the exhaust from the trains.

Looking around, he found a man in a dark suit holding a sign with his name on it. He identified himself to the driver, who took his bag and led him to a black car of a make and model Russ didn't recognize. Then again, he'd already realized he wasn't going to recognize a lot of things on this side of the ocean.

"Make yourself comfortable," the driver said. "We will be at château d'Eternité in about forty-five minutes."

Russ considered pulling his book back out, but then the architecture in Marseille caught his eye, and he stopped to remind himself where he was. He was in one of the oldest cities in France, founded by the Phoceans in 600 BCE. As a student of history, he could hardly justify burying his nose in a book, even a history book, when he could be drinking in the ambience and the reality of that

4

history played out in all its myriad layers. Driving through the city wouldn't be the same as getting out and exploring on his own, but maybe he could come down for a day or leave a day or two early and explore some of the historical sites he'd only ever read about in books. He'd kick himself later if he didn't.

As they left Marseille and began to climb into the mountains, the sense of being surrounded by history faded somewhat, but the natural beauty of the region took its place, and Russ left the book in his backpack, enjoying the sight of the jagged, snow-covered Alps and the narrow, winding roads that traversed them. They passed through the occasional small village, tucked in a valley here and there, but for the most part, they could have been in the middle of nowhere or several thousand years earlier, before people had settled this region.

Russ scolded himself for his flights of fancy, but the sense of timelessness lingered as they passed beneath a wrought iron gate between two stone pillars with the same coat of arms on them as Russ had seen on the front of the invitation he had received.

The car stopped in front of the château, as beautiful in reality as it had been in the pictures. The lawn was not quite as green, unsurprising in this season, and patches of snow still lingered under the trees, but hardy pansies bloomed in the beds on either side of the impressive front staircase, and the fine gravel driveway was freshly raked and well-tended, giving the impression of luxurious elegance, an impression carried over into the façade of the building.

The carved wood door swung open and a distinguished gentleman of indeterminate age descended the steps to meet them. "Russell Peterson, I presume?"

"Yes, I'm Russ."

"Bernard Dunevon, your host. Welcome to château d'Eternité."

The man's English was accented but flawless, easing one of Russ's concerns. "Thank you, but I have to admit I'm a little puzzled as to why I'm here."

"All things in good time," Bernard said. "Come inside and we'll get you settled. Then we'll have time for a nice long talk. Are you a student of history, Monsieur Peterson?"

"Russ," he corrected automatically. "And yes, I'm fascinated by history. Why do you ask?"

"Because that makes things so much simpler," Bernard replied, an answer that gave Russ no information whatsoever. "Do you have a favorite time period?"

"Not really," Russ said. "I mean, there are so many reasons to like so many different time periods. I'm focusing on the end of the Middle Ages right now."

"Then the François 1er room should suit admirably."

Bernard led Russ through the front doors and into the main hall of the castle. He was sure the older man would call it a manor house or something like that, but as far as Russ was concerned, it was a castle. Elegant rugs covered the stone floors and candles burned in the sconces, adding a sense of timelessness to the room. Glancing upward, Russ saw an electric chandelier hanging where a true chandelier full of candles had once resided, but at that height and in this day and age, electric was far more practical. It was, however, the only identifiable change to the castle. If candles had burned overhead, they could have been in the sixteenth century as easily as the twenty-first.

"Your room is just at the top of the stairs," Bernard said. "Hopefully it will be to your taste, but if it is not, please tell me and we will find something else that suits."

"I'm sure it will be fine," Russ replied.

The spiral staircase rivaled the one designed by da Vinci at the château de Chambord, a double helix of stairs that tricked the eye and the mind. The two men reached the upper floor, and Russ felt time slip away from him. His and Bernard's modern dress seemed completely out of place as Bernard opened the door to show Russ his room. He stepped inside to a medieval bedchamber, from the curtained bed on its raised dais to the fire burning in the fireplace and the heavy tapestries lining the walls to keep out the damp and chill.

"I will leave you to get settled," Bernard said. "When you have freshened up from your trip, please join me in the parlor for an aperitif. We have much to discuss."

Russ had a feeling that was an understatement, but he simply nodded as Bernard left, shutting the door and leaving Russ alone. He took a couple of deep breaths, reminding himself he hadn't somehow slipped through time to end up back in the Middle Ages. Bernard was dressed in a suit of modern, if slightly outmoded, style. The chandelier had been electric, even if he saw no electric fixtures in this room. The tapestries and rugs, beautiful as they were, had to be careful reproductions, because no one would actually use medieval pieces that way. No one could afford to. The originals in the museums were all so fragile they had to be displayed in climate controlled rooms or cases.

The best thing to do was get an explanation, and that meant "freshening up" and going down to talk to Bernard. He found a pitcher of water next to a basin on the dresser with a towel beside it, so he used that to wash his face and hands. His jeans and sweatshirt suddenly seemed out of place. He hadn't packed a lot of dressier clothes because they didn't travel well, but he had brought one suit, figuring the elegance of the invitation might correspond to some degree of formality. He hadn't seen any other guests, so he couldn't use that to judge what might be appropriate. Stripping down, he decided to err on the side of caution.

His suit wasn't new, but since he didn't have a lot of occasion to wear it, it was still in good condition, and it fit him well. He wouldn't ever be a dashing hero, but he was presentable enough. He brushed his longish red hair out of his face. He never gave it any thought until it fell in his eyes and interfered with his reading, but it was maybe time to get it cut again. He couldn't do anything about the paper cuts on his hands, the victim of too much time handling dusty, old books, but none of them were bleeding at the moment, so that was good. The lines around his eyes, which he'd developed from squinting to read the sometimes cramped handwriting of source texts, weren't overly obvious in the candlelight, although he wouldn't bet on them staying so well hidden under more modern lighting. All in all, he was as presentable as he was going to get.

After taking one final deep breath to steady himself, he returned to the front hall, hoping he would be able to find the parlor Bernard had mentioned.

"Ah, Monsieur Peterson," Bernard said, coming into the foyer from somewhere else on the ground floor. "I didn't expect you back downstairs so quickly. Our guests often take a little longer to settle in to the ambiance here at the château."

"It certainly is quite atmospheric," Russ agreed, "but fascinating. The attention to detail is astounding. You must have some incredible decorators to create such elaborate reproductions."

Bernard smiled. "As you say. Shall we retire to the parlor? It gets chilly here in the front hall in the evenings. The fire will be most welcome."

Russ nodded and followed Bernard into the parlor, another amazingly appointed room, this time in the Baroque style. The sideboards were heavily gilded with ebony veneer and beautifully lacquered scenes. The armchairs near the fire were similarly carved and gilded, the brocade on the cushions catching and reflecting the light of the fire. "I feel like I've walked into a museum," Russ said.

"Not quite," Bernard replied. "What can I offer you? A glass of champagne? Some sherry or vermouth? Or perhaps a kir?"

"Um, whatever you're having is fine," Russ said. "I… I'm not a big drinker."

"Then we'll have kir," Bernard said. "A sweeter flavor than champagne."

Russ shifted uncomfortably from one foot to the other as Bernard prepared their drinks. He wanted to explore the room, but he didn't want to seem rude. It struck him as equally rude to sit without being asked.

Bernard turned back around, glasses in hand. "Sit, sit," he urged, herding Russ toward the fireplace. "We are not a museum. You should never hesitate to use our pieces for the purposes they were intended."

Russ took one of the two chairs and the drink Bernard offered him. Bernard sat in the other chair and clinked his glass against Russ's.

"To open minds and new adventures."

"That sounds ominous," Russ said, but he took a sip of his drink nonetheless. The light fruit flavor surprised him. He'd expected something harsher. "This is good. What is it called again?"

"A kir," Bernard said. "Bourgogne Aligoté and crème de cassis. It's a regional specialty of Burgundy, but one that is well appreciated all over l'Hexagone."

Russ almost asked for a clarification of the last reference as well, but Bernard didn't give him a chance. "You must be wondering what you're doing here."

"I'll admit to a certain curiosity," Russ said, fully conscious of the understatement.

"You're here because your last round of medical tests at your physical indicated a genetic marker that is of particular interest to the denizens of château d'Eternité."

"Denizens?" Russ repeated, nerves jangling at the thought of some stranger having access to his medical records. He forced himself not to freak out yet, though. He would hear Bernard out before he decided if a meltdown was in order. "I haven't seen anyone but you."

"I am the only resident at the moment," Bernard admitted, "but there are about twenty people who live here for some portion of the year. The rest of the year, they are traveling."

"Traveling where?" Russ asked. "Look, I don't know what this is about, but stop talking in circles and just tell me. Am I sick?"

"You aren't sick at all, Russ. You're gifted, and to answer your question about where, the answer is anywhere, indeed any*when* they want."

Russ rolled his eyes. "Anywhen? That's not even a word, and you're implying… what? That they can travel through time?" The very thought was so ludicrous he felt stupid even saying it.

"Yes," Bernard said, "that's what I'm implying, and no, I don't expect you to believe it. Not yet, anyway. No one does when they first come here. I didn't believe it when I first came here forty years ago either. Now I'm the guardian of the château and its secrets."

Russ rose from the chair, pacing in agitation as he ran one hand through his hair. Time travel. If he understood correctly, the affable old man sitting next to the fire with a perfectly sanguine look on his face was telling Russ people could travel through time, that *he* could travel through time. "How? How is this possible?"

"That is a question for the ages," Bernard said, "but if you sit down, I will tell you what I do know. It won't answer all your questions, because some of them have no answers, but perhaps it will answer some of them."

Russ returned slowly to his seat, trying to open his mind to the possibilities of whatever Bernard would say. His ability to look beyond the obvious made him an asset at the university history department as he pored over old records, seeing not just what was there but what was missing. He needed to turn that same sharp mind to this new problem. "Okay, I'm listening."

"As I said, you have a genetic abnormality that was identified in your last routine medical exam," Bernard said. "That mutation allows you the ability to move through time. Before you ask, no, it appears not to be an inherited trait. We know of no instances of two people in the same family having the ability. It appears to be a completely random mutation. Once the mutation occurs, the ability will manifest of its own accord on the person's thirty-fifth birthday or, if it happens after that age, on their next birthday—if they haven't already learned about the ability, and how to control it, before then. And no, we don't know what it is about that age, or birthdays in general, that triggers the ability, but we have seen it happen consistently."

"Okay," Russ said slowly. "Assuming this is all true, assuming I believe you managed to get hold of my medical records despite all the layers of privacy surrounding them these days, that still doesn't tell me why I'm here. Why not just let it happen in three years when I turn thirty-five? Why go to the expense of maintaining this place and bringing me over and all the rest?"

"Because the dangers of time travel are not inconsiderable," Bernard said with a Gallic shrug. "Not only to yourself, but also to the stream of history and to life as we know it. Dangerous enough that the greater good supersedes those layers of privacy you mentioned. We can trace a number of catastrophic events in history to someone traveling back unprepared and leaving behind absolute chaos. The assassination of Julius Caesar and the ensuing war, the assassination of Archduke Ferdinand that triggered World War I, the sacking of Rome that led to the Dark Ages... there are others, but you begin to see the problem."

"The world would be a completely different place if those things hadn't happened," Russ said, his mind racing as he considered all that might have happened and not happened if the knowledge held within the Roman Empire had not been forgotten, if World War I had not reforged the face of Europe, if.... "God, the possibilities!"

"Indeed," Bernard said. "It is possible to shift through time without setting off such dire consequences, with training, care, and practice, but you can see why we might not want people discovering the ability without assistance. Once we identify them, we bring them here to teach them how to use their abilities before they manifest naturally."

"Assuming I believe the rest of it, then, yes, I can see that," Russ said. "So I'm here for two weeks of training?"

"Essentially, yes," Bernard replied, "but you are still skeptical. Perhaps a demonstration?"

"A harmless one?" Russ asked.

"I do my best to make all my time travel harmless," Bernard replied with a wry smile. He extended his hand.

Russ shifted his weight from one foot to the other, hoping his nerves weren't as obvious in his movements as they were in the racing of his pulse, and accepted Bernard's hand.

He couldn't have said what he was expecting since he'd never actually thought about what it would feel like to travel through time, but he would have expected something, some physical sensation of displacement, disorientation, movement… something.

Instead, everything got blurry for a moment, and when it came back into focus, they were somewhere else. Russ had no idea where, but the elaborate baroque furniture was gone, replaced by simple, almost rustic pieces, and only a few. A bed with a mattress over a rope frame, a plain chest of drawers with wooden handles, and a single, straight-backed chair with a wooden seat and no cushion were the full contents of the room.

"Where are we?"

Bernard didn't answer, gesturing toward the small, single-paned window on one wall. Russ went to the glass and peered out, but the quality was so poor he could barely make out the shapes of anything outside. It took him a minute to figure out the unfamiliar catch on the casement, but once he got it open and stuck his head out, the scene in front of him stole his breath.

He had never been to Versailles, but he had seen enough pictures to recognize it, except that he'd never seen it like this, with one wing still under construction—construction, not renovation— and the grounds only partially planted, with workers digging beds next to those other men were planting.

The men had horses and carts, shovels and picks, but not a single mechanical tool in sight. No electric wires, no tractors or backhoes—just saws and axes, shovels and the strength of their backs to carve out the gardens, levers and pulleys to lift the heavy stones, and mortar and trowel to fit them in place.

Russ pulled his head back in and sat down hard on the chair. "We're in Versailles, probably in the 1680s because they're still working on the gardens, and Le Notre died in 1700."

"Impressive," Bernard said. "You do know your history. It is, in point of fact, 1678. Jules Hardouin-Mansart is in the middle of adding the second story and the north and south wings. It will take several more years before everything is truly completed, but already Versailles is the crown jewel of the French royal palaces."

"And we are in…?"

"The servants' quarters," Bernard said. "Shall we return to the château d'Eternité? I imagine you have questions."

Russ wanted to protest leaving so soon, but they were hardly dressed to go exploring. He nodded and held out his hand. As Bernard took it, the door behind them opened and a man walked in.

The scene blurred out before Russ could speak.

When it cleared again, they were back in the parlor of the château d'Eternité. "That man," Russ said. "He saw us. Is that going to cause a problem?"

Bernard chuckled. "Why do you think I chose that room to take you to, still in modern dress and totally unprepared for what you might see? That is Gilles. He works at Versailles in the kitchens when he is not wandering through time looking for more interesting adventures."

"He's one of us?"

"You are taking this better than most," Bernard said, returning to his seat. "Yes, he is one of us and has given me permission to use his room during the day while he is working."

"So explain this to me," Russ said, sitting down again as well. "I can travel through time, or I can if you help me, anyway, but you said there were dangers, so there must be rules, or guidelines, at least."

"There are," Bernard said. "Would you care for another kir? Dinner will be served in an hour, and there may be others joining us. We never know when others will return."

Russ blinked a couple of times, trying to sort out everything in his head, but he quickly gave up. This wasn't about sense. It simply was.

"Um, no, thank you," he said when he realized Bernard was waiting for an answer. "I need to concentrate so I'll remember everything you're saying. I don't want to mess up later."

"You don't mind if I do?" Bernard asked. "Traveling is more exhausting than it used to be, and I find a little glass of something restorative upon my return makes quite the difference."

"Of course," Russ said.

Bernard refilled his glass and returned. "So, then, the rules, as you called them. The most important one, the one that you must not violate under any circumstances, is that you must not try to change history, your own or anyone else's. The repercussions of doing so could be cataclysmic."

"Isn't my simple presence in the past enough to change it?" Russ asked. "If I wasn't there before but am there now, doesn't that change it by definition?"

"Yes, but there are changes and then there are *changes*. If you go to the past and do your best to fit in, to blend in, any changes your presence generates will be small ones, the ripples caused by a raindrop on a large lake, but if you go to the past with the intention of, for example, assassinating Hitler before he can rise to power, the changes you cause will be like a storm on the ocean, so destructive and far-reaching that you might not even have a present to come home to. For better and for worse, Hitler's rise to power shaped the world as we know it today. Changing that would so change the present that you might not be able to get home. Indeed you might not exist anymore. It is a risk we will not take."

14

Russ nodded. "I understand the difference. No messing with the history books."

"Secondly, you must not return to a time in your own lifetime. Neither you nor your past self will survive that confluence. The universe knows there should only be one of you during the past thirty-two years. If you create a situation where there are two of you, something will happen to alleviate that overlap, and that will change your history irreparably as well."

"You know this?" Russ asked.

Bernard nodded. "It has been part of our lore as far back as I have been able to trace, but twice in recent years, people have disregarded the rule and not returned. When I checked later, I found no records of the person beyond the date to which they returned and no trace of either body."

Russ shuddered. His life hadn't been all a bed of roses, but he couldn't think of anything worth taking that risk to change. He hoped the people who'd disregarded the rule had gotten what they hoped for out of their sacrifices.

"Anything else?"

"The amount of time you spend in the past is the amount of time that will have elapsed here when you return to the present," Bernard said. "If you are gone for five minutes, like when we went to Versailles, chances are no one will even notice, but if you go for a week or a month or more, be prepared to explain your absence when you return, or prepare for it before you leave, so no one will worry about unanswered e-mails, unreturned phone calls, absences from work. Time as a whole is fluid. Your timeline is not."

"That doesn't make sense," Russ said. "If I can choose a time in the past to go to, why can't I choose a time in the present to return to?"

Bernard shrugged. "Because you can't. Because none of us have ever been able to do that, even when we have tried to do so deliberately. You can move from one point in the past to another point in the past, but your return home will always take you to that amount of time after your departure, no matter how specifically you attempt to control it."

"If you say so."

"I do," Bernard replied.

Laughter in the hall interrupted them.

"And if you don't believe me, you can ask our new guests at dinner," Bernard suggested. "I believe that will be Chou and Linda returning. They wanted to see the crowning of the Jianwen Emperor."

"So space is as fluid as time?" Russ asked. "I mean, we were here, then we were in Versailles. You're talking about them going to China."

"Only from here," Bernard replied, "and no, I don't know why, before you ask. If you are at home, you can travel back to that location at any point in the past, but only from here can you move to other locations. That is why we bring everyone here to begin. If you travel to the past and then move away from that place, you may not be able to return there safely. If you need to get out in a hurry, you need a safe place to come. You will always be able to come here as well, even if you left from home."

"That doesn't—"

"Make sense," Bernard finished. "I didn't say it made sense. I said it's the way it is. We didn't make up these rules. We have just learned to abide by them for our safety and the safety of the rest of the universe."

The door to the parlor opened wider and two people came in, obviously of Chinese descent and still wearing the garb of fourteenth-century China. "Hallo, Bernard," the man said. "Got a new one tonight?"

"Good evening, Chou," Bernard said. "This is Russ. Perhaps you should change before dinner. Your clothes are still in your room."

"But I like these clothes," Chou replied.

"The wardrobes are open for anyone to borrow from, but we expect them to be returned when you're done with them," Bernard reminded him. "We will see you at dinner."

"Wardrobes?" Russ asked when Chou left.

"You didn't think we normally jump back in time in modern garb, did you?" Bernard asked. "We would be found out before we got ten feet. The château has an extensive collection of costumes from times and places all over the world, as authentic as we can make them from our own travels and the travels of those who came before us. We even have a tailor on staff to help with adjustments. You can, of course, buy garments when you return to the past if you intend to stay that long, but anything created in the past must remain in the past."

"You've thought of everything," Russ said with a shake of his head.

"Certainly not," Bernard replied, "but we've taken as many precautions as we can for the situations we have thought of."

"What about communication?" Russ asked. "I speak English, and I read a little of some European languages, but that's not going to help if I'm trying to blend into ancient China."

Bernard chuckled. "You have no idea you've been speaking French since you got here, do you?"

"What?"

"The mutation makes it possible for you to understand what you hear and reply in the appropriate idiom. It won't keep you from saying something culturally inappropriate, but the words that come out of your mouth will be understandable to those around you."

CHAPTER
TWO

THREE days later, Russ stood in the costume room, searching through the seventeenth-century section to see if he could find something that would fit without too much hassle and that would let him blend in with the servants at the Louvre. Bernard had worked with him extensively until he had mastered the art of moving through time, but this would be his first chance to travel on his own, and he wanted everything to be perfect.

He wasn't worried about getting there or even about getting back as much as he was about fitting in while there. The extensive wardrobe at the château could make him look the part, but it would be up to him to act the part, to concentrate on the mannerisms and speech patterns of the people around him so he could blend in rather than standing out.

That was one reason he had chosen to go back as a servant. No one paid attention to servants except when they needed something, and even then, they wanted to give an order and have it carried out. He could remain mute most of the time and mumble the rest of the time until he got his bearings.

He settled finally on something he hoped would be appropriate. If not, well, he could always come home and change again after he saw what the servants were really wearing. As long as he was careful not to overlap himself in the past, he could travel to the same general time period more than once.

"Seventeenth century, but not well-to-do...." Bernard's voice broke Russ's concentration, and he looked up to see the château's caretaker standing in the doorway.

"It's a time I know enough about to be able to blend in well, I think, and besides, there's something I've always wanted to know for sure."

"And that would be?"

"Whether Louis XIII was really gay," Russ admitted.

"You won't seduce the king of France dressed like that."

Russ flushed. "I wasn't planning on seducing him. I was planning on mingling with the servants and seeing what I could overhear. I don't have a death wish."

"And you think seducing the king would be dangerous?"

"His favorite, the man reputed to be his lover, was a swordsman of some skill," Russ explained. "I'm not. Besides, I wouldn't think you'd approve of someone getting their jollies by going back in time to get laid."

"People go back in time for far more scurrilous reasons than that," Bernard replied. "Take your trip, see what you can find out. I'll be interested to hear your experiences when you return."

"You know something," Russ said. It had only been three days, but he recognized that tone of voice already.

"You are not the first to ponder such pressing questions and decide to find out the answers," Bernard said with a shrug. "I will leave you so you can concentrate on your journey. Have a good trip."

Russ frowned as Bernard left him alone again. Had someone else gone back to try to seduce Louis XIII? Was that how Bernard knew about the king's proclivities? Would that make Russ's current goal more dangerous? Telling himself to stop stalling, he closed his eyes and concentrated on where he wanted to go. Bernard had taught him how to focus his energy on a particular time and place in the past, how to blur the lines between past and present, here and there, and even how to stop just before he arrived in the past so he could make sure the area he'd chosen was safe and unoccupied, but this was the first time Russ had tried it alone.

The room around him blurred and the streets outside the Louvre came into view. The alley he had selected from poring over an old map was deserted and so Russ let everything come into focus.

He took a moment to steady himself, straightening his tunic and making sure his appearance would pass muster. When he had no more reason to delay, he stepped from the alley, blending in with the others on their way to the Louvre for work. The guards at the gate didn't look at him twice as he followed a similarly clad man through the servants' door and into the kitchens.

"His Majesty wants his breakfast," the cook shouted. "Where is Pouquelin? He should have been here by now."

"I can take it," Russ offered quickly.

"Not by yourself, you can't," the man said, looking around until he could grab another servant by the collar. "Here, each of you take one tray. Don't dawdle, and don't speak of anything you might see or hear."

That sounded promising. Russ hefted one of the sizable trays and waited for the other servant to do the same, hoping the other man knew where he was going since Russ hadn't the slightest idea.

The other servant didn't even glance Russ's way, walking through the servants' passages with enough confidence that Russ sighed in relief. He wouldn't have to worry about getting lost, at least.

The servant reached a final door and paused. "*Bon sang*, I hope he's alone," the other servant said.

Russ was dying to ask who he might be with, but he kept his mouth shut. His time travel gene gave him the ability to understand and be understood, but it didn't keep him from saying inappropriate things. Bernard had driven into his head repeatedly the precept that the less he said, the better, until he got to know his new environment enough to blend in.

The other servant tapped lightly at the door. Russ knew the man couldn't expect the king to answer, yet he'd said he hoped Louis would be alone, which left Russ more than a little confused.

"You're late."

The man on the other side of the door was clearly another servant, although one of considerably higher rank, given his attire. "You're not Pouquelin."

"No, monsieur, he wasn't there and the cook didn't want to delay," the other servant said with a bow. Russ did his best to imitate the movement without overturning the tray, something easier said than done.

"Very well," the king's valet—Russ assumed that was who he was—said. "Come in and put it on the table. His Majesty will be ready to eat in a moment."

Russ followed the other men inside and set the tray on the large table, set for two. Russ knew better than to imagine the queen would be joining her husband for breakfast, but that did not mean the place was intended for the king's lover. It could as easily be Richelieu coming to plot some new way to control the aristocrats. Indeed, with servants around, that seemed far more likely than the king's lover.

The door opened behind them and the servant Russ had followed stiffened. Russ didn't turn around, sure they should not in any way indicate they had seen or heard anything, but he caught a glimpse of pale trousers and black boots out of the corner of his eye as he finished unloading the tray. Taking his cue from his fellow servant, he waited until the outer door had shut again before picking up the tray and returning to the servants' passages.

"Who was that?" Russ dared to ask as they made their way back toward the kitchen.

"You must be new to the palace if you have to ask," the servant said. "That was François de Baradas, but you didn't see him. A word against him or the king and you're a dead man."

"I may be new, but I'm not stupid," Russ said. "I can keep my mouth shut when I need to." Even when he got back to the present, he wouldn't really be able to talk about what he'd seen. How would he explain it? *Oh, I just popped back in time and posed as a servant so I could get into Louis's bedchamber as de Baradas was leaving.* He'd be laughed out of the history department in disgrace. He found it didn't matter, though. He knew the truth, and that was the most important part. If he chose to argue the point with someone, he could use the historical texts that had given rise to the suspicion in the first place to support his position, letting his own knowledge give him the determination to keep arguing, no matter what others said in return. He wondered vaguely about the rumor that Louis XIV was the son of Cardinal Richelieu rather than the son of the king, but he decided against trying to find that out. Some chances weren't worth taking.

They returned the trays to the kitchen, and Russ spent the next several hours engaged in other menial tasks until he could find an excuse to slip away long enough to assure his privacy as he returned to the present.

"Was your trip successful?" Bernard asked, coming into the foyer as soon as Russ appeared.

"How do you do that?" Russ asked in return.

"Do what?"

"Know when someone arrives."

Bernard shrugged. "It comes with being the guardian of the château, I suppose. I sense a shift when someone arrives or leaves. You didn't answer my question."

Here, with Bernard, he could speak for once about what he had seen. "Yes, it was successful," he said with a grin. "Not only did I not make a fool of myself, but as I delivered breakfast to His Majesty, I encountered his favorite departing for the day."

"Well done," Bernard said, "though what you will do with that information is beyond me."

"It's not about what I'll do with it," Russ said. "It's just *knowing*. Isn't it that way for all of us? We go back to a particular time and place to see something or experience something we've always wanted to see or experience. We go back to satisfy a curiosity of some kind. Other than among ourselves, none of us can talk about our travels. Why else would we do it, then?"

"That is indeed the burning question," Bernard said. "Some people never tire of it. Others never do more than a trip or two. They have the ability, but once the novelty wears off and they realize they can't really share with their loved ones, they lose interest and stop."

"I think it would depend in part on the relationships they left behind every time they traveled," Russ agreed. "I have house plants. If I had my parents still, if I had kids, even if I had a dog, that would be different. It would be a lot harder to think about being gone for more than a couple of hours. As it is, I can easily take a two-week vacation and no one will wonder where I am."

"Yes, that is definitely part of it," Bernard said. "Having someone to travel with also often makes a difference. Chou and Linda often travel together, even though they rarely see each other outside of their trips. Others grow so close they end up staying together even in the present."

"Does anyone ever go back to the past and stay?" Russ asked.

"Yes," Bernard said, "although it's often hard to tell if that was intentional or accidental."

"Accidental?" Russ repeated. "How could it be accidental?"

"If something happened to them before they could return or that might keep them from returning," Bernard explained. "A head injury could well leave them alive but unable to travel through time, and death is irreversible, even for us."

"That sounds ominous."

"A bullet, an arrow, a sword thrust… they don't always give warning before they strike," Bernard said with a shrug. "Neither does a car accident or a house fire or any other accident that might befall a person in modern times. Life is never without risks. You take them now or you take them then, but you take them either way. Dinner will be served in half an hour. You will want to hurry so you can shower and change."

DINNER was one of the stranger affairs Russ had ever attended, a motley collection of travelers from the present, one traveler from the past who had tagged along with a modern-day traveler, and one from the future who had come to the château knowing he would find friendly faces and a free meal. Russ could tell from the look of complete relaxation on everyone's faces how pleasant they found it not to have to hide a part of themselves they rarely got to share, even if the traveler from the future was guarded in his descriptions of the way things would be at some later date. Stories flowed freely in every direction, something the historian in Russ greatly appreciated. While they regaled each other with tales of trips they had taken and adventures they'd had, Russ noticed none of them mentioned a life beyond traveling. The sense that they all lived otherwise with great isolation left him feeling completely unsettled as he climbed the stairs to his room.

He hadn't gone so far that he couldn't turn back. He could leave at the end of his arranged visit and never slip through time again. He could save up his vacation and travel once a year, at least as long as he was single. If he didn't mind exploring the past around Tucson, he could travel any weekend unless he was trying to meet a deadline for work, but when people asked about his weekend on Monday, he'd have to lie. They wouldn't be surprised if he shrugged and said nothing special, because they'd heard that for most of the past six years, ever since he'd finished his degree and started working there. No, the change would be internal. He'd actually have something to talk about and not be able to tell anyone.

Bernard had warned him that traveling was taxing, but he hadn't realized how much until he fell asleep mid-thought and didn't rouse until well past breakfast the next morning.

RUSS awoke feeling surprisingly refreshed. His thoughts were no less in turmoil, but he felt better equipped to deal with them and to make a decision. He pondered his choices over his coffee and croissant in the parlor where Bernard had first introduced him to this crazy concept.

"You look lost in thought."

Russ looked up to see Linda, one of the other time travelers who seemed to have settled into the château for the moment.

"No, not at all," he said, summoning a smile for her.

"It's hard at first to strike a balance."

"How did you know?"

"Because we all go through it," she replied with a shrug. "We have this fantastic ability, but using it has consequences, even if not huge ones. We disappear for periods of time with no explanation, and we have parts of ourselves we can share with very few people."

"You obviously have chosen to continue with it," Russ said.

"Yes, because I love it. I love the rush of it, the chance to see times and places I'd never be able to visit any other way, but I'm very strict about how I do it."

"How?" Russ asked. "I'm considering options and trying to decide what my options even are."

"Well, remembering that this is what works for me, I save up my vacation each year and come here for the month I have off. My boss wasn't sure at first about letting me take all four weeks consecutively instead of in two-week blocks like everyone else, but he came around. I tell people I come to France for a cleansing retreat, so no cell phones, no Internet, no outside influences," Linda said. "And for that month, I travel, alone or with others, depending on who's here and what they have planned."

"And no one questions that or asks to go with you or, I don't know, asks for details when you get back?" Russ asked.

"There's always a certain amount of curiosity," Linda said, "but I've worked at the same company for fifteen years and have been coming on my 'retreats' for twelve. People have figured out I'm not going to talk about them."

"You don't ever do a little weekend jaunt back in the area where you're from?"

"No," Linda said with an emphatic shake of her head. "For one thing, if I got in trouble and had to jump back to the present, I'd be as likely to end up here as anywhere else, and then I'd have the trouble, not to mention the expense, of getting home in time for work on Monday. Plus, I wouldn't have the resources of the château available to prepare for the trip. It's far more than just the wardrobe. The collection of historical texts here is unparalleled outside of a university library, and maybe not even then."

Russ had perused the château's library one afternoon and admitted it was impressive, even for a historian working in a university history department. "Thank you," he said. "You've given me a lot to think about."

"You're welcome. Once you leave, you'll have to deal with this alone, but you aren't alone here at the château. Whatever complications you have in your life, someone here has faced them or Bernard knows someone who has, even if they aren't here at the moment. Nobody requires us to help each other out, but it's sort of understood."

"Thank you," Russ said again as Linda rose and patted his shoulder, then left him alone with his thoughts.

He didn't know if he'd be able to get a month off at a time, although maybe if he took it in the summer when things in the department and at the journal were quieter, but even if he did two-week blocks, he could take his four weeks, tell people he was wandering around Europe and didn't know how often he'd be able to check messages, and come here. He could take a day or two to do some sightseeing so he'd have pictures to show anyone who asked, if they asked, and he could spend the other ten to twelve days wandering through the past. He could take Linda's model and make it work.

That left him nine days before he had to return to Paris to fly home. Nine days to take advantage of everything the château had to offer.

He finished his coffee, then went to browse the history books and decide where he was going next.

CHAPTER
THREE

DRESSED in a simple brown tunic, *subligar*, and sandals, Russ felt absolutely ridiculous, not to mention only half dressed, but he had studied Roman garb from the early first and second centuries CE, and this was the way a working Roman citizen would dress. Russ considered for a moment adding a plain toga, but while he didn't want to be mistaken for a slave, he did not want anyone thinking he was putting on airs. A simple laborer working in the fields or forest to make his living… nothing to attract anyone's attention for the few days he would be there. He would have to hope someone would hire him or hunger would drive him back to the present before long, but he would worry about that once he got to where he was going.

He closed his eyes and concentrated on the spot he had picked in the forest outside of Nîmes.

It took him longer to get his bearings this time, maybe because of the greater jump in time or for some other reason that escaped him entirely. As soon as he was steady, he started walking through the underbrush, hoping the lingering disorientation would fade before long. The sound of shouting and of dogs barking was his only warning before a huge wild boar broke through the bushes just a few yards away from him.

"Oh shit," Russ muttered, looking for a place to run, a tree to climb, anything to get him out of reach of the deadly tusks. The animal already had several arrows sticking out of its side, but it had not yet succumbed to its wounds, and Russ doubted he'd be that lucky now. He bolted, not knowing what else to do, his heart pounding wildly as the pained cries of the boar grew closer. He tried to concentrate enough to return to the château d'Eternité, but he didn't have the skill to run and travel through time simultaneously. A final loud squeal heralded the boar's demise. Russ collapsed to his knees, panting harshly.

"What is this?" Russ looked up to see a centurion crossing the glade where he had nearly met his end. "What are you doing here?"

"I'm sorry, sir," Russ said. "I was cutting through the forest on my way to Nemausus. I didn't mean to interrupt your hunt."

"Get up."

Russ nodded and forced himself gracelessly to his feet, keeping his eyes down respectfully.

"You are some distance from Nemausus still," the centurion said. "You will not reach there tonight."

Russ's shoulders slumped in defeat. He'd blown this trip entirely. He'd have to go back to the château and start over.

"You will share our tents tonight and we will begin the return to Nemausus tomorrow," the centurion declared. "What is your name?"

"Russ," he replied without thinking, still too fraught from his near-death experience to remember the story he had invented for himself.

"That is not a Roman name."

"Rastus," Russ said quickly, giving the name he had intended to claim. "My sister couldn't say it when she was little. She shortened it to Russ and it stuck."

"Very well, Rastus," the centurion said. "I am Quentus Maximus, adjutant to General Oeneus Septimus, the legatus Augusti pro praetore of Nemausus."

"It is an honor, sir," Russ said, not sure of the correct form of address. "Thank you for saving my life."

"The gods will find a way for you to repay me in time," Maximus said.

"We should go, Legatus," one of the other men called. "It will be dark soon, and we must dress the boar before nightfall so we don't attract wolves and other beasts."

Russ filed the proper form of address away for future reference and followed the men back to their camp, his thoughts racing the entire way. He hadn't blown it after all. Well, maybe he had, but Maximus had rescued him before the boar killed him anyway, and his benefactor seemed willing to continue in that role, at least as far as giving him shelter for the night. When they reached the camp, he expected to be put to work, but Maximus had other ideas. "Come dine with me and tell me how you came to be in the woods. You are a long way from anywhere."

Russ took a deep breath, trying not to stare as Maximus stripped off his hunting gear and reclined on the pillows in his tent in only his tunic, leaving his muscled legs bare. His brain—his ever busy, overactive, never at a loss for words brain—shorted out at the sight. God, how many men did he know who would kill for bodies like the one in front of him right now? Maximus's legs were like tree trunks, solid muscle without an ounce of fat, and Russ would bet good money the rest of him was just as solid. Certainly his arms, extending from the short sleeves of his tunic, continued the theme. Despite the precariousness of his situation, Russ felt his body react. He shifted nervously on the pillows, trying to adopt the same relaxed pose as Maximus.

A servant brought in a clay platter full of roasted meat before Russ could think of an answer to Maximus's question. Russ wondered if it was the boar they had killed earlier in the day or some other provision. Either way, it smelled fantastic, making his mouth water. He held back, though, waiting for a cue from his host. Another servant followed a few moments later with a bowl of some kind of tabouli or other grain-based salad. The servants served the dishes onto two plates and retired with low bows. Maximus leaned forward and took a bite of meat in his hand, licking his fingers as he ate. Russ swallowed hard, trying not to groan at the sight. Yes, it had been a while since he'd gotten laid, but he didn't usually react this powerfully to complete strangers. Maybe time travel messed with his libido along with his energy levels. Or maybe it was the brush with death earlier in the day.

Shifting to try to hide the erection the *subligar* did nothing to contain, Russ reached for one of the wooden spoons and took a bite of the salad, hoping Maximus wouldn't resume the earlier thread of their conversation. The flavors of mint and coriander dominated, along with cheese. He couldn't decide what the base of the salad was, but it didn't matter. It was delicious, and he was suddenly so ravenous it was hard to remember his manners. He forced himself to eat slowly, though, and to mimic his host's gestures, taking pieces of the meat with his fingers and taking care to lick the juices off after each bite so he didn't soil his clothes or the rug on the floor of the tent. He could feel Maximus's eyes on him, the gaze so bold it seemed nearly a caress. When he finally dared to look up, the centurion's expression was taut with desire, and Russ's cock surged with lust. The man looked at him like he wanted to devour him, and at the moment, Russ was a very willing treat. The question was how to indicate that to Maximus without crossing some class barrier that would get him killed. At least in ancient Rome homosexuality wasn't illegal, so he didn't have that concern to worry about.

The servants returned before he could figure out a way. "Will there be anything else this evening, Legatus?" one of them asked.

"No, that will be all," Maximus replied with a wave of his hand. Russ thought he saw surprise on the faces of the servants, but he kept his thoughts to himself.

When the flaps to the tent fell shut, enclosing them in near darkness but for the oil lamp burning in the corner, Maximus pushed the table to one side with his foot. "Come here."

Russ swallowed hard as he scooted closer to Maximus.

"Let's see if the rest of you is as pretty as your face."

Russ should have been outraged, insulted, or otherwise disgusted by the comment and the assumption behind it, especially given that he wasn't some eighteen-year-old twink anymore. If someone had come on to him that way in a bar in Tucson, he'd have laughed it off completely, knowing he was anything but pretty, but in the shadowy tent in second-century Gaul with the man who had saved his life hours earlier, the words only fired his lust. He nodded and reached for the belt around his waist.

Maximus shook his head. "I want to do it."

Russ nodded again, not entirely sure his consent was required, but he gave it nonetheless. It made him feel better, even if it didn't matter to Maximus. The centurion didn't bother with the belt, sliding his hands up Russ's legs beneath the hem of his knee-length tunic. Russ knew his legs were no match for Maximus's, but the centurion didn't seem to notice, intent on reaching his prize. He pushed aside the simple loincloth and stroked Russ's cock boldly, surprising a moan out of Russ. It had been so damn long since he'd been touched, and Maximus's motions had such authority, such dominance (where the hell had that need come from?) that Russ couldn't do anything but collapse back against the cushions and spread his legs, silently begging for more.

Maximus swatted him on the hip, more encouragement than punishment. "I'm not doing all the work," he said, spreading his legs to reveal a thick, heavy, fully engorged cock. Mouth watering at the prospect, Russ shifted around, burying his head beneath the centurion's tunic even as his hand on Maximus's cock continued to work him hard.

As he applied himself to giving Maximus a blow job to blow his mind, Russ had the stray memory of reading somewhere that the Roman depictions of oral sex always involved slaves because no Roman citizen would want his face deformed by the suction, but Russ couldn't have cared less what Maximus thought of his status. He just wanted more of the salty flavor assailing his tongue and the mind-blowing feeling of a cock sliding into his throat.

He never did things like this. He never went out and hooked up with some random guy in some random bar, but he couldn't seem to stop himself. When he felt Maximus flip his tunic up to reveal his buttocks, he simply moaned and sucked harder.

"As pretty as any pleasure slave I ever saw," Maximus crooned, stroking the skin of Russ's ass. One finger found his entrance and probed lightly. "And far tighter. You're going to give me a good ride, aren't you?"

Russ was going to have to discuss Maximus's attitude with him—after the centurion fucked him senseless.

The fingers disappeared for a moment, returning seconds later covered with something slick and wet. Russ relaxed muscles he hadn't realized were tense. Of course Maximus would have something to ease the way if he was a lover of men, and out on patrol or campaign as they were, he didn't have a lot of other choice. Russ hadn't gotten much time to look around, but he hadn't seen any women in the camp at all. Then Maximus's fingers pressed inside him with more force than finesse, but not cruel, just... determined.

Strong fingers slid beneath Russ's jaw and lifted his head despite Russ's moan of protest. "Turn around," Maximus said, his voice softer than Russ had heard it yet. Russ nodded and spun around so his backside faced the soldier. The fingers he'd dislodged to move returned to stretch him more insistently. Russ dropped his forehead to the pillows beneath him and braced himself for a hard, fast ride.

To Russ's surprise, Maximus didn't simply plow into him like it was his right and fate to do so. Instead he took his time, popping the head in and out of the ring of muscle, giving Russ that sensation of first penetration over and over until he couldn't stop the desperate plea. "More."

Only then did Maximus push deeper, but even still, he moved with the same tantalizing control, working Russ's ass with a command no one else had ever done. Russ lifted up onto his elbows, trying to push back, the need to be filled growing unbearable, but Maximus's hands, those big, heavy, hot hands, settled on his hips, holding him still. "I am fucking you, pretty."

There it was again, that attitude that should have set Russ's teeth on edge and had him fighting to get free. He didn't move, though, except to nod and drop his shoulders again, giving control back to the man behind him. He couldn't do anything else. Maximus seemed to have taken over his mind as well as his body. When Maximus hit his prostate, lingering there with the same determined control as when he had teased Russ's entrance, Russ decided letting Maximus be in charge wasn't such a bad thing. Not when it made him feel like this!

As turned on as he was from the foreplay over dinner and sucking Maximus's cock, Russ knew he wouldn't last long. Already he could feel his balls drawing up as his release loomed, and the constant stimulation to his prostate only added to his desire without giving him the final push he needed. Shifting his weight so he could balance on one arm, he reached for his cock, only to have Maximus swat him firmly. "None of that. You only think you need it for your pleasure."

Russ didn't need it for his pleasure—he was plenty pleased—but he'd never been able to climax just from being fucked. He only hoped Maximus would let him jerk off after he was done, because not getting to come at all would seriously suck.

Except Maximus didn't speed up and take his own pleasure in Russ's ass. He kept that same slow, determined pace, playing Russ's body like a lyre, until the need and passion and pleasure swirled through him like a maelstrom. He squirmed between Maximus's restraining hands, but he could only move so much, so he resorted to begging, but that had about as much effect as his squirming. Eventually words required too much concentration, lust reducing him to grunts and groans as Maximus kept fucking him, an inexorable thrust and withdrawal until Russ thought he'd go insane with the need.

"Stop fighting it."

The words flipped some switch inside Russ, shattering whatever inner resistance he hadn't known he had, and suddenly his climax slammed through him, shaking him like a rag doll and leaving him limp and trembling. The moment his orgasm began, Maximus unleashed his own control, pounding into Russ with all the veiled power that had drawn Russ to him over dinner. This was the fucking he'd imagined before they started, a pure possession of his body. He'd probably have rug burn on his elbows and knees as he rocked forward with every thrust, only to be drawn back by those strong hands so he was in the perfect position for the next inward drive, but he didn't care. It was a small price to pay for the soaring feeling of release prolonged by Maximus's continued movements.

The sudden, hot rush of fluid he felt inside sent a fresh burst of desire through him. He didn't do this. He'd *never* done this. He'd always been safe, insisting his partners use a condom, but they were in Gaul. Condoms weren't an option. As the sticky mess oozed over his balls, Russ realized it didn't matter. He'd been fucked like never before, and the chances of Maximus having anything were slim. Even if he did, it wouldn't be anything modern medicine couldn't cure upon his return.

He winced a little as Maximus withdrew, feeling the pounding he'd taken now in a way he hadn't while Maximus was inside him.

"Thank you, Legatus," Russ said, straightening his clothes.

"I think you can call me Quentus after what we just did," the centurion said with a lazy smile. He tugged on Russ's hand, pulling him back down onto the cushions and into a comfortable embrace. "And there is nothing to thank me for. I took as much pleasure from it as you did. Now sleep. Tomorrow will be a long day of marching if we're to reach Nemausus before nightfall."

"Sleep?" Russ said. "Here?"

"Unless you have a tent hidden somewhere I don't know about or would prefer the company of my men," Quentus said, his voice growing harsh.

"No, of course not," Russ said. "I didn't expect the invitation, that's all."

"Sleep," Quentus ordered, although his voice had softened again. "We'll discuss your 'expectations' in the morning."

Russ considered a sharp reply, but he decided against it and settled into the cushions and Quentus's embrace, doing his best to keep his tunic covering him decently.

Quentus swatted his hand away and adjusted the tunic once more, leaving Russ's bare ass pressed to his groin while one large hand splayed across Russ's lower belly in a possessive caress that couldn't be misinterpreted.

Oh yes, they were going to discuss expectations, that was certain.

THE sun had barely begun to lighten the eastern sky when Quentus rose from their nest of cushions. Russ felt the press of his erection before he pulled back, so he expected a repeat of the night before, or at least some relief for his own morning wood, but Quentus simply left the tent.

He returned a few moments later with a bucket of hot water. "It isn't the baths in Nemausus, but it will have to do," he said, offering a rag to Russ as he began his own ablutions, stripping the tunic off and then rubbing the wet cloth over his entire body.

Russ had been right. The rest of Quentus was as strong and muscular as his arms and legs. At a guess, Russ would place him in his midthirties, but it could have gone either way. His studies of the time told him that career soldiers generally served for twenty-five years, so if Quentus had joined at eighteen, that made him somewhat less than forty-five, but given his rank, he was almost certainly in the second half of his tenure.

"You are looking at me most oddly," Quentus observed.

"I'm sorry," Russ said, feeling his cheeks heat. "I was trying to decide how old you are."

"Thirty-eight," Quentus said. "Another five years and I will be able to retire if I choose. If I stay alive long enough to retire."

"You sound as if that's doubtful," Russ said, not wanting to examine the twinge the thought caused around his heart. "This part of Gaul is peaceful now, is it not?" He supposed there could be minor skirmishes that hadn't made the history books, even the local ones, but he didn't remember Gaul being a hotbed area after Caesar's conquest.

"As peaceful as anywhere," Quentus replied, "but there is political intrigue here as well. Perhaps not as much as in Rome, but enough to make anyone in a position of power a potential target."

"So what would they have to gain by replacing you?" Russ asked, mind racing as he searched his memories for everything he knew about the Roman Empire. "You aren't the governor of the province."

"No, but I am the governor's advisor, his friend, and often his voice," Quentus said. "There are those who believe he would be better served listening to other counsel."

Russ nodded. "That's why you're in a hurry to return to Nemausus. You fear someone will replace you in your absence."

"No," Quentus said with a short laugh. "I am eager to return because I miss the comforts of home. I am no longer a youth, and the ground grows harder with each campaign, no matter how pleasant the company in my bed."

"Do you often have company in your bed?" Russ asked more sharply than he'd intended.

"Often enough," Quentus said as he finished his wash and began to dress, "although the company of slaves and prostitutes cannot compare to the company of an honest lover."

Quentus's attitude the night before made a lot more sense in light of that revelation. Russ pulled his own tunic back in place, belting it around his waist. "I won't be a plaything for your convenience, used when you need me and then cast aside."

"And yet you had every intention of leaving last night exactly like one of those 'conveniences', as you call them."

Russ could hardly argue with that. "So what happens now?"

"Now we break camp and return to Nemausus," Quentus replied. "You will ride with me, as your sandals are in poor repair for a march. We will deal with the rest when we reach Nemausus."

"Will we reach there today?"

"It depends on how quickly we leave and what we encounter along the way. Come, we will eat and then we will ride."

Russ followed Quentus out of the tent into the bustling campsite. All around them, soldiers and slaves worked to break down the camp and pack the wagons for the day's march. Russ stayed close to Quentus, not sure where he fit in the sea of shouts. Quentus handed him a plate. Russ ate without noticing what it was, too overwhelmed by seeing history alive around him. He studied the men, the uniforms, the equipment, everything, as unobtrusively as possible, trying to commit the details to memory. He could postulate when he returned home. No one had to know he had firsthand experience with the Roman army.

Soon after he finished eating, Quentus gave orders to begin the day's march. A servant brought Quentus his horse, a great brute of a warhorse that snorted when Quentus swung up into the saddle. When he reached down and pulled Russ up behind him, the horse shook his head in protest, but Quentus ignored it, turning to make sure Russ was settled.

The saddle itself was a curiosity, with four horns, two in front and two in back to hold the rider in place, and no stirrups to assist with stability or with mounting. Russ wouldn't have wanted to try to ride unaided, but with his arms wrapped firmly around Quentus's waist, he felt completely secure.

The column of soldiers began the march, their sandals slapping on the stone roads that were the hallmark of the Roman Empire. The wagons creaked into motion as well, pulled by huge oxen and herded along by slaves in tunics of even poorer quality than Russ's. Quentus rode at the head of the column, occasionally dropping back to the side to monitor the progress toward the rear, always in command, always in control.

Russ didn't want to admit that every shouted order sent another frisson of need through him.

By the time they stopped, late in the afternoon, the novelty of riding on horseback had worn off, leaving Russ's legs chafed and his temper worn. Only the thought of another night spent with Quentus kept him from losing his temper entirely, but nothing could disguise how awkwardly he walked as he crossed the camp to where the servants were setting up Quentus's tent.

"When we get to Nemausus tomorrow, you can soak in the hot baths until the stiffness fades," Quentus said, appearing suddenly at Russ's side. "You are obviously not used to riding on horseback."

"No," Russ agreed, thinking of the conservative coupe he drove at home. He couldn't tell Quentus that, though.

"And yet I think you are not used to walking either," Quentus continued.

"What makes you say that?" Russ asked, worried now that he'd been found out.

"Your sandals rubbed blisters on your feet. I noticed them last night," Quentus explained. The servants finished the tent, holding the flaps open for Quentus to go inside. Quentus ushered Russ in ahead of him. "Last night I was too caught up in you to take care of them, but tonight I will treat them properly."

"I'm not a child you need to tend to," Russ protested as he went inside the tent. Just being out of the sun eased some of the tension in the back of his neck, as if the rays beating down on him all day had somehow heated his emotions as well as his skin.

"If you were a child, I would turn you over to your mother or sisters," Quentus said. "If I am caring for someone, it is my lover."

"You order me around like a child," Russ said.

"Were you not paying any attention today?" Quentus asked. "I order everyone around. It's my role within the legion. Everything that happens here happens by my command, either directly or indirectly."

Russ had noticed the commands, of course, because he'd spent the day reacting to them, but he hadn't made the final connection between Quentus's role and his personality. He shivered a little at the memory of Quentus giving him orders the night before.

"Lie down," Quentus ordered. He rummaged in a satchel and pulled out a clay pot and a spatula.

"What's that?" Russ asked nervously.

"An ointment infused with willow," Quentus said. "The ointment will soothe your skin and the willow will help keep the abrasions from getting infected. We will reach Nemausus by midday tomorrow."

Russ nodded, wondering what would happen then. He had dressed as a simple laborer thinking to find work that way, but he had already seen how ill-suited he was to that life. He had no other skills to allow him to find work except perhaps as a translator, if such services were needed, and he couldn't presume on Quentus's generosity forever, or even for the eight days he had left before he had to return to his real life. The thought of going back to the university library and studying old manuscripts for hours on end suddenly seemed bland next to the vibrancy of the present moment.

Quentus scooped the ointment out of the pot with the spatula, but he spread it over the blisters on Russ's feet with his fingers, massaging the soles with firm strokes and making Russ moan at the pure pleasure of the muscles unknotting. The smile on Quentus's face at the sound was positively predatory, sending a fresh round of shivers through Russ's body. "Stay right there," Quentus said. He returned with a small vial of oil. Pouring some into his palm, he began rubbing Russ's calves in earnest.

Russ slumped back against the cushions, letting his elbows slide out from under him as he groaned again. Quentus's smile widened and he massaged more deeply, his powerful fingers digging at the spots of tension hard enough to surprise a gasp from Russ. Instantly Quentus stopped. "Am I hurting you?"

Russ shook his head. "No, it's what I need. It just surprised me."

Quentus reached for Russ's chin, forcing him to lift it enough to meet Quentus's gaze. "Do not let me hurt you without meaning to. Tell me to stop if it hurts."

It was as much a demand as everything else Quentus had ever said to him, but Russ was finding he didn't mind. The tone of voice might brook no disobedience, but the words themselves revealed the thoughtfulness behind the shield of command. "I'll tell you," Russ said. "I swear."

Quentus stared at him a moment longer before releasing his chin and returning to the deep massage. Once or twice, Russ almost asked him to stop, but before the words could leave his mouth, Quentus had changed the pressure of his hands, moving away from the tender place or gentling his touch or otherwise averting Russ's need to speak. It was a good thing, too, because Quentus's extended attentions to his legs were uncovering all of Russ's sensitive spots: the arch of his foot, the back of his knee, the curve of his instep. He'd thought he was hot for Quentus the night before, when their foreplay had consisted of eye-fucking across the table, but it was nothing compared to what he felt now, every nerve in his body on fire. Then Quentus spread Russ's legs and knelt between his knees, reaching for the healing ointment again. He spread it along the inside of Russ's thighs with firm but gentle strokes, the caresses doing as much to ease the chafing as the ointment itself.

Then Quentus began kneading and Russ gave up trying to hide his arousal, instead sliding his hand beneath his tunic to stroke his erection.

"What did I tell you about that yesterday?" Quentus said, catching Russ's hand with his and pinning it to the cushions.

"Yesterday you were fucking me when you said it," Russ pointed out, not fighting Quentus's grip—that would be like fighting the tides—but not exactly giving in either.

"That can be arranged. I had thought to give you a rest since I used you so hard last night."

He could rest when he was back in Tucson with no one to make him feel like Quentus did. He scrambled onto his knees, offering himself to Quentus in no uncertain terms.

"You are eager. I like that in a lover," Quentus said, smoothing an oily hand over Russ's buttocks, "but I am not in the mood to rush tonight. Get undressed. I want to see the rest of you, not just your delightful ass."

Russ shivered in anticipation. He hadn't considered last night particularly rushed, certainly not once Quentus started fucking him. He could only imagine what tonight would be like. He'd probably be begging for relief before Quentus was done with him. Of course it hadn't gotten him anywhere last night. He didn't imagine it would make any difference tonight either. Then again, he'd never felt anything like what Quentus had made him feel, so maybe he should just relax and give Quentus what he wanted. The results would surely be worth it.

HOURS later—at least that was how it felt to Russ—finally sated and curled up naked in Quentus's equally naked embrace, Russ lay awake, staring at the roof of the tent. His entire body felt limp, the result of coming so hard he'd almost passed out, but his mind wouldn't settle. Quentus had been every bit as commanding as the night before, refusing to let Russ do anything that might speed up their union, but Russ had never doubted for a moment that Quentus had any motivation behind his commands other than making Russ feel as good as possible.

He wished he could meet a man like Quentus in the future, but they didn't make men like that anymore. The dominant kind were either into kinky shit or they were Type A personalities with too many control issues. Quentus was domineering because it was his job to take care of everyone and everything under his command, and that included his lover. He wasn't callous or cruel. No, the only place Russ was going to meet a man like Quentus was right now, in Roman Gaul, in the second century CE. He could take advantage of it for the next week until he had to return or until Quentus got tired of him, or he could leave now and always wonder what might have happened. Leaving would be hell, but he couldn't stay. He didn't have a life here, and he had responsibilities back in his old life. He could leave now. He could slip out of Quentus's embrace on the pretext of finding the camp latrine and simply not come back. Quentus would search for him, probably, but he wouldn't find any trace of him, and he'd give up eventually. Russ hoped he wouldn't search for long.

He took a deep breath and made a decision. He had seven days left. He'd live them to the fullest and let that hold him until he could take his next grand adventure.

CHAPTER FOUR

THE ride the next day was nearly excruciating. The ointment Quentus had used helped during the night, but it did nothing to protect his legs from more chafing when he settled once more behind Quentus, and while they rarely rode above a trot, even at a walk, the movement of the horse put pressure on his well-plundered ass. Enough pressure to make him wish he hadn't goaded Quentus to fuck him harder quite as vehemently as he had.

"What are your plans when you reach Nemausus?" Quentus asked after an hour or so.

"I don't have any," Russ admitted. "I had thought to look for work."

"What kind of work?" Quentus pressed. "You are clearly no laborer despite your lowly garments. Neither your hands nor your feet bear the calluses of physical labor."

"Whatever is available," Russ replied. He should have come up with a better cover story, but he hardly had the skills to do much of anything. Even simple physical labor would be a challenge for him because his body wasn't used to it. "I have a knack for languages." It was a lie. He'd nearly failed out of his master's program because of the languages component, but the mutation that allowed him to move through time had remedied that problem.

"You have nowhere to stay?"

"No."

Quentus shook his head, presumably at Russ's folly, and fell silent for a time. "Where is your family?" he asked eventually.

"I have no family left," Russ replied. "My parents and sister died a few years ago."

"No lover?"

"None worth keeping," Russ said honestly. "I was coming to Nemausus to start over, hoping I would find something better."

A grunt was Quentus's only reply before he spurred the horse to the front of the column of soldiers, yelling at them for dawdling when home was only an hour's march away.

An hour.

Russ's stomach sank. In an hour, he could well have to watch Quentus set him down on the side of the road, wish him luck, and ride away. If it came to that, he'd find a place to hide and return to the château, but he hoped Quentus would give him some way of seeing him again before he had to go back. Quentus had used the word lover last night, although perhaps that didn't mean to him what it meant to Russ. He still hadn't figured out all the limitations of his newfound abilities.

The hour passed far too quickly for Russ despite the pain of riding, but Quentus didn't stop when they reached the city gates to drop him off. He kept one hand firmly on Russ's wrist as he dismissed the men, and kept riding with Russ behind him through the city streets until they reached what seemed to Russ to be a rather grand house in comparison to the ones around it.

"Ah, it is good to be home," Quentus said with a deep sigh as servants came running to take his horse. He swung down from the saddle and pulled Russ down into his arms. "Let's go inside. We will rest through the heat of the day and then go to the baths this evening. A long soak will help you relax."

"I should—"

"You should accept my hospitality," Quentus interrupted. "Nothing you had planned for today is so urgent it can't wait until tomorrow. Or the next day. Or a week from now. Come. It is cooler inside."

Quentus was right, since Russ couldn't search for a job or a place to live or anything else, given he'd be leaving in a week. If Quentus was willing to have him there, Russ should shut up and be thankful. He nodded and followed Quentus inside.

The interior of the house as they passed inside the entrance hall was dim and cool, as Quentus had promised. Quentus removed his sandals, so Russ followed suit, relieved to have the leather straps off the blisters that had flared again. The atrium was brighter, the open roof above the impluvium letting in light as well as rainwater, but the air was still markedly cooler than it had been in the street.

"Come," Quentus repeated, leading Russ through the atrium to another open-roofed room, this one planted with herbs and flowers and decorated with ornate statuary.

"Your home is beautiful," Russ said.

"It is home," Quentus said with a shrug as he passed through one of the doors around the garden. Russ hurried to follow him inside. This room was much smaller, without nearly the amount of decoration the other two rooms had displayed. A simple bed and chest stood on one wall. The rest of the room was empty.

Quentus shrugged off his uniform, leaving only his tunic in place. He lay down on the bed and let out a long, slow breath. Russ marveled at the difference he saw now that they were no longer on patrol. He had thought Quentus relaxed in the evenings, but seeing him now, truly relaxed, Russ realized how on guard Quentus had been the entire time.

"I could return the favor of the massage you gave me yesterday, though my hands are not as talented as yours."

"I didn't bring you here to be my servant," Quentus said without opening his eyes.

Russ was tempted to ask why Quentus had brought him there, but he chose discretion over valor. "I wasn't asking as a servant," he said. "I was asking as your lover."

Quentus's eyes opened at that comment, with something unreadable flashing in their dark-brown depths. It could have been warning, desire, or both. Russ held his gaze, waiting for permission but refusing to back down.

"If I need a massage, I'll call a servant," Quentus said finally.

"Fine," Russ said. "I'll be going then, since you have no need of me."

Quentus was off the bed in a flash, his hand closing around Russ's wrist. "I didn't tell you to leave."

"I wasn't asking permission," Russ retorted, the dominance that so turned him on while they were having sex now grating on his nerves. "You told me I wasn't a servant. I'm certainly not a slave. You made it clear you don't want me as a lover, so why should I stay?"

"I don't see how I could have made it any clearer that I *do* want you as a lover," Quentus said, his tone demanding an explanation. "I brought you here."

Russ was tempted to roll his eyes, but he didn't want to be smacked down for being disrespectful. "You obviously need a reminder how to treat a lover," he said instead. "I admit it. I liked it when you manhandled me in the tent. That doesn't mean I'm going to let you make every decision about everything else. I'm not a child. I'm not stupid, and I'm not your inferior in any way, no matter what rank you wear on your toga. When we're out there where people can see, I'll be as deferential as you want. I'll let you fuck me six ways from Sunday, and love every minute of it, but don't expect me to be a doormat."

"Do you know who I am?" Quentus blustered.

"You're Legatus Quentus Maximus, second in command to the governor of the province," Russ said, "but that's out there. In here, you're either my lover, which means I'm your lover in return, or I'm leaving."

"How dare you!" Quentus roared, but Russ had worked up too full a head of steam to back down now.

"Me! How dare you assume you get to make all the decisions? Yes, I know, everything that happens on patrol happens because of your orders, but I'm not one of your soldiers." He emphasized his final few words with pokes to Quentus's chest.

"You are beautiful when you're angry."

The words took the wind out of Russ's sails completely. He knew what he looked like when he lost his temper. His cheeks flared red to match his hair, making his freckles stand out in sharp contrast. He saw nothing beautiful about himself in a snit, but to judge by Quentus's expression, the other man disagreed.

"I'm not giving in just because you give me compliments."

"No, you're giving in because you like it when I take charge," Quentus said, pulling Russ against him and sliding hard hands beneath his tunic. Russ could feel the ridge of Quentus's erection press against his own and realized he was as fully hard as the centurion. Determined not simply to give in this time, he grabbed Quentus's head, pulling him into a kiss, their first despite the two nights of heated fucking.

Quentus's face was rough with stubble from the campaign, the whiskers scratching against Russ's lips as he was sure his own stubble scratched Quentus's face. Quentus kissed with the same masterful touch he did everything else, even if Russ had initiated it. His tongue surged into Russ's mouth, claiming him, and Russ let it happen. They hadn't finished their discussion, but maybe it didn't matter. He was leaving in a week.

Wasn't he?

THE sound of Quentus's snuffling breathing as he dozed at Russ's side shouldn't have been comforting. It should have annoyed Russ the same way it had with all his partners who'd snored in the past, but somehow he had the exact opposite reaction to Quentus.

About everything.

He shifted a little, feeling his ass protest the movement. The kiss had led to another round of incendiary sex, with Quentus driving Russ wild with need and then pushing him even farther. His domineering attitude in bed made for some fabulous fucking, and given the argument that had preceded the sex, Russ figured he'd get all the lovemaking he could stand. All he had to do was prick Quentus's temper a little.

The argument, the kiss, and the lovemaking afterward had been a bit of what his mama had always called a "come to Jesus" moment, that moment of revelation when everything he thought he knew crumbled and came back together remade.

Quentus was an arrogant, domineering Roman centurion, a product of his upbringing and his livelihood in much the same way Russ was the quiet, mousy librarian because of his upbringing and livelihood, but Russ hadn't given in when Quentus argued with him. He'd found the gumption to argue back, at least until Quentus kissed him and stole every rational thought from his head except one.

He didn't want to go home.

The thought had come out of left field, catching him totally off guard, but lying in bed, his body still humming from the incredible climax Quentus had wrung from his body, Russ couldn't dismiss it.

He had a job in Tucson, a scattering of acquaintances, and two house plants.

In Nemausus, he had Quentus.

It seemed like a more than fair trade-off, except they'd only known each other for three days. Russ's innate caution reared its head and pointed out all the problems with the choice: the precariousness of his relationship with Quentus, the lack of a job to contribute to their livelihood, the possibility that Quentus wouldn't want him forever, leaving Russ with nothing to return to if he cut all ties, the differences in their personalities. Today, that had led to a round of hot, sweaty sex, but a year from now, or five years from now, those differences would be like the sores on Russ's legs from riding, swollen pustules just waiting for the right moment to break open and spill their filth all over everything. They had to find some way to compromise if they had any hope of a real relationship, and Russ couldn't cut all ties with the future if he wasn't sure what he had in the past would last. He might have found the courage to come back in time, to stand up to Quentus today, to consider a new life, but he didn't have the courage to abandon his safety net entirely.

RUSS had found quite a few things he liked about life in Roman Gaul by the time they made their daily visit to the baths three days later—five days into the nine he had allowed himself on this trip, but the baths were definitely his favorite. Quentus went every day, something Russ had always read about but had never completely trusted, but for Quentus, the baths were the center of his social and political life. Russ wasn't about to complain, even if he still felt a little odd sitting around in the nude in a room full of other men. Their complete nonchalance had helped him relax, though, and Quentus insisted the *unctores* (one of the few words Russ hadn't managed to understand even with the help of his mutation, perhaps because the role didn't exist in the modern world) treat Russ to the same deep massages as they slathered him in bathing oil that they did all the other men who came to the baths.

It had quickly become Russ's favorite part of the day.

When they arrived at the baths that day, the slaves were all aflutter that the legatus Augusti pro praetore and his entourage were in the baths. Russ tensed, realizing this would be more than a simple relaxing afternoon if Quentus's superior was there. He would do his best to stay silent and in the shadows so he wouldn't accidentally embarrass Quentus through ignorance.

"Ah, Maximus, welcome home!"

"Thank you, Legatus," Quentus said with a deep bow as they entered the apodyterium. Russ mimicked the bow, holding his silence. "It is good to see you at the baths again."

"Bah, enough with the formality. We were brothers in arms for enough years for you to call me Septimus still. You have a new companion, I see."

"Yes, Septimus, this is Rastus. We rescued him from a boar a few days ago. He has been keeping me company ever since."

"Welcome to Nemausus, Rastus," the legatus said. "You will take good care of my Maximus, won't you?"

"Of course, sir," Russ said with another deep bow.

"Good. I will leave you to undress. I am for the caldarium."

The moment Septimus left the dressing room, another of his entourage approached. The expression on Quentus's face put Russ on his guard, not that he knew what he'd do to help other than maintain his silence.

"Maximus," the man sneered, "and with a new Northern prostitute in tow. You should think twice about insulting the legatus Augusti with his filth."

Quentus's hand shot out almost before the man finished speaking. "Watch yourself, Domitius," he said, his voice harder than Russ had ever heard it, even when Quentus had dressed down a soldier during the march back to Nemausus. "You have no right to insult Rastus. He is a Roman citizen and enjoys all the same rights as you. I will not have him insulted in my hearing."

"Just because you have Septimus's favor doesn't mean the rest of us will turn a blind eye," Domitius said around the constriction of Quentus's hand on his throat.

"Was that a threat?" Quentus demanded, shaking Domitius roughly. "Try me, Domitius. I'll meet you anywhere you choose. Come at me as often as you want, because we both know how that will end, but do not think to come at Rastus because I will cut you down like the dog you are if you so much as think of touching him." He shoved the other man back against the wall. "Do we understand one another?"

Russ did everything he could to keep his face a stoic mask so as not to give anyone more ammunition to use against Quentus, but

Quentus's display, both his physical strength and the sheer overwhelming confidence behind his words, left Russ wanting to do nothing more than drag Quentus home and offer himself to the centurion.

He knew that wouldn't happen, not after Quentus's ultimatum. Quentus might still be the first to leave, but only after he had fully enjoyed his bath and made sure Russ had done the same. Russ wondered if they could find a private alcove, or he was likely to embarrass himself in the baths.

Domitius snarled at Quentus but slunk away without answering. Only when the man had left the room did Quentus turn to look at Russ, the temper in his expression swiftly changing to a different kind of heat. He stroked Russ's cheek gently. "Careful, Russ, or you will make them think they were right."

"It's not my fault you make me needy," Russ grumbled, but his words held no heat. Quentus had called him Russ, not Rastus—the first time he had done so. Perhaps it meant nothing, but Russ chose to take it as another sign that he had come to mean something to Quentus.

Quentus laughed. "Let us bathe and then I will take you home and take care of all your needs."

"Surely there's somewhere here where we could...?" He waved his hand around the room.

"I'm sure there is," Quentus said, "but I will not besmirch your honor any more than I will let them do so. Come. Let us bathe."

RUSS let the conversation in the caldarium swirl around him. At Quentus's insistence, they had stopped first in the cold baths to help kill Russ's erection, although he was still at half-mast, and that wasn't likely to change as long as his thoughts kept circling around the infuriating, dominating, amazing man sitting at Russ's side discussing politics with the Legatus Augusti.

Hot sex was one thing, but it had gone beyond sex. Quentus wouldn't have defended Russ the way he had if Russ didn't mean something to him. Maybe not everything Quentus was starting to mean to Russ, but something.

And if he meant something to Quentus, he might be in a position to influence the man's behavior in his regard, to convince Quentus to see him as a partner. Maybe, but not in four days, not conclusively.

No, whatever he decided, he had to go back. The questions were for how long and to do what?

He could go back, write the time in Gaul off as a pleasant vacation interlude, and return to his life. He could let this all go and hope he found someone in Tucson who made him feel all the things Quentus made him feel.

Or he could make plans, go back, and apply for a leave of absence. The departmental director would be surprised since Russ hadn't mentioned it before, but he could tell the man he'd had a breakdown and needed a year away from work to recover, that he might be back sooner, but he didn't want to rush the process. He could hire a moving company to put his furniture in storage and break the lease on his apartment. He only had a month left anyway and hadn't gotten around to renewing yet. He could roll the dice and take a chance on Quentus.

What did he have to lose?

CHAPTER
FIVE

"I HAVE to leave for a few days."

"Why?" The tone of Quentus's voice left no doubt of his displeasure.

"I have something I need to do," Russ said, trying to answer as honestly as possible without telling Quentus more than he could expect the man to believe. "It will only be a day or two. Three at the most." If he were more experienced, he could probably time his departure and return during the hours Quentus was at the forum, but Russ didn't dare take that chance. He didn't want to misjudge the timing and meet himself coming and going. Bernard had been too clear about what would ensue if he did that. No, taking a couple of days was safer.

"What?" Quentus asked. "What do you need to do?"

Russ had worried this would happen. "Nothing you can help me with," he said. "I will go, attend to my business, and be back before you have time to miss me."

"I will come with you," Quentus declared.

"You can't," Russ replied, hoping Quentus would let it go. They'd just finished another round of bone-melting sex, but Russ figured he could distract his lover if he had to. Quentus wouldn't turn down a blow job because he'd never had a lover willing to do that for him. Prostitutes, but not a lover. That made no sense to

Russ, but he wasn't going to complain about anything that set him apart from the people who'd come before him in Quentus's life.

"Why not?"

"Because you can't," Russ said. "I'll be gone a few days and then I'll come back and stay as long as you want me."

Quentus opened his mouth to argue again, but Russ took the initiative, even knowing that wouldn't last for long, kissing Quentus and pushing him back on the bed.

He snuck out of their bed and the house the next morning while Quentus was in the other room seeing to his ablutions. It was cowardly and he knew it, but it was that or argue with Quentus again and maybe lose.

THE minute the château d'Eternité coalesced around Russ, he regretted leaving Nemausus. He knew it was necessary, but everything about it felt wrong.

"Ah, Russ, you are back sooner than I expected. Was Gaul not to your liking?"

"On the contrary," Russ said. "It was so much to my liking I didn't want to leave."

"And yet here you are, three days early. It would seem there's a story to be told."

Russ had quite the story to tell, and he could relate it to Bernard. No one outside the château would ever believe it, but Bernard would. He'd listen to every moment Russ was willing to share and accept it exactly as Russ recounted it. "I met someone."

"Ah, that complicates matters," Bernard said with a sigh. "Take your time freshening up and then join me in the parlor. We will talk."

Russ didn't like the sound of that. He couldn't let Bernard dissuade him from his path, but he went upstairs dutifully to change into his own clothes.

The spray from the shower that two weeks ago had felt too weak, compared to the water pressure at home, now seemed like little needles striking his skin, accustomed as he'd become to relaxing in the baths. His trousers felt confining, squeezing his body in places the tunic and *subligar* left unhindered. He left the top two buttons of his shirt undone, but even that felt constrictive after the loose Roman garb he'd been wearing.

As he walked toward the parlor, he shored up his determination. Everything here felt foreign now. Nemausus now felt like home.

"So tell me about her," Bernard said when Russ joined him in the parlor.

"Him," Russ corrected automatically.

"So tell me about him," Bernard said, not at all flustered by Russ's correction.

That helped in some immeasurable way. Russ relaxed a little and gave Bernard a highly edited version of what had transpired while he had been away. Bernard didn't need to know how often or thoroughly Russ had been fucked while he was gone.

"And what do you plan to do now?" Bernard asked when Russ had finished.

"Take a leave of absence for a year," Russ said. "Go back and see what happens."

"And if something happens after that year?" Bernard asked. "If Quentus is killed or deposed or even simply decides to bow to the pressure of marrying to carry on his name, what will you do then?"

"I don't know," Russ said honestly. "I haven't thought that far ahead, because it won't be an issue if I don't get through this year first. I know what I want, but he's harder to read. I think he cares about me enough to let me stay, but I can't be sure after only a few days. That's why I want the year's sabbatical. It won't address the concerns you raised, but it will give me time to be sure of him, at least. If nothing else, I'll come back here and see about starting over

56

as an archeologist in the Roman ruins. I'll certainly know where to look and what to look for if I've lived there for a number of years."

Bernard laughed. "How do you think they found King Tut's tomb? All right, you've thought this through and are clearly determined to do it. So tell me what you're going to say to your employer."

"You aren't going to try to talk me out of it?" Russ asked, surprised.

"I'm not your keeper," Bernard reminded him, "just the keeper of the château. What you do with your skills once you've learned to use them responsibly is your choice, not mine."

Russ let out the breath he hadn't been aware of holding and let Bernard help him plan his approach.

RUSS sighed in relief when the familiar façade of Quentus's house came into view. He'd misjudged the location slightly and ended up in an unfamiliar part of Nemausus. He hadn't wanted to ask for Quentus directly, but he'd found the baths finally and made his way home from there.

Home.

The word felt right, the way nothing had felt right back in the twenty-first century. His clothes hadn't fit right. The shower hadn't felt right. Talking with his boss had seemed strange beyond words.

That was all done now. He had a year's leave of absence, albeit a grudging one. He had a moving company putting his belongings in storage for a year. He had everything in place. Now he just had to convince Quentus to forgive him for disappearing. He refused to accept any other outcome. If only his heart would stop trying to beat its way out of his chest.

He pushed open the door and stepped into the atrium. Quentus stood in the center of the room in full armor, shouting orders. Russ's heart fell. He'd only made it back and Quentus was leaving. He paused on the edge of the marble floor, wondering if he'd turned his life upside down for nothing.

Then Quentus turned, saw him, and crossed the distance between them in a few long strides. "You're back," he said, crushing Russ against his chest, heedless of the way the armor bit into Russ's body. "I couldn't wait any longer. I was coming to find you."

Russ sagged against Quentus with relief. "I told you I'd come back. I've only been gone a few days."

"A few days too many," Quentus growled, dragging Russ toward the bedroom, dismissing the servants with a wave of his hand. "You shouldn't have left at all."

"I'm sorry," Russ said, not sure why he was apologizing except that Quentus was upset and Russ wanted to appease him. "It's done now. I'm back to stay."

That wasn't strictly true, but he had a year before he had to worry about it again, and hopefully a year from now, Quentus would trust him more.

"Yes, you are," Quentus agreed, shutting the door behind them and then stripping off his armor. "If I have to chain you to the bed to keep you here."

"I'm not your slave," Russ retorted, not willing to give Quentus too much leeway, even in the wake of his own apparent desertion.

"No, you aren't," Quentus replied, "but you are mine."

Russ started to argue, despite the thrill that went through him at Quentus's words, but Quentus seemed to have learned Russ's trick, stopping his words with a torrid kiss. Russ had known Quentus had a dominant side; he had proven that every time they went to bed. It made sense that it would extend to being possessive as well.

Quentus licked into Russ's mouth, dragging a groan from Russ. He had only been gone a few days, but he had missed the feeling of Quentus's hands on his body, Quentus's mouth on his,

Quentus's cock up his ass. The need he felt around Quentus still surprised him. He had never had a particularly active sex life. He'd never needed it until the first time Quentus looked at him with those velvety dark eyes and Russ had melted like chocolate left too long in the sun.

Slick fingers probed Russ's entrance, bringing his thoughts back to the present. He broke the kiss to shrug off the clothes Quentus had not already pushed aside. Quentus herded him toward the bed, not that Russ needed any encouragement. He scrambled away and onto the mattress on his hands and knees, offering himself to Quentus in the most obvious way possible.

The crack of Quentus's hand against his backside was as unexpected as it was painful. Russ startled upward, trying to get free, but Quentus's grasp was as implacable as ever.

"You're mine," Quentus growled in his ear. "You don't get to disappear with no explanation. It's not allowed."

Russ opened his mouth to protest, but Quentus robbed him of the ability to speak once more, driving his fingers deep into Russ's body and finding his gland with unerring accuracy. The tingling from the blow lingered but the pain faded, leaving an afterglow of sorts in its place. Russ relaxed into the feeling, rocking back against Quentus's fingers as much as he could with Quentus's other hand clamped hard on his flank.

"Don't move," Quentus ordered. "You left me. You owe this to me."

Russ might have argued if he hadn't wanted Quentus as badly as he did, but he wasn't about to say or do anything to stop his masterful lover from taking his pleasure, not when he knew how much pleasure he would get in return.

The burn of a third finger made Russ moan and squirm, but Quentus stilled him with another slap to his ass. "Stay still."

Russ froze, not sure how he felt about the chastisement or the way his cock jumped this time in anticipation of the tingling warmth that would follow, but his body burned with need. The rest would have to wait until they were sated.

Quentus gave him what he needed, as always, playing Russ's body like a lyre, until Russ could do nothing but hang there between Quentus's hands, so taut with need he could hardly move. Quentus growled orders in his ear, and Russ obeyed without thinking. He already knew the heights of ecstasy to be found at Quentus's mercy. His mind clicked off and his body took over, until Quentus whispered for him to come and he did, his climax wringing him out like an old rag. He collapsed onto the bed as Quentus pounded into him and found his own ease. Russ didn't flinch at the final swat Quentus landed on his now lax buttocks. The slight jolt of pain simply blended with the other sensations inundating him.

Russ wanted to stay awake, to say something to Quentus about his departure, his return, Quentus's reaction, anything, but satiation and the release of tension he had not known he was carrying until Quentus welcomed him back were too much for his overloaded brain. He let his exhaustion lull him into sleep.

RUSS awoke sometime later, several hours, to judge by the position of the sun coming in the small window. He could get up and check the sundial in the atrium, but that would require moving, and he was far too comfortable for that. He wondered idly where Quentus was, but the space beside him was empty.

An ewer stood on the low chest against the far wall, clean cloths waiting next to it, so Russ took that as an invitation to rise and bathe. He hoped it wasn't too late for a trip to the baths, but he could at least get rid of the stickiness between his legs before he dressed and went in search of Quentus.

He hissed a little as he stood, the movement reminding him just how thoroughly he'd been fucked before falling asleep. He'd missed the feeling while he was gone. Maybe he'd try to lure Quentus back to bed for another round before they went to the baths.

He peered over his shoulder as he cleaned up, trying to see if any sign of the spanking Quentus had given him lingered, but from what he could see, his ass had returned to its usual pasty white color. He frowned a little, as he always did when he let himself think about his appearance, but Quentus didn't seem to mind his pale skin, so Russ pushed the negativity away. He had enough real problems to worry about without adding imaginary ones.

Like the fact that he'd let Quentus spank him like a child for something Russ had warned him about ahead of time. He wasn't sure who that spoke worse of: him for allowing it or Quentus for thinking he had the right to do it in the first place.

Russ wasn't so innocent that he hadn't heard of people playing those kinds of games for the pleasure of it. He'd had a housemate while he was working on his master's degree who spent some time in leather clubs and relished the thought of shocking Russ with descriptions of everything he'd seen or done each time he went out. It wasn't the idea of spanking that shocked him. It was his reaction to it. He didn't like pain. It had never done anything for him. He barely even tolerated love bites. His college roommate had teased him about being shy because, even when he was dating someone seriously, he never had visible marks above his collar. The roommate assumed they were just hidden, but Russ had always protested before his lovers could leave any kind of mark on his skin. It hurt too much, and he didn't like that.

"So why the hell did I let Quentus spank me?" Russ muttered as he found his clothes and pulled them back on haphazardly. He rubbed his hand over his ass again, realizing that unlike the bite marks he'd always shied away from, the swats from Quentus hadn't left bruises or even any tenderness. They'd hurt in the moment, but the soreness hadn't lingered, visibly or otherwise.

He wasn't sure that should make a difference, but just thinking about Quentus's hands on him was making him hard again. He tried to focus on the swats themselves to see if the reaction would change, but they were tangled up in everything else Quentus had done and said. The sense of being wanted, of being *claimed*, was so strong that it overwhelmed the wrongness of accepting the blows.

He let out a huff. "Now what do I do?"

Forcing away thoughts of sex for the moment, because he had already proven his body would react to Quentus's touch regardless of his past predilections, Russ focused on the larger situation. He had made the decision to come back to Nemausus, to stay with Quentus, but if this was to be his life now, he had to find a way to support himself. He couldn't stay dependent on Quentus forever.

He could understand and speak any language he heard, and he could read and write some Latin. With a little practice, he would get better at that too. He would never survive as a soldier, and he didn't have the skill to work in any of the trades he had seen practiced as he and Quentus made their way through town to the baths, but he could read and write, a useful skill in an age where only a portion of the population was literate. He had no idea how to go about establishing himself as a scribe or translator, but Quentus might know.

Now he just had to find his absent lover so he could get started. He rose and stretched, anticipation singing along his nerves as he envisioned his new life.

CHAPTER SIX

THE wooden doors between the peristylium and the atrium were closed, something Russ had never seen in the time he'd spent at Quentus's house, but he thought nothing of it as he looked around the garden for Quentus. He did not hear his lover's commanding voice in any of the smaller rooms surrounding the garden, although the curtains across the doorways kept him from seeing inside. He had started toward the doors and the atrium when a servant stepped between him and his goal.

"Excuse me, sir," the servant said, his head bowed slightly, "but Legatus Maximus said you were not to leave this area of the house without him."

Russ could almost see the servant bracing for a blow or a fight or some sort of retaliation, but the shock of the servant's statement kept him silent and still for a moment. As the words sunk in, anger surged through him, but he took a deep breath, reining himself in. The servant was only the messenger, not the source of the order or the object of Russ's ire. He could berate the man, possibly force his way out of the peristylium and even out of the house, but he would gain nothing from that show of force except to put the servant in the position of having to explain to Quentus what had happened. The man in front of him with the bowed head and apologetic expression had done nothing to deserve the punishment that would surely follow. Russ was not an expert on ancient Rome, but he knew enough to know that a man in Quentus's position would think nothing of disciplining his servants.

"Can I sit here in the peristylium or am I confined to the bedroom?" Russ asked, doing his best to keep his voice level. He doubted he succeeded completely, but the hunted look left the servant's eyes, which Russ counted as a victory.

"You are allowed in any of the rooms on this side of the doors," the servant explained. "The legatus was most explicit about that."

"Then I will sit here in the fresh air for a bit," Russ said, dismissing the man with a nod, although he was certain the surveillance would continue from behind the curtains of the rooms where the servants worked, preparing the evening meal and tending to whatever other chores they had.

When the servant disappeared back to his duties, Russ took a seat in one of the chairs beneath the shaded portion of the room. The day was still cool, but Russ knew better than to sit in the sun without the benefit of sunscreen, a luxury not found in his current time. With his fair skin, freckles, and red hair, he'd be the color of a tomato in ten minutes and have no way to relieve the pain either, since he didn't see any aloe plants growing in the garden. He had no idea if it was even known in this part of the world. Botany had never been part of his historical research.

His thoughts raced, despite the outward appearance of calm he tried to project so the servants would leave him alone. A part of him couldn't believe Quentus would give such an order, but he also recognized the command as the same kind of discipline Quentus would use with his soldiers, servants, or slaves. Russ wasn't at all sure how he felt about being lumped in any of those categories, and it rankled that Quentus had not bothered telling Russ himself. It wouldn't have made the edict any more pleasant, but at least it wouldn't have been a surprise and Russ could have avoided the humiliation of having the servants know he had been confined like a child.

That rankled more than anything. He had upended his life completely for Quentus. He had taken a sabbatical from work, broken the lease on his apartment, and left behind everything and everyone he knew to stay with Quentus, only to be treated like a disobedient child. He'd told Quentus he had to leave for a few days. He'd given the man fair warning, and he'd come back exactly like he said he would. Where did Quentus get off thinking he could punish Russ like one of his underlings? Russ had a PhD in medieval history, for God's sake. He wasn't some foundling Quentus had picked up off the street and taken in with no resources and no hope of an independent life!

For a moment, he seriously considered closing his eyes, concentrating, and returning back to the château d'Eternité. He couldn't go back to Tucson right away, but he could pick a different time period and explore it in a way that really could benefit his career. He could spend some time in thirteenth- or fourteenth-century France or Germany, maybe take a peek in Florence or Genoa. He could even head to London and catch some of Shakespeare's original performances. The entire world was open to him. He didn't have to stay here and put up with Quentus's bullshit.

He had taken a deep breath, steadying himself for the trip, when the doors swung open, startling him. He looked up and found Quentus standing in the archway in the most formal toga Russ had ever known him to wear. Usually Quentus dressed in his uniform or in a plain toga when they were going to the baths, but this was nothing so simple. Russ didn't know where Quentus had been, but it was clearly important.

The realization did nothing to blunt his anger at Quentus's orders, but it did ease his frustration at having to hear those orders from a servant. If Quentus was dressed this formally, he probably hadn't had a choice in his departure.

"Where were you?" Russ asked, biting back his anger long enough to confirm that one detail. He intended to have words— *strong* words—with Quentus, but he would do Quentus the courtesy of only upbraiding him for actual mistakes, not things out of his control.

Maybe.

"Legatus Septimus summoned me," Quentus said. "The regional governor wanted to meet with him and his generals."

"You couldn't have woken me up?" Russ asked. "Maybe told me where you were going or that you intended to confine me to quarters?"

"There was no time," Quentus said. "I was nearly late as it was, and that would have reflected poorly on Legatus Septimus and on me."

Russ nodded slowly, pursing his lips in frustration. "So instead I wake up to find you gone with no explanation and a servant gets to tell me I can't even go into the atrium. I'm having a bit of a problem with that."

"You disappeared," Quentus roared. "You snuck out of my bed and my house with nary a word."

"I told you I had to leave for a few days," Russ shouted back. "I told you I'd come back. And I did."

"You didn't tell me you were leaving," Quentus retorted. "You said you would have to leave, but then suddenly you were gone. I tore the city apart looking for you, but no one had seen any trace of you. It was like the gods had simply swept you up into nothingness." Quentus grabbed Russ's shoulders, shaking him slightly. "Do you have any idea how desperate I was?"

The idea that Quentus had missed him to that degree appeased some of Russ's feeling of being of minimal importance to the centurion, but it did not change the current restrictions on his movements. "No," Russ said, forcing his voice to return to his usual calm. "I don't have any idea how desperate you were, but you have to have faith in me."

"You're keeping secrets."

"Maybe I am," Russ admitted, because how was he supposed to explain to his Roman warrior that he could travel through time because of a genetic mutation? "We've known each other for a week, Quentus. You have secrets too, or at least there are things I don't know about you yet. That's not the point. The point is that you're treating me like a naughty child. I'm not a child. I'm a man, and I have the right to make my own decisions."

"Not when those decisions impact me as well," Quentus disagreed.

"I didn't think you'd care if I was gone," Russ said. "I wasn't even sure you'd notice."

"The gods gave you to me when they put me in the right place to save your life," Quentus replied. "I would never scorn their gifts that way. For as long as I live, I will watch over and protect you."

How was he supposed to argue with that?

"Could we discuss the way you do that?" Russ asked after a moment. "I am still not a child, nor a servant to be disciplined."

Quentus frowned but nodded. "What would you discuss?"

"Not confining me to the house, for one thing," Russ said. "I need to find a way to support myself."

"Why?" Quentus asked suspiciously. "I have more than enough to support a family."

There it was again, Russ thought, caught halfway between scowling and smiling besottedly, that assumption that Russ belonged right where he was, with Quentus. "That's not the point," Russ said. "I need to feel I'm contributing to our well-being. I'm not a woman. I wouldn't know the first thing about maintaining your house or overseeing your servants. I can't be useful that way, so I need to be useful some other way."

Quentus looked at Russ suspiciously, but Russ plowed on. "Think about how you would feel if I took your legion away from you. What would you do with your time and energy? How would you feel about suddenly having nothing to do?"

"I would be most unhappy," Quentus said slowly.

"I never had a legion under my command," Russ said, "but I need something to do, some way to contribute."

"And what would you suggest?"

"I write a fine hand," Russ replied, "and I have a gift for languages. I could find work either as a scribe or perhaps helping in discussions with foreign emissaries if you have those here in Nemausus."

"Not often," Quentus said. "We are not near the borders of the empire here, but we often host travelers from other lands on their way to Rome. The local tradesmen might appreciate the assistance when it comes time to negotiate for goods or services."

"I could do that," Russ said. "I saw the tabernae in the front of the house are empty. I could set up shop there and—"

"No," Quentus interrupted. "You have no need to sell yourself like the poorest common laborer. You will not demean yourself by hawking your skills that way, nor will you turn my house into a market. The tabernae here are for storage, not commerce. When we do this, we will do it more subtly. You will start by being my scribe. I will boast to my friends about the quality of my new scribe's abilities, and when they ask, I will bring them here to meet you."

"That hardly counts as me being independent," Russ protested. "You would still be controlling everything."

"You said nothing about independence," Quentus replied with a frown. "You spoke of contributing. You would be contributing this way, both to me personally and to the household."

Russ barely refrained from rolling his eyes. "Explain to me why I can't use a taberna," he said slowly. "Even if you don't want me using one of yours."

"You are a member of my household now," Quentus said. "Your actions reflect on me. I would not let a son of mine work in such lowly conditions. I cannot let my lover do so either."

"See?" Russ said. "That wasn't so hard. Now that you've explained, it makes sense, but I need you to explain things instead of ordering me about. I don't care if that's how you do things with the legion. It won't work with me."

Quentus's eyes narrowed. "I don't let my men challenge my orders. Why should I let you?"

"Because I'm not one of your soldiers or one of your dependents," Russ said.

Quentus raised an eyebrow.

"Fine. I'm dependent right now, but only until I can find work as a scribe."

"Even the best paid scribes would not have a home like this," Quentus pointed out. "You could work from dawn until dusk and beyond, and you would still be my dependent."

Russ could not argue with that assertion. He had walked the streets of Nemausus. Few houses were as grand as Quentus's. He had no idea what a scribe would earn, but it would be nothing compared to the salary Quentus earned as a Roman general. Few positions were more respected, especially outside of the capital. As long as he lived with Quentus, no matter how much he contributed himself, Quentus would earn the bulk of their income. "I won't be just a kept man," he said instead. "I need to feel like I'm contributing to our life together. Maybe I won't earn what you do, but I need to do something."

"And you will," Quentus promised, "but we must do it right or we will both suffer for it." He withdrew a missive from his toga. "We will start with this. There is paper and ink in the tablinum. We will read the news from Rome and see how to reply. Consider it your first job."

Russ started toward the tablinum, but Quentus stopped him. "We will work at the table here. You were gone for four days. You will stay behind these doors for that same length of time."

"That is stupid!" Russ burst out.

"I would say it is a fitting punishment for the crime," Quentus countered, "unless you would prefer I punish you the way I would a runaway slave? I doubt you would appreciate the whip the way you did my hand."

Russ bit his tongue. He had taken more enjoyment from the few swats than he would have believed possible, but not enough to want anything rougher. He considered arguing, but he had already learned what the mulish expression on Quentus's face meant. He could argue. He could scream and shout and threaten to leave, but short of actually going for good this time, he wouldn't change Quentus's mind. He could either accept the other man's orders or he could give up on this new life. Reminding himself that he could leave at any time and that four days at home was hardly the worst thing Quentus could order him to do, Russ nodded his acquiescence.

RUSS had never really thought about conveniences like running water until he traveled to Nemausus the first time, but even then, the baths at the center of town made that a negligible concern since they went to the baths every day. As he prepared for bed that night, sticky with sweat and still smelling of sex despite having wiped himself down earlier, he missed the convenience of slipping into a hot shower. If Quentus said anything, Russ would just tell him it was his fault for not letting Russ leave to go to the baths. The flippancy of the thought did nothing to keep him from scrubbing his underarms and groin to alleviate the worst of it, though. He hated going to bed dirty.

"Come to bed," Quentus ordered from the other side of the room.

"In a minute," Russ said, rinsing the cloth in the bowl and then rubbing at his face and neck.

"Russ," Quentus said. "Come to bed."

"I'm dirty and sticky and I stink," Russ protested. "Let me finish cleaning up."

Quentus huffed and rose from where he reclined on the bed. He crossed to Russ's side and took the rag from his hand. "I spend weeks on campaign with soldiers and no means of bathing. One day's layer of sweat and the smell of my own spend on your body are hardly enough to dissuade me. Come to bed."

Russ let himself be led, his head already spinning from the mere touch of Quentus's hand. He had intended to take the lead in their lovemaking tonight, if only to regain some sense of control over his own life, but all it took was Quentus touching him and already Russ felt himself giving in.

He sank to his knees at the slightest pressure from Quentus's hands on his shoulders, not waiting to be told as he leaned in and nuzzled Quentus's cock.

"You are the only person who has ever done that for me willingly," Quentus gasped, stroking his fingers through Russ's hair. Russ figured their loss was his gain as he focused on giving Quentus as much pleasure as he could. It wasn't what he'd planned (not that he thought Quentus would actually let him top or anything, but he'd intended it to be a little more his idea) but it was still something he could give Quentus that no one else would without either extra incentive or explicit orders. Russ didn't need either. The taste of Quentus's cock and his little groans of pleasure were all the incentive he needed to suck harder and take Quentus deeper into his throat. Quentus's hand settled on the back of Russ's neck, holding Russ in place as Quentus fucked his face. Russ just opened his mouth wider and closed his eyes, letting Quentus take control. "You are so beautiful like this," Quentus murmured, stroking Russ's cheek with his other hand. "I could watch you like this all night."

Yes, please. Russ couldn't answer aloud because Quentus hadn't pulled back enough to let him speak, but he looked up at Quentus with pleading eyes, hoping his eagerness would show on his face. "You would do that for me, wouldn't you?" Quentus asked. "You would stay right there and let me take my pleasure in your mouth or on your face. You would let me mark you as mine."

Russ wasn't so sure about having Quentus come on his face, but he'd never had any problem swallowing with a lover he trusted, and he trusted Quentus. He nodded as much as he could in Quentus's hold.

71

Quentus grunted and Russ braced himself against the coming onslaught, but to his surprise, Quentus stayed in control of his thrusts, only barely hitting the back of Russ's throat, never enough to even come close to triggering his gag reflex. He wanted to tell Quentus he could relax his control, but that would mean pulling away, and even if he could, he didn't want to. He tried bobbing his head forward to meet Quentus's next thrust, intending to show his lover in actions what he couldn't say in words, but Quentus caught him before he could move far enough, keeping him in place. "I won't hurt you," Quentus said, his voice like velvet against Russ's skin.

Russ relaxed into Quentus's control. He could talk to Quentus later, assure his lover he could take, indeed would gladly take, more. For now he would enjoy the salty taste coating his tongue and do what he could to add to Quentus's pleasure. When the flood of fluid hit the back of his throat seconds later, he decided he'd succeeded.

Quentus's grip relaxed as the aftershocks of his climax faded, but he did not release Russ entirely. Russ was tempted to stroke his own nagging erection since Quentus didn't seem in any hurry to take care of it, but he held back for the moment. Since becoming Quentus's lover, he'd started learning the value of patience, aided mostly by the fact that Quentus made him feel things he didn't feel on his own.

After a moment, Quentus sat down on the bed and patted the space beside him. "Come here."

Russ scrambled off his knees and onto the bed, waiting without even being told for Quentus's next order. Quentus urged him onto his back. "Do not touch yourself," he ordered, running long fingers down the length of Russ's cock before sliding lower to his balls and entrance. Russ planted his feet and lifted his hips instead, begging silently for Quentus to fuck him with his fingers. "You are eager."

"I just spent the past half hour taking care of you," Russ said. "It's got me a little worked up."

Quentus traced Russ's entrance with the tip of one finger, teasing rather than probing. Russ mewled in protest, but Quentus ignored him, as insistent as always at taking things at his own pace instead of whatever pace Russ would prefer. When he was not desperate for more contact, Russ could admit that Quentus's choices paid off in the long run, but at that moment, the featherlight touch and lack of something inside him left Russ too needy to rationalize away the pleas that fell from his lips.

"Patience," Quentus ordered when Russ pressed against Quentus's hand, trying for deeper contact. Russ ignored the word, arching his back more. The slap of Quentus's hand across his inner thigh, far too close to his balls for comfort, shocked him into collapsing on the mattress.

"What was that for?" Russ demanded, trying to sit up, but Quentus's hand on his chest stopped him.

"That was for not listening to me," Quentus said. "You know I will give you what you need and more, but I will do it my way."

"What if I don't like your way?" Russ demanded.

"Then tell me to stop," Quentus replied, "and I won't touch you again, but if you aren't going to say no, then I will touch you when and as I decide is best."

"I just spent thirty minutes on my knees for you," Russ reminded him. "I could use some relief here."

"And you will get it," Quentus said. "When I say you're ready. If I let you rush, it will be over until you are recovered enough for a second round, perhaps not until morning, if we fall asleep, or even tomorrow night if my duties call me away. If you let me control your pleasure, *my* patience will guarantee a far more powerful release because you will have waited for it."

Russ knew Quentus was right. He could lie there and force his rational mind to accept it, but his body, God, how his body ached. "It probably won't stop me from begging," he said by way of acceptance.

Quentus smiled, the expression so fraught with lust, dominance, self-satisfaction, and predatory intent that Russ shivered. "I never said you shouldn't beg."

Russ opened his mouth to ask what Quentus thought Russ had been doing since he got on the bed, but Quentus chose that moment to stab deep with the finger that had not stopped its teasing, finding Russ's gland and scratching over it with a blunt fingernail. The sound that came out was far more of a shriek than anything else. Russ thrashed on the bed as Quentus played over his gland, one tiny step shy of pain whenever his fingernail would catch the sensitive flesh instead of his finger. He couldn't think, couldn't speak, couldn't even manage incoherent begging. He needed to come, but just when he thought he couldn't hold it back any longer, Quentus clamped his other hand around the base of Russ's cock, stopping his climax.

He lost track of how many fingers Quentus had inside him. Two for sure, maybe three—he couldn't concentrate enough to judge the bulk filling him, twisting and stretching, plundering his ass and hijacking his senses. He was past the point of sensibility, so desperate to come he would have done anything, promised anything, just to get Quentus to offer him surcease. He took a deep breath in preparation for one last attempt at begging when Quentus released the pressure on his cock and leaned over to kiss him deeply. Russ cried out into the kiss as his climax blindsided him. He collapsed onto the bed, panting harshly as Quentus continued to stroke in and out of him with his fingers.

Russ shuddered through the aftershocks, a new one hitting each time Quentus passed over his prostate.

Finally it was too much and he flinched away. Quentus withdrew his hand immediately, settling Russ with tender caresses along his hip and side. The postcoital lethargy was so strong Russ struggled to keep his eyes open, but Quentus simply kissed his temple and whispered for him to sleep.

Russ's final thought before unconsciousness stole all thought was that having Quentus in charge was not such a terrible thing.

CHAPTER
SEVEN

THAT feeling lasted until Quentus got ready to leave for the forum shortly before lunch the next day. They had risen and prepared for the day, Russ feeling the aftereffects of both the fucking and the fingering Quentus had given him the day before. He was looking forward to soaking in the baths and said as much as Quentus was changing into his toga after breakfast.

"You have three more days of confinement," Quentus reminded him. "You will have to make do with the ewer and bowl for now."

"I'd be going with you," Russ protested. "I wouldn't ever be out of your sight. I'm more likely to disappear if I'm not with you than if I am."

"This isn't about you disappearing now or in the future," Quentus said calmly. "Although if you do such a thing again, I really will tie you to my bed. This is your punishment for disappearing last week. Now, will you accept it like a man or must you be locked in like a child with no self-control?"

Russ glared at Quentus, but limited his protest to that. "Fine," he said with a huff. "I'll stay in the house, but that doesn't mean I like it."

"The point of any punishment is rather that you don't like it," Quentus said, the twinkle in his eye rubbing Russ the wrong way. "It would be no deterrent against future bad behavior if you enjoyed the consequences."

Fuck that, Russ thought, but he kept his silence. He stayed in the peristylium and glared at Quentus as the centurion finished his preparations for whatever the day would bring and then stroked Russ's cheek one last time before leaving. "I will be home this afternoon," he promised. "I have letters to write, and I will be sure to praise my new scribe at the forum today so others will pay attention the next time they receive correspondence from me. You may not be there yourself, but I will ensure people are thinking about you."

The promise mollified Russ enough that he stayed where he was after Quentus left. Once the peristylium was empty again, Russ sat down at the table Quentus had ordered to be moved into the garden so he would have a place to write. He picked up the letter they had received the day before and took a deep breath, trying to concentrate on the letters themselves, on the way they were formed and the way they were spaced on the page. He picked up the quill and traced over them, forcing his eyes to see the Latin letters rather than the translation his brain supplied automatically now. He could not afford to make a mistake and insert a word in English instead of in Latin. If he concentrated, he could do it, but with Quentus in the room and at the speed he would have to take dictation in order to function as a scribe, he needed all the practice he could get. He didn't have blank paper, though, and he couldn't go get it because it was in the tablinum, and that was on the other side of those damned wooden doors.

"Excuse me, sir," a servant said, appearing from somewhere. Russ had been so lost in his thoughts he hadn't heard the footsteps approaching. "The legatus asked me to check on you from time to time to make sure you didn't need anything."

Russ briefly considered asking to leave, but he didn't want to put the servants in a bad spot today any more than he had yesterday. "Could you bring me some paper from the tablinum?" he asked instead. "I have a letter to write for the legatus, and since I can't leave this area, I can't do my work."

"That is most unlike the legatus," the servant replied with a shake of his head. "He may dole out punishments when they are merited, but he doesn't usually leave us unable to fulfill our duties."

"I'm sure he simply forgot," Russ said, "but I would not want him to think poorly of me on his return."

"Of course not," the servant agreed. "I will fetch paper for you."

The man disappeared through the doors and then returned moments later with the requested paper. "Thank you," Russ said. "I'm sorry. I don't know your name."

"Antony," the servant said. "My mother was perhaps overly optimistic when she named me."

"I'm Rastus," Russ said, remembering the name he had given when he first arrived in Gaul, "but most people call me Russ."

"I couldn't presume," the servant demurred.

Russ almost insisted, but his own background in medieval history was full of the class distinctions no one questioned at the time. He couldn't expect a servant in a Roman household to take the liberty of calling him by his first name, especially not the first time they met. "How long have you been with the legatus?" he asked instead.

"I have been with his family since his father was a small child," Antony replied. "I was only a few years older when I first began working here in the garden. Now I am too old for that, or for much of anything, but the legatus will not hear talk of me leaving. He insists he needs someone who knew him when he was in swaddling clothes."

Russ smiled. "I bet he was as stubborn as a boy as he is now." The image of a much younger Quentus with his face clenched up in a belligerent pout was almost worth being confined to the house.

"Not at all," Antony said. "He was a very biddable child, the center of his mother's world. His military training is responsible for his stubbornness. He came home from his first campaign a changed man."

Russ could see that. He had known more than one classmate in high school and college who joined the military, and he had seen the effects it had on them in an age of mechanized warfare, when much of what happened was at a distance. For the Roman legions, all the fighting would be at the other end of a sword or lance or, at the most, a javelin. Any sort of military campaign would be brutal and personal, with great cost on the winning side regardless of the cost to the losers. Quentus had returned, and Russ knew few armies had stood against the legions for long, particularly not at this point in the empire's history, so he was sure Quentus's legion had been victorious, but he had probably lost comrades during the battle and had certainly seen men dying and in great pain. He could easily imagine that changing Quentus from a bright, happy child to the controlled, dominating man he was now. "And he never changed back."

"He has no reason to," Antony said. "No wife now to bring softness to his life or his home."

So he had been married, Russ thought. He didn't know what had happened to her, nor did he think it was his place to ask. Russ had always rejected the idea of either partner in a gay couple being the "girl" in the relationship because they were obviously both men, but he wondered now about how Quentus saw him, especially if his presence kept Quentus from marrying. "He is old enough and established enough to marry again."

"Oh yes," Antony said, though Russ had not intended the words as a question. "His peers wonder why he hasn't married again, but he has never spent much time in the company of women, either prostitutes or the daughters of citizens. He prefers to spend his time training with his soldiers. He has served as a mentor to the sons of many of the leading citizens here in Nemausus. Several of them now have units of their own. He is quite sought after as a teacher."

"That doesn't surprise me," Russ said, thinking of the way Quentus had run things after he rescued Russ from the boar. "He seems very in control of everything."

"It makes him a good leader and it assures his place in Nemausus. Even after he retires from active military duty, he will remain in high esteem because of his many victories and because he has ties to so many of the leading families. He will probably continue to mentor their sons and grandsons for as long as he is physically able."

It didn't make him an easy partner, though, but Russ thought he understood a little more now. Quentus had no relationships other than those that involved him ordering people around: his soldiers, his servants, the young men he mentored. They all looked to him for commands, and so Quentus knew no other way of asking for things. Russ would have to see if they could work on that, because he wasn't willing to be ordered around.

"So what is the best way to persuade him to do something?" Russ asked.

"I am only a servant," Antony said. "I would never presume—"

"Sure you would," Russ interrupted. "Someone makes sure he eats. Someone makes sure he pays attention to things like paying his creditors. I haven't been here long, but I've seen what he thinks about without prompting, and it isn't matters like those. Yet dinner appears on time. No one is at the door demanding payment for goods or services. You've been with the family all your life. You know how to manage him."

"Manage him, yes," Antony said, "because simply telling him dinner is ready will make him realize he's hungry and so he will eat. No persuasion is necessary because he understands the importance of such things, even if he relies on me to make them happen. Persuading him is something different entirely."

"Do you know what happened to make him so set in his ways?"

"You mean besides the regimentation of the legions?"

"You said he was a biddable child. Following orders would seem an extension of that, not something that would change it," Russ replied.

"A friend of his was killed," Antony said softly. "The general gave an order Quentus thought was wrong, but he was too inexperienced for anyone to listen to him. They marched into battle as ordered, and his friend died a matter of hours later. Quentus had been right about the orders. The general fell as well, and the man who stepped up to rally the legion ordered them to fall back and continue the battle the way Quentus had wanted in the first place. They were victorious, and Quentus was promoted to an officer. Everyone praised the field commander for his quick thinking, who in turn praised Quentus, but Quentus knew only one thing."

"His friend was dead because he followed orders he didn't fight hard enough to change."

"You know him well already," Antony said. "I must return to the kitchens. Tonight's dinner is important and everything must be perfect."

Russ frowned as Antony left the garden area. Quentus hadn't said anything about dinner when he left that morning. Russ had no idea how he might be expected to act at a dinner that, from Antony's comment, would undoubtedly include other notables from the city. Deciding he would gain nothing from worrying about it, he focused back on his work. That would help him more than anything else he could do at the moment.

RUSS ended up so engrossed in his writing that he had stopped hearing the doors open and close as the servants made their preparations for dinner. He had suggested to Antony that they simply leave the doors open, but Antony insisted Quentus had ordered them kept closed and he could not countermand the legate's orders. Russ thought that was carrying the letter of the law a little too far when it would be easier for the servants if they didn't have to keep opening and closing the doors, but he didn't argue. Antony wouldn't listen, not about something that contradicted Quentus's orders. Therefore the sensation of lips on his neck startled him.

"I didn't hear you come in," Russ said, rising to greet Quentus.

"What were you working on so intently?" Quentus asked.

How to explain his reasons to Quentus? He could hardly tell his lover he had been practicing writing in Latin so he didn't accidentally write in modern English. "It has been some time since I worked as a scribe," Russ said instead. "I was practicing my hand to make sure I would not embarrass you when you showed my work to others."

"I will start doing that tonight," Quentus said. "Some of the fathers of men I've trained are coming here for dinner. I need their goodwill so others will send me their sons for training, but they can also be useful to us in establishing you as a scribe available for discreet projects."

"Discreet?" Russ asked.

"Anyone with two denarii to rub together can pay for the services of a scribe in the city, but those men are often worse gossips than old women with nothing better to do," Quentus explained. "No one would use them for anything they didn't want to be public knowledge in a matter of hours. Among the elite, there is still a need for scribes, but better ones, more discreet ones than you can find in the streets around the forum. That is where you will come in. You will promise discretion and they will pay you for it."

"If they want discretion, will it bother them that I'm here with you?" Russ asked, not wanting to put more of a label on their relationship until Quentus did. "I would never reveal anything to anyone else, but I might accidentally let something slip to you."

"That's why we will start with the people who are coming tonight," Quentus said. "Those men already trust me."

"Are you sure I shouldn't bathe before meeting them?" Russ asked.

"You won't meet them tonight," Quentus said. "This is not a family occasion. We will dine in the triclinium off the atrium rather than in the exhedra. You can meet them another time, perhaps even the next time we go to the baths."

Russ fumed. "This is ridiculous! They're going to be here tonight. Why should I wait to meet them?"

"Because I confined you to quarters for two more days," Quentus said, "and I always do what I say I will do. Besides, I would not introduce you so quickly anyway. They need time to get used to the idea of having someone we can trust as our scribe instead of having to meet in order to exchange news."

"You make it sound like there's someone out to get you."

"It's no secret that Domitius and I are not friends," Quentus said, "and while he will not attack me directly, he would have no qualms about plotting behind my back. With me out of the way, he would have much greater access to Septimus. The men who will be here tonight support me. They listen quietly for rumors of Domitius's plans. He has not yet tried to assassinate me, but he would stop at nothing to discredit me. I prefer to be aware of the direction of his attempts before he launches his attacks."

"I had no idea things were so complicated."

"The less said about it in public, the better," Quentus said. "I was going to tell you the morning you disappeared, since we had met Domitius in the baths the day before, but you weren't there to tell."

Russ had already apologized for that. He refused to do it again, despite Quentus's obvious pause.

"We will see what they have learned since the last time we dined together and decide how best to counter Domitius's newest plans," Quentus continued when Russ remained silent.

"You don't think I might like to hear your discussions as well?" Russ said after Quentus finished. "I have a vested interest in your well-being. I deserve to know if something is threatening you."

"I'm sure you'll find someone to take care of you if anything happens to me," Quentus said.

"Fuck that," Russ snapped, realizing too late that the colloquial phrase might not translate.

"What did you say?" Quentus asked.

"I said forget that," Russ said, hoping he hadn't alienated Quentus too badly.

"You weren't speaking Latin."

"I told you I knew other languages," Russ said, hiding his relief that his words had simply been indecipherable rather than mistranslated or misinterpreted. "It seemed more appropriate at the time."

"More appropriate than what?"

"Than cursing at you in a language you could understand," Russ mumbled.

Quentus quirked an eyebrow at him but otherwise let it go. "Why were you angry enough to curse?"

"You have to ask me that?" Russ said incredulously. "After the time we've spent together?"

"Obviously I do or I wouldn't have bothered putting it into words," Quentus said. Russ's stomach sank. He'd thought Quentus cared enough about him to want them together.

"I don't want someone else to 'take care' of me," Russ said, enunciating every word so there could be no misunderstanding. "I want you to be my partner. I want to help protect you just as you protect me. I want to be the one you lean on when you need support, just like I have leaned on you since we met."

The look of pain that crossed Quentus's face was nearly enough to make Russ regret his words, but he couldn't take them back. They had to resolve this, and that wouldn't happen if they kept ignoring it. "I have forgotten what it's like to rely on someone, it's been so long," Quentus admitted.

"Maybe it's time to learn again," Russ said softly.

CHAPTER EIGHT

QUENTUS smiled as a servant escorted Jacobus and Octavian into the atrium. His old teacher and his first student, they were his closest friends and staunchest supporters.

"Greetings, my friends," he said, offering them seats on the cushions around the low table with a wave of his hand. "I hope the gods have blessed you this evening."

"As always," Jacobus replied. Octavian helped Jacobus lower himself onto the cushions, setting aside the cane the older man used to keep his balance. "Hades has not yet called me, so I am blessed indeed."

"Hades is afraid of you, Father," Octavian said, taking his seat.

"Don't tempt the gods," Quentus and Jacobus said in unison.

"What the gods give, the gods can take away," Jacobus added. The words sent a chill through Quentus. The gods had better think again if they intended to take Russ from him.

"Who else are we expecting tonight?" Octavian asked. Quentus allowed the change of subject. Octavian did not like thinking about his father's age any more than Quentus did.

"No one sent word of an expected absence," Quentus replied, "so there should be eight of us, as usual."

"Gustavus made it back from his campaign, then?" Jacobus asked. "That is good."

"His legion returned yesterday," Quentus said. "Septimus mentioned it when I saw him at the forum."

"And how is our governor?" Octavian asked.

"He seemed in good spirits," Quentus replied. "The last news he had from Rome was good, and the petty scheming of his naysayers here in Nemausus cannot hurt him if he has the emperor's approval."

"Not if their schemes are political," Jacobus said. "The emperor's blessing confers no protection against a well-placed sword."

"Who would really challenge Septimus that way?" Octavian said. "He could beat any of us with one hand tied behind his back."

"You assume it would be a fair fight," Jacobus said. "Men who would conspire against someone like Septimus would not confront him openly."

"Have you heard something?" Quentus asked sharply. "If you have, we must warn Septimus immediately."

"Nothing concrete," Jacobus assured him. "There are those who are discontented with his leadership, but for now, they are satisfied with grumbling. Don't worry, my friend. If I hear anything, I will find a way to contact you immediately."

It was the opening Quentus had hoped for, but before he could bring up Russ and his idea for using Russ as their private scribe to guarantee the secrecy of their correspondence, the servant returned with Crius, Alvinius, and Leander, three of Quentus's comrades-in-arms, all of whom he had trained for their positions. Quentus greeted his friends and got everyone settled. The servants returned with wine for everyone, then poured glasses for the two who had not yet arrived as well.

"We will call for you when we're ready for dinner," Quentus said. "Show Gustavus and Thaddaeus in when they arrive and then return to the kitchens until we summon you."

"Yes, Legatus," the servant said with a bow.

"What news?" Crius asked when the servant had withdrawn.

"Petty scheming and empty gossip, as always," Jacobus said as he sipped his wine. "You are always so generous with your stores, Quentus. It is a pleasure to dine with you."

"It's the least I can do for my friends," Quentus said. "Have you heard anything of import, Crius?"

"I'm not sure," Crius replied. "Domitius was leaving the baths as I arrived, so I heard only the end of the conversation, but he seemed... pleased about something."

"His corruption gets worse with each passing month," Leander said. "We won't be able to simply ignore him much longer."

"The corruption is the problem," Alvinius said. "Too many people owe him favors or debts."

"He came at me in the baths a week ago," Quentus revealed. "I was there with a friend, and Domitius chose to insult him. If he would be open like that more often, we could challenge him publicly. He would have no choice but to face one of us."

"He's wilier than that," Jacobus said. "I don't know why he slipped up and came at you in the baths, but you won't succeed in drawing him out that way. He will always stop short of a public challenge because he knows he can't beat you—any of you—that way."

"You could try to draw him out," Crius suggested.

Jacobus chuckled. "You give this old body too much credit. Besides, Domitius knows any insult to me would be answered a hundredfold by all of you."

"And by every man who ever served with you," Quentus added. "Not even Septimus would be safe from retribution if he insulted you gravely enough."

"Which is why Domitius will never be anything but respectful to me," Jacobus said. "No, if we wish to take him down, we will have to play his game."

"Whose game are we playing?"

The men looked up as Gustavus and Thaddaeus, twin brothers currently under Quentus's tutelage, came in.

"Domitius," Quentus replied as the twins greeted everyone and took their seats.

"We need someone he doesn't connect to us," Alvinius said, taking back up the thread of the conversation. "Someone he has never seen dining with us or training with us. Someone he would reveal his plans to without fear of it getting back to us."

"How then would it get back to us?" Octavian asked. "We don't dare put any of what we discuss in writing for fear someone's scribe will be loose-lipped. If this person in your plan can't meet with us either, how will we get his news?"

Quentus smiled. "I might have a solution to that. I told you Domitius made comments about my friend while we were in the baths. I didn't tell you about my friend."

He paused for a moment to make sure he had everyone's attention.

"Rastus is a scribe and a translator," Quentus said. "He is also seeking work. While it would not be possible to keep secret that he works for some or all of us since he is living here, if he works for others with no connection to us, Domitius will have no way of knowing who, if any, of those people are our friends as well."

"Living here?" Thaddaeus asked with a sly smile. "Is there something you'd like to tell us?"

Gustavus swatted his brother's shoulder. "Don't offend our host," he scolded. "His personal life is none of our business."

"Is he trustworthy?" Jacobus asked, ignoring the twins' bickering.

"I believe so," Quentus said. "He has given me no reason to think otherwise. We would continue our dinners as usual, nothing to indicate any change. Perhaps Rastus would not even work with all of us, at least not regularly. He will have to have time to seek other patrons as well. Domitius would see the addition of a scribe to my household, but he would have no way of knowing anything beyond that."

"He could choose to say nothing to anyone Rastus works with," Leander said.

"He could," Quentus agreed, "and if that happens, Rastus will have a satisfactory income and we will find some other way to stay abreast of Domitius's plans. I don't see that we have anything to lose by trying, plus we have a way to communicate among ourselves without drawing Domitius's attention by dining together more frequently."

"That implies that he suspects," Leander said.

"I don't know that he does," Quentus said, "but we must assume he has some idea. He is always a little more circumspect when we are all in town, as if he knows more eyes are fixed on him then."

"If nothing else, he knows Quentus has more support around him when we are all in town," Jacobus said. "He may not realize we are actively seeking out his plans, but he knows we will all defend Quentus if necessary."

"More than that, he knows I will defend Septimus if necessary," Quentus said.

"Nothing I've heard recently suggests any interest in Septimus directly," Leander said. "Do you really think Septimus is the target?"

"He gains nothing from removing me unless he's trying to get to Septimus," Quentus reminded them. "Compared to his family's holdings, mine are small and relatively unimportant, and they would pass to Callistratus anyway, so he would have nothing to gain in that respect. Command of the legions would devolve to Octavian or one of the other generals, all of whom I trained at one time or another, so he would have no direct gain from that."

"He would have no indirect gain, either, except perhaps in the day or two of confusion that might follow your unexpected death or deposal as your son takes your place," Leander said. "The men most likely to take your place are as loyal to Septimus and as distrustful of Domitius as we are."

"Unless the emperor sent someone from Rome," Jacobus said.

"To Nemausus?" Thaddaeus asked. "Why would he do that?"

"Because we are the gateway to the rest of Roman Gaul," Jacobus explained. "Quentus, you have neglected the boy's geography."

"Tell that to his father," Quentus retorted. "His tutors should have seen to that before he ever came to me."

"Goods from all over Gaul and even Britain come down the Rhône to Massilia, and they have to come through Nemausus to get there," Jacobus continued. "The emperor must have someone he can trust in power here to ensure safe transport of those goods. If he thought Septimus wasn't watching out for his best interests, he could easily replace our current governor with someone else or send a general to make sure Septimus was loyal."

"But Septimus's loyalty isn't in question," Gustavus said.

"Not at the moment," Jacobus agreed, "but Domitius is wily. If he arranged for Quentus's assassination and cast it in the right light, he could perhaps convince the emperor of the disloyalty of everyone Quentus trained. His family is an influential one."

"Ill-gotten gains at every turn," Leander muttered.

"Money is power, no matter how ill-gotten it is," Crius said. "We have always known that. It's why we watch and work to stop his schemes before they see the light of day."

"He's the one who should be watching his back," Leander continued. "Some days I think it would be easier to assassinate him and be done with it."

"If we operate outside the law, we're no better than he is," Octavian said. "We made that decision before any of this started."

"There was no decision to make," Jacobus said. "We are law-abiding men, citizens worthy of our empire and our positions in this city. Perhaps we won't stop Domitius, but we will face the gods knowing we did not stoop to his level."

Quentus shared a sympathetic look with Leander. He agreed with Octavian and Jacobus, but he also understood Leander's zeal. Domitius's scheming had cost Leander's father his olive groves, leaving the family without the income they had always relied on. Leander had managed to scrape together enough with his military service to keep the family afloat and to purchase a plot of land perfect for a vineyard to replace the olive groves, but the sting of Domitius's plotting had never worn off. "Removing him will not undo any of what he's already done."

"No, but it will make me feel better."

"Has anyone heard what his current schemes are?" Quentus asked. He couldn't help Leander directly, but he could make sure Domitius didn't hurt his friends again.

DINNER was every bit as isolated and miserable as Russ had expected, left out behind closed doors with nothing to do but sit as close as he could and try to listen in. Unfortunately, he didn't know any of the players besides Quentus, so he couldn't keep track of who said what, nor could he begin to guess at the undercurrents in the room between the guests and Quentus and among the different guests. He could tell it was far more complex than what Quentus had said as he explained things to Russ that afternoon, but Russ could be patient. His house arrest would be over in two more days and then he could go with Quentus to meet the men in the other room, one or two at a time and with an eye to understanding everything he overheard tonight. He wasn't a soldier. He couldn't pick up a sword and wield it in Quentus's defense, but he was an intelligent man. He could work behind the scenes to protect his lover, and from what little he could hear, their "enemy" moved behind the scenes anyway.

The possessiveness of his thoughts surprised him. As annoyed as he was with Quentus for confining him to the house, he hadn't expected to feel much of anything else, but he couldn't stand the idea of someone taking Quentus away from him. He heard Quentus call for the servants and slipped back to the bedroom. He didn't want Antony telling Quentus he had been spying on them. He would tell Quentus himself as he asked about what he had heard and what needed to happen next, but he didn't want to embarrass Quentus in front of his guests.

That was another surprising impulse. He seemed to be full of them tonight. He frowned a little as he considered all the conflicting impulses running through his mind at the moment. He still wanted to kick Quentus for thinking he could control Russ's freedom of movement, but none of the servants had seemed at all surprised by Quentus's orders, so Russ figured it was fairly commonplace even if it rankled. At the same time, though, he wanted to keep Quentus with him in ways that went beyond the prospect of more sex.

"Excuse me, sir."

Russ looked up to see Antony at the entrance to the bedroom.

"Yes, Antony?"

"The legatus had us make a plate for you as well, if you would like to come eat in the garden."

Russ couldn't stop the smile that made his lips twitch. Even when he denied Russ the right to join their guests for dinner, he hadn't forgotten Russ was there or left his well-being to chance. One more conundrum to figure out. "I will be there in a moment."

The meal could have challenged any five-star restaurant Russ had ever eaten in, not that he had been in all that many. He tended to be more of a pizza and burgers kind of guy if given a choice, although he had certainly learned to appreciate a fine meal. Course after course, the servants came out, carrying platters into the main dining room, but always bringing a plate for him as well. It felt odd eating a meal alone without someone to share it with, but the servants were too busy serving the meal to linger at Russ's table. He didn't blame them. Russ was probably still an unknown quantity to most of them, whereas Quentus was their employer. Of course they paid more attention to him.

He finished the meal finally, reclining on the cushions as he waited for Quentus's friends to leave. He wasn't aware of dozing off, but he must have because the caress of tender fingers along his neck woke him. He blinked slowly, his eyes coming back into focus. He summoned a smile for his lover. "Did you have a good dinner?"

"Yes," Quentus said. "Next time, I will introduce you to everyone."

"I'd like that," Russ said. "This is my home now, which means your friends will be my friends."

"You will like them," Quentus said. "You might have to win over Jacobus, but he is like that with everyone. He still hasn't decided what he thinks of Gustavus and Thaddaeus."

Another time, Russ would ask for more information about the men who had come to dinner, but he was too lethargic from sleep to do it now. It would be in one ear and out the other tonight, and then he'd have to ask again. Better to do it when he was awake enough to absorb the information.

"Are you falling back asleep on me?" Quentus teased.

Russ nodded.

"Come, then," Quentus said, scooping Russ into his arms and starting toward the bedroom. "We will retire for the night."

Russ relaxed in Quentus's arms, trying to get his brain back online. Quentus would want sex when they got to the bedroom. They hadn't spent a night together yet without it, and Russ was already in trouble. He didn't want to make it worse.

Quentus set him down on the bed and undressed him gently before rolling him onto his side and pulling the covers over him. "Go to sleep," he said, pressing a kiss to Russ's forehead. "I will check the house and come right back."

Russ was already dozing off again when Quentus returned. He startled a little when he felt the heat of the centurion's body spooning along his back, but while he could feel the ridge of

Quentus's cock pressing against his ass, his lover didn't try to wake him, but simply curled around him and settled a heavy hand against Russ's lower belly to keep him in place. Russ relaxed into the embrace and fell asleep wondering how to interpret this new turn of events.

CHAPTER NINE

WHEN Russ joined Quentus for breakfast the next morning, he hadn't come any closer to having an explanation for Quentus's tenderness the night before, but he knew for sure it wasn't a lack of interest on his lover's part. Quentus had awakened Russ that morning with demanding kisses and probing fingers. Russ's lower body clenched at the memory of being held so tightly in Quentus's embrace and fucked the way they had slept. Quentus had not made Russ wait the way he usually did, instead wrapping a hand around Russ's cock and jerking him off as he fucked him.

"You seem flushed," Quentus said, his eyes dancing with pleasure, an expression Russ had not seen before. "Are you well?"

Russ could feel his flush deepening. "Just thinking," he mumbled.

"What thoughts would bring such high color to your face?" Russ knew what to do with the domineering lover. He had no clue what to do with Quentus's teasing.

"You," Russ answered, flushing even more. He silently cursed his pale skin. If he could just get a tan like everyone else, he wouldn't have to worry about this, but no, he got freckles instead.

Quentus snagged Russ's hand, pulling him closer until Russ was nearly as close to his lover as he had been while they slept. "Are you embarrassed by what we share?" Quentus asked seriously.

"Not embarrassed," Russ said, squirming a little as his body reacted to Quentus's touch.

"Ah, I see," Quentus said, slipping his hand beneath the hem of Russ's tunic and palming his awakening cock. "You should have said something. I will tell the servants not to disturb us."

Russ shook his head. "Then I'd be embarrassed. They don't know what to make of me as it is. If you send them away so we can have sex at the table, they'll think I'm some whore you brought home."

"Does it matter what they think? They're servants. They do as they're told."

"That's not the point," Russ said, although he did not pull away from Quentus's hands. "They may do as they're told even when you aren't around, but they'll think badly of me, and they'll talk about it when we aren't there to hear them, and word will get out, and if it does, no one will take me seriously as a scribe. They'll think you're just indulging your latest plaything."

"I have kept concubines in the past," Quentus said, "but I always set them up in an apartment of their own and visited them there. I have hired prostitutes at times, but again, I never brought them here. I have not shared this house with anyone since my parents died and my sister married. Until you."

Russ swallowed hard against the internal chaos provoked by Quentus's words. He noticed Quentus did not mention his wife, but perhaps the memories of her were too bitter to bear.

"Why?" He couldn't begin to formulate the rest of the questions he wanted to ask, but this was as good a place to start as any.

"Because you aren't a pastime," Quentus said.

That only discombobulated Russ more. He needed to think about that, but thinking with Quentus's hands on him was impossible.

"All the more reason not to make the servants think this is just about sex," Russ groaned as Quentus slipped his hand inside the *subligar* and stroked his bare skin.

"You're here and sleeping in my bed," Quentus replied. "And you are hardly quiet. I am not ashamed of my desire for you."

Russ gave up his protests, too overwhelmed by Quentus's words and the touch of his hand to concentrate on why this struck him as a bad idea. Quentus had answers to all his reasons anyway.

He tried to turn so he could reciprocate Quentus's caresses, but his lover kept him firmly in place, with his back pressed to Quentus's chest. "Stop trying to control everything," Quentus chided, swatting Russ's thigh lightly with the hand not stroking Russ's erection. "Let me take care of you."

"I want to take care of you too," Russ said, his voice rough with need.

"You took care of me this morning," Quentus reminded him. Russ wasn't sure lying there and letting Quentus do whatever he wanted counted as taking care of him, but it felt good at the same time to relax into Quentus's arms and not have to worry about anything but his lover's hands on his body.

Russ groaned in protest, although he did keep his hands at his side without needing to be told.

"See? You do trust me," Quentus said. "You don't know why I stopped, but you know I won't leave you this way. You know if you wait, I will make it good for you."

Russ nodded. He had learned that lesson well. He ached to be touched, but he knew Quentus would reward his patience.

A moment later, Quentus's hands returned to his erection, stroking him hard and fast, and then manipulating his balls almost to the point of pain. Russ gasped, arching at the unexpected and overwhelming sensation.

"Yes," Quentus said to the silent question. Russ cried out as Quentus squeezed once more. Russ could swear Quentus had just pushed his release out of him with that grip. His body seized up before he collapsed limply in Quentus's arms.

Quentus kissed the side of Russ's neck. "Beautiful," he murmured, his breath tickling Russ's ear and sending another shiver through him.

Quentus straightened Russ's tunic, smoothing it down modestly. With another kiss, on Russ's lips this time, he shifted so

Russ sat beside him rather than practically in his lap. "Antony, bring a bowl and a pitcher of water so we can clean our hands before we eat."

The curtain to the kitchen parted and Antony looked into the garden. "Are you ready to eat, then, Legatus?"

"As soon as we have washed up."

"Right away, my Lord."

Russ flushed again, realizing the servants had heard everything, even if they hadn't seen any of it, but he pushed aside his discomfort. Antony appeared a moment later with a bowl, pitcher, and cloths. He bowed as he set them within reach and then withdrew again. Quentus cleaned his hands and then gave Russ the other cloth.

"I need to go to the baths," Russ muttered as he cleaned his hands as well. He wasn't about to push his clothes out of the way and wipe himself clean at the table.

"Tomorrow," Quentus promised.

"I thought I had two days left," Russ said.

"You did," Quentus replied, "but I miss having you with me during the day, so we will compromise. You will stay here today because it doesn't do to be too lenient, but tomorrow you will join me at the baths again, although you will stay here when I go to the forum. It would be strange for you to accompany me anyway, but you will not wander the city without me for one more day. I will introduce you to people as we meet them."

"So tell me about your friends," Russ said as Antony returned to collect the water and another servant brought breakfast.

"There are eight of us," Quentus said. "Men I trust with my life. Men I would trust with your life. Jacobus is the oldest, and the wiliest. He was my mentor when I began learning to be a soldier and the model I look to when I imagine my life after I leave the army. He walks with a limp now, but his mind is as sharp as ever. His son, Octavian, was the first soldier I ever trained. More importantly, though, their family has been in Nemausus for generations. They have wealth and standing to rival anyone in Provincia Narbonensis.

Without their friendship, I would never have made it as far as I have."

"They helped you get promoted?" Russ asked.

"No, but they kept my detractors from stopping my rise in the army," Quentus explained. "They evened the odds for me. Octavian will take my place as second to Septimus when I retire, I am sure of it. Alvinius, Crius, and Leander are comrades-in-arms, the captains I rely on to carry out my plans in battle, but also to make adjustments if circumstances warrant a change. Jacobus mentored Alvinius after I left him. Crius and Leander are former trainees of mine."

"Yet Octavian will succeed you, not Alvinius, who is older?" Russ asked.

"Age is not the only factor," Quentus said. "Alvinius is a capable captain, able to understand strategy and implement it, even with changes, but he is not a strategist himself. He does not see the big picture the way Octavian does. He has no desire for my job. He will serve Octavian as loyally as he has served me."

"That's six."

"Gustavus and Thaddaeus are the final two," Quentus said. "They are my current trainees, not in swordplay now, since they excel in that regard, but in strategy. They are young for command, but they have a knack for it that I haven't seen since I worked with Octavian. Normally I would take only one person at a time, but they are twins and would not be separated."

Russ remembered the story of the founding of Rome, of Romulus and Remus, who had been left to die from exposure by their uncle and had been raised by a she-wolf until they learned of their heritage and returned to claim their birthright, and nodded. "And it is Domitius they help protect you against?"

"Say rather that we protect each other and Septimus," Quentus said, "but yes, against Domitius. His family is nearly as old as Jacobus's, but they are not as well respected. Domitius wants to change that, but he prefers to get there in other ways. He is corrupt through and through."

"Corruption is hard to fight," Russ agreed.

"We have not caught him doing anything illegal," Quentus explained. "We know he is underhanded, but that is not enough to stop him, so we settle for thwarting his plans whenever we can. The problem is that he knows what we're doing. He knows who we are and when we meet, and so often he changes his plans because of it. That's where you come in. None of us have scribes of our own right now, and we dare not use a public scribe for such sensitive matters so we must meet to discuss what we've learned, thus tipping Domitius to the fact that we have learned something. We can trust you, though, both to write and possibly to carry the messages, and if you take other patrons besides the eight of us, Domitius won't know if we have added to our number. He won't know when our information gets passed between us. If you are willing, of course, you would be contributing not only to our household but to something far larger than either of us as well."

"The others agreed to your plan?"

"They want to meet you first, but they agree it is a good idea."

"Then I will do my best to win their trust."

While Russ's words were simple statement of fact, the implications went far deeper. Quentus had moved beyond demanding Russ's obedience to discussing a way to integrate him fully into his life. Quentus trusted him not just personally but with his friends. The situation that led to this moment might be proof of how little things had changed between Quentus's time and Russ's own, but Russ had always been enough a student of history to know that. Helping the others fight Domitius's corruption wouldn't change history, but it might be enough to change Russ's life for the better.

CHAPTER TEN

"THIS makes no sense," Russ said as he wrote what Octavian had dictated. In the month that had passed since Quentus first introduced Russ to his friends, Russ had grown comfortable enough around them to question what he heard. Even better, Quentus's friends had gotten comfortable enough with Russ to listen when he did.

"What do you mean?"

"Domitius wants something. We know that, we just don't know what, and the things we keep learning about his plans don't connect."

"How so?"

"Quentus said Domitius wants power," Russ said, "but not necessarily directly. He wants sufficient influence to make things happen without being seen to be responsible."

"That has always been his preference in the past," Octavian agreed.

"So then his plans should involve gaining wealth or control of wealthy people," Russ said. "How else would he gain influence?"

"By decreasing the influence of those already in power," Octavian suggested.

"Yes, but this Stefanus he's targeting right now… he's a tanner. I don't see wealth or influence in that," Russ said. "Not unless something else is going on behind the scenes that we're missing."

"So what else could be going on behind the scenes?" Octavian asked. "You've put this much together. Quentus told us he had found a scribe. He didn't tell us he had found an ally for us."

Russ flushed. "I didn't mean to overstep my bounds."

"You are too intelligent a man to be relegated to nothing more than a scribe," Octavian said with a shake of his head. "I asked for your opinion because I wanted to hear it, and I will tell Quentus to include you the next time we dine together. Now, what do you think is going on behind the scenes?"

"This is all a guess," Russ warned, "but I hear things from others besides all of you. I think perhaps Domitius has changed his focus from the high-ranking citizens, who have the wealth and influence to resist him, to the tradesmen. If he can control them, he controls the flow of goods within the city and thus the flow of wealth. What would happen if Quentus went to Stefanus's shop to buy leather for new arm guards or a new scabbard for his sword only to be refused service?"

"He would go to a different tanner," Octavian said.

"And today that would work," Russ agreed, "but if Domitius gains enough control over the tradesmen who truly have no way to resist him, he could eventually make it impossible for his enemies to get supplies; or if not impossible, he could control the cost of things and hurt people that way."

Octavian whistled softly. "If you are right, that would be a disaster indeed. I believe I shall pay Stefanus a visit and see what I can learn."

"Tread lightly," Russ said before he could think to guard his words. "I'm sorry. Now I have overstepped my bounds."

"Tell me how you think I should approach it," Octavian said, not appearing to be offended by Russ's boldness.

"I'm not sure you should," Russ said, hoping he wasn't headed for a disaster of his own. Quentus would not be happy if Russ alienated his friend. "You aren't Domitius, but you're equally powerful, perhaps more so, even. If Stefanus is feeling threatened, he might confide in you, but if Domitius has offered protection, has implied that you or one of the others will threaten him, your presence could play into Domitius's game."

"Then how do we discover Domitius's plan?"

"We need someone Stefanus would trust," Russ said. "Another tanner, a farmer who sells him hides, even a customer of the same class who would be no threat to him. Someone Stefanus could talk to without fear of retribution, maybe even someone Stefanus would share Domitius's offer with, if it is indeed an offer and not a threat."

"Where would we find such a craftsman we could trust?" Octavian asked.

"On one of your family's holdings?" Russ asked. "Or if not yours, one of the others? Quentus's tabernae are empty, but not everyone's are. There are options. We just have to figure out what they are."

"We had not planned on meeting for dinner for another two weeks," Octavian said, "but we might want to reconsider that. Write invitations to the others for dinner tomorrow night, and include yourself on the invitation to Quentus."

Russ pulled out six sheets of paper and began to write the requested letters.

"WHAT is this?" Quentus asked when Russ handed him Octavian's invitation.

"An invitation to dinner," Russ said, his voice so mild that Quentus's suspicions grew.

"Why is Octavian inviting us both to dinner tomorrow night?"

"Why wouldn't he?" Russ asked. "I'm a part of your campaign against Domitius now."

"As our scribe," Quentus retorted. He saw the flash of anger that crossed Russ's face, watched as his lover drew a deep breath and steadied himself. Russ's self-control only flayed Quentus's temper. Russ should have been the one worried about upsetting Quentus, should have been the one stumbling for an explanation. Instead Quentus was left with the overwhelming urge to apologize for upsetting Russ, though he had no idea what he'd done to merit that look in the first place.

"Really?" Russ said, his eyes narrowing. "I haven't made other contributions? That's not what Octavian said today. He believes I have something to add to the discussion or he wouldn't have invited me to dinner. He asked my opinion today and listened when I gave it, unlike some people. Letting you fuck me every night doesn't make me less intelligent or capable than the rest of you. Being new to the city doesn't make me less aware of the way politics work in general. I may not know all the players, but I know when something doesn't fit, and being your lover isn't going to keep me from pointing those things out. I can't pick up a sword and fight in your defense, but I can protect you with everything at my disposal."

"You're mine," Quentus growled. "I'm supposed to protect you, not the other way around."

"Bullshit," Russ retorted. "You can protect me all you want— if someone wants a fight, you'd better protect me if you don't want to lose me—but you can't ask me not to do the same. I'm a man, Quentus. A grown, capable man, and I won't be relegated to a corner because I'm not a soldier."

"I don't want a soldier," Quentus said. "If I did, I could have had my pick years ago."

"Then what do you want?" Russ asked.

"You," Quentus replied simply, his heart pounding at the vulnerability of the answer, but he didn't know how else to explain it to Russ.

"If that's the truth," Russ said, ignoring Quentus's spluttered insistence that it was, "then you have to take all of me, not just my body. I can't turn off my brain just because it would be more convenient for you if I was just a biddable warm body."

Quentus didn't know how to refute that. He didn't just want a warm body, as Russ put it, although he certainly craved Russ's responsiveness. He didn't want to *share* Russ, and he had no idea how to explain that to his lover without making the situation worse.

"You're mine," he said instead, pulling Russ into a soul-stealing kiss. To his delight, Russ melted into his arms. Quentus took that as permission to prove to Russ once again how completely devoted he was.

RUSS straightened his toga, a gift from Quentus that afternoon when he returned from the forum. The drape of the cloth fortunately covered all the marks left by Quentus's teeth, but Russ could still feel the possessive sting all along his shoulders, around his nipples, and on the insides of his thighs. Every step he took reminded him of how often and how thoroughly Quentus had taken him since he had come home with Octavian's invitation the day before. His ass ached, not quite to the point of agony, but certainly to the point that he had to pay attention to how he walked so as not to appear to be limping. He ought to scold Quentus for it, except he had reveled in every possessive touch, goading his lover on the moment his hands or teeth had connected with Russ's skin. It felt good to be craved that way.

If it meant paying for it now, Russ only regretted the timing, not the effects themselves. He could have done without the distraction as he tried to order his thoughts so he could convince the others of the ideas he had shared with Octavian.

"The litter bearers are here," Quentus called. "It is time to go."

Russ smoothed his hands over his toga once more, hoping he would not embarrass Quentus with his appearance. He felt like a fraud dressed this way. He had grown accustomed to the tunic he wore normally, but this was the garb of a citizen, a rank Russ could not truly claim. Taking a deep breath, he joined Quentus in the atrium.

Russ stood still as Quentus looked him over carefully. When their eyes met, Quentus's gaze was dark with lust, his pupils blown wide. "I will enjoy taking that off you when we get home."

Russ felt Quentus's gaze like a touch, his nipples tightening against the wool of the toga, his ass clenching at the thought of being filled again. "When we get home," Russ said, trying to keep his voice firm. He didn't need Quentus getting ideas in the litter.

To Russ's relief, the litter that awaited them did not have curtains on the sides, only a roof to protect them from the sun and cushions for them to sit on. Russ took his place across from Quentus as Quentus told the litter bearers their destination.

It was an odd sensation, riding through the streets he had walked so many times both on his own and at Quentus's side, but he was not working tonight. He was a guest attending dinner at the house of a wealthy friend. On his own, he might still have walked, but Quentus's status dictated they arrive in style, and Russ had spent enough time with Quentus's friends over the past month to understand that appearances counted in this game of cat and mouse they were playing with Domitius.

Russ stayed a step behind Quentus as they descended from the litter and waited for Jacobus's servants to admit them. He might have been included in the invitation, but he did not share Quentus's rank. He might not agree with the class system, but he had learned Bernard's lessons well. He had returned to the past knowing he would have to live within the confines of the society he had chosen to make his own. He would do nothing to challenge the status quo for fear of changing history in disastrous ways, only to protect the man who had drawn him there.

Russ stayed behind Quentus as they went inside, letting the centurion greet his friends first and keeping his own greetings subdued. Octavian had invited him, but that did not make Russ the true equal of any of the men in the room. When Quentus had greeted everyone and took his seat, Russ took the empty spot beside him. Perhaps a time would come when he would feel comfortable sitting elsewhere, but tonight was not that time.

When everyone had arrived, Gustavus turned the conversation to the matter that had drawn them together. "What was so urgent that you changed our plans, Octavian? I had intended to spend the evening with a lovely lady of my acquaintance."

"Your paramour can wait," Octavian scolded, "or if she can't, you're better off without her. Domitius appears to have changed his plans from targeting us directly to targeting the craftsmen in the city."

"But that's good news," Gustavus said. "If he's given up on us, that's one less thing for us to worry about."

"I wouldn't be so sure," Octavian said. "Rastus, would you care to share your thoughts with everyone else?"

Russ gulped the wine he had just sipped and sat up a little straighter, the movement sending a twinge through his ass again. He was tempted to scowl at Quentus, but it would only be misunderstood by the others and wouldn't have any effect on its intended recipient anyway. "It struck me as odd that Domitius would change direction so completely," Russ explained when he could speak. "He wants power and influence, but whenever he tries to get it directly, you counter him. Maybe you aren't always successful, but you're successful enough that he hasn't gotten what he wants. He can't come at you directly because you're too well connected, either in the city or in the army or both. Even if he did it subtly, having one of you assassinated, your influence, especially in the legion, goes too deep. Every division of the legion is commanded by one of you or by someone loyal to one of you because you mentored him."

"That doesn't explain the craftsmen," Leander said.

"Let him finish," Octavian interrupted.

"If he can't take power directly, then he has to find another way to do it," Russ said. "If he can control enough of the craftsmen, he can control the city's access to goods, and if he can do that, he has the power, no matter who controls the military."

"That's quite a jump in logic," Thaddaeus said. "What craftsman in their right mind would deny a soldier needed supplies?"

"One who stands to lose everything if he defies Domitius," Jacobus replied before Russ could speak. "I had not thought of this line of attack because it reeks of cowardice, but Domitius has never had a shred of honor. Leander can vouch for that."

"It's a risky path to take," Russ said. "There will be a period of time before Domitius has enough control to influence the city as a whole when he could lose everything. He has to gain control over each craftsman individually, unless he can control the supplies coming in to them, but if he gets to the point that he has that control, it will be very hard to break it. Someone would have to stand up to him, someone from each trade, in fact, and that may be hard to do, depending on how he has gotten control of them."

"Then we must stop him before it gets to that point," Quentus said. "How do we do that?"

The question was directed firmly at Russ, and that sent a thrill through him. Quentus trusted him to help them.

"We find out how he is controlling people and we help keep them independent," Russ said. "If we can't keep them independent, then we tie enough of them to us that Domitius can't take complete control of trade within the city."

"Somehow I suspect that will prove harder than it sounds," Crius said with a grim chuckle.

"Probably," Russ agreed, "but the other option is no option at all."

"WHERE did you learn all of that?" Quentus asked Russ as they climbed into the litter at the end of the evening. This one, Russ noted, had curtains that fell shut behind them, enclosing them in complete darkness.

"Here and there," Russ replied. It was all fundamental economics, but he could hardly explain the basic graduation requirements of his college degree to Quentus. "I saw it happen once before. It's one of the reasons I was on the road when you found me."

"Only one of the reasons?"

Russ shrugged, despite knowing Quentus couldn't see it. "There was nothing left for me at home. Maybe I wouldn't find what I was looking for if I left, but I certainly wouldn't have found it if I stayed."

That much, at least, was completely true. Russ still didn't know if staying with Quentus permanently would fulfill him in a way his life in Tucson had not, but he would never know if he didn't take the chance.

"And have you found what you were looking for?" Quentus asked, pulling Russ into his arms and then rolling him onto his back.

"You'll make them drop us if you rock the litter too much," Russ hissed.

"They're better paid than that," Quentus insisted, nibbling at Russ's earlobe. "You didn't answer my question."

Russ wanted to say yes. He had discovered so much about himself since he had been with Quentus, but the vulnerability of such an answer froze the words in his throat. He turned his head, trying to derail the conversation with a kiss, but Quentus evaded him, pinning him to the cushion with the full weight of his body. "Answer my question, Russ."

"I hope so," Russ said after a moment. It wasn't the answer Quentus wanted, he knew, but it was the best Russ could do right now. Fortunately Quentus accepted it for the moment, giving Russ the kiss he had sought earlier, laying siege to Russ's mouth with his tongue. Russ surrendered immediately, offering himself to Quentus as he had every time Quentus had touched him from the very first night they met. He half expected Quentus to order the litter bearers to take the long way home so Quentus could ravish him right then, but the centurion did not break the kiss.

Or do anything else.

His hands remained wrapped around Russ's wrists, holding him in place but making no move to push aside his toga. He pressed his body against Russ's, keeping him there but not rutting against him. He continued to ravish Russ's mouth with his own, but he did not slide his lips down Russ's neck to bite at the skin there or elsewhere, as he had done so often over the past day. He seemed completely content to continue the deep, drugging kisses, ratcheting up Russ's eagerness without doing anything that would begin to muss him up. They would only have a short walk from the litter to the front door of Quentus's house, but with only the torches at the door for light, no one would be able to see Russ's kiss-swollen lips to suspect anything had passed between the two men during the ride home.

Only when the litter bearers set down their burden did Quentus lift his head and roll to the side, releasing Russ. He descended first, turning back to hold the curtain aside so Russ could clamber out as well. Quentus paid the litter bearers and then led Russ inside. Antony waited for them in the vestibulum, but Quentus waved him aside with orders to lock the house for the night and to see that he and Russ were not disturbed until they called for breakfast in the morning.

Antony bowed and withdrew, leaving them alone in the atrium. "You were magnificent tonight," Quentus said, stepping behind Russ and trailing his fingers along Russ's forearm up to the drape of his toga. "I should not have underestimated you."

Russ shivered beneath the teasing caress. "It was common sense."

"No," Quentus said, "it was far more than common sense. Logical, yes, once you explained it to us, but none of us came to the conclusion ourselves. We needed you to show us the right direction." He lowered his head to Russ's neck, nipping at the tendons there.

"Even now, it is supposition based on what we know, not concrete fact," Russ said, forcing the words out through quickened breaths. "Domitius could have some other plan entirely."

"He could," Quentus agreed, urging Russ forward without breaking the contact of their bodies. "And if he does, we will discover that as well, but your suggestion makes far more sense than anything we came up with on our own."

They passed through the tablinum and the garden into the bedroom. A single lamp burned on the chest, casting wild shadows on the walls. Russ stood frozen where Quentus had left him when the centurion pulled away for a moment. He almost reached for the clasp on his shoulder that held his toga in place, but something in Quentus's eyes stopped him. He waited, quivering with anticipation as Quentus stripped his own toga off, leaving himself in only his short tunic. He returned to Russ's side a moment later.

"You are such a mix of contrasts," Quentus murmured, finding Russ's neck again with his lips. "You wear the toga with the confidence of one born to it, yet you look like some exotic bird in it with your pale skin and red hair. I have never known anyone like you."

Russ let his head drop back against Quentus's shoulder as Quentus lifted the drape of the toga from one arm, baring his bicep to the cool night air. This tender attention was new. Quentus took his time most nights, but his attentions had always been sexual, rough and ready and designed to wind Russ up to a fever pitch and keep him there as long as possible. While Russ had no doubt he would end this evening with Quentus inside him again, this moment was more sensual, loving, almost, than any of their previous interactions had been.

Quentus unfastened the clasp at Russ's shoulder next, but instead of pushing the whole thing off Russ's arm and to the ground, he unwrapped the top layer, peeling the toga off Russ with the same care as the servants who had helped him put it on earlier that evening. Russ trembled, not sure what to make of the sudden new layer of emotion surrounding them. Quentus seemed to have no such hesitation, though, his every movement as exact and deliberate as always, just with different intent.

More than once, Russ had felt overrun with sensation until he had no choice but to surrender to it, but this time he felt seduced, which made no sense. Quentus surely had no doubt about Russ's willingness, yet he paused before each new caress as if asking permission. The touches, when they came, were strong and familiar but somehow weighted with more significance than ever before.

Even with the slower pace, Russ was naked before long, splayed out on the bed for Quentus's enjoyment. Every inch of his skin received attention, a kiss or a caress, sometimes both, until the absence of touch was as arousing as the presence, anticipation pulling him taut.

Quentus nipped at the juncture of Russ's hip and thigh, not hard enough to leave a mark, but the pressure of those sharp teeth wrung a hoarse cry from Russ's throat.

"What do you need?" Quentus asked, lifting his head so that his breath blew across Russ's cock as he spoke.

"You," Russ replied, his voice broken.

"You have me," Quentus replied, moving to cover Russ's body with his. Russ shivered reflexively as he wrapped his arms around Quentus's shoulders.

"Take me," he pleaded, spreading his legs to make more room.

"As you wish," Quentus said, pressing against Russ's entrance.

For one moment of sheer hysteria, Russ had a flash of Westley saying those words to Buttercup, imagined they meant the same from Quentus as they had in the film, but that was wishful thinking and he knew it.

Then Quentus thrust into him hard, the jolt of pain and pleasure from the movement stealing all thought. Russ grasped at

Quentus's shoulders, trying to steady himself, to right his world again, but he was completely adrift. His body took over, reacting without conscious thought to Quentus's lovemaking.

When he came down from the high, Quentus had rolled to one side and folded Russ in a tight embrace. Russ let his thoughts drift, poking desultorily at the unexpected revelation brought on by Quentus's words. He knew Quentus didn't mean anything by the phrase other than simple agreement. Russ's reaction came entirely from a cultural phenomenon that would have no meaning to Quentus. None of that changed Russ's reaction, though, or the import of it. He *wanted* it to mean more than it did, and that was far more critical than whatever Quentus might have meant by the words.

He'd made the decision to take the sabbatical and see what could develop with Quentus, hoping it would be something very much like what had happened. Maybe there were elements of it he wasn't comfortable with yet, but for the most part, he'd gotten exactly what it said on the tin: a dominant, sometimes domineering lover and a life in the Roman Empire with all its challenges, constraints, and pleasures, but most importantly, he'd found someone to love. He wasn't sure what it said about him that he'd had to travel back to Nemausus in the second century CE to find that person, but now that he had him, Russ wasn't letting go.

Now he just had to convince Quentus to feel the same way.

CHAPTER ELEVEN

RUSS stared down at himself as he prepared to dress for the day. He couldn't possibly go to the baths like this. He was covered in marks from Quentus's teeth and hands. He'd lose what little standing he had with the others if they saw him like this.

"Are you not going to dress for the day?" Quentus asked, coming back into the bedroom.

"I'm going to dress," Russ said, picking up his *subligar*, "but I won't be undressing anywhere but in the bedroom for days."

"Why not?" Quentus asked.

"Look at me!" Russ exclaimed. "I'm covered in bite marks."

"So?"

"Would you go to the baths covered in bruises?"

"I'm a soldier," Quentus replied. "I always have bruises."

"Not that are obviously from someone's teeth," Russ retorted. "I look like some cheap whore who's been used and tossed aside."

"You are not a whore," Quentus growled, advancing on Russ, "and I will have strong words with anyone who dares to imply such a thing. You are mine."

Russ appreciated the sentiment, so close to what he wanted to hear, but that didn't change the rest of his situation. "They won't say anything when you're around," Russ said. "Nobody is that stupid, but they will look at me and they will think it. They will wonder what it says about me that I allowed this, and perhaps some of those who were considering hiring me as a scribe will change their minds because this will cast doubt as to my standing and my independence."

Quentus frowned. "Your absence from the baths will be as detrimental as you claim the bruises will be."

"You should have thought about that before you went after me like a barbarian," Russ muttered.

"Mark me as well," Quentus said unexpectedly.

"What?"

"You fear people will look down on you because you bear the marks of my claiming," Quentus said. "If I am marked as well, there is no inequality between us."

"Do you really think they'll fall for that?"

"Perception is everything," Quentus said, shrugging out of the tunic he wore at home. "Leave your mark on me."

Russ hesitated a moment longer, but he could hardly deny his desire to touch Quentus. He so rarely got the chance other than hanging onto Quentus's shoulders for leverage if he was on his back, and since half the time he was on his hands and knees, he didn't always get that.

He stepped closer to Quentus, running his fingers over the strong pectoral muscles. He had finger-shaped bruises on his hips, but he knew he'd never manage to leave comparable marks on Quentus. His hands weren't that large or that strong, but he could use his teeth and leave marks that way. Finding a likely spot, he leaned in, nuzzling the skin over his collarbone before latching onto it with his teeth. They might have started this for purely practical reasons, but Russ intended to take full advantage of it.

Quentus still smelled of sex from the night before, and his skin tasted salty from sweat. Russ sucked harder, his hands roaming over Quentus's sides as he raised a mark to the surface. Lifting his head, he risked a glance at Quentus's face, not sure what kind of reaction he would see there. Quentus looked back down at him, eyes hot with need. Emboldened by Quentus's expression, Russ licked his way lower to one dark nipple. He didn't try to leave a mark there, simply sucking at it lightly before choosing another spot to bite. He didn't need to leave as many marks on Quentus as Quentus had left on him, just enough to make it clear to anyone who cared to look that they were lovers, not master and slave.

Quentus seemed in no hurry to have him stop, though, his fingers cradling Russ's head as he raised a second mark. Russ considered pulling away, but Quentus guided his head lower, until Russ's lips were near his navel. "Again," Quentus said.

Russ chuckled nearly silently as he did as Quentus said. Even in this, even with Russ leaving marks of his own claim to match Quentus's claim on him, Quentus was fully in charge. Russ found it bothered him less with each passing day. He didn't need to control their sexual interactions, not when allowing Quentus to do it led to the kind of lovemaking he'd experienced at Quentus's hands. He simply needed to feel valued outside of those interactions, and Quentus's willingness to let Russ mark him now, while surprising, was exactly the kind of affirmation Russ needed. He wasn't a toy or a tool to Quentus. He had value, a place in Quentus's life that surpassed his place in Quentus's bed.

Suddenly desperate, he went the rest of the way to his knees, nipping at Quentus's iliac crease and then biting down hard. Quentus groaned, bringing a smile to Russ's face as he turned his head and lapped at Quentus's cock. It was already hard, the tip shiny with proof of Quentus's reaction to Russ's attentions. "Not yet," he teased, winking at Quentus as he trailed his lips over the top of Quentus's thigh. The skin there stretched so tautly over muscle that he could not suck it into his mouth as he had done at Quentus's hip, but Russ bit down anyway, although that bruise would be partially concealed by the hair on Quentus's leg. At this point, Russ didn't even care. People would see the marks or not and think what they wanted. Russ knew Quentus cared enough about the way people perceived him to allow this. That was more than enough for now.

He managed to leave three more marks on Quentus's stomach and thighs before his lover grew impatient, guiding his head back to center. Russ opened his mouth and took Quentus inside. Quentus tried to thrust, and while Russ could have taken him, he wanted more than just to have Quentus fuck his face. He wanted to give his lover a taste of his own medicine. Putting his hands on Quentus's thighs, he pushed back so his lips ringed the tip of Quentus's cock. He sucked lightly, playing with the slit with his tongue. Quentus groaned, his hands settling on Russ's shoulders instead of his head, allowing him more freedom of movement. Russ didn't doubt Quentus could take control again at any moment, and the thought didn't bother him as much as perhaps it should have, but for now, Quentus had given him permission to play.

He settled in to give Quentus incentive to let Russ have this much control, using every trick he had ever picked up to give Quentus the best blow job of his life. Russ could feel the trembling in Quentus's legs as he kept himself steady and struggled not to thrust into Russ's mouth like he so clearly wanted to do. His control lasted far longer than Russ expected it to, right up until the moment Russ moved his hands from Quentus's hips to his ass. Whether Quentus took that as permission or whether he simply grew tired of waiting, Russ didn't know, but Quentus snapped his hips forward, hard enough to nearly cause Russ to choke. His eyes watered as he overrode his gag reflex and angled his head to ease ingress of Quentus's cock down his throat. He timed his breathing to the rapid thrusts so he could take what Quentus dished out. His own cock ached, but he would see to Quentus first. His lover had made it quite clear he wanted to be the one to bring Russ to release, whether he came first or whether Russ did. After the concession Quentus had made in letting Russ leave marks on him, Russ wasn't going to ask for anything more. Hell, he'd probably even agree to no climax at all in exchange for what he'd already received.

Quentus cried out and his cock twitched in Russ's mouth. Russ choked a little on it, but he managed to swallow most of Quentus's offering. He leaned back, gasping for breath as Quentus pulled him to his feet.

"Are you well?" Quentus demanded.

Russ nodded, still trying to catch his breath.

"Russ," Quentus said, shaking him a little.

"You are not a small man," Russ said by way of explanation. "You caught me off guard."

"And yet you seem to enjoy it."

"I do enjoy it," Russ said. "I like the way you taste, the way you smell, the way I get to steal your control when I suck you off. I know what you think when you see me on my knees, but you're the one who can't keep from coming in my mouth."

"Impudent wretch," Quentus said with a light slap to Russ's hip. "Just for that, I shouldn't let you come."

"It would be worth it," Russ replied. "You have bite marks too. That's pleasure enough for me."

"But it isn't pleasure enough for me," Quentus insisted. "I want to see your face as you come undone under my hands."

"Whatever you want," Russ said.

"Yes," Quentus agreed. "Whatever I want. And right now, I want you on your hands and knees."

Russ spun around, dropping onto the bed in the designated position. He didn't care what Quentus had in mind. He'd enjoyed everything his lover had done to and with him, even the occasional swat. Whatever Quentus intended, Russ knew it would be good.

Russ flinched a little when Quentus fingered his hole. Quentus had taken him frequently and with some force over the past day and a half, and he was tender now, but Quentus didn't push inside. Instead he left his thumb resting against Russ's entrance while he stroked Russ with his other hand. As worked up as Russ was, it only took a few strokes for him to shudder through his climax. Only then did Quentus press harder on his guardian ring, the slight bite of pain intensifying Russ's orgasm.

"How do you do that?" Russ asked when he could speak again. "How do you always know just what I need?"

"I pay attention," Quentus said. "I get pleasure from knowing I've left you completely sated."

TO QUENTUS'S surprise, Russ did not bother with his toga as they prepared to leave for the baths. After their conversation—and the sex, by all the gods, the sex got better every time—he had expected Russ to want every possible affectation of citizenry and status when they appeared in public together, but Russ put on only the simple tunic. Quentus noticed, however, that Russ walked more at his side than behind him as they made their way through the crowded streets to the baths. Even more than that, he held his head high rather than look down at his feet the way he had always done before. The change surprised Quentus. Had he cowed his lover so completely before now that Russ hadn't dared show his true self?

Quentus wasn't sure what to think of that. It had been such a long time since he'd had anyone in his life besides soldiers and servants under his command. He had grown used to having to be in control of everything, to shouldering all the responsibility. The success or failure of every battle the legion fought rested on his head. Every soldier who didn't come home was a stain on his soul, making him all the more determined to control what he could. It hadn't occurred to him to do anything less with Russ, whom he had far more motivation to keep safe and close.

"Quentus, Rastus, well met!"

Crius's greeting drew Quentus from his thoughts.

"Hello, Crius," Russ called back, not waiting for Quentus to speak first. Had Russ done that before? "How are you today?"

"Very well," Crius said. "Quentus, you are quiet."

"Rastus is doing so well speaking for me that I saw no reason to stop him," Quentus said, making sure to smile at Russ as he spoke. He did not want his teasing to discourage his lover's newfound confidence. "I am well."

"Good to hear. Rastus, when will you have time to come by my house? I have a letter that needs to be written."

"I am free this afternoon," Russ said with a glance at Quentus. Quentus nodded imperceptibly, giving permission, hopefully without Crius noticing. He had not realized how far under his thumb he had kept Russ. Certainly he wanted his lover with him as much as possible, at mealtimes, in the baths, when they slept, but he had been dictating far more than that. No wonder Russ had insisted on having a profession of his own. Quentus had been strangling him without realizing it.

"Wonderful," Crius said. "Perhaps after lunch we could attend to business."

"Of course," Russ agreed. "Are you going to the baths?"

"Not yet," Crius said. "I have business to attend to first, and I prefer to save my relaxation until I have finished with that. Depending on how long you stay, I might see you there. If not, we will talk this afternoon."

"I'll look forward to it," Russ said.

Crius waved farewell as Russ continued on toward the baths, Quentus trailing behind him this time. It made for a sufficiently odd switch in roles that it left Quentus feeling vaguely uncomfortable, yet as he looked around surreptitiously, he saw nothing on the faces of those they passed to suggest anyone else found it odd. Granted, he didn't see any acquaintances, anyone who would have a different expectation, but Quentus didn't worry about his friends. They knew Russ now and wouldn't think anything of Russ's behavior. Domitius and his allies would find fault no matter how Russ and Quentus acted, because Russ wasn't from an old Roman family the way Domitius was, so their opinion didn't matter. The men whose opinions could impact their lives were the other citizens, the ones not actively associated with either of the rival parties. The men who were walking to and from the baths right now and not paying the slightest attention to either Quentus or Russ.

Quentus frowned. Had he grown so out of touch with the world around him that he no longer knew what his peers expected from one another, or was Russ such an unknown outside quantity that he set all the rules on their ear by his presence alone? He didn't have the answer, but he needed to find it, and the sooner the better. He didn't have a traditional household. His wife Alexia had died eighteen years ago, giving birth to Callistratus. His mother had died of the plague right before Quentus had received his posting in Nemausus, when Callistratus was twelve. His sister lived with her husband's family in Arausio, and they saw each other only rarely. Callistratus was away with the legions at Hadrian's Wall. He had no family expectations pressing down on him, no demands that he order his life in a certain way. He had an army to command, but as Septimus's second, he rarely went far from town these days, keeping the peace in Provincia rather than establishing the empire at its edges. He had reached a point in his life where he could think about himself and his own comfort. Russ was part of that, indeed the center of that, but watching his lover converse with men of their acquaintance as they prepared for the baths today, Quentus realized he had to adjust his vision of what that would be like. He couldn't treat Russ like a servant and then expect others to respect him.

Russ undressed and set his garments aside, and Quentus saw the looks some of the others gave the bruises covering his torso. Quentus frowned, removing his own garb quickly and stepping to Russ's side. No one looked at him as directly as they looked at Russ. Regardless of their growing respect for Russ, Quentus had a long-established standing that none but Jacobus and Septimus could rival. He saw their eyes dart over his body as well, though, taking in the same kinds of marks on him, before darting away. When they turned back to Russ, all trace of disdain had disappeared from their faces. As much as Quentus relished the sight of his claim on Russ's fair skin, Quentus wouldn't be leaving that quantity of marks again. He wouldn't put Russ in that position a second time, not unless Russ asked him to.

"Someone had a good night," Gustavus announced with a grin when Russ and Quentus entered the sauna.

"Someone should mind their own business," Quentus snapped.

"If you didn't want them knowing, you shouldn't have left marks," Russ retorted. "I had a very good night and an even better morning."

Quentus fought to hide his surprise. Where had this saucy side of his lover come from? Russ had always been completely circumspect in public, letting Quentus carry any conversation not directed specifically at him. He had spoken up at dinner the night before, but even then, he had heeded the bounds of propriety, giving his hosts the respect they deserved. He looked at Gustavus and then back at Russ and realized suddenly that Gustavus was probably several years younger than Russ. If Russ weren't a stranger, new to the city and their circle, his comments wouldn't be the slightest bit out of line. Certainly Gustavus seemed to find nothing unusual about Russ's reply, giving Russ a conspiratorial grin. Quentus shuddered a little at the thought of Gustavus and Russ ganging up on him. Between Gustavus's knowledge of Quentus's weaknesses and Russ's sharp tongue, Quentus wouldn't stand a chance against them.

Maybe that wouldn't be such a bad thing.

"I'm going on to the caldarium," Quentus announced. "Gustavus, don't get in too much trouble without me. Rastus, keep him in line."

"Keep me in line?" Gustavus spluttered. "He's the new one around here."

"And you're the young one who acts before he thinks," Quentus retorted. "You could learn a thing or two from Rastus."

Quentus saw the gratitude on Russ's face along with the surprise and determination not to let Quentus down. He smiled at his lover and withdrew to the other room.

"Well, well," Domitius drawled as Quentus lowered himself into the cold water. "You're slipping, Maximus, if you let that little whore mark you that way."

"It's not my fault you have your bedmates so cowed they can't show you a good time in return," Quentus retorted. "Some of us appreciate a little spirit in our lovers."

"Some of us prefer our whores to know their place."

Quentus was on his feet, ready to lunge for Domitius's throat, when a hard hand grabbed his shoulder. "Greetings, Quentus," Octavian said, his eyes sharp with warning. "Domitius."

Domitius returned Octavian's nod with a short one of his own. The conversation was no less tense after that, but at least it revolved around politics rather than Quentus's sex life.

CHAPTER TWELVE

"I HEARD from two different craftsmen today that Domitius tried to bribe them last week," Russ told Quentus when he returned home from his daily routine of checking in with each of Quentus's friends as well as with the craftsmen they suspected Domitius of targeting. "They both declined, so he resorted to threats instead. For the moment, they're still holding out, but if he starts carrying through on his threats, they might reconsider."

"Did they say what threats?" Quentus asked.

"To vandalize their shops, to speak to the owners of their tabernae to get them evicted, to scare off customers," Russ reported.

"If he gets them evicted from their tabernae, we can move them into other ones. Mine are both empty at the moment, and I know of others that are as well," Quentus said. "Domitius won't vandalize a taberna because he won't want to alienate the owner of the house, but if the tradesman owns his own shop, Domitius won't have that holding him back."

"Can you alert the patrols within the city?" Russ asked. "Not to the point of giving our plans away to Domitius, but enough that they make sure their routes take them past the shops in question?"

Quentus smiled. "There are occasionally advantages to having a legion at my command. I will speak with the commander of the night watch and let him know we have reason to expect problems in certain areas of the city."

"That doesn't change the fact that he's still approaching shops and businesses," Russ said. "If he can get enough people on board, he can manipulate the prices enough to put the holdouts out of business, and then he can raise the prices as high as he wants. There has to be a more effective way to stop him."

"His plan of approaching those with relatively little power is a good one," Quentus said. "By going about it this way, he hasn't angered enough of the powerful citizens for them to make a move against him."

"Then maybe it's time to focus on those citizens who aren't allied with either side," Russ suggested. "Even if we don't succeed in bringing him down, awareness of what he's doing could give other craftsmen the courage to refuse his offer and stand up to his threats, and if we do get enough people on our side, we might bring enough pressure to bear to stop him for good."

"I wouldn't know where to start," Quentus said.

"I bet Jacobus would."

"GREETINGS, Rastus."

Russ looked around when he heard his name, startled out of his thoughts. He rarely encountered people he knew in the streets unless he was with Quentus. "Hello, Gustavus."

"Where are you bound for today?" Gustavus asked, falling into step beside Russ.

"My usual rounds," Russ replied. "Checking to see if anyone has work for me, visiting those craftsmen we would like to keep on our side, perhaps finding a few new ones to resist the scheming of others. And you?"

"I am at loose ends today," Gustavus admitted. "I thought I might walk with you. The craftsmen have taken much at your word.

It might help us all for them to see that you do have the allies you claim."

"Most of them have been convinced by the presence of the night watch near their shops and homes," Russ said, "but I won't refuse your company."

"I don't know if anyone has thought to tell you," Gustavus said as they continued along Russ's route for the day, "but Quentus is so much more relaxed since you've joined us. Before, he was always sharp, always on the verge of a bad mood, but now he saves those scowls for people who actually deserve them instead of inflicting them on everyone. Thaddaeus and I have noticed it, of course, since we spend so much time studying with him, but even the foot soldiers have commented on it. They don't know you to make the connection, but they know something has changed for the better."

"I'm glad," Russ said because the comment needed some acknowledgment, but inside he was dancing at the thought that he had somehow made Quentus's life a little better. He could list the myriad ways his life had improved since coming to Nemausus, but he had a much harder time quantifying what he brought to Quentus. Contentment seemed as good a place as any to start.

Shouting behind him drew his attention a scant second before Gustavus pushed him into a doorway and drew his sword. "Stay there," Gustavus ordered. "Quentus will kill me if anything happens to you."

Russ chose not to argue, making himself as small as possible in the shelter of the doorway. He had no idea who Gustavus was fighting or why, but he wasn't about to do anything to distract the other man. Russ didn't want to be the one to tell Quentus something had happened to his captain, either.

The fight was brutal, all thrusting swords and clanging armor, and then Gustavus took down his assailant. He raised his sword to strike the final blow, but Russ caught his arm.

"Wait! Do you know him?"

"I've never seen him before," Gustavus replied.

"Then maybe you should ask why he attacked you," Russ suggested. "It might be important."

"He wasn't after me," Gustavus said. "I just got in his way."

"Who was he after, then?"

"You."

The shock left Russ momentarily speechless. "Why would anyone attack me?"

"I don't know," Gustavus said, "but I'm sure Quentus will find out. Let's go. I want you somewhere safe in case he wasn't working alone."

Russ was shaken enough to let Gustavus escort him home. He did his best to pointedly ignore the man Gustavus dragged along behind them.

They'd passed through the vestarium of Quentus's house and into the atrium before Quentus heard the commotion and joined them. He took one look at Gustavus's face, his drawn sword, and the man on his knees behind Gustavus, and flipped. Russ had the stray thought—he was pretty sure he was in shock—that the word was too modern for their current context, but he wasn't in any shape to come up with another one.

"Why did you attack Rastus?" Quentus demanded, putting his sword at the man's throat. "He's never done you any harm."

"It wasn't personal," the man said hoarsely. "I had a debt. Taking this job repaid it. Or it would have if I'd succeeded."

"Who hired you?" Quentus asked.

"He'll kill me if I tell you."

"I'll kill you if you don't tell me," Quentus snarled.

Russ wanted to ask him to calm down, but he didn't know enough about the justice system to know if there was another option. Their conversations about stopping Domitius hadn't covered the rest of the legal system.

"And if I do tell you?"

Russ suspected that was the wrong question to ask, but Quentus didn't attack the man. "I want the man responsible for the attack," Quentus said. "If I have him, I don't care what happens to you."

"Domitius," the man replied.

Quentus's eyes narrowed, his focus so fixed on the man on the ground that Russ wondered if he saw anything else.

"He's a dead man," Quentus growled.

"Not in cold blood," Gustavus said. "Do this right, so it can't come back and hurt you or Rastus."

"Get him out of here," Quentus ordered Gustavus. "Keep him somewhere we have access to him and Domitius doesn't. I want him to testify when we take Domitius before the magistrate. I don't want Domitius getting out of this one."

"Yes, sir, Legatus," Gustavus said with a salute. The man on the ground paled even more, if that was possible, upon hearing Quentus's title.

"On your feet," Gustavus ordered, jerking upward on the man's bonds. The man stumbled to his feet and Gustavus dragged him away.

"I swear, I can't let you out of my sight," Quentus muttered when they were alone again. "I let you out alone and someone tries to kill you. Am I going to have to keep you under lock and key to keep you safe?"

Russ wondered if he should protest as Quentus stalked toward him and propelled him into the bedroom, but Quentus wasn't angry at him. Quentus wanted to protect him, and that was an entirely different thing. When he wasn't so shaken, he'd discuss some realistic safety options with his lover, but for now, he was content to let Quentus manhandle him out of his clothes and into bed.

"Mine," Quentus growled, climbing onto the bed after Russ. "They can't have you."

Russ shivered with the aftereffects of the adrenaline from the fight and the always arousing sensation of Quentus hovering over him. Quentus braced himself on one elbow so he had his other hand free to inspect Russ. There really wasn't any other word for it. Quentus ran his palm over every inch of Russ's skin, starting with his hands, moving up his arms, across his chest and then down the other side, back up, over his chest again and then down his stomach to his legs. Russ lay there quietly and let Quentus look and touch to his heart's content. Russ wasn't going to complain about anything that got his lover's hands on him, and truth be told, he needed the reassurance right now as well, that he was alive, that he was unscathed. Quentus rolled him onto his stomach and repeated the process with Russ's back, checking for injury and finding none.

"Gustavus pushed me to safety," Russ said when Quentus neared his feet. "I bumped up against the doorway a bit, but not even enough to scrape my shoulder."

"I owe him a great debt," Quentus said, "for I would be lost without you."

"Let me turn over?" Russ asked.

Quentus lifted up enough to allow the movement.

"I'm safe," Russ said. "I'm right here with you and I'm not going anywhere. I promise."

"You make promises it might not be within your ability to keep," Quentus said.

"I'll never break it willingly," Russ replied.

"Domitius won't get a second chance to take you from me."

Russ didn't get the chance to answer. Quentus kissed him and all rational thought fled.

"RUSS!"

The sound of his name startled Russ enough that he dropped the pitcher of water he was carrying. It shattered at his feet, clay shards going every which way, propelled by the splash of water. He needed to clean it up before someone slipped in it or cut themselves, but the panic in Quentus's voice overrode all else. He had left Quentus sleeping off the hard, fast round of sex and had gone to fetch water so they could wash up later. He didn't know what could have happened in the few minutes he was gone, but it didn't matter.

"I'm here. What's wrong?" he said, skidding through the curtain that separated the bedroom from the peristylium.

"I woke up and you weren't here," Quentus said, grabbing Russ and then practically tossing him onto the bed. "You weren't here!"

Comprehension dawned. "I just went to get some water." He sat up and reached for Quentus. "I'm here. I'm fine. Lie back and let me make it up to you?"

Quentus looked at him suspiciously, but Russ pasted on his most innocent, beguiling smile and hoped it would work.

"Very well," Quentus said, joining Russ on the bed. Russ nudged him until he reclined comfortably. He thought for a moment about straddling Quentus's hips, but in this mood, he doubted Quentus would leave him there for long, and that defeated the purpose. He settled for kneeling next to Quentus's side and lifting his lover's hand to his mouth. He had no idea how long Quentus would let him remain in control, but he would take advantage of it for the time it lasted, soothing his lover in every way he could think of, returning all the pleasure Quentus had ever given him. He sucked on one long finger, his own digits loose around Quentus's wrist, supporting his hand, not confining it. He ran his other hand up Quentus's arm, pausing to trace the cut of his forearm and bicep. He'd had those arms around him. He knew how strong they were, but now they were expanses of skin, responsive to his touch, the veins popping as Quentus gasped.

Russ moved to Quentus's middle finger, using every trick he could think of to arouse Quentus further. He stroked and squeezed Quentus's arm, digging deep and then easing back, and all the while, he kept his gaze locked with Quentus's, letting his lover see his own arousal and how much he enjoyed touching Quentus this way.

Quentus growled and reached for Russ, but Russ stopped him with a gentle hand on his chest. "Let me love you?" he asked softly. "When I'm done, you can do whatever you want to me. Just let me have this moment."

"I can do whatever I want to you now."

"You can," Russ said. "You're strong enough, but wouldn't it be better to know I wanted it? Wouldn't it be better to know I gave in to you willingly?"

Quentus's eyes darkened, his pupils blown with lust, and Russ pressed his advantage, licking along the vein from Quentus's wrist down toward his elbow. "Let me play now and I'll take anything you want to give me later."

"And if that's nothing?" Quentus asked.

"Then I'll take that too," Russ promised. He didn't think that would happen, but if it did, he'd consider it a reasonable price to pay.

He followed the vein up Quentus's bicep to his shoulder and across the broad expanse of his lover's chest. Quentus's body was a marvel to him. He'd known muscular men in his own time, but it had always felt fake, either the product of too many hours in the gym, too many steroids, or both. Quentus wouldn't know a gym or a steroid if it bit him in the ass. His body came from years of hard campaigns and rigorous military training. It came from life, and Russ found that incredibly attractive.

He found one of Quentus's nipples hidden beneath the thick pelt of hair on his chest and nuzzled it softly. Quentus gasped, giving Russ the courage to continue. He licked and nibbled on the little nub, worrying it to full hardness. Quentus held eerily still beneath him until Russ finally lifted his head. He couldn't read the expression on Quentus's face.

"Has no one ever done that to you before?"

"Not in a very long time," Quentus said roughly. "I had forgotten how good it could feel."

Russ poked him in the side. "Remember that next time you don't want to let me touch you."

"Insolent pup," Quentus muttered.

"And you love me for it," Russ retorted, leaning toward the other nipple. Quentus caught his head before he could connect and drew him into a demanding kiss.

Russ knew the minute Quentus's hands closed around his head that his moment of control had ended. He discarded the idea of trying to wrest it back before it had even fully formed. He enjoyed pushing Quentus's control, but only because he knew this moment would come, the point at which Quentus would take back control and Russ could slide into submission.

He half expected Quentus to flip them and simply pound into Russ without prelude. It hadn't been long enough since the last time they made love for him to need much, if any, preparation, and they were both fully hard and ready for it, but Quentus surprised him, pulling Russ on top of him.

QUENTUS stared up at the face of the man above him, the man he'd *put* above him. He'd believed Russ was a gift from the gods from the first moment, but he had never expected a gift of this magnitude. Russ had upended Quentus's life from the very beginning, and now... now he was forcing Quentus to revisit everything he'd accepted as given about his life. Everyone else jumped to obey his orders. Russ challenged him before turning around and giving Quentus the gift of his submission. No one had done that for him in twenty years, not since Viator died in battle. Viator had usually ended up on the bottom, but only after fighting Quentus for it. The knowledge that it could have gone the other way had always made the victory sweeter. Russ couldn't stop Quentus physically, but a

131

word would be enough, and that made this victory the sweetest of them all.

Russ was hot and tight around him, no different than every other time they had made love, except that it *was* different. Always before, Quentus had taken what he wanted and needed. Russ hadn't fought him, hadn't discouraged him in any way, but Quentus had still been the one taking. Now, for all that Russ squeezed him as sweetly as ever, Quentus was fully aware of the difference. This time, Russ was giving, not simply being taken, and the magnitude of the gift of his surrender struck deep within Quentus.

He urged Russ to move, to set the rhythm of their lovemaking, and matched the movement of his hips to Russ's beat. He could give any order right now and Russ would obey it. He could send him to his hands and knees, ass in the air for Quentus to plunder. He could tell him to pull off and suck Quentus until he found release. He could make any demand, and so he made none, choosing instead to accept what Russ was already giving him. When his release stole up on him, minutes or hours later, it was the most fulfilling of his career.

CHAPTER THIRTEEN

"Is IT done?" Jacobus asked.

"It will be," Quentus said. "Septimus listened to us, and Domitius could not argue his innocence with the assassin there to accuse him."

"Did he issue a verdict?"

"No, but he ordered Domitius imprisoned for the night," Octavian said. "He has to be thinking about the consequences of ordering Domitius's execution."

"He tried to have Rastus assassinated. I don't see why there's anything else to discuss," Quentus said. He'd been repeating that refrain since Septimus had delayed the verdict.

"Because eliminating Domitius will leave a vacuum of power," Russ said. "A hole in the power structure," he added when he saw their blank looks. "With Domitius gone, someone else will rise to take his place."

"You're so sure," Quentus said with a shake of his head.

"He has brothers, sons, nephews, something," Russ said, "and they may not agree with what Domitius did, but he's still part of their family." He turned to Jacobus. "His holdings will pass to someone, correct?"

"Yes," Jacobus said. "If you had been killed, some portion of his estate would have gone to your family as reparation, but since you were not injured, much less killed, I doubt Septimus will dissolve even part of the property. Domitius's son will inherit if he is executed."

"I don't know anything about the son," Russ said, "but he's not going to be happy about his father's public humiliation and execution. He'll have to decide for himself what to do with his father's legacy, but he'll either take over his father's role in society or someone else will. People were allied with Domitius. They were taken in by his lies or they shared his philosophy. Those people won't go away just because Domitius miscalculated and tried to kill me while I was with someone who could protect me."

"Anytime, Rastus," Gustavus said with a tip of his goblet. "We don't keep accounts around this table."

"We owe each other our lives so many times over that we stopped counting," Crius added. "One small sword fight barely even registers."

"It does for me," Russ said. "You're all warriors, or you were. For you, a fight is normal."

"Not in town," Thaddaeus said with a smile.

"Perhaps not," Russ agreed, "but fighting together, fighting for one another, that's what you do. That's what soldiers do. It's what makes the empire so formidable." Russ was enough a student of history to know it was both more and less than that, but his knowledge stretched far beyond what he could expect the men around the table with him to know or accept. "I'm not a soldier. I'm a scribe. It's not what I do."

"And yet we sit here tonight in a more secure position than we've been in for years because you helped us thwart Domitius's plans," Octavian said with a smile. "We may be soldiers and even tacticians, but only my father is a politician."

"Yet," Russ insisted. "The other citizens of Nemausus don't see me, and furthermore, they don't need to see me. They do, however, see all of you. We may not know who will step up to fill the void left by Domitius's downfall, but I know who will step up to counter him, and furthermore, after today, the citizens of Nemausus are beginning to realize it as well."

"That will make us even more targets for their ire," Jacobus said. "We must all be careful as we go about our business. Even the best trained soldier can be felled by an unexpected blow."

"If the soldier is well trained, the blow will not be unexpected," Quentus said.

"Not all of us are as adept at staying on our guard as you are," Alvinius said. "Sometimes I wonder if you sleep."

"He does," Russ said with a chuckle. "I've seen him."

Gustavus and Thaddaeus grinned, as Russ had known they would, and even Jacobus seemed amused. Quentus, on the other hand, looked perturbed. Russ braced for the explosion, but either Quentus was mellowing or the presence of his friends held him back.

"Only when I know it is safe," he said. Russ counted the relatively mild retort as a win.

"So we must consider even Nemausus as unsafe now?" Leander asked. "I am not so sure that is an improvement."

"It depends on how you define improvement," Russ said. "Whereas before, Domitius considered you his adversaries but did little other than snipe at you; now his allies know you are capable of more. There is a proverb where I come from. 'To whom much is given, much will be required.' We have the ability—the connections and the will—to make Nemausus a better home for everyone, but people will test that, thinking we aren't as committed to the cause or to each other as they are to their own gain."

"And we will be ready," Octavian replied, pinning the others with his gaze. "We have come too far and proven too well what we can do to stop now."

The servants brought dinner then, which forestalled further conversation. Russ relaxed into the camaraderie of the evening, letting the sense of belonging wash over him. He had attended collegial dinners in Tucson, but he had never fit with a group of people like he fit with these eight Roman citizens, men of another time but whose basic honor and determination to do what was right called to him in a way all the intellectual rivalry between colleagues had never done in his past. He might have been born in the twentieth century, but he belonged here in Nemausus. All that remained was making sure Quentus felt the same way.

"You shouldn't go out alone," Quentus said as they were walking toward home later that evening.

Russ bristled at the thought, but at least Quentus had phrased it as a suggestion, not an order. "I can hardly expect you or one of the others to follow me around on my daily business, and if I can't go out at all, how am I supposed to do what needs to be done? We didn't foil Domitius's plans because we sat back and waited for him to come to us."

"You can't expect me to simply let you walk into another trap," Quentus insisted. "I don't want you to get hurt."

"I don't want to get hurt either," Russ said. "I just don't want to feel like a prisoner. Maybe you could teach me to defend myself. I know I'll never be a soldier, but if I knew enough to hold off an attacker long enough for help to arrive, I'd be safer than I am now."

RUSS knew intellectually that the Roman legion was one of the most advanced and best trained military units prior to the seventeenth century or even later, depending on which military historian one believed, but that didn't prepare him for the sheer size of the training fields on the outskirts of Nemausus. Hundreds of youths gathered around instructors, holding wooden swords and wicker shields, waiting for directions.

"Maybe this isn't such a good idea after all," Russ said. "I'm never going to be up to their level."

"And we aren't throwing you in with them," Thaddaeus said. "You aren't here to be a soldier, but Quentus would kill us if we ruined his peristylium practicing there, and our father wouldn't be any happier to have us practicing at our house. Besides, they have practice swords and everything here, so we might as well use them. Come on. Quentus will be joining us later, and I want to show him we're serious about teaching you."

Russ still doubted this was a good idea, but he followed his two teachers to the armory, where they fitted him with a wooden sword and shield of his own. "You won't have the shield if you're just in town on business, but it doesn't hurt to learn the basics."

Russ took them and groaned under the weight. "If the practice equipment is this heavy, I'm afraid to feel what a real sword feels like."

"The real swords are only about half the weight," Gustavus said. "If you can fight with that sword, you can fight with anything." He picked up a practice sword of his own and showed Russ how to hold it.

Russ sighed and prepared to get his ass kicked.

Gustavus and Thaddaeus were better teachers than that, though. They held back the strength of their own blows, coaching Russ through the thrust and parry of swordplay. They still landed far more hits than he did, not hard, since he didn't land any against the two experienced soldiers, but as the hours dragged on, he could at least pretend they had to work a little harder to get past his guard.

Finally Russ called a halt. His arms were trembling so hard he could barely lift the sword again. "Please. Can we take a break?"

"There aren't in breaks in battle."

Russ looked up to where Quentus stood watching them. "I know that. I really do, but this is my first day and I can't even lift the sword right now. If I get hurt, that's only going to slow my training down. Besides, I'm not training to fight any battles, just to defend myself enough to get away or get help."

"The more you learn, the easier that will be," Quentus said.

"Just give me ten minutes to catch my breath," Russ said. "Then I'll start all over again."

Quentus looked unimpressed, but he nodded. Russ collapsed right where he stood, ignoring the concerned looks as he stared up at the blue sky. The sun beat down on him, but it was cooler now than it had been over the summer, for which he was grateful. He didn't think he could have done this in July. He'd always considered himself in decent shape. He ran or swam a couple of times a week at home. He wasn't sharply defined, like some of the athletes at the university, but he wasn't a pudgy desk jockey either. This, though, was far beyond any workout he'd ever dreamed of undertaking. He didn't like what it said about him that Gustavus and Thaddaeus had hardly broken a sweat while he was completely winded.

His whole body ached from the strain of holding the sword as Gustavus and Thaddaeus had taught him, and that didn't even count the bruises where their practice swords had made contact. He knew they were holding back, but that didn't make the impacts from their hits hurt less. Quentus would chide him if he complained after being the one to suggest this, so Russ took another deep breath and forced himself back to his feet. He picked up the sword and nodded to his instructors. "Start at the beginning again."

QUENTUS stood at the foot of the bed and stared at the unmoving lump not even covered by the sheets. After Russ had finished training with Gustavus and Thaddaeus, Quentus had taken him to the baths to soak his tired muscles. For all that Quentus had pushed Russ to keep going today, he did remember what it felt like to be a new recruit. The first few weeks had been miserable, and that was before they'd even been allowed to start working with weapons. Then it had gotten even worse. Russ hadn't wanted to leave the hot water, but eventually they had no choice. They got home, Russ collapsed onto the bed, and he hadn't moved since.

Quentus knelt on the bed at Russ's feet and picked one up, holding it between his palms. "Relax," he murmured as he started to massage Russ's instep. He had done this for Russ once before, the first night he spent under Quentus's roof, but he hadn't taken the time since then to linger this way. He could hear Viator's voice chiding him for getting complacent. From the time they were children, Viator had pushed Quentus, making him consider his actions from every angle, making him think through the consequences of his choices. It had been an asset in their military beginnings, and his death was a loss Quentus had never recovered from. He couldn't bring his old friend back, but he could learn from the mistakes of his past.

Russ just groaned and let his foot rest in Quentus's hands. Quentus smiled as he worked the sore muscles and stiff tendons, coaxing the stiffness out of them. When he had finished with that foot, he switched to the other and then worked his way up Russ's legs. He worked across the muscles of Russ's buttocks, tempted to do more than massage, but he needed Russ to relax so he would be able to continue training tomorrow. He had attended Domitius's execution, but he had taken Russ's concerns to heart. One enemy might be gone, but others would rise to take his place.

They had to be prepared to meet the next threat, whatever form it might take.

He pressed his thumbs hard into the muscles on either side of Russ's spine, knowing from experience where the stress of training built up. Russ winced and hissed at the pressure, but Quentus didn't let up until he felt the knots give beneath his fingers. Russ's sigh of relief went straight to Quentus's groin. He loved the little noises Russ made when they were in bed together. He had hired prostitutes who were more theatrical in their appreciation, but with Russ, Quentus knew every sound was real.

Finished with Russ's back, Quentus moved to his arms. Next to the warriors Quentus spent most of his time with, Russ's arms were positively spindly, but Quentus knew that could be improved with time and effort. He hadn't been even as developed as Russ when he had started his military training. He massaged Russ's arms deeply as well, backing off a bit when the yelp Russ let out had more pain than pleasure in it. He had delivered pain on his enemies and even on servants he'd had to punish, but he didn't want that tonight in bed with Russ. He wanted to make his lover feel good, so good that he would stay. They hadn't talked about it after Russ's return from wherever he had disappeared to. They had left things vague between them, let the assumption that Russ would stay stretch out. So far, Russ had shown no sign of being restless or wanting to leave again, but Quentus watched him like a hawk. He had been caught off guard by Russ's first disappearance. If Russ disappeared again, Quentus intended to know it was coming so he could do everything in his power to stop it.

"Feeling better?" he asked when he had finished massaging Russ's arms.

"Yes, much better," Russ mumbled against the mattress.

Quentus chuckled and rolled Russ onto his back. As tempted as he was by the crease of Russ's buttocks, Russ would never manage to hold himself up in that position tonight, and Quentus wanted his hands free for more than holding Russ's hips in place. Besides, with Russ on his back, Quentus could kiss him while he took him. He lowered his head to do just that.

Russ opened for him immediately, sending a rush of desire and gratitude through Quentus. He had no idea what he had done to deserve this gift from the gods, but he intended to cherish it to the best of his abilities. He lingered over Russ's mouth as he had lingered over the massage.

CHAPTER
FOURTEEN

RUSS let himself into the house, whistling to himself as he untied his sandals and walked deeper into the house. He set down his papers in the tablinum and checked to make sure no new letters had arrived. Finding everything in order, he wandered into the peristylium, intending to relax there until Quentus came home from the forum. He'd gotten halfway to his favorite chair when someone grabbed him from behind and put a sword to his throat. "Who are you and what have you done with my father?"

"My name is Rastus," Russ said, not moving other than to talk. He might have learned a few things from Gustavus and Thaddaeus, but he wasn't stupid enough to get himself killed when he had no hope of winning a fight. "I live here. Ask any of the servants. Ask Antony."

"Antony!" the man behind him shouted. "Where are you?"

The elderly servant came in from the kitchens. "Master Callistratus, you are home! We weren't expecting you."

"Who is this, Antony?"

"That is Rastus, your father's scribe and friend. You should let him go. The legatus would be most upset if you hurt Rastus."

Callistratus lowered his sword and shoved Russ away from him. "Where is my father?"

"He went to the forum today to attend to business. He didn't tell me he had a son."

Russ rubbed at his throat and studied the man across the garden, who was still glaring at him like he was the intruder. He supposed to Callistratus, he was.

"My father never tells anyone anything. He just gives orders."

Russ frowned at the bitterness in the young man's voice. "He's getting better about that. Antony, could you send a messenger to the forum? I'm sure the legatus will be eager for the news of his son's return."

"Of course, sir," Antony said with a bow.

The moment he withdrew, Callistratus advanced on Russ. "You've made yourself at home, walking in like you own the place, ordering the servants about. What hold do you have over my father?"

Russ was tempted to tell Callistratus where he could shove his attitude, but Quentus wouldn't appreciate it if Russ ran his son off before they could even see each other. "He saved my life and invited me to stay here with him. Antony told you I'm his scribe. We've been working to decrease corruption in the city."

"In other words, you're his latest diversion in his attempts to forget about my mother," Callistratus said with a sneer. "You won't last any longer than the others."

"He already has, Callistratus, and I'll ask you to keep a civil tongue in your head. Rastus is my guest. As such, he deserves that much from you." Quentus's voice startled Russ. He had only now asked Antony to send a servant to find Quentus, but Quentus must have been nearly home already. Russ was tempted to move to Quentus's side for the assurance, but he suspected Callistratus would see that as a sign of weakness.

"So he is your concubine."

"No, he's my lover," Quentus said. "He is here by choice, not because I've paid him, and he stays because he wants to be here, not out of any sense of indebtedness. That makes him different even from your mother, who was only ever here out of duty. Now, are you here to insult me or did you have another purpose in mind?"

"Stop it, both of you," Russ said, annoyed at the ridiculous posturing. "I've been here six months and this is the first time we've met, so obviously you've been away for quite a while. Maybe you should sit down and talk, listen to each other's news, something besides this silly arguing."

"Always so wise," Quentus said with a fond smile for Russ. "What say you, my son? Will you leave the past behind us where it belongs?"

Callistratus shot Russ another murderous glare, making Russ wonder just what he'd gotten himself into, but when he turned back to Quentus, he nodded sharply. "Very well."

"How goes the campaign in the north?" Quentus asked. Russ let him guide the conversation. Callistratus's clothes proclaimed him a soldier. If they could discuss battles and strategy, it would give them some common ground. Russ didn't need to understand the details to know that they were finally speaking the same language.

Once he was fairly sure they were not going to return to shouting insults at one another, Russ slipped into the kitchen. "Antony?"

"Sir?"

"Tell me about Callistratus."

"You should really ask the legatus about that," Antony demurred.

"Antony, they're out there talking for what I suspect is the first time in a long time. I'm not going to interrupt them with questions about a past they seem inclined to leave behind for the moment, but if I don't know their story, I'm as likely to make matters worse as to help. The last thing I want is to make matters worse."

"I suppose it would be all right," Antony said. "The legatus married young, soon after his first campaign. His parents arranged the match to the daughter of a powerful family. They tolerated each other, which is better than I can say for some matches, but that was the extent of it. He had lost his friend Viator in that campaign and was not himself, but he honored his parents' wishes. Callistratus was born a year later. His mother died giving birth to him. The legatus's mother was still alive at the time, and she and his sister took over raising the child while the legatus returned to the legions. Eventually his sister married and moved to Arausio, leaving Callistratus alone with his grandparents. When Callistratus was twelve, the legatus rose high enough in the ranks to be posted here in Nemausus instead of on the borders of the empire, and by that time, Callistratus had already started training as a soldier himself and was hardly home. They barely know each other. The legatus was perhaps less subtle than he should have been in seeking companionship when Callistratus still lived at home. Coming home and finding you here was the worst introduction you could have had."

God, if he'd known, he could at least have handled it better when he did find Callistratus there. He could have been prepared for it somehow. He could have tried to diffuse the situation. Quentus always complimented him on how well he controlled social situations (which Russ found hilarious since he'd always been somewhat inept back home), but he'd blown this one completely.

"Thank you, Antony. I'll get the rest of the story from Quentus."

Russ returned to the peristylium, where Quentus still sat talking with his son. Partially hidden by the shadows, he stopped and studied them. He could see the resemblance in the set of their shoulders and the lines of their faces, but where Quentus was dark, from his hair to his skin and eyes, Callistratus was fairer. Not as pale complected as Russ, by any means, but not nearly as dark as his father. His hair was a lighter shade of brown, and Russ thought his eyes might be green, although it was hard to tell at this distance. It made Russ wonder again about Quentus's wife. Antony said she was from another powerful family in the city, but everyone Russ had met was swarthy like Quentus, very much what Russ would consider Mediterranean. Callistratus didn't stand out the way Russ did, but for him to have eyes and hair that much lighter than his father's, his mother must have been fair indeed.

"Will you join us, Russ?" Quentus called.

"Only if I won't be intruding," Russ said, stepping into the light so Callistratus could see him as well. "You haven't seen your son in some time. You have much catching up to do."

"Yes, but I would like for him to get to know you as well."

"Another time," Callistratus said, rising from his seat. "I have traveled many days to get home. I am tired and dirty. A trip to the baths is in order. Father, Rastus, I will take my leave."

"Will you return for dinner?" Russ asked. He might want some time alone so he could yell at Quentus, but this was Callistratus's home. Russ didn't want him to feel unwelcome.

"Not tonight," Callistratus said. "I told my commander I was coming to announce our arrival. I didn't tell him I would be staying. I will come for dinner another night."

"You are welcome anytime," Russ said, when Quentus didn't say anything.

"Send word if you can, so we can prepare your place at the table," Quentus added.

"I won't show up unannounced again," Callistratus said, the glare reappearing on his face.

Russ was sorely tempted to kick Quentus, but instead he walked with Callistratus to the door. "Your father didn't mean to imply you weren't welcome. He simply meant he would prepare a special meal if he knew you were coming."

"So you're an authority on my father now?" Callistratus asked.

"Not an authority," Russ said, "but an avid student. I've had time to learn that what he says and what he means are not always the same thing."

"Then you should teach him to say what he means," Callistratus said. "We would all be happier if you could."

"Believe me, I'm trying," Russ said. "Enjoy the baths and welcome home."

The moment the door closed behind Callistratus, Russ pivoted and stalked back into the peristylium. "You didn't think it was a good idea to tell me you have a son?" he demanded, poking Quentus in the chest. "I could have handled it so much better if you'd bothered to warn me. Even if you hadn't told me that you don't get along, just not being surprised by his existence would have been nice."

"It didn't seem important," Quentus said with a shrug. "He is stationed in Britannia. It will be years before he rises high enough in the army to choose his own station, unless he chooses not to make a career of his service. For all I knew, you could be gone again before he ever came home."

"Gone?" Russ repeated. "Where exactly do you think I'm going? You made it abundantly clear I was staying right here."

"I don't know," Quentus said. "You had a life before I found you. You say I haven't told you about my life, but you've wormed your way into every part of my life, and I still know nothing about you. Whatever brought you here, it could take you away from me at any second. I can't fight an enemy I can't see, and your past hangs over me like a shade, just waiting to snatch you away."

"My past is in the past," Russ said. "There's nothing to draw me back. I swear."

"Then why won't you talk about it?" Quentus demanded. "When I ask you about it, I get evasions or outright lies. You just discovered the only secret I had from you. What are you hiding from me?"

Russ swallowed hard. Quentus would never believe the truth. "Nothing that matters," he swore. "When I left for those few days, I did it so I could put my past to rest, so I'd be free to stay here with you. That life is as foreign to me now as... as the wilds of the barbarian empires would be to you. The only way I would go back is if you didn't want me anymore."

Russ tensed when Quentus didn't reply right away, but after a moment, Quentus reached in his pouch and drew out a package.

"I don't want you to leave," Quentus said. "I thought I'd made that clear already, but obviously I didn't. I had that made for you. I was going to give it to you when the time seemed right, but I'd rather give it to you now than have you doubt how I feel about you."

Russ unwrapped the package carefully. It wasn't large or particularly heavy, but something in the way Quentus watched him with eagle-sharp eyes made Russ treat it with gravitas anyway. Whatever it contained, this was important to Quentus. He folded back the last piece of cloth to find a heavy gold ring inside. Russ picked it up carefully and examined the symbol on the flat side. It matched the seal on Quentus's signet ring, the one he always used to sign and seal anything Russ wrote for him.

"This is… your ring."

"A copy of it," Quentus affirmed, holding out his hand so Russ could see the matching ring on his own finger. "It's yours. If you want it."

"If I want it?" Russ repeated. "Of course I want it!" He threw himself into Quentus's arms, nearly knocking them both to the floor in his enthusiasm.

"It won't make me any less demanding or any easier to deal with," Quentus warned.

"I didn't think it would," Russ replied, his voice muffled against Quentus's shoulder, "but it means you want me. It means you trust me. I could sign your name to anything with this and no one would question it."

"I know," Quentus said. "You haven't steered me wrong yet, and it's your life too. I rely on you for so much. I never would have taken on Domitius without you, much less brought him down. And yes, maybe others will rise to take his place, but I did it. I made a difference here. You brought me that. It only seemed right to give this to you."

"Thank you," Russ said softly. "You won't regret it."

"Callistratus won't be happy about it."

"Does it matter what he thinks?" Russ asked seriously. "I mean, I know he's your heir. Everything will pass to him when you die, but for the time before that happens, can he challenge your right to give it to me?"

"No," Quentus said. "Not as long as I'm alive and of sound mind. He might try to argue that giving you the ring is proof that I'm not of sound mind, but Jacobus, Octavian, and the others will vouch for you and for my actions since meeting you. I may be hopelessly taken with you, but it has not impeded my judgment."

"Hopelessly taken?" Russ said. "I like the sound of that."

"I do too," Quentus said as he reached for Russ to pull him into an embrace. "I had forgotten what it was to have a companion, a true one, not simply a friend or someone with whom to find release. I haven't had that in many years."

"Twenty?" Russ guessed.

"Antony told you about Viator?"

"Only that he died during your first campaign and you came home a changed man," Russ replied. "I guessed the rest."

"Viator was my best friend, but he was more than that. We became lovers almost before we realized what that meant, but we knew each other so well it was inevitable. We played together as children, trained together as youth, and marched to war together as young men. He fell in battle because a commanding officer gave a bad order. I promised his shade I wouldn't let it happen again. That I would never again follow an order I knew was wrong."

"And you never let anyone else close to you?"

"I couldn't," Quentus said. "I couldn't take another lover, not a true lover, until I could control my world enough that I wouldn't lose him the way I lost Viator."

That explained so much, Russ realized. With a past like that, of course Quentus would be a control freak. It also made the few times Quentus had relaxed his control enough to let Russ touch and tease him all the more remarkable.

"How about we agree to work together on controlling things so we can stay together?" Russ asked. "I might not be a soldier, but I can help with other things."

"Like Domitius."

"Like Domitius," Russ agreed. "You're nearing retirement from the legion. You said so yourself. I can't help you there, but I can help you with everything that's politics here in Nemausus. If you'll let me, that is."

CHAPTER
FIFTEEN

RUSS lay awake listening to Quentus's breathing as he slept. He fiddled with the ring on his hand, not quite at the point of accepting its presence as a given. He'd started to wonder if he'd ever get any definitive sign from Quentus after six months. He hadn't given up hope exactly, but he'd started negotiating with himself about what would be enough, what it would take for him to stay. He'd played mental games with himself for weeks now, trying to convince himself he had enough reasons to stay. If Quentus gave him another massage like he'd done the first night of Russ's training, if Quentus included him in dinner without one of the others explicitly inviting him, if Quentus asked his opinion where Septimus could hear… except Quentus had done all of those things and still Russ hadn't felt like it was enough.

The ring, though, was something that couldn't be misinterpreted. It was the key to the kingdom. With it, Russ had as much control over Quentus's life as Quentus did. It was a show of trust, of faith, that couldn't be misunderstood. Quentus might not have said he loved Russ in so many words, but he wouldn't have given Russ the ring if he hadn't wanted Russ to be a permanent part of his life.

Russ still had six months left in his sabbatical. He didn't *have* to make a decision until March, and if he'd had any doubts left, he would have taken that time, but the doubts were gone, chased away by the gold band around his finger, and the longer he delayed, the less time his department chair would have to find a replacement for him.

Leaving to take care of it, though, would require an explanation to Quentus. He couldn't simply disappear like he'd done last time. For one thing, he didn't want to end up locked in the house again, but more importantly, he didn't want to abuse Quentus's trust. They had finally achieved a balance in their relationship that he wasn't willing to sacrifice. The problem remained, as it had been from the beginning: how to explain the situation to Quentus. He couldn't do it with science, but perhaps he could do it with religion.

Quentus frequently left offerings at the temple of Mars. Russ didn't know the Roman myths as well as he knew the Greek ones, but instances of the gods interfering in the lives of mortal were plentiful. Quentus already believed the gods had sent Russ to him. Russ could build on that, making his presence in this time a gift of the gods.

He would talk to Quentus tomorrow and see how it went. He had time to convince Quentus of the necessity of a few days' absence.

"COME sit with me," Russ said when Quentus came home from the forum the next day. "I have something to tell you."

Quentus looked concerned at that, but he came and joined Russ on the cushions spread out to one side of the peristylium. "Is something wrong?"

"Not wrong," Russ said, "but something I should perhaps have told you before. You have asked once or twice before yesterday about my past, and I always gave a vague answer. I didn't know how to explain. I wasn't sure you would believe me."

"Believe what?" Quentus asked.

Russ took a deep breath. This was it. If Quentus didn't accept the basic tenet of his explanation, the rest of this would be a mess.

"You know how you've always said the gods put you in the right place at the right time to save me from the boar?"

"Yes," Quentus said.

"I don't know if the gods put you there, but Venus put me there," Russ said. "She brought me from my time and my home because I was alone there, without someone to share my life with. She offered me a chance to find love in another time and place than my own. I just had to trust her."

"Why didn't you tell me sooner?"

"I wasn't sure you'd believe me," Russ replied honestly. "It's not every day the gods interfere in people's lives so directly."

"So why are you telling me now?" Quentus asked. Russ wasn't quite sure what to make of Quentus's calm acceptance, but he'd go with it as long as he could. His life was certainly easier if Quentus wasn't freaking out about this.

"Venus gave me a set time to make a decision about staying where she put me. Once I made it, she said, I could return to my time to set my affairs in order and say good-bye before settling permanently in the time she picked for me," Russ explained. "I've made my decision. I want to stay with you, but I can't abandon my past completely without making some arrangements. When I left before, it was to make plans to be gone for a year, the time I would need to make my choice, but people are expecting me back at the end of that time. I need to tell them I won't be coming back. I need to let them know I'm leaving for good."

"So you don't actually have to do this now," Quentus said. "It hasn't been a year yet."

"No, it hasn't," Russ agreed, "but I don't need the remaining time to make my decision. I want to stay here with you. The sooner I do this, the sooner everything will be settled and we won't have to worry about it anymore. We won't have it hanging over our heads, unresolved."

"What the gods give, the gods can take away." Quentus sounded more worried than Russ had ever heard him.

"That's true." Russ hadn't considered that aspect of choosing this way to tell his tale. He'd intended to put the story at a level Quentus could understand and accept, not add to his concerns. He knew his decision wouldn't change, but he had invoked the gods with all their capriciousness. "But Venus is the goddess of love. Why would she separate us after she worked so hard to bring us together?"

"Who knows why the gods do anything?" Quentus retorted. "I have always been conscientious in my devotion to Mars. Perhaps it is time to add a shrine to Venus in the atrium. I would not have her think we were ungrateful for her role in our lives."

"We can rearrange the atrium whenever you want," Russ offered. He knew it wouldn't change anything, but he would do whatever it took to make Quentus comfortable with this revelation and secure in their future together.

"I will make my devotions to Venus on the way home from the forum today," Quentus declared. "The priestess there can tell me how best to please the goddess."

"YOU are back much sooner than I expected," Bernard said to Russ as he walked into the entrance hall of the château d'Eternité. "It hasn't been anywhere near a year yet."

"I know," Russ said, "but I've made my decision. There didn't seem to be a reason to delay making it official."

"You are welcome here as long as you need to stay, of course," Bernard said. "Your original room is available at the moment, or we have one that's more in the style of a Roman villa if that would make you feel more at home."

"After six months, it does seem odd to be surrounded by medieval architecture," Russ admitted. "You'd think Nemausus—Nîmes would feel strange since I lived in this era for most of my life and have only been there for six months, but it feels like home."

"As it should, if you're planning on making a complete break," Bernard replied. "Have you thought this all the way through?"

"What do you mean?" Russ asked. "That's where I want to be. What is there to think through?"

"Your lover in Nîmes, how old is he?"

"I don't know for sure," Russ said, "but he has a son who's already an adult, so he can't be much younger than forty."

"Life expectancy in the Roman Empire was only about fifty," Bernard reminded him. "You, however, have had the benefit of modern nutrition and healthcare. Your life expectancy might decrease some in that era, but nothing compared to the average Roman. Your lover might exceed expectations as well, but you are a number of years younger than him. A time will almost certainly come when he is no longer there. Will you be able to survive without him?"

"I'm hardly likely to die of grief," Russ said. The thought of Quentus's death unnerved him, but not enough to dissuade him from his path. He would rather have a few years with Quentus and lose him than never have anything more than what he had already shared.

"I was thinking more along the lines of exposure or starvation," Bernard retorted. "You are living in his home, a home that will pass to his sons upon his death. Will you be able to support yourself without the benefit of his assistance?"

"I have a job there," Russ said. "I won't get rich doing it, and I might not be able to afford a house as nice as Quentus's, but I won't starve."

"That's good to hear," Bernard said. "I didn't want you to cut all ties to the present without considering what will happen farther down the road. There could be ways to make this move for the rest of Quentus's lifetime without making it permanent."

"There probably are," Russ said, "but I don't think they'll be necessary."

Bernard nodded. "The current château is obviously of medieval origin, but it was built upon a foundation that predates the

Roman Empire. If the worst comes to pass, you can seek aid from the guardian at the time."

"That's good to know," Russ replied. "I should get settled and dress for dinner. I have a busy few days ahead of me."

"The resources of the château are at your disposal," Bernard offered.

"Think you can figure out how to convert my life savings into either gold or Roman coins?" Russ asked jokingly. "It seems stupid to leave it sitting in a bank account here where I can't get to it."

"You could leave it against your possible return," Bernard reminded him, "but if you truly don't want to keep that avenue open, I can make arrangements. Just remember that you won't be able to bring anything back to the present with you unless you find the exact same pieces of gold. Not the quantity. The actual gold itself."

"I know," Russ said. "I'm not doing this lightly, Bernard, however it might seem to you. I've thought this through. I don't belong here anymore. I belong in Nemausus."

"And I'm not actually discouraging you," Bernard said. "but it is my responsibility to ensure you understand the choices you're making and that you make them fully cognizant of the possible outcomes."

"Some kind of code for being the château's guardian?" Russ joked.

"Something like that," Bernard replied. "Let me show you to the Caesar room."

Bernard led Russ up the stairs and down a different hallway than the one that led to the François 1er room. It was more ornate than Quentus's room—Russ didn't know if the austerity was Quentus's choice or truly a Roman preference, not having been in any bedroom but Quentus's—but the general feel of the room fit the era he wanted to call home, with a low table and cushions instead of a couch or chair near the fireplace. "Thank you," Russ said, turning to Bernard. "This feels much more comfortable."

"I will have someone bring your bag to you," Bernard said as he withdrew, leaving Russ to get ready for dinner.

Russ walked into the en suite bathroom and was relieved to see a bathtub instead of just a shower. He turned the water on hot and let it begin to fill while he waited for his bag to arrive. He dreaded putting on a suit after months of wearing tunics and togas, but while everyone at the château would probably understand if he arrived in his period clothing, he would feel out of place, and that would make him more uncomfortable than the unfamiliar clothes.

A knock at the door drew his attention. He retrieved his bag from the man on the other side, someone he didn't recognize, but the château had to have staff. They were time travelers, not magicians. Food, laundry, supplies didn't appear out of thin air. Digging out his toiletries bag, he went back into the bathroom and climbed into the tub. It wasn't as comfortable or as spacious as the baths in Nemausus, but it was still better than the stinging spray of a shower. He soaked for a few minutes, but without the conversation that was as much a part of the communal baths as the bathing, he grew bored. He grabbed his soap and washed quickly before rising and drying off.

As predicted, his suit felt strange on his shoulders. He took the jacket off, shook it out, and tried again, but it still didn't fit right.

"The training," Russ said to himself after a moment. "I must have built up some muscles after all."

He had continued his work with Gustavus and Thaddaeus, even sparring with Quentus on occasion, although his lover still disarmed him every time. While he didn't have—and would probably never have—a body honed to perfection like theirs, he had definitely gained muscle mass. He grinned and tossed the jacket on the bed. He'd just have to go down without a jacket tonight. It would only be for a few days. They could deal with seeing him in his shirtsleeves.

He didn't recognize anyone other than Bernard when he arrived in the salon to wait for dinner to be announced, but more had changed than just the size of his muscles while he was gone. The awkwardness that had always plagued him had died a swift death as he'd come into his own as Quentus's partner.

"Hello," he said to the man closest to him. "I'm Russ."

"Paolo," the man said. "Nice to meet you."

"Where are you from, Paolo?" Russ asked, committing the name to memory. He'd found that knowing people's names had encouraged them to trust him. Domitius and his men had never bothered. When Russ knew the names of all the craftsmen he approached, it set him apart from the other man.

"Sicily," Paolo replied.

"Is this your first visit to the château?"

"Yes. Bernard has been very helpful, but it is all… overwhelming."

"Yes," Russ said, "it is a lot to take in at first. I'd say you get used to it, but I'm not sure that's accurate. More like it stops being the focus of everything you do."

"You've been here before?"

"This is my third visit," Russ said, "but I suspect it will be my last."

"Your last? Why?"

"Because I've found the time and place I was meant to belong to, and I'm only here to tie up loose ends so I can go back there guilt-free."

"People really do that?" Paolo asked. "They really give up everything for some other time?"

"I don't know about 'people'," Russ said, "but it's what I'm doing. It's not all that different from moving to a different state or country to be with the person you love. It just makes staying in touch a little harder, but I don't have anyone here to stay in touch with, and there, I have friends, a lover… a life."

"It sounds like you were lucky," Paolo said.

Russ smiled and thought of the explanation he had given Quentus for his presence. "Lucky or blessed," he replied. "It all depends on your perspective."

QUENTUS detoured away from the forum when he left the baths three days after Russ's departure. Russ had explained to him that he would need at least seven days in his own time to make all the arrangements for a permanent relocation to Nemausus. He had made Quentus promise not to worry until at least a fortnight had passed. Quentus had made the promise to appease Russ, but the worry had started the moment Russ left.

Quentus reached the temple of Venus and paused outside, a bundle of myrtle in his hand. He was hardly a devotee of the goddess, having always made offerings at the temple of Mars, who watched over soldiers, but Mars could not help him now. Venus had brought Russ to him the first time. Venus would be the one who could bring him back. Taking a deep breath and hoping his devotions now would be enough to retain her favor, he removed his sandals and entered the temple.

He laid the offering at the foot of the statue and knelt, bowing his head as he prayed.

"Venus Caelestis, goddess of love and fertility, hear my prayer. In your beneficence, you brought Rastus—Russ—to me. You gave me the means to secure his affections as I saved him from the boar, and you gave us the time to build on those affections, to establish a life together. I did nothing to earn your favor. I know that, but still I would beseech your blessing once more. Bring him back to me, gentle goddess. I will spend the rest of my days treasuring your gift. You will never be disappointed in my devotion to him or to you if you will see him safely back into my arms."

The prayer seemed little enough in the face of the depths of Quentus's emotions, but he didn't know what else to say or do, so he rose and left the temple. He would return tomorrow and repeat his offering and his prayer. And the day after, and the one after that, until Russ returned to him.

"I never thought I'd see the day when Legatus Maximus forsook Mars for Venus."

Quentus flinched and looked up to see Alvinius grinning at him from across the street. "Not forsook," Quentus insisted, "merely added. You can hardly deny how Venus has blessed me these past months. I thought it prudent to show some gratitude."

"Where is Rastus?" Alvinius asked. "I would have expected him to join you in your devotions."

Quentus bit back a curse. He hadn't come up with an explanation for Russ's absence. "He is... busy," Quentus said. "He said he would stop by the temple himself later."

"Who is with him?" Alvinius asked. "I just left Gustavus and Thaddaeus at the training grounds, and Octavian is on patrol. I thought Leander said he had been summoned to speak with Legatus Septimus today. Is he with Crius?"

Quentus was tempted to say yes just to end the line of questioning, but it would be too easy to be caught in that lie. "He is doing so much better with his training, and there's been no new threat. He assured me he could go alone."

"Are you sure that's a good idea? Perhaps we should go look for him."

"I'm sure he's home by now," Quentus said. "He's not a child, after all. He will be fine."

He had to be.

"If you say so," Alvinius said. "I'm for the baths. I deserve a chance to relax after the morning I've had."

"Enjoy," Quentus said automatically. "I'm going home. I need to talk to Callistratus before he leaves for Britannia again."

Alvinius waved farewell as Quentus headed toward home. He knew better than to hope Russ would be there, although he would give much to come home to the sight of his lover bent over his table writing letters, but he could hope Callistratus would be there. Russ had done his best to smooth matters over between them, but Callistratus had even less use for Russ than he did for Quentus, and that was saying something. Quentus had never been terribly bothered by it before, but now, he had someone else in his life, someone who could be hurt by their animosity if something happened to Quentus.

The house was empty but for the servants when he returned, so he took Russ's place at the writing desk, composing a report to Septimus about the status of his legion. Normally he would have dictated it to Russ or some other scribe, but Russ was gone and Quentus wanted to be here if Callistratus came home. Septimus would just have to deal with Quentus's less than perfect handwriting.

The shadows had lengthened considerably and the report had grown to three pages when the door opened and Callistratus came in.

"Doing your own dirty work now?" he sneered.

"Writing reports is hardly 'dirty work'," Quentus replied, determined to keep his calm. "If you hope to advance in the legion, you will write your share before your tenure ends."

"Isn't that what scribes are for?"

"A scribe is a wonderful and useful thing," Quentus agreed. His hand ached from struggling to maintain a fine hand while he gathered his ideas. "However, one is not always available, and the absence of one doesn't negate the need for a report. You may rise in the ranks, but do not ever think yourself above the men you lead or you will find out how helpless one man is against thousands, no matter how well trained he is."

"You really believe that, don't you?" Callistratus asked.

"Of course I do," Quentus said. "I've seen generals give bad orders and foot soldiers save the day because they had a better sense of the flow of battle than the general who stood in the rear protecting himself rather than protecting his men. I've seen a 'lowly' scribe topple a powerful citizen who had aspirations that would have hurt us all. Intelligence is not the sole privilege of the rich or titled, nor is competency. You could do worse than learning that from Rastus."

"That's a little hard when he isn't here."

Quentus took a deep breath. He had to address the resentment dripping from all of his son's words. "Your grandparents arranged my marriage to your mother because it was advantageous to both families. You know this. I never kept it a secret from you. While she lived, I did my best to honor and respect her as my wife. I was faithful to her even when I was on campaign. I did my duty by her as befits a citizen of my standing. If she had lived, I would have continued that way, but she didn't live, and I had to think of you and your future. I had a career in the legion. I didn't have one anywhere else. I don't know what else you want from me, Callistratus."

"I wanted a father," Callistratus said. "You were never home."

"You're a soldier. You know I had no choice but to go where my orders took me," Quentus protested. "I made sure you were well cared for. If I had stayed, I couldn't have done even that."

"The family has an estate. You could have overseen it or something else to stay here. Not everyone spends their lives in the legion."

"But it is where my talent lies," Quentus reminded him. "I bring my men home so they can keep seeing their wives and children, so they can keep supporting their families. I lost a dear friend to bad orders before you were born. If I step aside, that could happen again, to people who looked to me to make sure it didn't happen."

"When was the last time you fought a real battle?" Callistratus demanded. "Not just a routine patrol to put down bandits or unrest, but a real battle to expand the empire?"

"Not so long that I've forgotten what it's like," Quentus replied coldly, "or are you suggesting I've grown weak in my old age? I can still take you or any young whelp who thinks he's something special."

"Prove it. Meet me at the training grounds tomorrow morning."

"Do you really want to make our private dispute public that way?" Quentus's heart ached at the thought that he had lost his son so completely.

"Yes."

"Then what are the terms?" Quentus asked, not completely able to keep the frustration and resignation out of his voice.

"Terms?"

"If you win, what do you expect from me?"

"Give up Rastus."

"No," Quentus said. "That is not for you to decide."

"Your signet ring, then," Callistratus said. "If I win, I take control of the family estates."

"And who will run it in your absence?" Quentus asked.

"I'm sure I can find an overseer to run it for me. Isn't that what you did?"

"Your grandmother was still alive when I was stationed at the borders of the empire," Quentus replied. "She oversaw the estate until her death, and by that time, I had returned to Nemausus. If you take the ring, you will request a transfer to Nemausus so you can oversee our affairs properly."

"Very well."

"If I win, on the other hand, you will agree to spend time with Rastus upon his return. You will be respectful to him and you will learn from him," Quentus decreed. "I can't order you to like him, but I can put you in a situation where you will be able to see his value."

"Then it's a good thing I will win, isn't it?" Callistratus asked. "Since I'll never see the value of your boy."

Quentus bit back his retort that Russ was at least a decade older than Callistratus. He knew the insult was deliberate, debasing Russ because of the way Callistratus viewed him rather than because of his age, but understanding it did nothing to soften the blow. "We will settle this at first light, at the training grounds. Don't be late."

"I'll be there... Father."

The word hit Quentus like a blow, the venom in Callistratus's voice as painful as any viper bite. He waited in stony silence for Callistratus to leave.

"By Jove, what is wrong with that boy?" Quentus muttered when Callistratus had gone, slamming the door behind him. "I know my mother wouldn't have tolerated that attitude when he was a child."

He didn't have time to dwell on that, though. He had a fight to prepare for.

Fortunately, Gustavus and Thaddaeus were at home when he sought them out.

"Quentus, what brings you out at this time of night, and alone, no less?" Gustavus asked. "Where is Rastus?"

"Rastus will be back in a few days," Quentus said, "but I have more pressing problems. Callistratus has crossed a line I cannot ignore. He's challenged me to face him tomorrow on the training grounds. If I lose, he takes control of the family estates, and given his attitude since his return from Britannia, he will probably turn us out. He's too hotheaded to oversee the estate by himself yet. I can't afford to lose."

"No, of course not," Thaddaeus said. "What do you need from us?"

"Two things," Quentus replied. "First, have any of the recruits who came back with Callistratus said anything that would explain his sudden change in attitude? I don't remember him being this bitter when he left for the border."

"Not in my hearing," Thaddaeus said, glancing at Gustavus, who shook his head in confirmation, "but we could ask around. Just because we haven't heard about something doesn't mean there isn't something to hear about. We haven't spent as much time with Callistratus's unit as we have with some of the others. What else?"

"Have any of them brought back new moves I should be on guard against?" Quentus asked. "I still train regularly, but with my own men, men whose tricks I know because they learned them all from me."

"We might be able to help you with that," Gustavus said with a grin. "I imagine you don't want to go to the training grounds now, so we will have to push the furniture out of the way so we can practice here."

"Your father will not approve."

"He would approve even less of you losing the fight and your position," Thaddaeus retorted. "Help us here so we can get started."

BY THE time they finished three hours later, it was nearly midnight, and Quentus was as exhausted as he could remember being in recent years. He had to remember to spar with Thaddaeus and Gustavus more often. They had shown him enough new tricks that he felt like a new recruit again. He didn't know if Callistratus knew any or all of them, but Quentus was glad he'd sought out his friends' help because he would have been hard-pressed tomorrow if Callistratus had pulled any of those against him. He wondered now how Russ had survived if Gustavus and Thaddaeus had pushed him this hard when he started training with them. He would have to remember to express his appreciation for Russ's dedication when he returned.

He briefly entertained the thought of going to the baths, but as much as he would enjoy sinking into the heated water, he needed to sleep so he would be awake in the morning and ready to face his son on the field of combat.

He let himself into the house, not at all surprised to see Antony waiting for him in the atrium.

"Welcome home, Legatus," Antony said. "Will you want dinner?"

"Yes," Quentus said, "but bring a second plate. I have questions for you, and I would rather not eat alone."

"Sir?"

Quentus sighed. "You heard me, Antony. Rastus isn't here. I need someone to talk to, and I suspect you're the only person who can answer my questions anyway."

"Very well, sir," Antony said. He withdrew and returned with two plates. Another servant carried in the tray with dinner on it. Once the other servant had retired, Quentus gestured for Antony to sit.

"What was it like while I was gone?" Quentus asked. "When Callistratus was a child, I mean. I thought I knew him, but after today, I'm not so sure."

"Your lady wife's death came swift on the heels of the death of your father," Antony reminded Quentus. "Your lady mother took the dual loss very hard. She maintained appearances in public, but in private, she was not the woman you remember. She spent most of her time in her room, leaving the care of the household to your sister before her marriage and to me after your sister wed. She would put on her best face when you came home, but that was not the side of her Callistratus saw."

"I didn't know," Quentus said quietly.

"She didn't want you to," Antony replied, "and it was not my place to say anything. Your sister might have if you had returned while she lived here, but she was so happy to be away from your mother's bitterness. She must have decided not to say anything to you on the eve of her wedding either."

"So instead of growing up surrounded by care and guidance as I did, he grew up feeling abandoned and unloved," Quentus said. "But why choose now to act on those feelings?"

"That would be a question for him," Antony said, "but when he was a child, he was dependent on you for everything. He is a man now, capable of making his own way in the world. Even if you disowned him, he would still have his place in the legion, and from that, a way of supporting himself and even a family. He is no longer a helpless child."

"A fact he thinks to prove to me tomorrow," Quentus said. "So now I must not only win the fight, but I must do so in a way that doesn't strip him of all pride. When did my life get so complicated, Antony?"

"I'm not sure you want me to answer that, sir," Antony said with a smile. "When will Master Rastus be home? He will make you feel better."

"In a few days," Quentus said, "Venus willing."

CHAPTER SIXTEEN

"D<small>ID</small> you get everything arranged?" Bernard asked Russ when he arrived back at the château d'Eternité after a quick trip to Tucson.

"Yes," Russ said. "My department chair wasn't happy about it, but at least he has the rest of the year to find a permanent replacement before the temporary one leaves. That's far more than he would have had if I'd waited until my year was up, and if I ever did decide to come back and try for another academic position, it's a little less of a black mark on my name than shorter notice would be."

"You really don't think you'll do that, do you?"

"No, I really don't," Russ said. "Even if I don't stay in Nemausus after Quentus's death, I just don't fit here anymore. My life's different now, and I like my new life, not my old one."

"Then you're a very lucky man," Bernard said. "Too few people find happiness in their lives, in the present, past, or future, and end up wandering through their days with a vague discontent that isn't enough to push them into changing anything but also isn't enough to leave them feeling fulfilled. I've seen much in my tenure here as guardian of the château, and much of it I wish I could forget."

"I hope I've given you one thing you'll want to remember," Russ said, not knowing what else to say.

"You have," Bernard said. "I've been working on converting your savings for you. It will be tomorrow before it's all ready, but then you'll be able to return to Nemausus and the life that makes you happy."

Russ thanked Bernard once more and then withdrew to his room. Looking around at the Roman-style furnishings, he shook his head a little at the unexpected turn his life had taken. When he'd received the mysterious invitation to come to château d'Eternité for a "retreat," he couldn't have imagined this end result. He had never been adventurous, never been one to take risks, and yet here he was, six months later, gambling his entire future on a man from the ancient past. Now the only surprise was how little that decision felt like a gamble. The modern touches in the room—the cleverly disguised light switch, the electric lamps in place of the oil lamps, the thicker mattress on the bed that wasn't quite the right height or length—weren't sources of comfort to him the way they would have been when he first arrived at the château. Instead they were reminders that he was not in Nemausus, in the room he shared with Quentus, waiting for his lover to join him.

Tomorrow, he reminded himself. He would be going home tomorrow, and then he would have the rest of their lives to spend together. He only had to make it through one more night in the too soft, too large, too empty bed.

THE training grounds were crowded, as they always were at that hour of the morning. Quentus frowned as he tested the weight and balance of one of the practice swords. He would not risk injuring Callistratus, even if the dulled and unfamiliar blade put him at a slight disadvantage. He had used his real sword to spar with Gustavus and Thaddaeus last night, but that had been practice, not a true fight, and he trusted them to pull their blows as he had done. He could not rely on that today. He would have to strike hard and true, fighting Callistratus as he would fight any enemy, or Russ would be coming home to a very different life than the one Quentus had promised him. Quentus didn't think that would matter to Russ, but he couldn't take that chance. He couldn't give up everything he had worked so hard for because Callistratus was in a snit.

"Are you ready, Legatus?" Gustavus said, coming into the area where Quentus was preparing. "Your opponent has already taken to the field."

His opponent. He needed the reminder, but the words broke his heart, that he could face a day when his son and heir was also his opponent. "I am ready."

He donned his helmet, picked up his shield, and prayed to Mars for the speed and skill to end this quickly before either of them got hurt.

The crowd had grown in the time Quentus had been preparing, he saw as he stepped out onto the grassy field. All around the edges of the lea, soldiers had gathered. Whatever the outcome, they would have plenty of witnesses to the results. Quentus couldn't decide if that was good or bad. He sought Callistratus with his gaze, lifting his sword in salute.

Callistratus returned the salute and then rushed Quentus.

The boy had strength, Quentus had to give him that, as their swords clashed together for the first time, the power behind Callistratus's blow resonating down the sword to Quentus's hand. Quentus was too experienced a warrior to be overcome by sheer strength, though. He parried the thrust, sending Callistratus sprawling from the momentum of his attack.

If he had been tutoring a new recruit, he would have counseled the man on the wisdom of patience and control in battle, but Quentus saved his breath. Callistratus wouldn't want to hear it, and even if he did, Quentus intended to use every advantage at his disposal to end this quickly.

Callistratus scrambled back to his feet, his expression wary now. Quentus wondered who he had been training with to expect so little from his father, but that was a worry for another time. Right now, he had an angry opponent to defeat.

The blows came fast and wild after that, with no pattern to them that Quentus could discern. He parried the ones he could with his sword and caught those he couldn't on his shield, letting Callistratus wear himself out pounding against Quentus's defenses, another mistake he would have corrected if this had been a less serious situation. He could identify Callistratus's fellow soldiers by the way they cheered with each strike of the sword, as if any hit mattered, as if they had seen Callistratus win many a fight in just this manner.

When the rain of blows began to slow, Quentus pressed his own attack, slowly, testing Callistratus's defenses with a feint here, a thrust there. Again, the mentor in him sighed at the lack of response. Callistratus was all attack and nothing else, it seemed, a situation that didn't bode well for his survival in any prolonged combat, but perhaps surrounded by comrades-in-arms, he would do better. As it was, Quentus bided his time until he found his opening, batting the sword from Callistratus's hands and taking him to the grass in one smooth move that elicited gasps and cheers from one half of their audience, boos and catcalls from the other.

"Do you yield?" Quentus asked.

Callistratus bucked against Quentus as if to throw him off, but he was still little more than a youth, while Quentus was a man in his prime. He outweighed the younger man by more than enough to subdue his struggles. "Do you yield?"

"Yes," Callistratus said after a long moment.

"I will send word when Rastus has returned so you can join him in his daily routine," Quentus said as he pushed to his feet. "I expect your compliance with our agreement."

"I'll be there," Callistratus said, his resentment clear in his voice. "It won't change anything, but I'll be there."

"You're not too old for me to take you home and thrash you properly," Quentus muttered. He gave Callistratus one last glare and stalked off. He needed a bath. He needed an outlet for all the frustration and aggression he had not been able to let loose against his son. He needed Russ.

Deciding he was in no fit state to carry on conversation at the baths, Quentus tossed the practice sword back in with the others and headed toward home. Fortunately no one tried to stop him to talk about the fight. He thought he caught a glimpse of Thaddaeus and

Gustavus, perhaps heading off well-wishers, but he didn't wait long enough to check. He didn't have any patience left, even for his friends.

He passed the temple to Venus on his way from the training grounds and detoured inside. He was a mess, sweaty from the duel, temper out of control, and with empty hands, but he had to stop. He needed the goddess's blessing now more than ever.

"Gentle goddess," he prayed, falling to his knees, "hear the pleas of a humble soldier. You brought me such blessings, but now he is absent. I understand why, but I beseech you, bring him back to me. I'm nothing without him. I fought a duel with my son this morning because he wasn't here to help me find another way to remedy the situation. I fought a duel with my *son*. Oh, blessed Venus, I have nothing left without him. My son is lost to me right now, but Russ would know how to fix it. He fixed my broken heart. I have nothing to offer you right now but my promise, but I give you my most solemn oath. If you will return Russ to me, I will be your most faithful servant for the rest of my days. I will guard and cherish him like the most precious gift that he is to me. He will never know a moment's want. He will be the center of my life, as you will be the center of my devotion. Just please… send him back to me."

His voice broke as he spoke, but he was beyond caring. Perhaps if the goddess realized how deep his emotions went, she would be more inspired to answer his plea, and even if she wasn't, the temple was empty. No one else had heard his impassioned supplication. Rising slowly and feeling every one of his thirty-nine years, every battle he had fought, every injury he had ever sustained, he bowed before the altar once more and then trudged toward home.

RUSS paced the peristylium, trying not to let his nerves show. Antony had been delighted to see Russ and then had proceeded to tell him of the argument between Quentus and Callistratus that had led to a challenge and this morning's duel. Antony had not said how he knew things, but Russ had learned how easily voices carried inside the house. With only curtains to separate the rooms, Antony would have heard their words as clearly as if he had been standing next to them. They would be fighting right now, Antony explained. Russ shuddered again at the thought. He hated being the root of this kind of tension between father and son, but he didn't know what he could do about it now. If he'd realized it was so bad before he left, he could have delayed his departure, perhaps been here to diffuse the situation, but he hadn't known, and so he'd left, and while he was gone, tempers had flared beyond control.

"Fuck," he muttered. "If I've screwed up the one good thing in my life, I'm going to be really pissed."

He wanted to go the training grounds, to be there if the worst happened, but he couldn't do that to Quentus. He couldn't let their reunion take place in public, and he couldn't let his presence be a distraction to his lover. He wouldn't be the reason Quentus lost this fight.

Antony had told him the stakes Quentus and Callistratus had agreed on, but Russ couldn't have cared less about that. He didn't need an estate, especially not now, with the pile of gold bullion he had brought back with him hidden safely in a cache outside of town. He and Quentus could easily afford to start over in Nemausus or somewhere else. He was worried about Quentus's pride. If Callistratus beat him, Quentus would question everything about himself and his position as general of the legions, and that would destroy him.

Not that winning would be much better, since winning would mean defeating his son, hopefully without serious injury on either side; but if Callistratus had made this as public as Antony seemed to think it would be, everyone would be aware of the rift in the family, and that would wear on Quentus nearly as badly as losing would.

"I should have waited," Russ said to the statue of Venus that had taken up residency in the atrium while he was gone. "I shouldn't have left him alone knowing Callistratus was here and the situation was tense, but I wanted it resolved for good. This is what I get for wanting things."

If he thought leaving now would help, he'd do it, but it wouldn't change anything between Quentus and Callistratus. The damage was already done, and Russ's departure would do nothing but make the argument meaningless. He'd just have to find a way to heal the division between them. He was a resourceful guy. He could think of something. He was sure the others in Quentus's circle would help as well, because any kind of crack in their united front was harmful to their efforts. Maybe he'd go see Jacobus. The wily old fox would surely have some suggestions.

He didn't want to be gone when Quentus got back, though, so maybe he'd wait and visit Jacobus later. It would be better to announce his arrival than show up uninvited.

He sat down at his writing table and pulled out a clean piece of parchment, noticing as he did that the stack was somewhat smaller than when he'd left. He would have to ask Quentus what he'd been writing and see if Quentus wanted him to rewrite any of it. That could wait until later, though. Right now he needed to write his note to Jacobus and send it.

Dear Jacobus,

I have returned from my short trip, and imagine my surprise and dismay when I discovered that the tension between Callistratus and Quentus reached a breaking point during my absence. Such a rift cannot be good for any of us, but as I am unfamiliar with the history of their falling out, I find myself at a loss for how to fix it. If you would be amenable to discussing the situation and especially to exploring solutions, I would be free to call on you at your convenience. If there is someone else I should speak with instead of you, please make me aware so that I can proceed accordingly.

Respectfully,

Rastus

Russ blew on the ink to dry it and then sealed the scroll. He hesitated a moment over pressing the imprint of Quentus's signet ring into the wax, not knowing the outcome of the fight, but he pushed the worry aside. Quentus would win, and they would find a way to make things right with Callistratus. Everything would work out for the best.

"Antony," he called. "Could you have a servant deliver this to Jacobus?"

"Of course, sir," Antony said, taking the letter.

That done, Russ leaned back in the chair, trying to think of other ways to pass the time until Quentus returned home.

CHAPTER SEVENTEEN

QUENTUS pushed open the door to the house and stepped inside. He was tired in a way that couldn't be attributed to the fight he'd just won. A crackle of energy raised goose bumps on his skin as he looked through the atrium to the peristylium. Hardly daring to hope, he walked deeper into the house until he could see into the garden, could see Russ slumped in the chair at his writing desk like he'd never been gone.

"Thank you, gentle Venus," he whispered as he rushed across the space between them and swept Russ into his arms. "You're back."

"I shouldn't have left," Russ said, burying his face against Quentus's neck. "I should have waited until everything was settled with Callistratus. I'm sorry."

"No, don't apologize," Quentus said, smoothing his hands over Russ's back. "None of this was your fault. Mine, maybe, for not realizing how bad the situation had gotten, but not yours. If you hadn't been here, he would have found some other excuse to be angry with me."

"If I had been here, I might have helped you resolve it," Russ disagreed, but Quentus had no real interest in talking anymore. Russ was here. Venus had granted Quentus's prayer, and he had a promise to keep to the benevolent goddess.

He lifted Russ off his feet into an embrace. Russ wrapped his legs around Quentus's waist, heedless of the armor Quentus still wore. Quentus slipped his hands beneath Russ's tunic as he braced him, coming to rest on the firm muscles of his buttocks, and all resolve to talk to his lover before taking him to bed melted away. He needed Russ beneath him, begging and pleading for more. They could talk later.

He carried Russ toward the bedroom, peppering Russ's face with featherlight kisses the entire time. He needed Russ now, but he *had* to do this right. He'd made a promise to Venus, and the last thing he wanted was to lose Russ because he couldn't keep it.

They tumbled onto the bed. "Stay there," Quentus growled, standing long enough to strip his armor and tunic aside. Russ didn't move, thankfully, except to reach up and pull Quentus, now naked except for his *subligar*, back down on top of him.

"I missed you," Quentus said roughly before nipping at Russ's neck. "You're mine. You're supposed to be here with me."

"I'm here now," Russ promised, "and I won't leave again. I made all the arrangements. There's nowhere else I want to be."

The words pierced every wall around Quentus's heart, and he poured his emotions into a kiss, trying to convey the depth of his devotion in the contact of their mouths.

Russ's tunic rubbed against his skin in a way that might have been pleasurable if they hadn't been separated for nearly a week, or if Quentus's emotions hadn't been running so high. As it was, though, the cloth was an annoyance Quentus dealt with swiftly. When he lowered himself back onto Russ again, only hot, smooth skin met his touch, and that was perfect.

Beyond perfect. It was a gift from the goddess.

He licked and nibbled his way down Russ's chest, trying his best not to leave marks since he knew Russ preferred to keep their love life private, but struggling against the need to bite, to mark, to *claim* Russ as his own. Venus had given Russ to him, by all the gods, and Quentus wanted the whole world to know it.

Russ bucked beneath Quentus each time his teeth connected with tender skin, but when Quentus lifted his head to ask if Russ wanted him to stop, Russ grabbed his hair and pushed him back down. "Don't stop."

Quentus smiled against Russ's belly and sucked skin into his mouth, worrying at it until he raised a bruise that would be unmistakable the next time they went to the baths.

Russ just moaned and pressed harder against Quentus's scalp, so Quentus took that as permission. He had promised Venus he would cherish Russ if she returned him. Russ wanted bite marks. Quentus fully intended to give his lover anything he wanted, especially when it was so in line with his own desires.

He bit at the crease of Russ's hip, the jolt of pain causing Russ to rock beneath him. Russ's cock bumped Quentus's cheek as he moved, the musky smell beckoning to him in a way he had always refused to consider before, but this was Russ. This was his gift from Venus. His own considerations of status and propriety could not take precedence over that. Turning his head, he nuzzled the hard shaft, working up the nerve to take the risk of trying something new with Russ. With a casual lover, he would never have made himself vulnerable this way, would never have tried something he could not be assured of doing with his usual mastery, but this was no casual lover. This was Russ.

The way Russ caught his breath, like Quentus had offered him the sun and the moon and he could think of nothing he wanted more, convinced Quentus to try.

He licked along the length of Russ's erection, learning the texture of the skin with his tongue as he had learned it already with his hand. The smell and taste of Russ's essence was stronger here as Quentus's nose bumped against Russ's sac. He hesitated for a moment, the intimacy almost too much for him, but he had never been one to do anything by half measure, so he pushed onto his hands and knees and hovered over the tip of Russ's cock. A bead of fluid nestled in the slit, beckoning to him. Reminding himself that nothing he did with Russ in love could be a mistake, he lowered his head and licked away the tiny drop. Russ cried out at the contact, startling Quentus enough that he rocked back on his heels, but when he met Russ's eyes, he understood. His lover's eyes were blown, pupils so wide they swallowed all the green in his eyes. His mouth was open as he panted for breath, and every muscle in his body was trembling with need.

All that from one little lick. He wondered what Russ would look like if Quentus found the courage and skill to drive him to the brink that way. It was a thought to explore another time, though, because he couldn't contain the surge of desire he felt at seeing Russ this way, desire he knew only one way to release.

"Turn over," he said hoarsely.

Russ scrambled onto his hands and knees with such speed that Quentus knew he had made the right call. Russ had no more patience for protracted oral play right now than Quentus did.

Even shaking with need and knowing Russ felt the same, Quentus couldn't bring himself to mount his lover immediately. It had been nearly a week since they had been together. Russ would have tightened up in that time, and while it might feel incredible around Quentus's cock, he wouldn't risk hurting Russ that way. He reached for the oil with trembling hands, wondering as he did what had happened to his vaunted control. Russ, it seemed, had the gift for reducing that to ash. When Russ looked back and whispered for him to hurry, Quentus decided he could live with that.

He stretched Russ hastily, with none of his usual finesse, but it didn't matter because Russ pleaded and rocked back against his hand, obviously in as much of a hurry as Quentus. After a final cursory swipe of an oily hand over his own cock, he nudged Russ's knees farther apart and slipped between them, covering Russ with his body and joining them with one inexorable thrust.

Russ cried out at the ingress, but Quentus had learned his lover's noises enough by now to recognize relief and fulfillment when he heard it. He reached beneath Russ, encircling his cock and shunting his hand up and down its length in time with his rocking hips. Russ's cries changed to sharp little mews each time Quentus hit that spot inside him until neither of them could take anymore. Russ undulated around him and collapsed onto the bed. Quentus pounded into him a few more times before his own release blindsided him, and then it was all he could do not to crush Russ as he collapsed as well.

"You came back," Quentus said when he could speak again.

Russ turned into his arms, curling against him. "I told you I would. I'll always come back to you."

"DID all go well when you went home?" Quentus asked later as they reclined at table for lunch.

"As well as can be expected," Russ replied. "My former employer was not happy to lose me, but there wasn't really anything he could do about it. There wasn't a lot else to take care of. I had some furniture to give away, and I had my estate, such as it was, to convert into something of value here in this time. When we have a chance, we should take a wagon or something and go out to where I hid it. It was too much to carry into town with me."

"Too much what?" Quentus asked.

Russ grinned. "Gold."

Quentus quirked an eyebrow at Russ. "I thought we had discussed the matter of your contributions to the household."

"We did," Russ said. "But it seemed wasteful to leave it all sitting there unclaimed and unused. This way, I have something of my own if Callistratus continues to make trouble for us. Something he can't take away from us even if he manages to wrest the estate from your control."

"Antony told you, I presume?"

"Not all of it, but enough that I knew what you were facing," Russ said. "I'm sorry. I didn't mean to be the cause of that."

"You weren't," Quentus assured him. "Callistratus's mother died when he was born. My mother raised him while I was away at war, but apparently she was less of a nurturing mother to him than she was to me. He's angry I wasn't here. An empty house is at least testament to the fact that I married. A house with someone else in it makes him feel like I'm trying to deny that. I'm not sure where that logic comes from, but that's apparently the way he feels. He lost the duel. He'll be spending some quality time with you for a while. I won't leave you at his mercy if something happens to me."

"I won't be at his mercy," Russ said. "I have my gold, and I have a place to go if it comes to that. A place he can't reach me."

"Where?" Quentus asked.

"The place where Venus found me," Russ replied for lack of a better explanation. "Even in this time, it will be a safe haven for me. It's in the mountains to the east. Even if he kicked me out with nothing but the clothes on my back, I could walk there before hunger or exposure became too much."

"He still needs to learn to keep a civil tongue in his head," Quentus said. "I won't inflict him on you today, but I'll send word that we'll expect him tomorrow. He's so blinded by his anger at me he can't see your value. Maybe this will change that."

"If he learns to be civil, I'll be satisfied with that," Russ said. "I don't know that we'll ever be friends, but anything will be better than worrying about him coming back from battle and attacking me again."

"He'll learn," Quentus said. "He doesn't want to know what I could do to him if he doesn't."

Russ shook his head. "It won't come to that. I won't have our lives reduced to a battlefield. There's a solution out there somewhere. We just have to find it."

"If anyone can, it will be you."

"Together," Russ said. "We'll find it together."

EPILOGUE

BERNARD awoke to the feeling of something being different. He had long since grown used to the fluidity of time, but the château itself was usually the one constant in a universe that flowed in more directions and veins than most people could imagine, much less begin to comprehend.

He took stock of his room as he rose from his bed, but nothing appeared different there. Once dressed, he worked his way through the rooms in the château, checking each one for any differences since the last time he had visited them, but they, too, seemed unchanged until he reached the Roman-era room. The furnishings were much more authentic than they had been yesterday. Bernard smiled. He could guess what had happened. Now to confirm it and establish the extent of the changes.

In his office, he opened the ancient tome that contained the records of the guardianship of the château and began to read.

In the second year of the reign of Caesar Marcus Aurelius Commodus Antoninus Augustus, a new guardian took power at the shrine. Rastus Petronius, former advisor to legatus Augusti pro praetor Quentus Maximus, accepted the position and ordered the construction of a villa on the site for the lodging of all supplicants, regardless of origin.

"Well done, Russell Peterson," Bernard said as he closed the book. He doubted he would find the barest hint of stonework to mark the existence of that villa, but it placed the roots of the château several centuries farther in the past than had been previously established. He didn't need to see the changes to know they existed. He had all the proof he needed right there.

It was a relief to see a testament to Russ's survival in black and white. He had seen more than one person off to the past, never to be heard from again, some by choice like Russ, others with no explanation whatsoever. He could glean little from the stark words on the page, but Quentus had not been the legatus Augusti when Russ was last here, so they had clearly thrived together before Russ arrived at the site of the château. Bernard would have to crosscheck the date, but if his history hadn't failed him, Russ would have gotten a good fifteen, maybe even twenty years with his lover before the date recorded in the book. Of course he could have been at the shrine for some time before taking over as guardian, but even so, it reassured Bernard that the decision had been worth it for Russ.

He put the book away and stood. "Adieu, Russ."

ARIEL TACHNA lives outside of Houston with her husband, her daughter and son, and their cat. Before moving there, she traveled all over the world, having fallen in love with both France, where she found her husband, and India, where she dreams of retiring some day. She's bilingual with snippets of four other languages to her credit, and is as in love with languages as she is with writing.

Visit Ariel at her website http://www.arieltachna.com or e-mail her at arieltachna@gmail.com.

Also from DREAMSPINNER PRESS

Lycan Partnership

A Partnership in Blood novel

ARIEL TACHNA

http://www.dreamspinnerpress.com

Also from ARIEL TACHNA

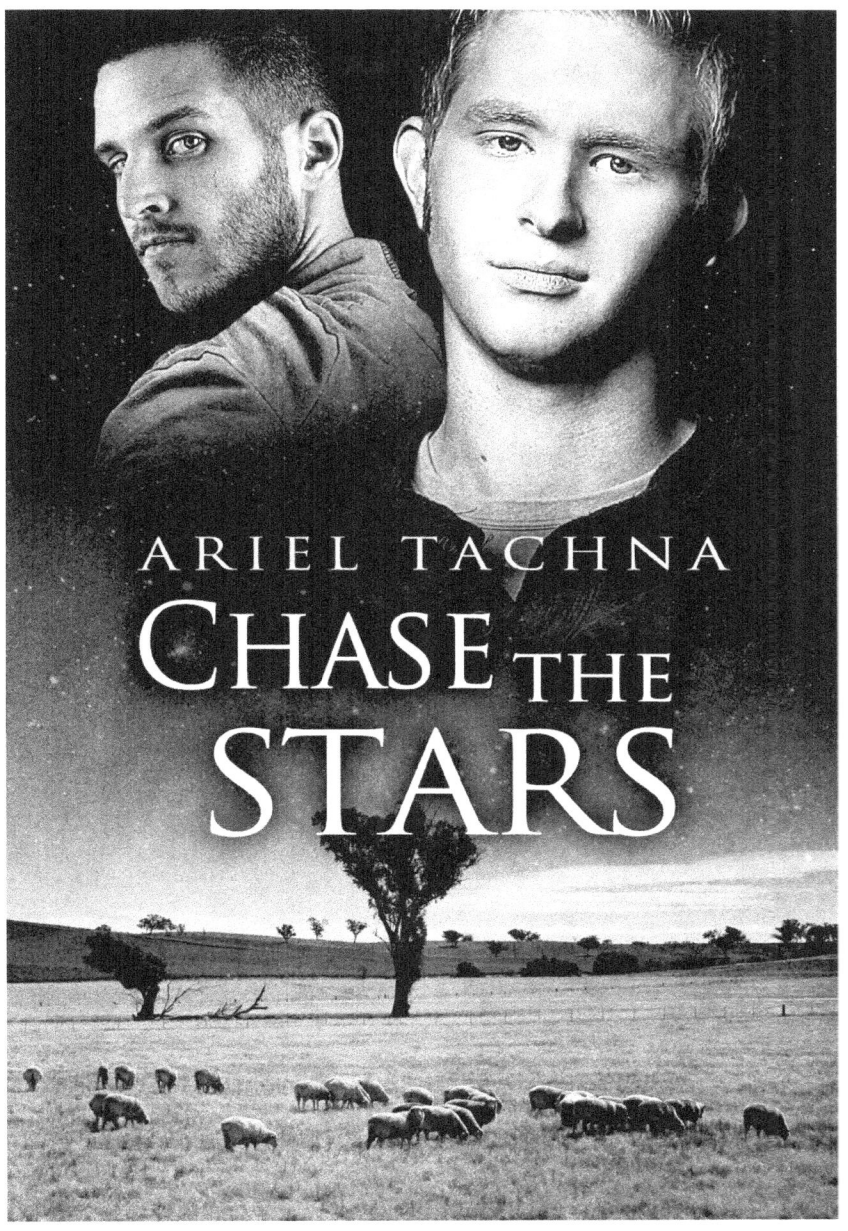

Also from ARIEL TACHNA

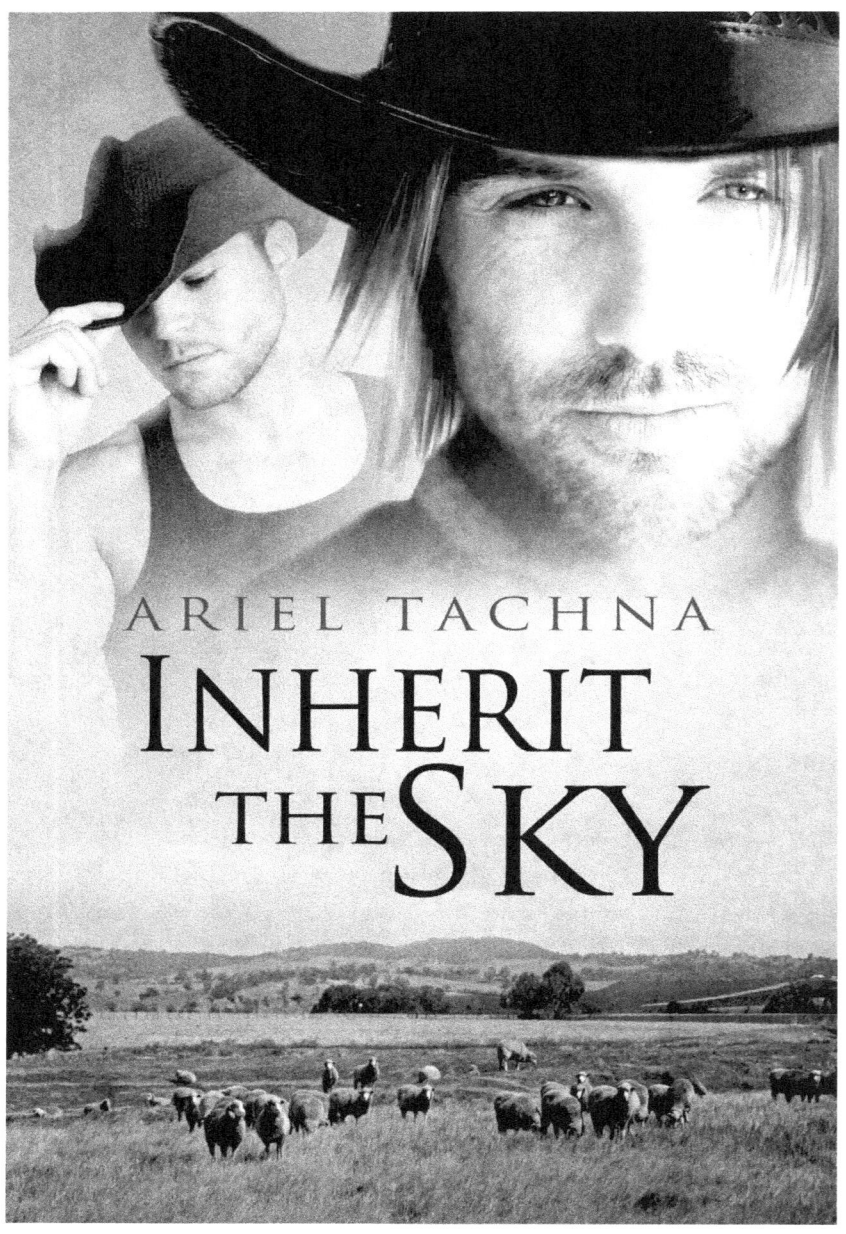

ARIEL TACHNA

INHERIT THE SKY

Also from ARIEL TACHNA

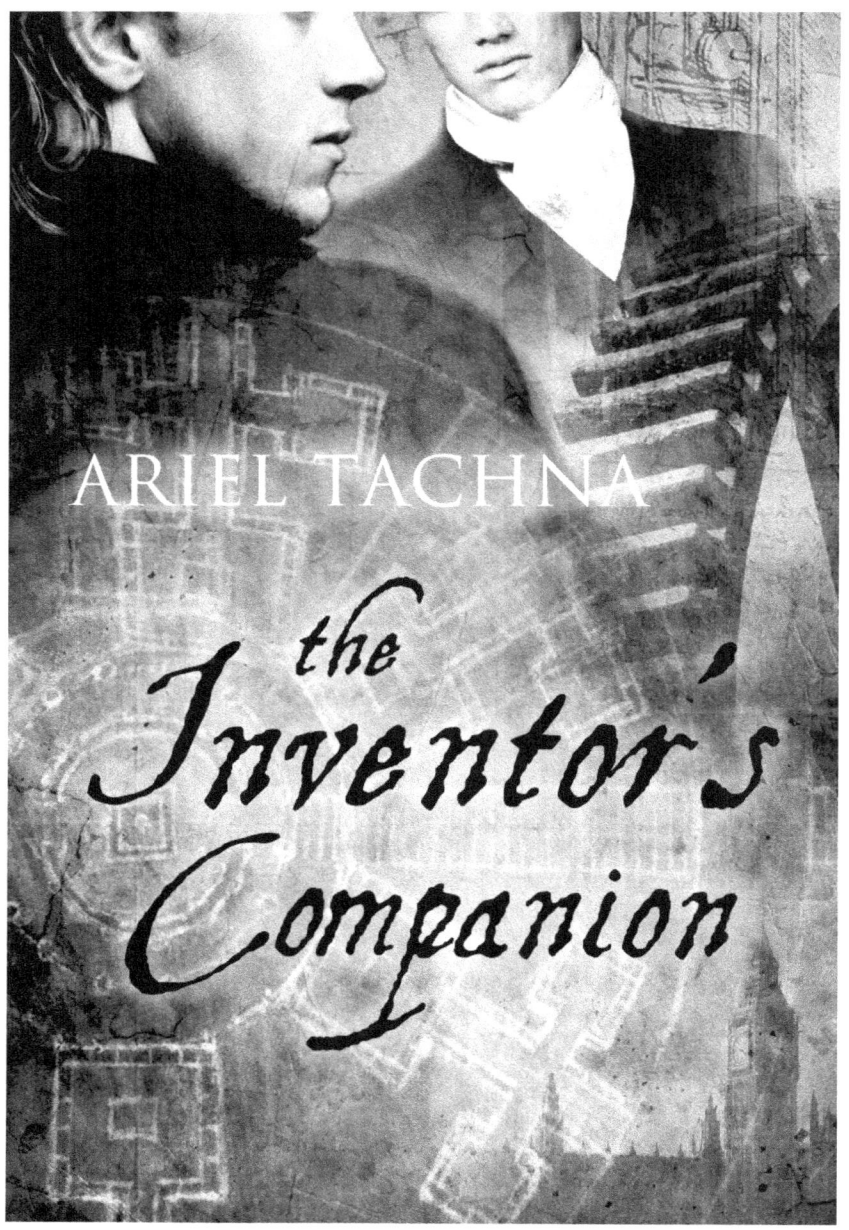

Also from DREAMSPINNER PRESS

http://www.dreamspinnerpress.com